AN
ECHO OF
OBLIVION

THE FRAGMENTED

AN ECHO OF OBLIVION

SOFI AGUILERA

Paperback ISBN: 978-1-63337-835-3
Ebook ISBN: 978-1-63337-836-0

Printed in the United States of America
1 3 5 7 9 10 8 6 4 2

TO THE LOST.

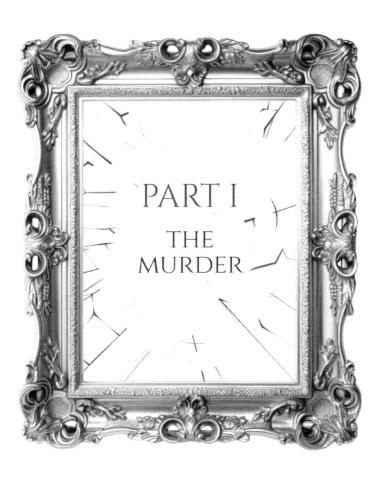

PART I

THE MURDER

WOLF TRIED TO CONTAIN the urge inside his chest to kill everyone around him.

He felt their lives pulsing with every beat of their hearts, and his instincts raged at him to take that pulsing and make it his own. Wolf ground his jaw and pushed through the crowd. The music blared around him in dizzying beats as blue and red lights danced around the room in bright flashes. At the far end of the nightclub, the DJ pumped his fist in the air as he switched from one jarring song to the next. Wolf's nose itched as the scents of sweat, cheap perfume, and alcohol drifted into his nostrils. He was a head taller than everyone around him, but that didn't help as he tried to spot his target.

Whirls of color blinded him as one of the rotating lights shot beams at his face. His skin trembled from the blasting music. Bodies pressed in behind him, and before he knew it, he was being swallowed onto the dance floor. Wolf stood stiffly like a boulder among clashing ocean waves. For a second, he feared he would attract people's attention with his height, then realized everyone around him was too drunk, high, or both to even glance his way. A woman stumbled into his chest and bounced back as if she had hit a brick wall. She looked up at him, her eyes glassy, then turned away.

A string of curses flared through Wolf's mind. He hated nightclubs and hadn't set foot in one since they were invented, but they had become the favorite playground for many of the others. He breathed deeply as the sharp pull in his chest urged him to make a kill.

Just one, it demanded.

He whipped his head around as he tried to spot a tall and slim man with midnight black hair. Wolf hadn't seen him since the Second World War, but his image was still intact in Wolf's mind. Unlike the others, Wolf was the only one whose memories hadn't been devoured by oblivion.

Warm liquid splattered onto his shoes and soaked into his socks as someone next to him puked. A growl escaped from his throat, but the music quickly drowned it out. Using his broad chest and shoulders to barrel through the throng, Wolf pushed his way out of the crowd and pressed himself against a wall to separate himself from the mass of bodies by a couple of feet. He forced himself to not glance down at his shoes and tried to ignore the acidic smell of vomit. He shut his eyes to gather his thoughts.

A melodious laugh sliced through the music. Wolf opened his eyes and snapped his head to the side. A man's back was to Wolf, but Wolf recognized him immediately. The man's dark hair had been cut short. It was meticulously combed and reflected the red and blue glares of light. His powerful physique was wrapped tightly in a black shirt. He gently but possessively held a woman by her arm. After another laugh, the man pulled the woman to the side, and they disappeared into a hallway.

Wolf pushed himself off the wall. The club blurred around him as he followed the man. Wolf turned right, then left to walk through a corridor that ran parallel to the dance floor. Dark blue light dripped from the top of the black walls and bathed him in an eerie hue. A deep voice with a British accent echoed through the hallways, but it was cut short when a door slammed shut. Wolf hurried to the end of the corridor and turned right again to face a bathroom door. Muffled voices seeped from the crack underneath. He opened the door and walked inside.

The man's shirt had already been fully unbuttoned, and the woman pressed her hand onto his muscled chest. Her other hand

4

was buried in his hair as he kissed her jaw. The man's head snapped toward Wolf, his eyes a roiling sea of green.

"Hey," Wolf managed, his throat tight.

The other man went so still he stopped breathing. As he scanned Wolf's face, his eyes widened, then narrowed.

"Do you know him?" the woman asked, her gaze bouncing between the two men. "Rafe?"

"Rafe," Wolf repeated, testing the word on his lips. He must have changed his name since Wolf had known him by another name when he had last seen him.

Wolf expected Rafe to ask what he was doing here or how Wolf had found him. Or to even tell Wolf to fuck off.

"Could you close the door?" Rafe simply said.

"Sure." Wolf shut the door slowly, his heart thumping nervously. "We need to talk. There's a . . . family emergency that—"

"Yeah, yeah." Rafe waved his hand. "Just give me a second." He turned back to the woman with a slow, predatory smile, his eyes glimmering like two emeralds. "I'm sorry to have to end our night so soon."

"You can call me whenever you're done with—"

Rafe's long fangs shot out of his mouth before he clamped his jaw around her neck while holding the back of her head with one hand and her waist with the other. The woman screamed, but Wolf knew no one would come save her. He glanced away, finding a very interesting spot of yellow moss under the sink. The scent of blood caused another pull inside Wolf's chest, and he gritted his teeth so hard his jaw ached. He focused on his shoes instead, noting the vomit had dried and left tiny white specs behind.

Wolf winced as the dead body thudded loudly onto the floor. He turned back to face Rafe. Blood spilled from Rafe's chin as his gaze drilled into Wolf, then scanned him from top to bottom. The woman's body now lay sprawled between the toilet and the wall.

"I should have saved some for you," Rafe said, his fangs still out and smeared with dark blood. "You've looked better." Wolf didn't reply and remained silent as Rafe wiped his mouth clean with some toilet paper and then washed his chin and hands at the sink with exasperating calmness. "Seriously," Rafe continued as his fangs retracted, "you've let yourself go."

Wolf's eyes darted to the mirror. He had broken his nose a few months ago, and it was still angled slightly to the side, making the bump on it more noticeable. His golden-blond hair had bleached to show a few white strands, and a few wrinkles curled around his dark eyes, but he looked no older than forty-five. His face was still lean, and he had maintained a toned physique. He thought he looked fine, until he turned back to Rafe to examine him more closely.

Wolf wasn't sure how old Rafe looked. The gleam in his green eyes created a childish and playful air. But the hard line of his chiseled jaw gave him a more mature appearance. His smooth, flawless skin seemed to have been carved from ivory and pearl. And his midnight black hair didn't have a single white strand in it.

"There's another club down the street we could go to," Rafe said as he buttoned up his shirt again, his powerful muscles flexing like taut wires under his skin. "It's mostly for younger people, but maybe—"

"Gabriel is dead," Wolf said in a monotone, which didn't match the avalanche of emotions that slammed into him as he spoke those three words.

Rafe's hands went still, clutching the neck of his shirt before he finished smoothing it out. He blinked, then chuckled. "He's been dead to me for a long time. I'm glad you've shut him out of your life too."

"He was murdered," Wolf continued.

Rafe didn't laugh this time. His hands went slack at his sides. "That's impossible. We don't die."

"He just did."

"No, that . . . that can't be right." Rafe finished smoothing his shirt.

Wolf took a deep breath. "Gabriel. Is. Dead." The words dropped from his mouth like stones. "Someone murdered him."

Rafe remained silent, but Wolf felt the other man's power coiling tightly around him. It was easy to have fake thoughts inside one's mind—lying to oneself, and to others, was easy—but emotions were impossible to fake. You could suppress them and even ignore them, but there was no running from them.

Rafe tensed, most likely at whatever he sensed in Wolf's emotions. The other man let out a long breath as if exhaling a burst of ashes that had been lodged in his lungs. "Let's go for a walk," Rafe said. He turned back to the dead woman. Rafe touched her forehead. Her body twisted at unnatural angles. Wolf blinked, and she was gone. It took him a second to realize that there was now a dead cockroach on the floor.

His legs turned to rubber, and his heartbeat roared in his ears. Wolf had forgotten how shallow and merciless the other man was. Rafe smiled at him, and Wolf knew Rafe had detected some fear from him.

Good, Wolf thought. It was better for Rafe to think he was afraid of him.

The two men silently exited the bathroom. The blue lights in the hallway made Rafe's eyes look sunken, like two voids. Wolf followed him back onto the dance floor, and they edged around the mass of people until they were outside.

Wolf's ears rang slightly at the sudden absence of noise. He exhaled. Mist curled out of his mouth and evaporated into the air a second later. Silence stretched between him and Rafe as they walked down the street. The dark-stoned facades of centuries-old buildings stood between skyscrapers with sleek glass exteriors. Yellow and white lights filtered through some windows, reflecting off puddles that rippled with the cold wind. A dog barked in the distance, and laughter echoed behind them as another group exited the club.

"He's truly dead?" Rafe asked.

"Yes," Wolf replied.

They arrived at the Thames River and walked parallel to it. Rafe looked out at the rushing dark water. "I can't say I'll miss the old grouch."

Wolf took a deep breath. "Someone found a way to kill us," he said.

Rafe glanced up at the crescent moon that sat atop a small cloud like a pair of horns. "How?"

"That's the same question I was going to ask you," Wolf said.

"Are you insinuating I had something to do with this?" Rafe locked gazes with him in a challenging stare.

"No," Wolf said. "I'm insinuating you're smart enough to help me figure out who did this and how."

Wolf couldn't be sure Rafe wasn't behind the murder. Coming to find him had been an act on a hunch—a very risky bet. But Wolf was out of options, and Rafe was the only one who could help him find the answers he needed.

"Who else knows about the murder?" Rafe asked after a few seconds of their silent walking.

"Just the two of us. And the killer, I suppose," Wolf replied.

"Why me?" Rafe asked, probably sensing Wolf's doubts about him. "You could have gone to anyone else first."

"I have my reasons," Wolf said. "Will you help me or not?"

Rafe looked up at the sky again, scratching his neck. "Sure." Even though Rafe's tone was playful, Wolf knew the other man understood the seriousness of the situation. "I'm assuming you have a plan to find the killer and deal with this mess?"

"I do," Wolf said. "I was thinking we could start with—"

Rafe held up a hand to silence him. They rounded a corner,

entering a dark alley cutting between two gray-stoned buildings. A lightbulb hung above a door on the left and flickered like a giant firefly. Rafe kicked Wolf. Sprawled on the ground from the pain that erupted in his ribs, Wolf growled as fear coursed through him.

"You've let yourself grow weak," Rafe said.

Wolf rolled to the side. He barely avoided Rafe's foot from colliding with his face. The cement cracked slightly under Rafe's force.

"You should be ashamed," Rafe hissed.

Wolf lifted himself from the ground.

Rafe placed his hands behind his back, circling Wolf with exaggeratedly long steps. "When was the last time you drank?"

Tying to ignore the blasting pain in his side, Wolf clenched his teeth. He had to have at least one broken rib, maybe two.

Rafe continued, "Even after you knew Gabriel was dead and that someone might come hunt the rest of us, you refused to feed." He jerked his chin toward the corner of the alley, and Wolf spotted a homeless man wrapped in dark blankets that blended with the ground.

"You didn't even see him, did you?" Rafe stepped closer to the man, who didn't wake up from his slumber. Wolf finally began to feel the pulse of life emanating from the man.

"I'm not going anywhere with you until you feed," Rafe said. "If we're going to hunt down the killer, you'll need to be in full strength." Rafe's eyes seemed to glow green. "Drink. Then we'll talk about where to start."

"You didn't have to beat my ass to prove your point," Wolf said as relief swept through him. If Rafe was the killer, then he would have taken advantage of Wolf's weakened state and killed him there and then.

"That was much more fun though." Rafe smiled wickedly, a crescent moon forming between his lips. "Drink."

His throat suddenly dry, Wolf gulped. It had been about a

year since he had last fed, and even then, he had only drunk a little. At the thought of fresh, warm blood, the *Aether* began stirring and trembling in his bones.

The pull inside him grew until he felt it would tear off his rib cage. Tugged by the invisible gravity that emanated from his chest, Wolf slowly walked toward the man and then kneeled next to him. Sweat and piss scents curled into Wolf's nose, making it itch again. The arteries in the man's neck throbbed softly as they pumped blood out of his heart. Wolf's fangs instinctively shot from his mouth. Behind him, Rafe gleefully said, "Let's remind the killer why people used to call us gods."

Wolf's power surged within him, the *Aether* a relentless force clamoring to be free. He had unleashed it fully only once before, and he had nearly destroyed the world. That was why he had started starving himself—to make sure it didn't happen again. But Rafe was right. He needed more strength to face their new enemy. Wolf took a deep breath and asked himself if he was willing to risk destroying the world again rather than letting it destroy him.

He thought about that for a second. Then he sank his fangs into the man's neck.

2

I SLOWLY WALKED TOWARD the Victorian-style mansion, the gravel crunching beneath my feet. It stood regally in the middle of a clearing edged by redwood trees. The dark walls contrasted beautifully against bright white accents, and the multi-gabled roofline had steeply pitched roofs and elaborate wooden shingles. The home had several tall, narrow chimneys that sent thin columns of dark smoke drifting into the thick gray clouds that hid the afternoon sun. Typical of Bay Area weather.

I exhaled. White mist puffed out of my mouth. My backpack seemed to become heavier, pulling me down, but I straightened my back and continued toward the mansion. My hands trembled, and I couldn't tell if it was from the cold or nervousness.

It's just a job interview, I told myself. But if I didn't get this job, then I would have to move back with my parents.

My hands tightened around the straps of my backpack. I couldn't go back home without a job or any money and ask for my parents' help after they had spent most of their savings to get me through college. They had never asked me to pay them back, but I felt obliged to give them something so, for once, I could help them like they had supported me throughout my whole life.

I took a deep breath as I climbed the porch steps. The porch itself was wide and welcoming with a roof that extended out from the house and was supported by a series of columns.

The wooden floor squeaked as I headed toward the grand double doors. A small bell hung on the side. I rang it. The sound echoed off the porch before fading into an uncomfortable silence. I waited, but no one came out. I was about to ring the bell again when the door swung open.

I startled back, then quickly composed myself. "Hello." My voice sounded much smaller than I had intended. I blamed my sore throat for that.

The girl at the entrance seemed younger than I, maybe seventeen or eighteen, and stood half a head shorter. Her straight midnight black hair was cut right below her sharp jawline, and her dark brown eyes accentuated her solemn expression. Her lips were pale and thin under a small and slightly upturned nose.

"Are you Isa?" the girl said before I could ask if this was the right address.

"Ah, yes," I said, trying not to stumble over the words.

She swept me from head to toe with her gaze, then stepped to the side. "Come in."

I thanked her and walked into the house, which was not much warmer than the outside. Wearing only black leggings and a dark blouse, the girl didn't seem to mind the cold. I unzipped the top of my jacket because it suddenly felt like it was choking me, but I didn't take it off. I breathed out, catching my reflection in a mirror as I passed by it. The smoky edges were framed by an elegant bronze frame. I smoothed out my dark hair, which had tangled as if the wind had tried to tear it off my head. My brown skin seemed a bit pale, which was expected with the cold, but my cheeks had turned blazing red, almost like the wind had scratched them. At least my blue eyes didn't betray the nervousness I felt, and a calm gaze stared back at me.

I took another deep breath and turned away from the mirror. From the high ceiling hung a chandelier, its crystals reflecting the light that filtered through the windows. A fireplace stood on the far right with a lively fire crackling inside of it and bathing dark sofas in a warm light.

The girl headed to the grand staircase across from the front door. After hesitating for a second, I followed her.

"I'm Sue," she said as she climbed the staircase without glancing back at me.

"Nice to meet you," I said.

The girl stopped at the second-floor landing. Tall and narrow windows had beautiful latticework. Hallways on either side of us branched deeper into the house, and I followed Sue down a corridor on the right. She knocked on the door at the end of the hallway.

"Come in," someone said from the other side.

She opened the door, then motioned for me to step into the room. I was expecting her to come in with me but instead felt a breeze at the back of my head as she closed the door behind me. A man, maybe a few years older than I, sat on the opposite side of a dark wooden desk. Bookshelves lined every wall except the one on the right that had a large window with a view to the forest.

"You can sit down, Isa." The man's voice was deep and husky, and I noted a British accent.

I nodded, unhooked my backpack, and placed it on the floor next to the chair in front of the desk. For a long, awkward moment, the man simply stared at me. I examined him too. He was like winter. His hair was the deep black of a cold, starless night. It created a stark contrast to his snow-white skin. Although his eyes were gray like two frozen ponds, there was a certain energy in them that made his irises shine as if lightning was frozen inside thick clouds. He had an elongated face with a long, straight nose, thick eyebrows, and a strong jaw. He was easily the most handsome man I had met. I was glad my cheeks were already reddened by the cold so he couldn't notice my face warming as he stared intensely into my own eyes.

"I'm Lucian Holt," he finally said. He glanced down to read a piece of paper, and it took me a second to realize it was my resume. "Dr. Herring provided a stellar recommendation of you." He raised his head again. "I wanted to hire him, but he strongly insisted that you would be a better fit for this specific job." Although his flat expression didn't reveal anything, I could sense from his tone that he was displeased to have me instead of a more professional translator. "In your resume it says you are fluent in English, Spanish, French, Attic Greek, Latin, and Egyptian."

"That's correct," I said. I was about to add *sir*, but he didn't look old enough to be called that. He was twenty-eight, at most.

Lucian nodded slowly. "I have some Greek, Egyptian, and Latin texts that I need translated into English as quickly as possible," he said. "I'll show you part of the texts right now. If I like your translations, I'll pay you to work on the rest."

Dr. Herring had already shared some details about the job with me, so I had come prepared. But the emphasis on the *if* made my stomach swirl with anxiety. I nodded.

"Good," he said as he stood. "Let's go to the library."

He stepped around the desk, and I quickly followed him with my backpack. Lucian was over a head taller than I and had a powerful physique. He wore a dark blue shirt and a long black coat. After exiting the office and walking through several corridors, we arrived at the library. The grand room had a high curved ceiling and ornate carvings that framed the tall bookcases lining the walls. The shelves were filled to the brim with leather-bound volumes. Dim gray light filtered through the stained-glass windows at the top of the room. A thick patterned rug covered the hardwood floor, and plush armchairs and sofas were arranged in cozy groupings around a massive fireplace.

Lucian led me to a mahogany desk in the far-right corner. A thin stack of papers was already waiting for me. I had imagined some ancient parchments or books, but maybe he had copied the passages from their original source for me to work with. A few dictionaries lay on the table, but I had brought my own.

"Where should I write the translations?" I asked.

"You can use your own materials if you brought any. If not, I'll give you some paper," he said.

"Yeah, I have a notebook," I said.

"Translate those pages." He motioned to the stack of papers. "I'll be back in a few hours." He regarded me for a second, almost challengingly, then walked out of the room.

I started the translations right away. Lucian clearly doubted my ability to do this assignment, but I couldn't lose out on this job. And if Dr. Herring thought I was the perfect fit for this, then I knew I could do it.

Two pieces of paper had writing in Attic Greek. The next two papers were in Latin, and the last ones were in ancient Egyptian. I marveled at the beautiful hieroglyphs that had been drawn on the paper and wondered if Lucian had written them.

I started by reading all the papers to get a general idea of what they were about. I began with the Latin text but quickly felt confused. The sentences didn't seem connected to each other and were written as if they had been randomly selected from different sources. I couldn't decipher an overall theme. I moved on to the Greek papers, but those, too, made little sense. The writings weren't from any classical work I recognized and seemed akin to phrases a drunken man would have scrawled on a wall or to a scary story told to children.

I know the names of the gods who live on those who cherish evil and gulp down their blood.

I wondered if the writings were part of an occult manuscript and found it strange that Lucian would hire someone to translate such weird text. But as long as he paid me, I didn't care what his hobbies were. I was nearly done reading the Greek page when I found a sentence that was the same as one in Latin.

Tell me my name.

My blood chilled. I didn't know why. Those words didn't hint at anything sinister, but something about them simply felt wrong.

I finally moved on to read the Egyptian text, which took me a bit longer even though I had always been very good at translating Egyptian. I had been better at it than my professors, who had been surprised with my skills. It was the first ancient language I had been drawn to. I had spent countless hours as a teenager in the Natural Sciences Museum chasing down a scholar who could translate ancient Egyptian until he agreed to teach me how to read it. In exchange for his lessons, I had become his assistant, so it had been a win for both of us.

Tell me my name.

That was the last sentence in the Egyptian text. Was the writer trying to invoke someone? Ancient civilizations, especially the Egyptians, had believed that names held power and that if you knew a being's true name then you could control them.

I went back to the Latin text and began writing down my translations, hoping that a second, more in-depth reading of the material would help me understand it better.

For you have life, your soul has health, your corpse is long-enduring, you see the flame, you breathe the air, your vision is clear in Darkness which is set in the entrance of the sky without seeing a storm.

I stared at the English translation for a few minutes, willing my brain to find meaning in those words.

I have given you your flesh, I have gathered your bones together for you, I have collected your members for you, I have thrown you off the earth which was on your flesh.

Definitely creepy, I decided.

Death is my destination, and I will enter into the place of execution.

I translated the Greek next, then moved on to the Egyptian. Lucian had only asked for a translation, but he hadn't said it had to make sense. Still, it bothered me that I couldn't understand the overall meaning or purpose of these pages.

You shall be for millions on millions of years.

Whoever had written these pages also switched between the first- and second-person point of view, which made everything more confusing.

Tell me my name.

Beyond sharing that one sentence, the three different texts seemed to be connected by an invisible thread. They all felt the same, although I couldn't logically explain why. Could they all come from the same source? Lucian hadn't mentioned that. Was he testing me to see if I could make that connection?

May she grant your soul to be strong and your corpse to be intact like the gods.

Where had Lucian even found these texts? They didn't resemble anything I had encountered before. Something nudged at my mind as if trying to make me remember where I had read this before. It was probably just my own frustration.

Tell me my name.

"Are you done?" Lucian's voice startled me, and I almost dropped the dictionary I had been holding.

He stood right behind me, looking down at my notebook and emanating predatory intensity. The warm yellow light from the lamp had created a circle around the table that pushed away the darkness within the rest of the room.

"Uh, yeah, mostly . . . I think," I said.

I handed him the notebook. His eyes darted through the pages as he read the translations. I pulled out my phone and realized it was seven in the evening. I had been so absorbed in the translations I hadn't felt the time pass by.

"Is this all?" Lucian asked as he looked away from the notebook. His piercing gray eyes were cold like two bits of an iceberg.

"For now," I said quickly. "I can keep translating them and—"

Lucian shook his head. "That's all for now."

My heartbeat sped up as panic shot through my veins. He hadn't liked the translations and wouldn't be giving me the job. Maybe I could offer to stay here overnight to redo the translations and—

"You're hired," he said.

"But—" I caught myself, then blinked.

One of Lucian's brows shot up.

"Really?" I asked.

"Yes," he said. "If you can handle it."

"Yeah, I can definitely handle it."

"I wasn't talking about the translations," he said. "You're clearly good at that. It's the rest of the job you might not have the stomach for. But if you can handle it, I'll pay you twenty thousand dollars for the next week or so."

My mouth went dry. That was a lot of money for one week of work. This job was starting to seem too good to be true, and a sliver of fear cut its way through me.

Lucian placed my notebook back on the table and met my gaze again. "I haven't told you why I need these translations."

"Why do you need them?" I asked.

Lucian's gray eyes seemed to swirl. "Because I'm a private detective, and I need your help to solve a series of murders."

3

"WHAT?" I asked Lucian.

Helping to solve a series of murders was not the job description I had expected. From his pocket, Lucian pulled out a black badge. It had his picture and name at the top and a metal shield on the bottom with the words *Private Detective* carved into it.

"I'm a private detective," he repeated. "And I need your help translating texts to solve some murders."

My heartbeat echoed inside of my ears. "Why would you need to translate texts to solve a murder?" I asked.

"I can show you," Lucian said.

He motioned for us to walk out of the room. After a stunned second, I followed him. Lucian led me downstairs just as Sue was walking upstairs.

"Where are you going?" she asked.

"The basement," Lucian responded.

"Definitely not creepy," Sue said as she turned around and began walking at Lucian's side. "You don't take young ladies into your basement, Lucian, especially not right after you met them."

"Why not?" Lucian asked. "It's a nice basement."

Sue rolled her eyes.

We arrived at the first floor, then walked toward a door at the side of the staircase.

"I take it she did brilliantly with those translations?" Sue asked.

Lucian didn't respond as he opened the door and switched on the light, revealing another staircase. Sue descended the stairs behind Lucian, and I went after her. The temperature lowered with every step I took until I reached the bottom and saw a basement that was a wine cellar with enough bottles to throw a party every night for the next year. Lucian walked to the right toward an open door between two wine stacks. He passed through it without a glance behind him. Sue followed right at his heels. I took a deep breath, then walked into the room.

I stopped at the threshold, my heart skipping a beat. A large whiteboard covered most of the opposite wall. My eyes darted from one picture to the next. I balled my hands into fists to keep them from shaking.

"Are these . . . ?" My head felt light.

"Victims," Lucian said. "The police found the first two yesterday and the third one this morning. All of them were women aged between fifteen and twenty-five and who lived in the Bay Area." Lucian pointed at one of the pictures, which showed a woman's bare back. I gulped down a sudden wave of nausea. "The killer has been carving Latin, Greek, or Egyptian text onto the victims. That text was what I asked you to translate."

He turned back to me as if assessing my next reaction.

"Did Dr. Herring know all this?" I asked.

Lucian hesitated for a second. "No." His gaze held me steady. "I told him I needed urgent help translating a private collection." Lucian paused. "I would have told him the truth if he had agreed to help."

"He's the most distinguished scholar in this area who knows all three of those languages," Sue said, pulling my attention to her. Her eyes narrowed at me. "He couldn't help on such short notice but said that you were his best student and that you would be able to do the job. So will you?"

I didn't respond. Lucian and Sue exchanged a quick glance.

"And you never know," Sue said as she turned back to me, "with a serial killer murdering young women around the city—you're in danger too." She paused. "You'll be doing yourself, and other young women out there, a big favor if you help."

"I know this is a lot to take in," Lucian said as he walked closer to me. "But I can promise you one thing. Whatever happens, I will keep you safe." His towering physique dominated most of the room like a pillar holding up the ceiling.

"And there's no one else who can solve the murders?" I asked. "Like the police?"

"The police asked me to help them," Lucian said.

Sue crossed her arms, her eyes narrowing as if assessing me for a challenge.

I looked back at the pictures of the dead women. I didn't recognize any of them. My heart thudded heavily. I didn't recognize any faces for now, but if the killer continued with the murders, then I might in the future.

"What exactly do you need me to do?" I asked.

Lucian turned back to the boards. "The carvings seem to be important to the killer's modus operandi. We can't understand their motive unless we understand the inscriptions. I need you to help me figure out why the killer is carving that text."

Silence settled in the room as Lucian and Sue looked at me. I met Lucian's piercing gray eyes. Could I trust him? I had no way of verifying that he was a private detective and that this was a real murder case. But those pictures looked very real, and I didn't think anyone would fake a murder case to lure me into a scam job. If I left, I was back to having no job, and if my skills could truly help solve a murder case, then it was worth the try.

"Alright," I said. "I'll help you."

Sue smiled.

"Good," Lucian said. "Let's get to work then."

My feet sank into the hot sand that pulled me deeper into the earth. I thrashed my arms wildly, trying to escape, but the desert kept swallowing me like a hungry mouth. The bruised purple sky disappeared as my head went under the sand. My chest was squeezed tightly.

I had lost something and had come to look for it. *Where are you?* I asked but received no response. I continued to slide deeper and deeper into the darkness. Then my bare foot hit something soft and cool.

"Tell me my name," it whispered.

I tried to say that I didn't know their name, but I couldn't get the words out of my mouth. My body began buzzing, the grains of sand vibrating against me. My toes curled, and whatever was beneath me shifted, moved, and slithered.

I awoke with a start, bolting upright as I squinted at the lamp on the desk. I didn't recognize my surroundings, other than it was a large, dark library. Then the memories of the last few hours came rushing back. A pang of guilt swelled in my chest, and I was glad Lucian hadn't realized I had fallen asleep while working. Something in my pocket buzzed. I fished my phone out.

"Hello?" I said with a yawn.

"I told you she would be asleep," my dad said from somewhere in the distance. I must have been on speaker.

"Why haven't you called me?" my mom exclaimed at the other side of the line. "You didn't even text if you were back in your apartment."

"Hey, Ma. I was busy," I said.

"How did the job interview go?" she asked. Even through the phone I sensed her nervousness.

"It went really well," I said. I banished the images of the dead bodies from my mind and glanced at the disorganized papers and dictionaries strewn across the desk. "I got the job and will be translating some ancient texts for the next couple weeks."

"That's wonderful," Dad said. "I told you they would see how smart and talented you are. It's impossible not to."

"Yeah," I said, my tongue suddenly dry.

"Are they paying you well?" Dad asked.

"They are," I said. Right after I had agreed to help, Lucian had paid me ten thousand dollars as an advance. "I can send you some—"

"No." Mom's tone was sharp. "That is your money. It's important to start on your savings."

I thought of the worn-out chairs around the living room, the main door hanging on the hinges for dear life, and the leak dripping from the kitchen ceiling.

"Are you sure you don't need a bit to—"

"No," Mom cut in again. "We can take care of ourselves like we always have, and now you can take care of yourself too."

"That's right," Dad said.

"Okay," I said. "Just let me know if you need my help."

"Hmm," Mom said and paused a bit before adding, "We're so proud of you, Isa. So, so proud."

A knot bulged in my throat. "Thank you, for everything."

"Hmm," she said again. "Also, I sent you some pictures of new chicken recipes."

"Try not to burn the chicken into coals like last time," Dad said.

"That was one time," I complained.

He laughed.

"The recipes are super easy," Mom said.

"So easy it might only take you three hours and thirty ingredients," Dad added.

"Anyway," Mom said, "let me know if you want me to send more recipes from your grandmother's cookbook."

"Or you can just get those frozen chicken nuggets again," Dad said.

"No," Mom said, "that's not healthy. You need to cook real food."

"I'll try. Thanks, Ma," I said.

"Alright, we'll let you go now," she said. "Good luck with the new job."

"Thanks. I love you," I said.

"Love you too," they both said, then hung up.

The screen went dark for a second, then showed the clock. It was four in the morning, around the time my parents got up for work. While Lucian hadn't said I needed to keep working overnight, I hadn't wanted to leave after he had revealed the terrible truth about the job. I must have fallen asleep at some point, and no one had come to wake me up.

I skimmed through my unread messages and opened the chat with my mom. The *easy* recipes she had sent could have been part of a gourmet cooking show.

Next, I opened a text from Mya.

I'm back! Trip was long but it went well. When are we going out again?? My soul needs some dancing.

The air grew thick, suffocating my breath. I wanted to tell her to leave the city because a serial killer was on the loose. But Lucian had been very clear about the confidentiality of this assignment.

"You can't tell anyone about this," he had said. "Not your parents, not your friends, no posting on any social media platform. Nothing."

They didn't want to alert the killer they were onto them, or so Lucian had claimed. Guilt tore at my chest, and my hands trembled as I typed a reply.

I've been feeling sick.

There's something going around, but we could go out in a couple weeks maybe?

Would a potential airborne disease prevent Mya from going out? Hopefully she was too tired from her trip for any outings. And in the meantime, I would be working with Lucian to catch the killer. I didn't know how long it would take, but I hoped it was soon.

After texting Mya, I noted three missed calls from Aura and a few texts from her.

How did the job interview go????

Are you back home yet?

Let me know how you're doing.

I sighed and quickly wrote a response. The claws of guilt sank deeper into my chest.

Doing good! I got the job but went to sleep late working on some things. Will update you later.

I looked through the other notifications I had missed.

Save your streak before midnight!

Oops. Well, there went my 135-day Duolingo streak to learn German. I sighed, then put my phone away. My stomach grumbled. I hadn't eaten anything since lunch the day before, and my mouth was so dry I felt like I had been walking in the desert for hours.

At the thought of the desert, I remembered the strange dream I'd had before waking up, but I didn't give it a second thought as I stood and made my way out of the library. All the lights were out, casting the mansion in a deep, oppressive darkness. I pulled out my phone and turned on the flashlight because I couldn't spot any light switches. I didn't expect anyone to harm me and didn't think the serial killer would break in somehow, but my heart still stuttered in fear.

After descending the stairs and walking through a couple of rooms, I finally found light casting a halo around a large double door. I approached it carefully, then slowly opened the door. A man I hadn't met before stood on the opposite side of a kitchen counter cutting carrots. He stopped as soon as I walked in. I turned off the flashlight.

"Hello," I said.

"You must be Isa," the man said. He seemed to be in his mid-thirties and spoke with an American accent. "Sue told me you would be helping Lucian with translations."

"Um, yeah," I said.

"I'm Dario," the man said, eyeing me with warm hazel eyes. He had a wolfish face with a high forehead and sharp cheekbones. The man's lips were thin under a pointed nose. His caramel blond hair was a few shades lighter than his skin.

"Nice to meet you," I said.

I wondered why he was cooking so early.

"You must be hungry," Dario said as he dumped the carrots into a salad bowl. "I made you some dinner." He glanced at the wall clock. "Breakfast, I guess. Did you sleep well?"

"Oh, I fell asleep on the library desk," I said sheepishly.

Dario glared at the salad as he mixed it with two large spoons. "That man has no manners," he muttered under his breath. "I thought you had slept in one of the guest rooms."

A tense second of silence thrummed in the air.

"Do you need any help with the food?" I asked.

"No, no," Dario said. "You can just wait in the dining room."

"I can help with something," I insisted. I glanced around the kitchen, trying to find a dirty dish that I could wash but didn't see any.

"Well, if you really want to, you can help me heat the soup." Dario motioned at a pot on the stove.

I spent a few minutes stirring tomato soup before Dario pulled a large piece of steak out of the oven and cut it into smaller pieces. My mouth began to water at the smell. He served the soup into two bowls, and I helped him carry the rest of the food to the dining room adjacent to the kitchen.

We began eating in silence. The food was wonderful, much better than anything I had cooked for myself in the last couple of months.

A door somewhere deep inside the house banged shut. Had that been Lucian or Sue? Or were there more people here?

"Is anyone else joining us for an early breakfast?" I asked.

"No," Dario said. He glanced at my almost-empty plate. "I'm glad you're enjoying the food."

"Thank you," I said after I swallowed.

He hadn't touched the soup and had only taken a few bites from the meat while pushing around the rest with his fork. A large grandfather clock chimed behind me indicating it was four thirty in the morning. Roman numerals adorned the clock's face, and the long second hand moved at a steady pace. The pendulum swung back and forth, its rhythmic motion hypnotic and soothing.

"It was my father's," Dario said as he stared at the clock. "It's one of the first things he bought when we moved into the house."

"This is your house?" I motioned around us.

Dario nodded. I stared at him for a few seconds. He didn't seem old enough to be Lucian's father, and they didn't resemble each other. If Lucian was made of winter, then Dario was like summer. Dario sounded American, but Lucian was European, and Sue was Asian.

Dario must have noticed my confusion because he laughed. "The three of us aren't related by blood," Dario said. "But we're like a family." He didn't elaborate more, and I didn't ask.

I was just finishing my salad when the door behind us burst open. Lucian walked in. He wore the same clothes as the day before. If he hadn't slept, it didn't show. His eyes burned with an intense determination. He also didn't seem surprised to see I was still here, and I wondered if he would say something about it.

"Welcome back," Dario said.

Lucian nodded in acknowledgement, then turned to me. "Did you finish the translations?" he asked.

"Yes, but I'm trying to reorganize the text to—"

"That's fine," he said. "I'm driving into the city to examine a new scene. I want you to come with me. You can tell me what you've discovered on the way."

"Sure," I said. "When do we leave?"

"Now," Lucian said.

He left the room like a draft of wind.

Dario shook his head once Lucian's footsteps had faded. "No manners," he muttered again. I lifted my plate intending to take it back to the kitchen, but I stopped when Dario said, "I'll clean up. Don't worry about it."

I hesitated, but Dario only smiled and jerked his head toward the open door.

"Thanks." I hurried out of the dining room. I was disoriented for a second before finding my way to the front door. The engine of Lucian's sleek black car was already on when I stepped outside. I climbed into the passenger seat and buckled my seat belt.

Even though the sun hadn't yet risen on the horizon, a considerable amount of traffic clogged the highway into San Francisco. Lucian's phone rang a few minutes after we left, and he quickly answered it using the car's hands-free system.

"Where are you?" Sue asked.

"I'm taking Isa to the new crime scene," Lucian said.

"Oh joy," Sue responded and paused for a moment. "We tried to pull up the camera footage but didn't find anything. The building owner was too cheap to repair the cameras, which have been out for a few months."

Lucian huffed, squeezing the steering wheel until his knuckles turned white.

"Mm-hmm," Sue said. "Check if any of the neighbors have wireless cameras. I asked the officers, but they didn't remember."

Lucian nodded. "Will do."

"I'm in the morgue now. I'll let you know what I find on the body," Sue said.

She seemed a bit young to be examining corpses, but I refrained from saying that.

"Great, thanks," Lucian said before hanging up. He breathed deeply as if trying to calm a storm of emotions brewing inside of him. "So, what have you discovered in your translations?"

I didn't want to show my confusion and tried to sound as confident as possible.

"Some passages were repeated across all three languages," I said.

"Such as?" Lucian asked before I could continue.

"Tell me my name," I said. "That phrase is repeated often. There are also sentences that speak of gods who gulp down blood, of corpses that remain intact, and of souls that have strength."

Lucian's grip tightened on the wheel.

Prompted by his silence, I continued. "The passages are in either first or second person, like *I have walked* or *you have walked*. They also mention several houses, caverns, and mounds but don't include specific locations, which makes it harder to find the origins of the passages."

Lucian didn't speak for a long moment, the roar of the car engine filling the silence as we slowly advanced through the traffic. The lights from the cars and distant buildings pierced the early morning fog like fireflies casting a gentle, hazy glow.

"Why?" Lucian finally asked.

"Why what?" I asked.

"Why is the killer inscribing such text onto the victims? What are they trying to do?" Lucian asked.

I shifted uncomfortably. "I don't know."

"That's what you need to find out."

I nodded but had no clue how I would discover that.

Lucian's phone rang again, and he answered.

"Detective Holt," a deep male voice said on the other side.

My heart immediately sped up. So he *was* a detective. It made me feel better to hear it from someone else.

"Officer McGowan," Lucian said. "I'm on my way to the scene. Is it clear?"

"As clear as it can be," McGowan said. "The body's at the morgue for inspection. Have you decoded what the inscriptions mean?"

"I'm working on it," Lucian responded.

There was a short silence on the other side as Lucian stopped at a red light. "I have never seen anything like this, and there is no indication that the killer will stop."

"I've never seen anything like this either," Lucian said.

"Coming from you, that's even more concerning," McGowan said.

"I'll find the killer," Lucian said. The way he said it made it sound like a promise.

"I know you will," McGowan said. "Let me know if you discover anything new."

"I will," Lucian said before hanging up. He exhaled, his shoulders sagging a bit, but he quickly composed himself. "We should be the only ones at the scene."

"Where is it?" I asked.

"Downtown in the victim's apartment."

"She was murdered in her own apartment?" I asked.

"Yes, last night," Lucian said.

Spikes of fear shot through me. It was one thing to get murdered when you were out and about, but getting killed in your own home seemed to violate a sacred law to me. If you weren't safe in your home, then where were you safe?

"We'll be safe, don't worry," Lucian said as if reading my thoughts.

Our eyes met for a second before he turned back to the road. Lucian's phone rang again, and he answered.

"Just took a look at the body," Sue said. "This time the MO is different. The inscriptions were carved after the victim was killed."

Lucian frowned.

"She was tased, then asphyxiated while she was unconscious. No bruises on her neck so it could have been with a pillow or plastic bag." The way Sue said that so casually made shards of fear crystallize in my chest. "And we found a little piece of a knife embedded into her skin." Sue paused. "It was pure silver."

Lucian's muscles locked into a rigid stance. "Are you sure?"

"Yes."

"Was there a mark?" Lucian asked, making me wonder what kind of mark he was expecting.

"No," Sue quickly said. "That doesn't confirm anything though."

Lucian exhaled. "We'll talk about this later."

"Yeah," Sue said. "Good luck at the scene. Keep me updated."

"Will do," Lucian said, then hung up. "Do any of the texts mention silver knives?"

"No," I said.

Lucian exhaled but didn't say anything else, leaving me wondering what could possibly be so important about silver knives.

4

THE SUN HAD BARELY peeked over the horizon when Lucian and I arrived at the apartment building. A man walked out the front door with his dog, and a couple of children played tag in the lobby. If anyone knew someone had been murdered, they didn't show it. I didn't spot any police cars either. Lucian and the police must have really been working hard to keep the murders secret so the killer wouldn't suspect anything.

After riding the elevator to the fourth floor, we made our way down the hallway. Lucian fixed his gaze on every door. I did the same but didn't spot any wireless cameras. He stopped before a door at the end of the hallway, analyzing it carefully. I wondered if he was looking for signs of forced entry, but I didn't see anything wrong with the door. Lucian turned the knob and walked in, motioning for me to follow.

The metallic stench of blood wafted into my nostrils. Lucian switched on the light. My legs turned to lead, and I regretted not asking Lucian if I could stay in the car. A large bloodstain coated the carpet next to the dining table. Cold sweat slicked my palms as a knot of anxiety tightened in my gut. I felt the blood drain from my face, leaving me feeling slightly lightheaded. Lucian blocked the light as he towered above me and stared at me. He didn't say anything. There was nothing he could have said to help me feel better. I squeezed my eyes shut, took a deep breath, and opened them again. I nodded at Lucian, who pulled his gaze away after a second.

He examined every room, and I silently trailed behind him. He never touched anything but merely observed things as if he were walking through a museum. We ended up in the kitchen, and Lucian offered me a stool to sit on.

"The lock on the front door wasn't broken," Lucian said, "which means the victim willingly let the killer in. Why?"

After a couple seconds of silence, I realized he had asked me the question.

I shrugged.

"Who would you open the door for?" Lucian asked.

"Only someone I know," I said.

Lucian said nothing.

I chewed on my cheek, thinking. "Or maybe a package delivery person."

"Did you see any packages around here?" Lucian asked.

"No," I said, "but they could have used a decoy package."

"Don't you check your name on the package as soon as you receive it?" Lucian asked.

"Sometimes," I said. "When I'm expecting a package, and someone just hands it to me, then I usually don't." I paused. "We should ask at the front desk whether there's a package room or if people receive packages at their door."

"Good idea," Lucian said.

He walked over to the fridge, opened it, and carefully analyzed its contents. The smell of blood was less intense in the kitchen, but it was still present and making my head spin.

"The killer could be a woman," I said.

Lucian's intense gaze bore into me. He closed the fridge. "Why?"

"Assuming it wasn't a package delivery person, I wouldn't open the door to a man I didn't know, no matter what," I said. "But if a woman knocked on my door and asked for help . . . maybe I would."

Lucian's lips formed a slight smile. "That's good. I had also guessed the killer was a woman."

"Why?" I asked.

"Generally, female killers tend to use methods that require less physical strength and use smaller weapons," he said. "Sue mentioned the victim was tased, then asphyxiated. Men tend to choke their victims by crushing their windpipes, but the victim was killed another way." He looked out the kitchen door toward the bloodstain that was thankfully out of my view. "This is just a generalization, so we can't be sure the killer is female. And it's always good to keep our minds open. But at least this part of the evidence points to a female killer or to someone who doesn't have a lot of physical strength and relies on other methods to over-power victims."

Lucian's gaze settled on something behind me, and his eyes narrowed slightly. I jumped to my feet, my heart lurching into my throat.

"Sorry," he said. "Didn't mean to scare you."

Lucian leaned down to retrieve a black piece of paper that had fallen next to the stove. It had been ripped, but I could still make out the gold foil vines that edged it and the number five right next to the rip. Lucian held the paper by its edge, pulled a plastic bag from his coat, carefully dropped the paper inside the bag, and sealed it.

"Might be important," he said.

He walked over to the trash can and opened it. I peeked in, too, but didn't spot the missing part of that black paper. There was, however, a large plastic bag at the very top of the trash. My breath caught. Lucian went utterly still.

"Do you think that . . ." I couldn't finish.

"Possibly," Lucian said. "We should take it for evidence too."

He closed the trash can.

"What did you observe?" Lucian asked as he turned back to me.

"What?"

"As we went through the rooms, what did you observe?"

"I . . ." Too shocked to do anything except follow Lucian, I had tried to not look around.

He walked out of the kitchen, and I followed him. "I want you to tell me what you observe in this scene and what that tells you about the victim and the murder."

He raised his chin ever so slightly and his eyes narrowed with a challenging edge, daring me to push beyond my shock.

My mind scrambled for a response. "Sue mentioned the inscriptions had been carved after the victim's death, so that's where the bloodstain comes from if she died of asphyxiation," I said, trying to form a coherent sentence. "If those wounds were inflicted after she died, then there would be less bleeding since the heart wasn't pumping blood anymore. The bloodstain isn't big enough to indicate the victim bled out either." I turned back to Lucian. The weight of his stare made my heart speed up. "But how did Sue know the inscriptions were carved after the victim's death just by looking at the body?"

"If wounds are inflicted postmortem, there's usually no redness or swelling around them because there's no inflammatory response anymore," Lucian said. "So it tends to look like a cleaner cut."

I nodded.

"Keep going," Lucian said as he motioned to the room.

"The table and the chairs have not been disturbed, even though the bloodstain is right next to them, which indicates no signs of struggle," I said. "So either the victim knew the killer or felt safe around them."

"Good," Lucian said. My heart shouldn't have made a little leap at his approval, but it did. I had nothing to prove to him, yet I wanted to show him that I could be helpful.

We walked through the apartment again, and this time I paid attention to the details inside every room—the made bed, the clean and spotless bathroom, the organized desk. According to Lucian, the victim usually got home from work between five thirty and six in the evening.

"If you had to wake up at seven in the morning for work, at what time would you go to sleep?" Lucian asked.

"Before midnight," I said.

Since the bed was made, the murder could have happened before midnight if the victim usually slept seven or eight hours. That left a window of six hours between the time she got home and the time she went to bed for the murder to occur.

We continued walking through the apartment, and I began noticing more subtle details—a stack of mail envelopes on her nightstand, the open laptop that had been left on at her desk, a phone and a half-full cup of tea on the living room table, an unwashed plate in the sink, a pot of soup still sitting on the stove.

"What was the victim doing before the murder?" Lucian asked.

Back in the kitchen, I felt too nervous to sit. Instead, I paced back and forth in front of him.

"She had just made herself dinner," I said. "She must have left the soup on the stove because it was still hot and she wanted to wait for it to cool before putting it in the fridge. She didn't clean her dishes, but the rest of the kitchen is clean and tidy, so she probably wasn't someone who left her dishes out overnight." I paused. "Her phone was in the living room so that's probably where she was, drinking her tea, before the killer knocked on the door."

"What time do you think she ate dinner?" Lucian asked.

"Maybe between six and seven, after she came home," I said. "So the murder must have happened when she finished, around seven or eight."

Lucian was silent for a few seconds. I stopped pacing to face him. A subtle smile graced his lips. "Good," he said again. "Now we have a time frame. If we had some camera footage, we could have confirmed this. Unfortunately, we don't have that evidence, so this all just remains an estimate." He exhaled, walked over to the trash can, and picked it up carefully from the sides. "Let's go."

After leaving the apartment, we went down to the front desk. They confirmed that there was a package room, so it was less likely the killer would have pretended to be a package delivery person. They must have used some other cover to convince the victim to open the door.

"I was thinking," Lucian said as he placed the trash can into the trunk of his car and used some duct tape to close the lid so it wouldn't spill. He was careful where he added the tape, maybe trying to avoid erasing fingerprints if there were any. "It would be safer and more efficient if you stayed with us at the mansion while we find the killer. We have several guest rooms."

I hesitated for a second, but only a second. "I agree."

I gave Lucian my address, and we rode in silence to my apartment. Once there, I quickly ascended the steps to the third floor and hurried to my door. My hands shook slightly, making the keys clatter, as the images from the murder scene flashed through my mind.

I opened the door and turned on the light, then shut the door behind me and locked it. I stood there for a moment, catching my breath. Nothing seemed to be out of place in my studio apartment. Knowing it might be a few days before I came back, I walked over to my potted plants next to the window and watered them with the bottle I had left on the floor.

Then I packed some clothes. I glanced at the bookshelf, overflowing with dozens of books, and considered packing one but knew I probably wouldn't have time to read. And if I did have some free time, I could just read an ebook on my phone.

I walked over to my desk to check if I was missing anything and packed one extra notebook, more pens and pencils, and a thick stack of sticky notes. Leaving my other personal notebooks and journals on the desk, I debated whether to take my diary but opted for just leaving it in a drawer.

On my way to the bathroom, I passed by my unfinished paint-by-numbers canvas depicting a tall mountain range behind a lake. The paint-crusted brushes that I had used the day before seemed to stare at me accusingly. While I was packing some toiletries, I received a call. I considered not answering, since Lucian was waiting for me and he didn't seem very patient, but I fished out my phone to check who the caller was. I immediately responded.

"Hi, Dr. Herring."

"Isa," he responded in his lively tone. "Did you get the job?"

"Yes, I did."

"That's wonderful," he said. "The moment Holt explained he needed someone to translate that private collection, I knew you would be the perfect fit. I'm glad that you finally found something and that it gives you some time to figure out what comes next."

"Yeah," I said. "Did you know Lucian before he offered you the job?"

"He's friends with a friend of mine," Dr. Herring said. "I don't know much more beyond what my friend told me—he belongs to a very wealthy European family and is visiting the States to purchase some ancient manuscripts. He'll be leaving soon and wanted those translated urgently, but he refused to send digital files and have someone do it remotely."

I wondered if Dr. Herring's friend was a cop, or someone involved in that world, who had lied about Lucian to cover his real identity. Or maybe Lucian was such a good undercover detective that even his own friends didn't know the truth. Although he didn't strike me as the type of man with a lot of friends.

"Has everything worked alright with him so far?" Dr. Herring asked as if sensing my anxiety.

"Yes," I said, maybe a bit too quickly. "Thank you for calling to check in on me."

"Of course. Keep me updated on how things go."

"Will do," I said.

I hung up after we both said goodbye. A small pang of guilt bubbled inside my chest. Part of me felt like I should have told Dr. Herring the truth, but Lucian seemed to not want others to know his identity, and that wasn't my secret to tell.

I finished packing and headed back to the car. Lucian was on the phone with Sue when I climbed into the passenger seat. Sue went silent. I felt that I had interrupted a conversation they didn't want me to hear.

"Let's stay vigilant just in case," Lucian finally said.

"Always," Sue said.

She hung up. Lucian started the engine again, and we began driving back toward the mansion.

"Dario already copied the new inscriptions," he said. "We'll need those translated as soon as possible."

"Sure," I said. "What will you be doing in the meantime?"

"Sue and I are following some possible suspects," Lucian said.

He didn't elaborate more, and I didn't ask. The ride back to the mansion was silent, and I tried my best to look out at the other cars instead of letting my thoughts wander back to the victim's apartment.

I glanced away from the window when my phone pinged with a text from Mya.

Oh no! I hope you feel better soon. Let me know if you need anything.

I opened the text to answer, but my thumbs remained hovering over the screen. I put the phone away again. Any other lie I told her would just make me feel worse.

Once at the mansion, I stepped out of the car, but Lucian remained inside.

"After translating the new inscriptions," Lucian said, "try to figure out why the killer is so interested in those passages."

"Okay," I said.

A new piece of paper was already waiting for me when I returned to the library. This one was in Egyptian, written in the same careful script as the others were.

As soon as I sat down, Dario walked into the room holding a tray in his hands. He set the tray down at the edge of the large desk. "I assumed you would want some lunch." He motioned to a sandwich.

"Thanks," I said, although I wasn't particularly hungry after visiting the murder scene. But, I would probably be hungry later.

Dario looked at the small duffel bag I had brought. "I can take that to one of our guest rooms."

"Sure," I said.

"Let me know if you need anything else," Dario said. "I'll be around the house."

"Thanks."

As soon as he was gone, I started translating the new text.

I have hidden the one whom I found missing.

The image of the bloody carpet kept flashing inside of my mind. But having it hovering over my thoughts gave me a strange focus I hadn't felt before.

I have risen as a possessor of life because of that day of cold blood, fresh wounds, and burial.

Blank pages quickly filled up with new sentences.

Their knives shall hold no power over me, because I know them, I know their names.

It didn't specify a silver knife, but I made note of the weapon since it had interested Lucian.

Yesterday, which is pregnant with the one who shall give birth to himself in another time, belongs to me.

I ate the sandwich while I continued. Even though I still wasn't hungry, I was beginning to feel lightheaded, and the ham sandwich was pretty good. I had just finished eating it when my phone rang.

"Hey, Aura," I said. "Can we talk later, I'm in the middle of—"

"Just wanted to check in on you," she responded. "You didn't call me last night like you promised. I tracked your phone location, but you never left the address you gave me. I got worried. I literally would have called the cops if you hadn't texted me this morning. What happened?"

"Sorry," I said. "I got busy with . . . onboarding stuff."

"No worries," she said. "We can talk tonight after Book Club. I want to hear all the tea."

Shoot, I thought. I had forgotten about Book Club. I glanced at the translations. The image of them carved on someone's back burned through my mind. I could help Lucian prevent that from happening to someone else, but the clock was ticking. Time closed in on me, squeezing the air out of my lungs, every second pulsing through my body like an extra heartbeat.

"I . . . I don't think I'll be able to make it," I said.

"What? Why?" she asked. "You've never missed Book Club in two years."

"I know," I said, yearning to spend some time with Aura and the group to off-load some of the tension from the past day. "I just have a lot of work."

"You're going to be working until eight at night?" she asked.

"Maybe," I said.

"Sounds like a toxic work culture," she said.

I glanced at the cryptic inscriptions. "A little."

"Are you sure you can't stop working for a few hours to join us?"

"Sorry. I can't. But I'll be back next month. I promise."

A moment of silence stretched through the line. "Okay. Let me know when you're free so we can talk. Hopefully soon."

"Will do," I said.

"Alright, bye."

"Bye."

I hung up the phone and took a deep breath. It would only be a couple of intense days and then my life would be back to normal. I pocketed my phone and returned to the inscriptions.

I have been reborn, I have gone forth in a shape whom the common folk worship.

Death and rebirth seemed to be a common theme in the texts, I thought.

My body is everlasting, my shape is eternity.

The immortality of the gods was also mentioned several times. But how did that tie in to the killer's motivations?

Tell me my name.

And what did names have to do with anything? The ancients had thought names could give them complete power over another individual, but how was that connected to the murders?

I am one who gave birth to myself yesterday, one who created my own name.

On a new piece of paper, I wrote out the passages from all the texts, then highlighted the similarities—anything that I felt could have come from a single source. Then I rewrote the text, rearranging the sentences so they flowed more concisely. But I still couldn't make sense of them.

Why had the killer used these ancient languages? Were they fluent in all three? Very few people were, which made me think the killer wasn't, and if they were, that narrowed down our suspect list. But I assumed Lucian had already investigated that. Maybe the killer had copied these sentences without knowing what they meant. But why?

I went back to the original inscriptions, highlighting syntactic irregularities and sentences where the grammatical structure was incorrect. But how could I find the killer's motivations from text they might not even understand? The killer could have just murdered the victims and been done with it. So their goal went beyond killing—this was some sort of macabre ritual that they believed important. Was it some sort of sacrifice? But for what purpose? The more I read and reread the translations, the less I understood them. The light outside dimmed as the afternoon dragged by. My mind went around in circles trying to find answers, like a dog trying to bite its tail.

"Did you find anything?" Lucian asked.

I startled. He walked so silently I could never tell when he was in the room.

"Maybe," I said.

Lucian stepped closer, staring at the translations, then his eyes slid to me. "You should get some fresh air," he said. He motioned at me to follow him, and together we walked out of the library. He led me to the third floor where we exited onto a terrace. The sun was mostly obscured by clouds, but it still cast a warm yellow glow on our surroundings. I couldn't believe most of the day had already gone by. We sat on a pair of chairs overlooking the clearing and the towering trees beyond, both of us silent for a time.

"The inscriptions seem to focus mostly on death and rebirth," I said. "And there was one mention of a knife, although nothing specified it was silver. But I'm still struggling to understand how this ties in to the killer's motivations. I don't think the killer understands these ancient languages."

"What makes you say that?" Lucian asked.

"Greek and Latin use a case system," I said, unsure of how much he knew about the languages. "Case endings on nouns and adjectives determine the meaning and function of a word in a sentence. But in some of the sentences, the case endings don't match up to create a coherent sentence. So my guess is that the killer copied the sentences from another source and might have tried to make some edits, but they don't know how to use the case system, so now the sentences are gibberish. At least that's what it seems like."

"Hmm," Lucian said. "But even if they don't understand the inscriptions, they must have a belief that they mean something."

"Yeah," I said. "I'll have to keep thinking about that."

"Have you eaten anything?" Lucian asked abruptly as he looked at his watch.

"Dario gave me a sandwich," I said, "but I haven't been hungry since visiting the murder scene." I suppressed a shiver. "I should have stayed in the car."

Lucian shook his head. "No. I wanted you there."

"Why?" I asked.

"It's one thing to see pictures and another thing to see a real crime scene," Lucian said. "I wanted to motivate you."

"I was already motivated," I said.

"Were you?" Lucian asked.

I opened my mouth to retort, then realized he was right. Yesterday morning, this had just been a job that I needed to keep myself afloat. But being at the crime scene had grounded me in the grim reality we were facing and had made me feel more determined to find answers.

"Did you find anything new while you were gone?" I asked.

"Another victim."

My lungs contracted painfully. "So soon?"

Lucian nodded.

My eyes burned with tears. What if this time it was someone I knew? Lucian pulled out his phone, and relief swept through me when I didn't recognize the face in the photo. But that feeling was short-lived because whether I knew the victim or not, another young girl's life had been brutally ripped away. Lucian put the phone away. I turned back to him. His expression was calm even though there were already multiple victims in three days. Then I looked into his eyes, and I realized I had mistaken calmness for a very still rage that simmered like a thundercloud about to drop a storm.

"How do you do it?" I asked.

Lucian's expression softened. The wind ruffled his dark hair, and a strand curled onto his forehead.

"You can't save everyone," Lucian said. "This job is not about saving everyone." He paused to take a deep breath. "But you can save someone. The hardest part is that you never know who that someone is going to be. Once you find the killer, all you see are the ones you failed and not the someones you will probably never meet because the killer never got to them. And you just have to make peace with that."

I nodded slowly, unsure if I could make peace as easily as he made it sound.

"How long have you been a detective?" I asked.

"A long while," he responded.

It couldn't have been that long if he was in his late twenties, unless he had been a teenage Scooby-Doo prodigy.

Lucian exhaled slowly. "I know this must be hard for you, and that it wasn't what you expected to be doing after college, but I really appreciate your help."

"It definitely wasn't what I was expecting," I muttered.

I looked back at the clouds and could feel Lucian's gaze on me but refused to meet it.

"What were you expecting?" he asked.

I shrugged. "I don't know. I still have to figure out what I want to do."

I finally turned to face him. His brows knitted together as if I were another puzzle he needed to solve.

"I think people focus too much on what they want to do instead of who they want to be," Lucian said. "You're clearly very good with ancient languages, and your resume shows you enjoy studying them and ancient civilizations. But who do you want to be, Isa?"

"I . . ." That was a much harder question to ask myself, and I hadn't truly thought about it that way before. "I've always loved ancient languages, ever since I was a little kid." I paused. "I'm just not sure how I could turn that into a career, at least not in the immediate future." I had applied to work at museums and academic institutions but hadn't received a single offer, and I didn't know what else I could be doing with my talents.

"That still doesn't tell me, or yourself, who you want to be," Lucian said. He leaned closer to me. "If you focus too much on what you want to do, then you'll be frustrated because what you do is not always up to you. Life may close some doors for you and open others, but we can't always control that." He paused. "But if you focus on who you want to be, no one and nothing can take that away from you."

I considered that. "And how do you figure out who you want to be? Doesn't what we do determine who we are?"

Lucian pulled his hair back with his hand. "Our actions determine who we are. Actions stem from doing, yes, but also from our beliefs, thoughts, and feelings. So being is more than just doing, Isa." He pulled back a bit, bracing his arms on his legs, but his eyes never left mine. "Whenever you think about ancient languages, what are the beliefs and emotions tied to that?"

"I feel happy," I said, then thought deeper about it. "Passionate, inspired, motivated, independent, curious, creative, free." The words had flowed out of me. A smile quivered on Lucian's mouth. "I feel those emotions when I believe I might be the first person in millennia to understand something that someone left behind and when I feel I'm giving a voice to those who can't speak anymore."

A smile finally parted Lucian's lips. "So you do know who you want to be—a translator. You can do many things as a translator, but don't worry too much about specific jobs. Something will find you."

"I hope so," I said, hoping it was as easy as he made it sound. I turned to face him again. "What sort of emotions do you feel as a detective?"

Lucian turned away as something flashed in his eyes, an emotion I couldn't quite place. It took him a few moments to respond, as if he hadn't expected me to turn the questions back to him.

"Safe," Lucian said, his voice so low I had to lean closer to listen. "I felt so powerless and defenseless for such a long time that the only thing I wanted was to feel safe. And when I decided to become a detective, I wanted to help other people feel the same when I caught killers they couldn't fight against."

I opened my mouth to say something, then realized I didn't even know how to respond. I wondered what Lucian had lived through to make him feel like that.

His muscles flexed as if speaking strained his entire body. "But when I started, I was just angry. I felt lost, and catching killers was the first thing that gave me a purpose—to hunt the monsters that had once hunted me." He chuckled, pulling further away from me and crossing his arms over his chest as if to cover up an open wound in his heart. "This probably makes no sense to you."

"It does, a bit," I said. "I know what it feels like to be lost. I've felt like that for a while."

"Why?" he asked.

I shrugged. "I don't know it's just . . ." I shook my head. "I know, I know—I should focus on who I want to be instead of what I want to do. But it seems that everyone around me knows exactly what they want to do, that they're happy with it, and that they have their entire lives figured out." I paused, meeting Lucian's gaze briefly. "And even though I'm still young, it feels like time is slipping from my fingers like water, like I can barely keep up, and the next thing I know I'll be old, my entire life will be behind me, and I'll wonder what I've really done with my time here." I shook my head. "That probably sounds so stupid."

"It doesn't," Lucian said gently, bracing his hands on his thighs as he leaned toward me again. "That's the most accurate description of life I've heard." A sharp gust of wind blew toward us, making the trees rustle. "I didn't think anyone else would feel that way."

"Not even Dario and Sue?" I asked.

His expression hardened slightly. "We don't talk about these things," he said. A howling wind filled the silence that stretched between us for a few seconds.

"What should I do to find the killer's motivations?" I asked, feeling that I needed to change the subject. "I've read the translations ten times but feel like I'm going in circles."

"Take a step back," Lucian said. "Try to figure out where the passages come from or if they're related to other ancient texts."

I nodded. "Sure. I can try that."

And I had no idea where to start.

Lucian turned around, and I followed his gaze as Sue opened the terrace door.

"We should go," she said to Lucian. Her eyes traveled between the two of us. "Don't want to keep the police waiting."

He nodded, then stood as Sue walked back into the house.

"Good luck," I said as I stood too.

"Thanks," Lucian said. He fished something out of his pocket, then handed it to me. It was the black piece of paper with gold foil that we had found. "It didn't have any fingerprints, so it's useless now, but could you store it somewhere safe? Just in case."

"Sure," I said as I grabbed the paper.

Lucian stepped closer to me. His gray eyes held me steady as his gaze turned slightly challenging again. "You're a translator. Go give a voice to those who can't speak anymore, Isa. I know you can do it. You just have to believe you can do it too."

I nodded, smiling. Lucian walked back into the house. From the terrace, I watched him and Sue climb into the car and drive away. I took a deep breath as the gold foil glinted in the faint sunlight. I wondered what the five meant and what the full number was. I pocketed it away after a minute, then walked back to the library.

I couldn't give the victims their lives back, but I could give them a voice.

PART II

THE
REUNION

5

WOLF AND RAFE SAT outside at a café as the morning mist cleared to a sunny day. The peak of the Eiffel Tower seemed to poke through the roof of the building at their side. Strangers passed by them as they walked down the old narrow street. Their lives pulsed like faint echoes. Wolf tried to ignore them but couldn't fully suppress the craving in his chest that demanded more blood. One body hadn't been enough to satiate him, but it had fully awakened the *Aether*, which now flowed through his body like a second circulatory system.

"Have you talked to Helios?" Rafe asked.

"No," Wolf replied.

"Nicholas?"

"No."

"Sekhmet?"

"Nope."

"Laius?"

Wolf shook his head. Some of the other Athatos had changed their names, and only a few of them retained their original ones. It usually depended on how fragmented their minds had become.

Rafe pushed back his hair with a sigh, his eyes staring intently into Wolf's. Not wanting to shy away from the challenge, Wolf didn't dare look away. He knew what Rafe was trying to find in his eyes—a sliver of Wolf's power that glowed in his irises. But Wolf had enough control over his power to not let it show.

A young waitress placed a steaming cup of coffee before each man, her gaze settling on each of them longer than it should have.

Shifting uncomfortably at the woman's attention, Wolf turned away from Rafe. Wolf knew he looked much younger than he had the night before, maybe now around thirty or so, and he had to admit that it felt invigorating to live in a younger, more agile body. But he also drew more stares from humans, which he didn't like. And it didn't help that he could feel the waitress's heart beating like drums pounding against his skin. Wolf clenched his jaw to prevent his fangs from shooting out, and it was a considerable effort to sit still until the young woman left.

"What?" Rafe asked with a laugh once she was gone. "Are you worried she might think we're a couple gazing lovingly into each other's eyes."

"No," Wolf immediately retorted. "That hadn't even crossed my mind. Why would you even—"

"That might be a good cover actually," Rafe said.

Wolf didn't bother responding. "Have you been in touch with anyone else?"

Rafe shook his head. "Not since the eighties."

Wolf didn't believe him but decided not to push. He took a deep breath, gathering his thoughts. He had kept track of some of the Athatos, but that didn't mean one of them couldn't have slipped past his attention to kill Gabriel.

"So how exactly do you plan on finding the killer?" Rafe asked as he stirred his coffee.

"I intend to ask Gabriel," Wolf said.

"How are you going to ask him if he's dead?" Rafe asked, but as soon as he finished speaking his eyes went wide. He tightened his grip on the spoon, bending it backward. "Is it possible?"

"If it's possible for humans and half-bloods, then I don't see why it wouldn't be possible for us," Wolf replied, knowing that for seven days after his death, Gabriel's soul would be in the Underworld before it moved on to somewhere else. Wolf was certain of it but didn't say so because it would make Rafe ask questions he didn't want to answer.

Rafe nodded, his gaze becoming distant. Wolf knew the other man was beginning to understand his plan. That was the main reason why he had come to Rafe, even if he didn't fully trust him—Rafe could lead him to Gabriel's dead soul. The other two Athatos who could have helped Wolf didn't have enough power in their current states to do it.

Rafe exhaled. "Do you think the killer is one of us?"

"Maybe, but we can't rule out the possibility that the half-bloods are behind this," Wolf said.

At the mention of half-bloods, Rafe's gaze darkened. Just like Wolf, Rafe was the only other Athatos who had never created a half-blood. Rafe had opposed their existence and had tried to wipe them out. But the other Athatos had become attached to their half-bloods, and Rafe had paid the price for hurting their children.

"Half-bloods have been wanting to overthrow us for millennia, and they haven't because we're supposed to be indestructible," Wolf continued. "But now that someone figured out how to kill us, that dream could become a reality."

In Wolf's opinion, the half-bloods had more motives for murder than any of the Athatos. Sure, the Athatos had fought and battled, and their interactions had, more often than not, been fueled by hate, envy, and jealousy. But what would killing Gabriel accomplish? He wasn't even one of the ruling Athatos anymore, so the killer couldn't have been after his throne. Had the murder been personal? Or was one of the Athatos out to kill the rest of them to take full control? Wolf's mind spun as he tried to understand the killer's motives.

"But Gabriel is—was—mightily powerful," Rafe said. "Which makes me wonder which half-blood could have killed him. Even an Athatos would have struggled to overpower Gabriel. We're missing something."

Wolf had wondered about that too. "We need to discover how they managed to overpower Gabriel and to make sure they don't do the same to us."

Rafe dropped the crooked spoon on the table and took a sip from his coffee. "Do you think the killer knows you're onto them?"

"No," Wolf said. Wolf and Gabriel had been very careful with their meetings in the last few weeks. If the killer had known they were in touch, then they would have come after Wolf too. He would have been an easier target than Gabriel. Fear coated Wolf's bones at that thought. He could have been killed too—and he wouldn't have been strong enough to protect himself. The *Aether* swirled inside him, but Wolf pushed it down. He wouldn't use it unless necessary.

"Right now, the element of surprise is the only thing we have in our favor," Wolf said. "The murder was intended to stay a secret or else everyone would have known by now. We need to be careful about what we do, so the killer doesn't know we're onto them."

Rafe nodded. "Regardless of who the killer is, this situation will detonate at some point. Gabriel was our king. He was once the mighty Zeus." Rafe spread his arms wide to emphasize the last word. "That's symbolic. This isn't just a murder—it's the start of a war."

Dread curled inside of Wolf. Their table rattled slightly as Wolf's power leaked out of him, but he quickly pulled the *Aether* back to him. A war hadn't been the first thing that had come to mind when he had set out to find Gabriel, but now that Rafe mentioned it, a war seemed to be inevitable. But he knew there were other elements at play influencing the situation. He just didn't want to share them with Rafe.

"You're hiding something from me," Rafe said.

Wolf bit his tongue, cursing himself for letting his emotions reveal that.

"If you don't trust me, then why did you come find me?" Rafe asked. Green tendrils of light danced mischievously in his eyes.

Their cups began to shake, the coffee inside them vibrating. The silverware rattled against the table. Wolf gritted his teeth and reeled the *Aether* back to him.

"I trust you want to survive," Wolf said.

Rafe raised a brow.

"The half-bloods hate you more than any other Athatos," Wolf said. "Regardless of who the killer is, if the knowledge that we can be killed spreads, who do you think will be the next one the half-bloods assassinate? You've been torturing them for millennia, and they'll want revenge." The table trembled as the *Aether* trickled out of him. Wolf felt like he was trying to hold a liquid in a broken container. "I've never trusted you, and I know you would love to kill some of the other Athatos if you knew how. But I know you enjoy being alive more and wouldn't want to risk getting killed by the very beings you've fought so hard to destroy."

Rafe dropped his smile and pressed his lips together. Wolf knew Rafe would likely become a threat later, but for now, Wolf could trust Rafe to fight on his side—at least long enough to find the answers he needed.

"We need to keep this knowledge a secret," Rafe said. "We need to crush this war before it starts."

"Agreed," Wolf said.

"Do you think Hera knows?" Rafe asked.

"I don't know."

It bothered Wolf that he hadn't heard anything from her. Hera had the power to see the future. Gabriel and Wolf had known that, and Wolf had used a bit of his power to shield them from her visions whenever they met. But Wolf hadn't been there when Gabriel was murdered. Hera must have seen that, so why hadn't she done anything to stop the killers? Hera hated Gabriel, but did she hate him enough to allow someone to kill him and make them all vulnerable? She was the Queen of the Immortals—she couldn't possibly be planning to start a war. Or could she? What if there hadn't been any signs of struggle at the scene because Gabriel had known the killer and had felt safe around them? Wolf suppressed a shiver. Whether Hera was the killer or not, she was planning something, and Wolf felt anxious not knowing what it was. She was one of the very few Athatos who Wolf feared.

"How long do you think we have until they kill someone else?" Rafe asked. "If this is a war, I think it's safe to assume they'll come after the rest of us."

"I don't know," Wolf said as his chest tightened with fear. A streetlamp burst on the other side of the sidewalk. At least no one had been standing below, and Wolf sucked the *Aether* back to him. After some startled cries and suspicious stares, people continued down the street giving wide berth to the streetlamp and the shattered glass around it.

"Was there any evidence at the murder scene?" Rafe asked. He hadn't even turned to see the small explosion.

"No," Wolf said.

Rafe's eyes narrowed. "How did you find Gabriel's dead body?"

"He called me," Wolf said. "Said he wanted to talk."

"Do you think he knew someone was coming for him?" Rafe asked.

"Maybe," Wolf said.

"How long had you two been in contact?" Rafe asked. Wolf didn't respond, which prompted a smile from Rafe. "Were you feeling so lonely that you went to Gabriel for some company? He didn't strike me as your type."

Wolf clenched his jaw. The cup exploded in front of him, and coffee sprayed everywhere. The waitress rushed in their direction, and a few moments later, a waiter showed up with a broom to sweep the bits away. The waitress apologized for the inconvenience and made Wolf and Rafe move to another table.

Rafe grinned with his cup still in his hand as they sat down again.

"I didn't contact him out of loneliness," Wolf said, then cursed himself for responding.

Rafe's smile held.

Wolf knew the other man could sense the gaping hole inside of him. Their table began rattling again as if an earthquake were shaking it.

"Oh, do you have a girlfriend then?" Rafe asked. "Is she mortal, half-blood, or Athatos?" He ignored the trembling table, his eyes set only on Wolf. "Or have you started dating men now, in which case I happen to be single and—"

Rafe turned to his right only a second before Wolf turned too, and they watched a young man walking down the street completely oblivious to their presence. Wolf was glad for the distraction before the *Aether* destroyed the entire block, and he pushed down his anger. He shouldn't have let Rafe roil his emotions, but the pain of heartbreak still felt fresh in Wolf's chest. He buried it deep.

"Damn," Rafe said as he shook his head. "He's really let himself go."

The last time Wolf had seen him, his name had been Jake, but Wolf had the suspicion he went by a different name now. Jake looked to be in his mid-twenties and had shaggy blond hair and blue eyes big as an owl's. His cheeks were speckled with pimples, his lips cracked with the cold. He walked with a slight hunch that made his back look curved.

"How long do you think it's been since he last fed?" Rafe asked.

"I would say a couple of years."

Jake's face was still sharp and handsome, even with the imperfections, but it was just . . . human. Jake's shoulders tensed

61

as if he sensed someone watching him. He tightened his grip on a rolled-up newspaper. Jake's gaze swept around him but never settled on Wolf or Rafe.

"Not even a flicker of recognition," Rafe muttered.

Wolf stood, and Rafe followed him. They tailed Jake for a couple of blocks until he stopped in front of a building and pulled out a clattering ring of keys. Jake finally turned to the two men when they cast a shadow over him.

"Hello?" Jake said. Even his voice had a higher pitch.

"Jake?" Wolf asked.

"I think you have the wrong guy," he said with a slight French accent. "I'm Pierre."

Pierre inserted the key into the lock with a shaky hand and opened the door. Wolf and Rafe followed him before he could close it. Pierre's eyes widened, and he clutched his keys.

"We need to talk," Wolf said.

Pierre scanned the two men as if expecting to see a gun poking out of their jackets. "About what? Who are you?"

Wolf exhaled, and a sense of fatigue swept over him. How many times had he had these conversations with the others? He had lost count.

"How about you take us to your apartment," Rafe said.

If Pierre's mental state had been intact, he would have probably refused, but his mind was weak enough for Rafe to influence his emotions. Pierre nodded, and the two men followed him into an apartment on the third floor. Pierre left the keys and newspaper beside a stack of books spread on a table next to the kitchen. On the opposite side of the room was a couch facing a small TV. A clear door beside it led to a small balcony overcrowded with plants like a miniature jungle.

"Do I know you?" Pierre asked. He narrowed his eyes as if a memory was tugging at the edge of his mind.

"You should," Rafe said. "Don't you remember your own great uncle"—Rafe pointed a finger at Wolf—"and your cousin?" Rafe gestured toward himself with his arms.

"I . . ." Fog swirled in Pierre's clear eyes like mist concealing the morning sky. It cleared for a second. "Wolf?" Pierre took a step back.

Wolf nodded. "Yeah, it's me."

"I changed my name to Rafe," Rafe said before Pierre could ask.

"What are you doing here?" Pierre looked around his apartment as if he was wondering why he was there. He blinked a couple of times, biting his lower lip. His gaze became distant again, lost in some unseen horizon. Wolf had never experienced a fragmentation, but when the others recovered from one, they had explained that it felt like waking up from a dream.

"We need your help," Wolf said.

Rafe looked at Wolf with a raised eyebrow.

Pierre slid his eyes back to the two men. "With what?"

"How would you break into Alec's home?" Wolf asked.

"Who's Alec?" The fog in Pierre's gaze evaporated once more and his irises seemed to glow. "Oh, you mean Hades." He straightened his back, standing taller. A phantom wind flipped a few pages on the books that lay open on the table. The newspaper swirled in the air as if a ghost of Pierre's power had swept through the room. Pierre laughed, throwing his head back.

"You're trying to break into Alec's home." He said each word in between a laugh. His skin emitted a soft golden glow. "He will flay the skin off your bodies, watch it heal, and do it over and over again for the next century."

"How would you do it?" Wolf asked.

Pierre whistled. "I'm assuming you want to get out of there in one piece. Let me think about this." Pierre plopped down on one of the couches and kicked off his shoes. He exhaled, lost in his thoughts for a few seconds. "Max throws a party at his castle every year for his birthday. You should definitely get an invitation this year." Pierre flashed his perfectly white teeth in a smile. "There's an underground tunnel that leads from his castle to the Underworld, and if I remember correctly, there's a specific route that takes you directly to Alec's. That should be the easiest way to get in."

"Who's Max?" Rafe asked. Some of the others changed their names so often that Wolf had a hard time keeping track.

"Dionysus," Pierre said.

"Ah," Rafe replied.

"How do we find the tunnel?" Wolf asked.

"There's an entrance in the kitchen next to the big stove. It's hidden in one of the cabinets. The path that takes you to Alec's is the one that's not marked with runes." The words spilled quickly from Pierre's lips. "The party may be your only chance to get in because Max's children guard that entrance quite heavily. But during the party, there should be enough distractions for you to get through undetected. I hope that helps."

"It does," Wolf said.

"You'll still need to get an invitation though," Pierre said. "You can't get in without one, even as an Athatos."

"Where do we get one?" Wolf asked.

"They usually mail them out," Pierre said.

"Well, that's not going to work," Wolf said. He walked over to the books and ripped out a page.

"Hey," Pierre exclaimed.

Wolf walked back to him and handed him the paper. "Make this an invitation."

Pierre glared at him as if Wolf had torn off one of his fingers instead. Pierre snatched the paper from Wolf while muttering a curse in French. As soon as Pierre touched the page it began to shift. It shrunk, the letters disappeared, and a black background spread over the paper like spilled ink. Golden foil appeared at the edges, framing the paper with gleaming vines. At the very center of the page appeared the number 5,480 in gold. After doing some mental calculations, Wolf realized that number was Dionysus's age. He was one of the youngest Athatos.

"There you go." Pierre handed the invitation to Wolf.

The timing would be close, as the party was on the start of the seventh day after Gabriel's death. Wolf found that timing strangely coincidental but didn't dwell on it too much. He was more worried that he wouldn't have much time with Gabriel but felt sure they could find him before his soul moved on.

The fact that Gabriel had apparently been overpowered so easily held Wolf back from even thinking about breaking into Dionysus's home before the party. If Dionysus and his half-bloods were involved in the murder, Wolf didn't want to raise their suspicions. He didn't feel comfortable confronting anyone until he knew who the killer was and how exactly they had killed Gabriel. It was better to play it safe and wait a little. Besides, the party would be happening soon enough, so he wouldn't have to wait long.

Pierre leaned back on the couch, crossing his arms. "Why do you want to break into Alec's house?"

Wolf opened his mouth to respond, but Rafe spoke first. "How long have you been in France?" Rafe asked.

"A couple of years," Pierre responded.

The fog began to creep back into Pierre's gaze. He blinked a couple of times, then eyed Rafe as if wondering what the man was doing in his living room. Wolf clenched his jaw hard, trying to ignore the painful beat of his heart. Hermes had once been so powerful, so mightily cunning and strong. Now this was what was left of him—a shadow of his former self.

A tiny, broken fragment of a god.

If a war with the half-bloods or another Athatos was brewing, then Wolf wasn't even sure who was left to fight on their side.

Pierre wasn't the only one who would be an easy target. Maybe if Death was knocking on their door, that would force the power inside the others to awaken from whatever slumber it had fallen into during their fragmentations. But if Gabriel had not been able to fight the killer, then how could Wolf hope the others would defend themselves?

"Well then," Rafe said. "It was great seeing you again. We'll just let ourselves out now."

Pierre stood again. "Thanks for the visit." He smiled, but the outer corner of his eye twitched. His back hunched over again as he leaned forward to wave them goodbye. The glow from his skin vanished.

Rafe walked to the front door. Wolf stopped as a picture on the newspaper caught his eye. He picked up that page, then followed Rafe down the stairs as he read the article. His hands trembled slightly with fear. The doors at his sides rattled. Wolf quickly folded up the page, holding it tightly inside his fist as they walked outside.

The two men walked onto a crowded street. Wolf's nails dug into his palms as heartbeats vibrated against his skin. He clenched his teeth so hard his jaw ached. The ground beneath them began to tremble slightly. The people didn't notice. Rafe did, though, and he pulled Wolf into a deserted alley that led to an emptier street. Trash lined the sidewalks, but Wolf welcomed that pungent odor as it tamped down his need for blood. He was usually better at controlling that craving, but as the *Aether* swelled in his veins, it became more demanding. The *Aether* wouldn't be satiated until Wolf drank more—but then it would be nearly impossible for Wolf to control the *Aether*.

"You knew Pierre was here, didn't you?" Rafe asked after a minute. "That's why you made us travel from London to Paris overnight."

"Yes," Wolf said.

"I thought you said you weren't in contact with the others?" Rafe asked, a dangerous edge to his voice.

"I'm not," Wolf replied. "That doesn't mean I didn't keep track of a few of you."

Rafe stared at Wolf but didn't say anything.

Wolf had known exactly where Pierre was because he had been Wolf's first choice to lead him through the Underworld. But after seeing Pierre so fragmented, Wolf knew he wouldn't have been able to guide him to Gabriel. That's when he had gone looking for Rafe. Only after he had found Rafe had it occurred to him that they still needed a way to find an entrance to Alec's house, which is why he had returned to Pierre.

"What a sad sight Pierre was," Rafe said as he brushed a leaf from his jacket. "I don't know how any of you do it, how you can ignore the craving and live such insignificant lives. You let your bodies grow weak and waste away for a few years. You let yourselves fragment even further, shattering into so many pieces you forget who you are and who you were."

Wolf hadn't minded letting his body go weak. For a time, it had made him feel more alive. He had begun enjoying the little things in life—a walk in the park, a meal at a restaurant, a movie at the theaters. The world had changed, but it was hard to change with the world when time passed by so rapidly. He understood why Pierre, and some of the others, had stopped feeding. The fragmentations had made it possible for them to forget their past and pretend they weren't immortal. It was a release, a fresh new start. They could erase millennia of accumulated, painful memories. In a world that didn't worship gods and monsters anymore, not feeding was a way to remain relevant, even if it was temporary. Even if, as time passed by and their bodies grew old, they came to a point where they couldn't ignore the pull inside them any longer and made a kill.

Wolf was the only one who had never forgotten his past since he had never experienced a fragmentation. He wasn't sure if he regretted that or not.

"So what now?" Rafe asked, pulling Wolf out of his thoughts. "You seem to have a plan for everything we have to do to catch the killer." Rafe's tone was sharp as a dagger, and Wolf knew that the other man was aware he was keeping something from him but was willing to play along for now. "I assume you're not going to take me on a date around Paris until Dionysus's birthday party."

"No."

"I'm devastated," Rafe said, then added, "Not even dinner?"

Wolf tightened his grip on the newspaper, crushing it to ash as the *Aether* ebbed out of his hand. "We're going to meet some new people." He opened his palm and let the dark ashes fall onto the cobbled stones. "Depending on how things go, maybe you can have them for dinner."

Rafe smiled.

6

IN THE QUIET of Lucian's basement office, I pinned another translation on the board, trying not to cover much of the notes and pictures. Footsteps echoed behind me as Lucian walked into the room. I hadn't expected him back so soon, but I was ready to share my new discoveries. After he had left, and feeling like a flame had been lit inside me, I had chugged some coffee Dario had offered and gone straight back to work.

I was a translator.

Lucian had said go give a voice to those who can't speak anymore. And I had.

"I think I know the killer's motivations," I said to Lucian. Even though his lips didn't move, his eyes crinkled slightly as if smiling. "I think they're trying to attain immortality."

Lucian tensed, and I couldn't read his carefully guarded expression. "Walk me through the process of getting to that conclusion," he said.

"Okay," I said, feeling jittery. "Out of the three languages, Egyptian is the oldest, so I assumed the original text came from there. Then I started researching ancient Egyptian texts that talked about death and immortality, and I came across the Book of the Dead." I paused to see if Lucian had any questions, but he nodded at me. "It's not a single text, but a collection of different texts. Egyptians believed that they could attain immortality in the afterlife and be like the gods if they had some of those verses inscribed on their coffins or if they were buried with parchments containing that information."

Lucian frowned, but he didn't say anything.

"I downloaded an online version of the Book of the Dead to read it. Some of the sentences we found on the victims match it almost exactly." I pointed at the verses on the board that I had found so far.

Lucian stepped closer to read them.

"I confirmed that the Book of the Dead was the primary source," I continued. "In later times, it was translated into Latin and Greek to make it more accessible to other cultures, so some specific verses may only survive in those languages."

Lucian's eyes never left the board as I talked.

"So I think, and I know this sounds crazy, but I believe that the killer is performing some sort of ritual to try to make their victims immortal by inscribing the Book of the Dead onto their skin." I paused to take a breath. "Or maybe they're trying to make themselves immortal, and they're experimenting with the victims first to get the right version of the text. That could be why some of these verses are repeated on different victims while others are new."

Still, Lucian didn't speak. I wondered if he thought I had gone mad, but I continued.

"One thing to note is that all the bodies have the phrase *tell me my name* or make some reference to the narrator knowing someone's name. In ancient cultures, and especially in Egypt, if you knew a being's name, then you could make them do things for you. The Book of the Dead mentions that you must ask certain gods for help to attain immortality, so the killer must believe they're summoning the gods to help them."

Lucian finally ripped his gaze from the board to meet my own. Something dark whirled in his eyes. "But no one ever did, right?"

"Did what?" I asked.

"Attained immortality with these verses?"

"Not that I know of," I said. "But immortality was supposed to be for the afterlife, which is another realm beyond our own that can only be accessed after death. The Book of the Dead gives immortality of the soul and not of the body."

"Then why include these passages on bodies?" Lucian asked as he pointed at one of my translations. "Didn't the Egyptians mummify their bodies to better preserve them?"

"They did," I said. "And eventually, they decomposed in this world. But they believed that their bodies in the afterlife would be intact."

"What if those interpretations are wrong?" Lucian asked what every Egyptologist who had come before me would have felt offended by. "What if the true purpose of the Book of the Dead was to attain immortality in this life, to die but be reborn in your own body and to become one of the gods."

"Uh, I don't think so based on the history and mythology I've learned."

"History is wrong most times," Lucian said.

How would he know if history was wrong? The intensity in his gaze made me pause when I was about to challenge that comment. Lucian pulled back from the board, nodding to himself.

"That's what the killer is trying to do then," he said. "They're trying to find another way to achieve the immortality of the gods. And they're using these victims to experiment."

"I believe so," I said, which was bonkers. I wondered what had driven the killer to believe it was possible.

Lucian's frown deepened even further, cutting through his smooth skin. "I have never seen anything like this," he whispered, seemingly more to himself than to me. He turned and met my gaze. "This is good. This is a very impressive interpretation of the inscriptions and the killer's motives."

My heart jumped at the compliment.

"Thanks," I said.

"I need you to keep comparing the passages from the Book of the Dead to the ones we found on the victims. And write down any other passages from the Book of the Dead that refer to immortality of the body that we haven't found in the murders yet."

"Sure," I said.

My stomach growled, and Lucian paused. He cocked his head to one side like a confused dog. "You're hungry."

"Yes," I said. I had been so absorbed in the translations that I had forgotten to eat dinner.

"Let's go to the kitchen so you can grab some food."

"Sure."

"How old is the Book of the Dead?" Lucian asked as we walked up the stairs.

I tried to think of an estimate, knowing that initially those inscriptions had belonged to the Pyramid Texts. "Around five thousand years old," I said.

Lucian nodded to himself. "That seems about right," he muttered.

I frowned, unsure of what he meant. We arrived at the main floor, then walked to the kitchen. Night had plunged the mansion into darkness once again, but the warm light of the kitchen pushed back on the cold.

"Can I just grab something from the fridge?" I asked.

"Sure," Lucian said.

There was surprisingly very little food considering three people lived in the house. I only spotted two Tupperware containers with some leftovers. There were no eggs, ham, or cheese, which to me seemed like basic items, and no fruits or vegetables either. Maybe they had cleaned out the fridge and someone would be buying groceries soon.

I grabbed one of the containers, hoping no one minded I ate the leftover pasta. Lucian watched my every move. I took off the lid and placed the container in the microwave for a minute.

Lucian still didn't leave. He clearly wasn't hungry and seemed anxious as his hands fidgeted with a pen he had found somewhere. I didn't feel like going to the dining room, so I placed the food on the kitchen island in front of Lucian. I was about to begin eating when my phone buzzed. I pulled it out of my pocket and considered ignoring it but knew Liz would keep calling until I picked up. I answered the call.

Liz started speaking before I could say anything. "Aura said you're missing Book Club, but I couldn't believe that."

"Yeah, sorry," I said. "I'm busy with work, but I'll be back next month."

"Why are you working so late?" she asked. "Where is your new job? Wait, hold up, let me look at your location."

"No, you don't need to—"

"Why are you in the middle of the forest?" she asked.

"I'm in a manor," I said. "That's where I'm working on the translations."

"And your boss is making you work during the night too?" she asked.

"It's a temporary contract with a tight deadline," I said.

Lucian made himself busy looking through some drawers on the other side of the kitchen. I considered stepping out while I was on the call, but at that point, that would have been more awkward.

"Worst boss of the year," Aura said somewhere in the background.

If Lucian heard that, he gave no indication as he rummaged through a drawer.

"Do you want me to fake some emergency so we can pick you up?" Liz asked.

"I can take us all in my van," Bobby exclaimed.

"Am I on speaker?" I asked.

"We can have Book Club in the van," Liz said, ignoring me.

"It's a thirty-minute drive. We can totally do that," Aura said.

"No," I said.

Lucian slid a ripped piece of paper across the kitchen island.

If you want to go with your friends for a bit, feel free.

I looked up at him. He nodded, but I shook my head. My friends didn't understand the urgency of the work I was doing, how we were in a battle against time to find the killer. Besides, I would have rather gotten some rest than driven to the city and back.

"Are you sure you don't want us to pick you up?" Liz asked again.

"Yes."

There was a short pause. "Do you want me to water your plants while you're out?" Liz said. That was the secret sentence we had come up with in college in case one of us was in an emergency but couldn't say it out loud.

"No, my plants are fine. I already watered them," I said.

"Are you sure?"

"Yes."

Someone mumbled something in the background. "Alright, we'll miss you tonight," Liz said. "You better be here next month."

"I promise."

"Alright, good luck with your new job."

"Thanks, bye."

"Bye."

I hung up and put the phone away.

"Sorry for keeping you away from your friends," Lucian said.

"It's alright," I said.

"Do they usually know where you are?" he asked.

"We have an app that tracks each other's phones," I said.

"I've heard of those but thought only mothers used them," Lucian said.

SOFI AGUILERA

I shrugged. "I've seen several friend groups use it in college for safety."

"That's smart," Lucian said.

A tense silence settled between us as I began eating the pasta.

"How often do you eat?" Lucian asked after a minute.

I stopped mid-bite, then shrugged. "I don't know. Every four hours or so?"

Lucian nodded thoughtfully. "What do you usually like to eat?"

I shrugged again. "I'm not picky, so I'll eat whatever."

"And how many hours do you sleep?" he asked.

"I try to sleep eight hours," I said unsure of where he was going with the questions.

"You haven't had enough sleep then."

"No," I admitted. I was no stranger to pulling all-nighters, but the intensity of the work we were doing was starting to wear me down.

Lucian placed the pen on the counter. "What do you usually do with your free time?"

My mouth was full so I couldn't immediately reply.

"Sorry," he said after a second. "I didn't mean to pry too much. I'm just . . . trying to understand you better."

"That's okay," I said. "How much do you sleep?"

Lucian chuckled. "Not as much as you."

Our eyes met for a second. In the light of the kitchen, his irises were a dark gray.

My phone rang again. It was my mom. The phone stopped ringing as I considered not answering. Her text pinged me a second later.

It's an emergency.

I immediately called back.

"What's the emergency?" I asked, my heart battering against my chest.

Lucian went still.

"I need you to help me choose which dress to wear tonight," she said.

"Mom," I said, annoyed. "I thought it was a real emergency."

"Fashion is always an emergency."

I ground my teeth. Lucian glanced away, but he didn't leave.

"Okay," Mom said, "I just sent you two pictures. Which one do you like more?"

I pulled my phone away from my ear to look at the pictures. "I like the yellow dress more."

"Really?" she asked. "But doesn't the pink one look better?"

"Then wear the pink one."

"But you said you liked the yellow one more."

"If you like the pink one, then you should wear that one."

"Hmm, I don't know," she said. "Why do you think the yellow one looks better?"

I glanced at the pictures again. "I like the color, and the design is more elegant."

"But I already wore that dress last week," she said.

I released an annoyed breath. "The pink one looks great too. I like the embroidered design on the sleeves."

"Oh yes, it's lovely. I'll wear that one then."

"Great."

"Have you tried out any of the recipes I sent you?"

"Not yet," I said as I poked at the pasta.

"Please tell me you didn't buy more frozen chicken nuggets."

"I didn't," I said. "I get food at work."

"Alright." She didn't sound convinced. "I'll talk to you later then."

"Okay, love you."

"Love you too. Bye."

I hung up and went back to eating my pasta.

"Your parents?" Lucian asked without meeting my gaze.

I nodded.

"Do you speak to them often?" he asked.

"Every day."

Lucian nodded thoughtfully.

"Where do your parents live?" I asked him.

"Oh, uh, my parents died a long time ago," Lucian said.

"I'm sorry. I shouldn't have asked."

"It's alright," Lucian said. "No one has asked me about them in a long time." He buried his hands in his pockets. "I'll admit it has been awhile since I last thought of them."

I took another bite, letting him continue.

"I don't remember my father much, but I've never forgotten my mother," he said. "Everyone always said I looked exactly like her—the dark hair and bright eyes, my nose and eyebrows." Lucian smiled, his gaze becoming distant. "She used to make all my clothes, wove them together from scratch. She cooked and baked all our food and grew herbs and vegetables outside the house." Lucian seemed to pull away from a trance. "I miss her sometimes."

"I'm sorry you lost her," I said.

Lucian shrugged. "That's life." He glanced at me. "What's your mom like?"

"She's the strongest woman I know," I said. "Always willing to do anything for our family to pull us through hard times, even if that means she has to make some sacrifices." I took another bite and swallowed. "She taught me how to read and write, and sew, and cook, although I'm terrible at cooking. My dad taught me how to drive and to fish, and he always sat with me at night to help me do my homework even if he didn't fully understand it."

Lucian moved closer to the kitchen island, placing his elbows on the counter. "My parents didn't know how to read or write, so I didn't either for a long time. I taught myself to read much later, and then started writing."

"Do you enjoy reading?" I asked.

"I enjoy it more now than I did before," he said. "I'm assuming you like reading."

"I do," I said. "And I have that monthly Book Club with my friends."

"What do you read?" Lucian asked.

"Mostly fiction," I admitted.

"Any good book recommendations?" Lucian asked.

"I'm not sure you're the type of person who would enjoy reading romance fantasy novels," I said teasingly.

Lucian's brows furrowed together. "Don't I seem like a romance guy?" A playful smile tugged at his lips.

My cheeks felt warm. "Not really."

Lucian laughed. "And what makes you say that?"

"Hmm," I said, trying to come up with some coherent response before my face could redden further. "You seem too focused on your work to have time for romance."

Lucian pulled back slightly, and I immediately felt bad for saying that. "You're not wrong," he said.

Lucian's gaze became distant again. I finished eating in an uncomfortable silence, then I washed the container and left it to dry.

"Do you have any weapons for self-defense?" Lucian asked.

I turned back to him as I dried my hands. "Not really. Some of my friends had pepper spray, but I never got one. Why?"

Lucian shrugged. "Just curious. It's a dangerous world out there." He paused. "I could give you something, if you want."

"Yeah, sure," I said.

We made our way back to the basement, and Lucian pulled a large pen from a drawer. He slid a switch and clicked a little button on the side of the pen. I startled when electricity crackled at one end.

"A Taser pen?" I asked. "I was hoping for a magical sword or a bow and arrow like in my books, but a Taser pen can be cool too."

Lucian smiled. "It's thin and small enough to carry without anyone noticing." Lucian turned it off with the little switch below the button. "If you tase someone on the upper shoulders, upper hips, or below the rib cage, it will have maximum effect." He pointed at each spot with the pen, then handed it to me.

"Thank you," I said.

I switched it back on and clicked the button once, watching the electric blue lines sizzling between the contact probes, then turned off the switch and put the pen inside my jacket.

"Don't you want to practice?" Lucian asked. "I would feel irresponsible if I gave you a weapon and didn't teach you how to use it."

I pulled the pen out again but didn't turn it on. "Let's try it then."

Lucian stepped closer to me. "Okay, so if I faced you like this"—he towered over me—"where would you tase me?"

"Not sure," I admitted.

"Go low," Lucian said. "They're less likely to see that coming. So try the upper hip or below the rib cage, preferably below the rib cage since people aren't used to protecting that area."

I nodded.

"Try it," Lucian said.

I met his gaze, then broke away as I slowly poked him below the rib cage. My heart echoed inside of my ears.

"You'll have to be faster next time," Lucian said. "But you get the idea."

I chuckled, and a smile settled on his lips.

"Okay, now"—Lucian stepped around me—"what would you do if I attacked you from behind?"

My back brushed against his chest.

"Hip again?" I asked without turning around.

"It depends," Lucian said. "You'll want to be as far away from their hands as possible so they can't take the taser pen from you. May I?"

It took me a second to realize he was asking whether he could put his arm around me. He already had his hand at my side, hovering inches away from me.

"Yes," I said.

Lucian wrapped both of his arms around my waist, gently, and pressed my back against his chest. My heart beat furiously, and I wondered if he could feel my frantic pulse. If he were a real attacker, I wasn't sure how much damage the pen would actually do, but if Lucian seemed to think it an effective weapon, then I wouldn't doubt him. One of the victims had been tased unconscious, hadn't she? I pushed that mental image away as Lucian tightened his grip slightly, his arms coiling against my stomach.

"If you want to keep the Taser pen as far from my hands as possible, where would you hit?" Lucian asked.

"Your shoulder," I said as I struck him on the upper shoulder.

"Good," Lucian said. "What if I had my arms here?"

He slung one arm around my neck, the other still at my waist. My breath quickened even though his grip around my neck was loose. "Below the rib cage," I said as I tapped his torso.

He pulled his arms away, then wrapped them around my upper arms, his hands pinning me immobile against him. "What if I have you like this?"

"Upper hip seems the most accessible," I said.

"Yes."

Lucian's hands lingered on my arms for half a second before he let go. His brilliant gray eyes met my own. "The pen should be helpful if anyone attacks you. But every situation varies, and you might not be thinking clearly as shock and adrenaline take over. Try to keep practicing, even if mentally."

I nodded. "Thank you," I said. "This was a useful exercise."

"Of course," he said. "Anything I can do to help you feel safer."

Footsteps echoed from the stairs, and a few seconds later, Sue came into view.

"I found some leads," Sue announced. She eyed the Taser pen in my hand. "That's a fun one," she said.

"Let's go then," Lucian said. He glanced in my direction as he walked out of the room. "Get some sleep, then you can continue looking for clues in the Book of the Dead."

I nodded. "I will."

Lucian climbed the steps, disappearing from view. I waited for a few moments, then headed back to my room. The house didn't feel so cold anymore.

7

TELL ME MY NAME, he whispered.

"I don't know your name," I said.

The suffocating darkness seemed to be alive, breathing, pulsing. It was so dense that I felt it embracing me with skeletal arms. I couldn't see him, but his voice brushed against my ear.

Tell me my name.

Something nudged at the edge of my mind. I did know his name, but I had forgotten it. I extended my hands before me trying to feel my way through the dark, but I didn't find anything for a long while.

I tripped over something and tried to break my fall with my hands, but when I kneeled, they felt sticky with a warm liquid. The metallic tang of blood wafted into my nose. The body came into view a second later. He lay face down, his body covered in ancient Egyptian symbols. His head was turned sideways, his glassy eyes looking straight at me.

Tell me my name. Blood dripped from his lips.

I screamed.

I sat bolt upright on the bed, breathing heavily. The room was bathed in deep darkness, and I fumbled with the lamp on the nightstand until I found the switch. Golden light burned my eyes, and I squinted at its brightness. I lay back on the bed, keeping the light on, and closed my eyes, but sleep had already run away from me. I checked the time on my phone. It was almost two in the morning.

I pushed the sheets away and pulled a hoodie over my paja-mas. The hallways seemed to hold an oppressive darkness as I headed toward the kitchen to grab a snack, my phone's flashlight cutting through the blackness like a slender knife. I turned the kitchen light on, welcoming its warm glow, and I was pleasantly surprised when I found the fridge stocked with food. After some searching, I grabbed some cheese sticks and ate them quietly, then munched on a pack of cookies that had been left on the counter. I headed back to my room, retracing my steps through the old mansion.

An open door caught my attention. It hadn't been open when I had walked through the second-floor hallway earlier, and I curiously peeked in. Lucian sat with his back to the door and looked down at something on the table before him. He had lit a candle that cast moving shadows across the room.

He turned around sharply, making me startle.

"Sorry," I said. "I saw the open door and peeked in. Didn't mean to disturb you."

"No worries," he said. In the candlelight, his face seemed gaunt as if the shadows had hollowed out his cheeks. His eyes had lost their silvery fire.

"Are you okay?" I asked.

Lucian didn't respond and turned back to the table. I stepped inside the room, walking closer to him. A drawing lay before him that depicted a beautiful woman with long dark hair.

"Is that your mom?" I asked.

Lucian nodded, something like pain flashing in his eyes. "I hadn't thought of her in a long time until you asked about my parents yesterday."

"I'm so sorry, I didn't know—"

"I'm glad you did," Lucian said. His eyes hadn't broken away from the drawing. "I realized I didn't fully remember what she looked like."

I sat on the chair next to him.

"I wish I had a picture of her," he said. "I'm not entirely sure this drawing is accurate." A couple of pens lay on the table next to Lucian, one of them broken and dripping black ink that stained the desk. "It's been so long that I don't know if I'm remembering her how she was or how I want her to be." The flame reflected in his eyes, mingling with the gray like fire melting ice.

I wanted to say something to comfort him but couldn't think of anything. Hesitantly, I laid a hand on his shoulder. Lucian didn't move. He closed his eyes, and a tear rolled down his cheek.

"Thank you," he whispered, his eyes still closed.

"For what?" I asked.

"Just for listening," Lucian said.

I pulled up my sleeve and wiped the tear off his cheek. For a second, I worried I had crossed a line I shouldn't have, but Lucian didn't move as I placed my hand back on his shoulder.

"I don't remember her voice," he said. "She used to sing beautifully and had a laugh that could warm up the coldest days, but I can't recall how that sounded." He opened his eyes again and looked at the drawing. "I have nothing left of her except my memories. But memories are fragile things that can be broken easily by time."

Filling the dark with its flickering dance, the candle's flame continued to burn as we sat in silence.

"The only thing I remember with absolute clarity is her name," Lucian said. "Maybe you were right, and names do have power, at least in our memories."

"What was her name?" I asked.

"Emer," Lucian said. "Her name was Emer."

"That's a beautiful name."

A small smile edged his lips. He took a deep breath, looked away, and then met my eyes. His gaze was so raw with emotion that it made my chest stir as my heart sped up. He turned away after a second and grabbed the drawing, then after looking into the flame for a moment, he blew it out. The room was plunged into darkness as the scent of smoke filled the air.

I should have said good night and gone back to my room but couldn't. I didn't want to leave Lucian alone. He placed his hand on top of mine, his calloused palm holding on tightly to the back of my hand as if that was the only thing grounding him here.

Part of me felt this was inappropriate, but there had been something familiar and genuine in our conversations that now made me feel comfortable with him.

After a minute, Lucian began humming.

"Is that a song your mom used to sing?" I asked.

"Yeah," he said. "I still remember her lyrics, but like I said, I don't remember her voice."

"What are the lyrics?" I asked.

Lucian took a deep breath. As my eyes adjusted more to the darkness, I was able to make out the drawing held delicately in his hand as if it was the most precious artifact he owned. Lucian began singing softly. His voice was rich and deep in a language I didn't understand. A haunting melody emerged from his words, weaving through the air like a ghostly lament. Even without understanding him I could feel the sorrow and longing in the song—a mournful ode to loss. The language had a steady emphasis on vocals, adding a more lyrical element to his chant, and I noted he pronounced his *r*'s softly, but I couldn't understand individual words. The notes and phrases blended seamlessly, creating a beautiful tapestry of sound that wrapped around us both and bound us in its melancholic embrace. After a minute, his vocals faded softly into silence.

"She made that song the day my father died," Lucian said. "And she kept singing it every night afterward as if the song would keep him alive with her. I was too young when he died, which is why I don't remember him, but I've never forgotten that song." He let out a shaky breath. "I sang it for the first time the night she died. I used to sing it a lot but haven't done so lately. I guess I got busy." He exhaled deeply again. "Thank you, Isa, for helping me remember."

I wasn't sure I had helped with anything but squeezed his shoulder in response. He tightened his grip on my hand, the heat of his skin pressing against mine. I could have stayed like that all night, but Lucian finally pulled away as he slowly stood up.

"I don't want to keep you from sleeping," he said softly.

"It's okay," I said as I stood too. Lucian stood rigidly, like a towering statue, and he still clutched the drawing. I stepped forward and gave him a hug—he definitely seemed to need one. "I'm so sorry for your loss, Lucian. I really am."

After a second, he wrapped his arms around me, too, and held me close. His breath brushed the top of my head as his chest rose and fell slowly.

"Thank you," he finally whispered.

I pulled away, and he did too. "Good night."

"Good night, Isa."

"What else can we do to find the killer?" I asked.

His gaze fixed on the road, Lucian didn't respond. Neither of us had mentioned what had happened during the night, and Lucian's eyes shone with a powerful determination again.

After an early breakfast, he had asked me to come to another crime scene to look for clues. I wasn't super excited about it, but Lucian had promised that this one would be less gruesome and that I might have some useful insights.

"Serial killers tend to get sloppier as the killings progress,"

Lucian replied. "They start feeling safer and stop taking precautions. So I'm hoping that we'll be able to find something."

The new murder scene was in another victim's apartment with a similar situation as last time—no camera footage and no witnesses. The victim had been found dead in the morning with the inscriptions carved on her back.

I hadn't had time to look further at the Book of the Dead but would do that once we returned to the mansion. Hopefully, that would give us more answers.

"I don't think—" Lucian was cut off as the phone rang. He quickly answered, "Hello?"

"Detective Holt," Officer McGowan said. I recognized his voice, but his tone seemed more alarmed. Lucian must have noticed it, too, because he immediately perked up, and his grip tightened on the wheel.

"We have another victim," McGowan said. "She's still alive, for now."

"Where?" Lucian demanded.

"Midtown in—"

I didn't hear the rest as Lucian stepped on the gas and I shot backward, the seat belt digging painfully into my ribs.

"The killer fled the scene, and we have ambulances on the way," McGowan continued.

"I'll be there in five minutes," Lucian said.

He hung up and drove through the streets like a madman. People honked angrily at us, and Lucian nearly ran over some pedestrians by swooshing through several red lights, but no one stopped us. We arrived at a tall concrete building with a giant FOR SALE sign at the front. Lucian parked on the side and bolted out of the car.

I raced after him. My mind felt strangely detached from my body as we rushed inside the building, climbed two stories, and arrived at a floor with several police officers. They lowered their guns once they saw Lucian, then eyed me carefully.

I followed Lucian into a barren room, then froze at the doorway. A girl, maybe around eighteen, lay on the floor in a pool of blood. She had several jackets covering her body and cried loudly as a female police officer kneeled at her side and talked to her gently. If her body looked anything like the bodies of the other victims, then her skin must have been carved with inscriptions. Torn pieces of fabric bandaged her wrists, and I imagined the officers had tried to stop the worst of the bleeding.

The girl saw Lucian as he approached her and immediately curled away from him.

"It's alright, sweetheart," the officer said. "This is Detective Lucian Holt, and he's going to find the person who did this to you."

Lucian kneeled next to the girl, opposite the female officer.

I tentatively stepped closer, my legs feeling as if they would dissolve at any second. One of the jackets slid down from the girl's shoulder, revealing a crude inscription. I had read it so many times that even though a few of the letters were marred with blood I could make out what it said.

Dic Mihi Nomen Meum
Tell me my name

I shivered.

"The ambulance should be here soon," said a police officer with salt-and-pepper hair standing next to a window. I recognized his voice as Officer McGowan.

"What's your name?" Lucian asked the girl. His voice had never been that gentle.

"I'm Ana," the girl said with trembling voice.

"I promise I'll catch whoever did this to you, Ana," Lucian said. "Can you tell me who that was?"

"She had fangs. She bit me." Ana whimpered and closed her eyes. She extended one of her arms out to Lucian. My heart skipped a beat as Lucian pulled at the makeshift bandage to reveal the wound. Two sharp holes dug into her arm, and the skin around them was an angry shade of red and slightly purple as if the bite had injected poison into her bloodstream. "Then she cut me with a knife."

"What did she look like?" Lucian asked.

"She had long blond hair. A scar . . . on her chin. She seemed . . . thirtysomething." Her sentences were short as her breaths caught. More tears streamed down from Ana's eyes. "I don't want to die."

"It's alright," Lucian whispered to her. "You'll be alright."

"I don't want to die," she repeated.

Lucian held her hand gently. The distant wail of the ambulances echoed outside. The girl's breaths became quicker and hoarse. Lucian tightened his grip around her hand as if that was the lifeline that could keep her alive. He kept holding on to the girl's hand even after she went still.

8

I SAT OUTSIDE Ana's apartment building holding on to a blanket an officer had given me. I hadn't stopped shaking in the last ten minutes since I had exited the building. Ana's words kept repeating inside my head like a song on repeat.

She had fangs. She bit me.

But what that implied seemed impossible.

"How are you holding up?" I flinched at the voice and shot to my feet, then I realized it was the female officer.

I didn't answer as I sat back down. The officer had tanned skin and flowing dark hair tied back in a high ponytail. She was tall and lithe, but her grip was soft as she held on to my shoulder.

"It's not easy working in this business," she said.

I nodded in agreement.

"Especially when you're fighting against monsters like these. At least we have Lucian." She chuckled. "A monster hunting monsters."

A sharp tingling sensation crawled up the back of my neck, like countless tiny pins pressing into my skin. I gripped the blanket tighter as I felt the ground tilting beneath me.

She cocked her head to one side and let go of my shoulder. "He probably won't hurt you. But still, I would advise you to stay away from him and his kind. He's never killed any innocents, as far as I know, and he's caught hundreds of criminals. But he's still a killer, and even though he'll never admit it to himself, he's a monster just like the rest of them." The officer stared at my face, then frowned. "He hasn't told you the truth, has he?"

"I . . ." I couldn't form a sentence because my thoughts were too distracting. *He's a monster just like the rest of them. She had fangs. She bit me.*

The officer's brows shot up. "What do you know?"

"I'm helping him solve a murder case," I said.

"But do you know what the killers are? What he is?" she asked.

My heart pounded furiously against my chest. "No," I responded, although I was afraid I already knew the answer.

The officer's eyes traced over me. "Has Lucian hurt you?" she asked.

"No," I said.

"Good," she responded. "I didn't expect him to but still wanted to ask." She huffed. "Not that I could protect you from him. He's too powerful." Her gaze softened. "I don't know why he hasn't told you, but you deserve to know the truth and to understand who you're really working with."

Blood rushed into my ears as my heart hammered painfully against my chest.

"Lucian Holt," she said slowly, "and his partner Sue, are vampires."

I blinked in response. The sheer absurdity of those words didn't allow me to fully believe it.

"I know," she said. "It's crazy. But that's the world we live in. Vampires are real, and they've been around for millennia killing us for food. Lucian is a rare exception. He uses his skills to hunt down criminals we can't deal with ourselves and to kill other vampires who murder innocent victims for fun."

The truth was hilariously absurd yet terrifying.

"Do what you want with that information," the officer said. "And again, be careful. Even though he's saved countless lives, we're still his food."

The officer patted me on the back, then walked away, leaving me alone buzzing with questions. In the minutes that followed, I tried to convince myself that I had imagined our conversation and Ana's words and that seeing Ana die had been traumatic enough to cause me to misunderstand everything.

But I couldn't have imagined something like that, right?

"We're leaving," Lucian said behind me.

I jumped to my feet again, my heart lurching. Lucian's expression was neutral as he walked past me. Feeling like I was in a trance, I followed him back to the car, still holding on to the blanket. I climbed into the passenger seat and put on my seat belt. We drove in silence for a while until Lucian stopped at a random parking lot. I didn't know where we were and didn't particularly care at that point. Lucian turned off the engine, gripped the wheel tightly, leaned forward and rested his head against the back of his hands, then breathed deeply.

Cars raced past on the street. People chatted as they exited a grocery store. Rain began splattering onto the windshield.

"If I asked you a question, would you answer me honestly?" I asked.

Lucian raised his head from the wheel, then turned to look at me. I didn't meet his gaze, but I could feel his eyes burning into me.

"What did the police tell you?" Lucian asked.

My heart stuttered in my chest like a hummingbird trapped in a cage.

"The truth," I said. "But I want to hear it from you."

I finally mustered the courage to look at him. It was the first time I noticed the unnatural brightness in his eyes and his smooth, flawless skin. Lucian turned away from me to stare ahead at the passing cars.

"You said most of history was wrong," I prompted him.

"It is," he said. He met my eyes again, weariness weighing down his gaze. "What do you think happened to the ancient gods?"

"What do you mean?" I asked.

"The ancient gods," Lucian repeated. "Where do you think they went?"

I shrugged, unsure of where he was going with the conversation. "They weren't real. People made them up to explain natural phenomena they didn't understand."

"Do you really believe that?" Lucian asked.

I didn't respond.

"Well, they're real," Lucian said. "The gods are flesh and bone beings that have lived among us since the beginning of time."

That made no sense. "But no one has seen them in millennia. They disappeared, and people stopped believing in them."

"They never left," Lucian said. "They began to grow old, losing their power and becoming hungry. Then they realized that they could regain their youth by drinking human blood." Lucian's eyes held my own. "They didn't disappear. They simply hid because instead of protecting humans they began to hunt them. Humans forgot they had been gods once and began calling them vampires."

I realized I had stopped breathing when my chest began to burn.

"Does that mean you—"

"No, I'm not a god," Lucian said. "The gods also discovered that after draining a human's blood, they could feed the victim their own blood and turn them immortal." He tapped his finger on the wheel. "Humans called these new beings demigods, and the gods loved them as their own children. Or as their wives and husbands. The power this second generation of immortals inherited was weaker, and unlike the gods, they could be killed—but they were still highly dangerous."

My head began to pound painfully.

Lucian continued, "And then the demigods bit their favorite humans, too, and turned them immortal. This third, weaker, generation did the same and so on." Lucian finally broke his tight grip on the wheel and pulled his hair back with both hands. "Anyone fourth-generation and beyond is closer to the modern perceptions and beliefs of what vampires are since they have lost most, or all, of the power inherited from the gods."

I sat in stunned silence wanting to scream, cry, and fall asleep all at once.

"That's the full truth," Lucian said quietly.

"Do you kill humans for blood?" I asked.

"Yes," he said. "Only human blood can keep us alive. Animal blood isn't enough to sustain us." He added that last sentence as if he knew what my next question would be. "I kill criminals," he said. "I made a deal with the police a long time ago, here and in other major cities. They know what I am. They know that I have to drink blood and that no matter how hard they try they can't kill me. So I kill criminals that they want off the streets, and I solve cases when others like me are involved."

The rain pattered down harder on the windshield.

"Why would you solve murders caused by vampires if you all need to kill humans for food?" I asked.

"There's a difference between killing for food and killing for fun," Lucian said. "You eat chicken, yet I assume you don't go to a farm to torture them before you take a bite."

"No," I said. "But don't you get in trouble for killing other vampires?"

A smile curved at the edges of Lucian's lips. "If anyone has a problem with what I do, they can take it up with me."

I suppressed a shudder.

"Are you still willing to help me?" Lucian asked, his gaze softening. "I know the truth is a lot to take in. You deserved to know it to understand the full implications of this murder case, but I understand if you want to leave. I can drop you off at your apartment right now if that's what you want. But if you stay, my promise still stands—I'll keep you safe."

The image of Ana as she lay on the floor dying flashed into my mind. How would my parents feel if it had been me instead? How would Ana's parents feel when they heard the news? How would I feel if next time the victim was one of my friends? The killer would continue to murder innocents, and if there was anything I could do to help find them, then I was willing to do it.

Lucian's gray eyes sparkled with lightning. But he wasn't the monster I was afraid of.

"Yes," I said.

"Good," Lucian said with a nod. "Let's go then."

PART III

THE
MEMORY

9

WOLF SAT NEXT TO RAFE on a train, his eyes closed as he attempted to doze off for a bit. He had tried to ignore his loneliness, but Rafe's words earlier that day at the café had cleaved open a wound he didn't realize had been bleeding for some time. He couldn't stop the rush of memories that invaded his mind . . .

"Are you going to show me that?" he asked.

She peeked at him from behind the canvas as she sat crosslegged on the floor, her smile making his heart flutter.

"It's not finished yet," she said.

He leaned back on the couch, picked up the book beside him, and continued reading. She had recently gotten into painting, and now the room was full of the beautiful landscapes she had created. Splotches of paint marred the hardwood floor and some of the walls. They would have to clean those before they left, but for now, he let her enjoy her creativity.

"I can't believe you read this," he said as he leafed through the pages. "My brain is rotting, and I'm only on chapter three."

She laughed. "I never said they were good books, but they're entertaining."

He huffed. She had already finished reading the books he had bought last week. Tomorrow morning, he would slip away to buy her new books and surprise her when she woke up. He had wanted to know what she was reading so he could find similar books, and now he, too, was entertained by the silly fantasy stories humans made up.

He placed the book beside him and picked up their phone. They didn't have anyone to contact, but he enjoyed being able to use the internet on a small device. He opened a new tab and looked for new craft ideas. She had enjoyed weaving before, so maybe she would like knitting and crocheting. He made a mental note to get supplies for that too.

Satisfied with that thought, he went back to reading, although he kept shooting glances in her direction. Every time she noticed, she smiled and hid behind the canvas, making him smile too.

"Okay," she said after an hour. "I think it's done."

He dropped the book on the couch and went to sit next to her. She had painted an indoor garden, one that was all too familiar to him. The painting had exquisite detail—the tall fountain in the middle of the atrium, the frescoes on the walls, even a few birds resting on the trees.

"You remember," he said.

She leaned closer and wrapped her arms around him. "Of course I remember," she said. "That's the place where we first met."

He looked at her and smiled. He had fallen in love the moment he had first seen her, a deep, blooming sensation that he couldn't logically explain. It was as if they had been born to be with each other. But she was already engaged when they had met, and it had taken many years for them to finally end up together.

He kissed her, and she held him tighter. He pulled away to look at the painting again, nostalgia taking ahold of him. No ruins had been left of that garden, but it would always hold a special place in his memory. He pulled her into his lap and kissed her again, heat building up in his chest. She pulled away with a chuckle.

"Can we go to the beach first?" she asked.

"Can we go to the beach after?" he asked as he tugged at the edge of her leggings.

"No." She sprung away from him with a laugh and raced out of the room.

He laughed, too, but didn't immediately go after her. He picked up the canvas and left it next to the window, hoping the dying rays of the sun would help it dry sooner.

When he walked out the back door, she was already waiting for him at the beach and looking up at him as he descended the stairs. He stripped off his clothes, leaving only his swimsuit on. She made sure he was looking at her when she pulled down her leggings, removed her blouse, and let them drop onto the sand. She stepped toward the edge of the ocean. Watching the waves warily, he walked to her.

"Afraid of sharks?" she asked with a teasing smile.

"I don't like getting wet," he said as the waves licked at their feet.

"I do," she whispered into his ear before pulling back with a smile.

His length strained against the swimsuit. Her smile widened. She skipped away before he could pull her into his arms and take her back to the house. He exhaled, his body burning, and followed her into the ocean. The cold water stung, but the feeling quickly evaporated. She waded further away from the beach.

"If you keep going, you might find some sharks," he said when only her head bobbed up from the waves.

She stopped, and he quickly caught up. He was much taller than her, so his feet were still planted in the sand. She swam closer to him, and he finally pulled her in for a kiss. Her lips still tasted like the wine they had drunk earlier. He slipped his tongue between her teeth, and she sucked in a breath, pulling him closer.

The sun, the sand, the ocean—it all dissolved as their bodies pressed together. A groan escaped from his lips when she rubbed against him.

"Can we go back?" he asked breathlessly.

"We just got here," she said. "Let's watch the sunset."

Frustration tore through him. He had been looking at sunsets for millennia. The only thing his eyes couldn't get enough of was her.

She turned around, and he pulled her back against his chest with a hug. Her hair still smelled like honey, and he let that smell float around him as he settled his chin on her head. He tried to simply enjoy the moment, to let her warmth seep toward him. As the sun continued its descent, it cast a warm glow across the vast canvas of the sky. A palette of soft pinks and oranges painted wisps of clouds that hung like cotton candy against the fading blue.

An abrupt surge of fear coursed through him. He tensed slightly and pulled her closer. This moment felt too perfect to last. What if she remembered her past? She had remembered the garden, and he wondered if other memories were bubbling up to the surface in her mind. He had loved her for so long, and now that he finally had her, it seemed bittersweet that he would spend his days fearing this perfection would dissolve.

As the sun descended further, it touched the horizon and set the sky ablaze with hues of fiery red and deep violet. Each wave that rolled around them carried the reflection of the sinking sun, creating a dance of liquid flames beneath their gaze.

He didn't know how long he had until her memories would come flowing back. But once they did, she would forget again. Guilt sliced through his chest, but he suppressed it. She was much happier with him, her tragic past forgotten like a stolen dream. If anything, he was doing her a favor.

At least the *Aether* hadn't bothered them in a while. They had both chosen to stop feeding, but with her at his side, the craving for blood seemed insignificant. They had both aged in the last couple of years without fresh blood, but nothing would ever take her beauty away.

She placed her hand over his as the ocean seemed to hold

its breath, caught between day and night as if savoring the last moments of the sun's embrace. She turned her head to face him and planted a kiss on his jaw.

"Let's go back," she whispered.

They walked out of the ocean holding hands. He ground his teeth as his legs began to itch. Sand stuck to him everywhere like leeches. When he tried to wipe it off, it stuck to his hands instead. She laughed as they stepped under the outdoor shower to wash the sand away. When he walked into the house, the cold air conditioner made him shiver, but heat immediately overtook him when she pulled off her swimsuit.

"Are you just going to stand there and watch or—"

He ate up the distance between them and pressed his mouth against hers. She reached out to pull down his shorts, but he grabbed her hands before she could touch him and pushed her onto the bed.

"Not yet," he whispered into her ear. "You made me wait. Now it's your turn."

"But—"

"No buts," he said as she lay sprawled under him.

He started with a kiss on her lips, then another one next to her ear, and the next one on her throat. Her skin was still salty from the ocean, but he didn't mind as he slid his tongue down her chest until he reached her breasts. He sucked on her nipple, palming her other breast with his hand as she gasped.

How many times had he fantasized about this ever since he had met her? He had never desired her so badly than when she had walked down the aisle at her wedding to marry her husband. He still remembered the golden dress she had worn, which had made her sparkle like a star. In that moment, he would have destroyed the entire world except for her if that meant he was the only one who could have her. He had never wished death on anyone so badly than on her husband. Why had she chosen him—an average-looking, weak, and mostly powerless being? He knew he could love her better than anyone else in the world, yet she hadn't seen that.

It didn't matter anymore, he thought as he pulled his lips away from her breast and planted soft kisses on her stomach. Now she belonged only to him.

He pulled himself lower, shoving her legs apart. He licked her entrance with a wide sweep of his tongue, then gave smaller licks until his tongue found her clit. He grazed it softly with his teeth, earning him a gasp. He held her thighs at the sides of his head as he sensed the heat building up inside of her. Just when he knew that desire was about to break through her, he stopped. She groaned but then gasped as he slid one finger into her.

"More," she demanded.

He pumped his finger into her as her hips rocked in a steady rhythm. He held her down with one hand, pinning her steady. She grunted, but to appease her he slid a second finger inside. He could sense the desire coursing through her as he pumped slowly, and just as it was about to burst again, he stopped.

He stood from the bed, stepped out of his swimsuit, then crawled back toward her. Grabbing her thighs, he flipped her over. Her back now to him, she kneeled in front of him and parted her legs. He dug his fingers into the soft skin of her thighs.

"Please," she begged as he hovered at her entrance.

He leaned forward. "Tell me you're mine," he whispered into her ear as he pushed his tip inside.

"I'm yours," she said breathlessly.

He thrust inside of her, and she moaned.

"I'm yours," she repeated. "Just yours."

All his worries melted away as he lost himself inside of her and heard her moans and screams as he drove her to a climax. He felt it shake through her, and that made him come, too, pleasure roiling from him in waves. He growled, then pulled away from her slick entrance as she became limp in his grasp. He embraced her, and they lay together as their ragged breaths became even.

"I love you," he said as he kissed her on the lips. "I love you so much."

"I love you too," she whispered into his ear before planting a kiss on his cheek.

He would never get tired of hearing those words. He kissed her again, savoring every piece of her. They lay in silence for a while, simply enjoying each other's company. Then, after the automatic lights outside turned on, she gently pulled away from him.

"Want some hot chocolate?" he asked.

She nodded. She had once told him that chocolate was the best food to be invented by humans. He put on a pair of shorts and a loose shirt while she changed into new sweatpants. They headed to the kitchen together where he turned on the stove to heat up some water. While he prepared their drinks, adding some extra cocoa the way she liked it, she wandered over to the large map they had hung on the wall. He joined her a few moments later and handed her a mug.

"Wondering where to go next?" he asked.

She nodded. Her eyes traced through the pins on the map. They had nearly one hundred by now.

"There's no rush," he said. "We can stay here for a while until we decide."

It was so peaceful at the beach house with no one to bother them and their days spent entirely with each other.

"Let's go somewhere cold next," she said.

"Tired of the heat?" he asked.

"A little."

He turned back to the map, studying it carefully. "What about Greenland? It should be cold but not too bad if we go in a few months during the summer."

"That would be nice," she said as she took a sip from her mug.

He planted a kiss on her forehead. She smiled at him. A few wrinkles had begun to form at the sides of her eyes, and he kissed each of them. They continued drinking as they stared at the map.

"Come on, let's go see the stars," she said after their hot chocolate was gone.

They stepped out of the second-floor window and climbed onto the roof. The stars were relatively bright above them. But they had been so much brighter before, and he couldn't see most of them now, which he found tragic.

They both gazed up at the night sky in companionable silence. He had always felt a certain kinship to the stars. Just like them, he had survived the ages as the world had changed around him. Maybe she felt the same, and that was why she enjoyed watching them every night. He pulled her closer, wrapping her in an embrace with her back to his chest. He kissed the top of her head.

"I forgot to tell you," she said after awhile. "I spoke to the neighbors this morning."

"What did they say?" he asked, glancing at the house that stood about a hundred yards away from theirs. They hadn't interacted much with mortals in the past few months, and he didn't expect them to bring any trouble. But still, he was wary about humans. They always seemed to sense there was something different about them.

"Not much," she said. "They asked for our names."

"And what did you tell them?"

"I said yours was Wolf," she said.

"Wolf?" he asked. "Why?"

She must have had a minor fragmentation he hadn't noticed—their names were usually the first things she forgot.

"I don't know," she responded. "I've always thought that if you could turn into an animal, you would be a wolf. You have that strength and cunning intelligence, and you've always been more of a loner. You don't need anyone."

I need you, he thought, but didn't say it aloud. "Wolf." He said the name to taste it on his lips. He liked it.

"What did you say your name was?" Wolf asked.

She didn't respond immediately. "You tell me."

"Tell you what?"

"Tell me my name," she said.

So Wolf gave her a new name.

10

THE DRIVE BACK to the mansion from the murder scene felt interminable, thanks to the heavy traffic. We didn't speak a word the entire way, and once we arrived, I quietly followed Lucian down to the basement. Lucian walked past his office and stopped before an empty wine shelf. He slid his hand through the side. Something clicked, and the shelf swung outward like a door.

"A secret room?" I hesitantly stepped closer.

"Something like that," Lucian said.

It was more of a narrow depression in the wall. Knives, two swords, and one axe hung from the wall. Lucian pointed at one of the knives.

"Take that one," he said.

The knife was the size of my palm with a black handle and a double-edged blade. Lucian stepped back as I reached for it. The cold from the handle seemed to seep into my bones. The blade gleamed brightly from the light above us.

"You can take one of the sheaths too." Lucian pointed below the weapons.

I tried a few until I found one that fit.

"Nice collection," I said as I held the sheathed knife.

"It's all silver," Lucian said. "Not a magical weapon but close enough. Silver is the only metal that can kill a vampire. Even touching it burns us."

"Really?" I asked as I gripped it tighter. "So the silver myth is true?"

"It is," Lucian said.

That explained why he hadn't grabbed the knife himself and had stepped away from me.

"It wouldn't kill any of the gods. They're basically immortal and silver doesn't affect them. But anyone second-generation and below will die if you stab them with that," Lucian said. "Including myself." He had added that last sentence like an afterthought.

I met Lucian's eyes, which had softened. I wasn't sure I could fight a vampire hand-to-hand even with a silver weapon, but it did make me feel safer to have it. Lucian must have known how vulnerable I felt knowing the truth, so he had given me the one thing that made him vulnerable.

Lucian exhaled. "Okay, let's get back to the inscriptions."

We went back into the office and read through the translations. Now the murders took on a different meaning, and I understood what Lucian had been getting at with his questions about immortality the night before.

"Here." I pointed at one of the inscriptions.

Lucian walked closer to me but was careful to keep some distance between us.

"This mentions the gods drinking blood," I said. "Do you think the Book of the Dead is trying to explain how the gods made humans immortal?"

"That's what I thought about yesterday," Lucian said. "You said the Book of the Dead was about five thousand years old, correct?"

"Yes," I said.

"That's around the time that the gods discovered human blood kept them youthful and that they started creating the second-generations," Lucian said. "So the timing of when this manuscript began appearing makes sense. What I don't understand is why the killer believes the inscriptions in the Book have any power."

"What about this part?" I said while motioning to the paragraphs that invoked specific names. "Could the killer be trying to summon the gods to force them to turn the victims immortal?"

Lucian frowned. "As far as I know, calling a god's name won't bring them under your control." He paused. "I don't believe in the concept that names have power, but maybe the killer does. *Tell me my name* is repeated quite often, so it must mean something important."

Footsteps echoed behind us as Sue walked into the room. She pulled her windblown hair back with one hand and was breathing hard.

"Could we talk in private?" Sue asked.

"No need," Lucian said. "She knows the truth."

"Good," Sue said. "Now we don't have to keep stocking up the fridge to pretend we're normal."

"I don't think I would have guessed the truth based on that," I said.

"Oh yeah?" Sue said. "What else would have given us away?"

"I never saw you go to sleep, which would have gotten weird after a few days," I said. "Do you even own pajamas?"

"I do. I love pajamas," Sue said.

"Pajamas are overrated," Lucian said.

"Says the man who's never worn them," Sue said. "Seriously. They're so comfy nowadays. I'll buy you some for Christmas. I bet there's some cute vampire ones out there that have silly faces with little fangs."

Lucian only rolled his eyes, but a smile tugged at his lips for a second. "What were you going to tell me?"

"I started trailing some strays," Sue said. "No strange activity from them yet, but I would like your help tracking some of them. If we don't find anything, it might be worth spying on some of the smaller covens in the area."

Lucian nodded to Sue before turning back to me. "We'll be back in a few hours. Let me know what you discover from the Book."

"I will," I said.

Lucian and Sue left, leaving me alone with the board. I headed to the bathroom quickly, then came back into the room. Dario was there looking at the board when I returned.

"Hey," I said, my heartbeat echoing in my ears. If Sue and Lucian were vampires, I assumed Dario was too.

"Is the killer really trying to turn their victims immortal?" Dario asked.

"We think so," I said.

A golden blaze appeared in Dario's eyes, but it was gone in a second. Dario raked a hand through his hair.

"How can I help?" he asked.

"Well, I'm currently reading the Book of the Dead to find clues."

"The Book of the Dead?" Dario asked.

I told him what Lucian and I had discovered, and Dario listened attentively. He didn't startle when I mentioned vampires, so Sue or Lucian must have told him I knew the truth on their way out.

"Hmm," he said after I finished. "I never heard anyone mention the Book of the Dead, not even Helios."

"Helios?" I asked. "The ancient Greek Titan of the sun?"

"Yes," Dario said. "I used to belong to his family, which is one of the twelve ruling covens."

That was fascinating, but I didn't say it out loud. "So he bit you?"

"No," Dario said. "A second-generation bit me, so I'm third-generation."

Dario extended his hand in front of him. Golden-red light rose from his palm and materialized into an orb the size of an apple. It was as if fire had split into very fine silk fibers and then woven into a sphere. The strands of light shifted, restless and thrumming with life. A wave of warmth washed over me. It wasn't the same fire that would burn in a fireplace or that could be lit with a match. This was much more powerful.

"It's solar energy," Dario said. "I can set things on fire, but I can also make plants grow."

"That's amazing," I said.

It vanished after a few seconds. "It's not good to stare at it for too long."

"Oh, right," I said.

"I can also turn things to gold," Dario said. He grabbed a pen from a table. It immediately began shifting as if gold were spilling from Dario's hand onto the plastic pen. I didn't remember Helios being associated with gold but was still mesmerized by Dario's power. He set down the pen, eyeing it for a few seconds.

It was one thing for Lucian to tell me the truth, but seeing Dario use his power so easily, that was something else entirely. It confirmed everything Lucian had said, even though I had already believed him.

The ancient gods were alive.

Vampires were real. And some of them had inherited the power of the gods who had bitten them.

"So . . . the Book of the Dead," Dario said.

"Oh yes," I said. "What do you know about it?"

"Not much," Dario admitted. "Like I said, no one ever talked about it. What I do know about it is from visits to museums."

"So it's not an important book for vampires?" I asked.

"Not that I know of," Dario said as he scratched his head.

I crossed my arms. "How did the gods discover that human blood kept them alive?" I asked.

"I don't know," Dario said. "Helios never talked about that either. I know as much as everyone else does. One day they just discovered it."

That seemed . . . wrong. I didn't think the gods would have

woken up one day deciding to drink some blood. Had they discovered it by accident?

"I'm just trying to figure out how that knowledge ended up in the Book of the Dead," I said. "Ancient Egyptians must have believed that those inscriptions would compel the gods to give them immortality, and now the killer is trying to do the same."

"Interesting interpretation," Dario said. He shook his head. "But regardless of whether this works or not, we need to stop the killer." He looked at the pictures again. "No one deserves to die like that, and no one deserves to have immortality forced upon them." His tone was bitter, and I sensed his comments were rooted in his past.

"I have my computer upstairs," I said. "I'll get it so we can do some reading."

Dario glanced at his watch. "It's almost lunchtime," he said. "You should take a break, then we can continue working."

At the mention of food, my mouth watered. "Good idea."

I followed Dario to the kitchen where he had left some sandwiches on a couple of plates.

"That looks good," I said.

"It's an Italian panini," Dario said as we made our way to the dining room.

"Do vampires still eat?" I asked as we sat down.

"We don't need food, only blood, but some of us still eat just for pleasure. When we get turned, we begin losing our appetite for food," Dario said. "I always loved cooking and have tried to keep eating, but as time passes by, food begins to lose its taste." He took a bite. "Sue and Lucian haven't eaten in a long time. They've probably forgotten how often humans need to eat."

That explained a couple of things about Lucian.

"How old are you?" I asked after a few seconds. "If you don't mind the question."

"I don't," Dario said. "I'm seventy-four years old. Sue is

ninety-five, and we don't know how old Lucian is, but he's much older."

I managed to swallow a piece of panini without choking. How old could Lucian be?

"How long have you been with Lucian and Sue?" I asked. I assumed he had been the last to join their little coven.

"About six years," Dario said. Even though Dario had been with them for a while, there seemed to be a certain coldness about his interactions with Lucian. I had only seen them together once so I couldn't know that for sure, but I did wonder how well they got along. Considering my conversations with Lucian, it didn't seem like he talked about his emotions with the other two.

"How long have Sue and Lucian known each other?" I asked.

"She joined him about twenty years ago."

That was a long time. "Are Sue and Lucian—"

"In a romantic relationship?" Dario finished. "No. He's always been like an older brother to Sue and to me."

"And why did you choose to join them?" I asked.

"It's safer," Dario said.

"Why would it be safer?" Dario shifted in his seat at my question, so I quickly asked something else. "What are Sue and Lucian's powers?"

"Sue is fourth-generation," Dario said, "so she still has a bit of power and can manipulate sound waves by amplifying them to hear conversations or by canceling them to make herself completely silent. But Lucian is second-generation. He's—"

My jaw nearly dropped to my plate. "He's a demigod?" I asked.

Dario nodded. "I guess he technically is."

"Who bit him?" I asked.

"We don't know," Dario said. "He's never told us."

"What are his powers?" I asked.

"He can manipulate weather patterns—storms, hurricanes,

earthquakes, tornadoes. He can summon lightning in his palm or turn the earth upside down with a flip of his wrist. He's incredibly powerful. But I wouldn't ask him that question though," Dario added quickly. "Lucian hates the gods, and any mention of them will make him mad."

"Why?" I asked.

"I think he was turned against his will," Dario said. "He also thinks that the gods are too old to be ruling the world and that they should let the world rule itself."

I didn't dare ask whether Dario thought the same about the gods, having come from one of the main ruling covens. I tried to think which god or goddess had powers over weather phenomena. Zeus was the obvious first choice, and I wondered if he had been the one to bite Lucian.

After we finished eating, I helped Dario clean the dishes. Then I grabbed my computer from the library, along with the sticky notes and another notebook, and headed back down to the basement office.

We read a full translation of the Book of the Dead from a digital book I had downloaded. Every time a passage seemed to refer to the ancient gods attaining their immortality through blood, Dario wrote it down on a sticky note. I remembered reading some of the passages for one of my classes, but most of the Book talked about how the deceased soul should traverse through the afterlife and which gods would be able to help them. The Book used a considerable amount of pages explaining the dangers of the afterlife and the monsters that could kill a soul. It took us a couple of hours to get through it, and in the end, we had a chaotic spread of sticky notes on a new whiteboard.

"Does any of this make sense to you?" I asked.

Dario cocked his head to one side. "Helios was called Ra in Egypt, so they're the same god, and he's mentioned a lot along with Osiris. But again, from my personal interactions with Helios, he never mentioned anything about this book, the afterlife, or any of this." He motioned at the notes.

"Do you know anything about Osiris?" I asked, trying not to freak out at the fact that Ra was a real being and that Dario had lived with him. "He's the god most frequently mentioned here. His myths say that he died and came back to life briefly before he became the ruler of the Underworld."

"I've never heard anyone talk about Osiris," Dario said. "But there are a lot of other gods I haven't heard about either."

We continued to discuss specific passages, taking the sticky notes with phrases we had found on the victims and pasting them in their respective places. There didn't seem to be a specific pattern. All the phrases the killer had used came from different sections of the book.

"Why would some of these inscriptions be in Latin or Greek?" Dario asked.

"Maybe because the Book of the Dead got translated to make it more accessible, so some versions may only exist in those newer languages," I said.

We rearranged some of the sticky notes and found that the inscriptions carved in Latin and Greek were missing from the Egyptian translation, confirming that theory.

"Hmm," Dario said.

"It feels wrong," I said.

"What?" Dario asked.

"That the killer would use Greek and Latin translations," I said. It wasn't something I had put too much thought into before, but now it bothered me. "Ancient civilizations believed that symbols had power. By translating the text into another language, you use different symbols for the letters and the text would lose its original power." I tapped a pen on the notebook. "The killer must believe that the meaning of the words has more power than the words themselves, but that doesn't sit right with me."

"Interesting observation," Dario said. "But from my experience watching Lucian catch killers, their actions don't usually make sense."

I exhaled. "True."

Dario's phone rang, and he quickly answered it. His features tightened with concern as Lucian's voice sounded through the phone.

"Yeah," Dario said. "Send the pictures. I'll help Isa with the new translations."

He hung up.

Exhaustion crawled through my muscles, but I pushed the fatigue away. I let out a deep breath as Dario began writing Greek words on a spare sheet of paper.

I sat down on the floor and began the new translation.

11

"SHOTGUN," SUE CRIED before jumping into the passenger seat and forcing me to sit in the backseat, which I didn't mind.

Dario and I had been working on the translations for a couple of hours when Lucian had asked me to come with him to another scene where the police had found carvings on a wall that matched those from the murders. Driving into the city for the second time that day felt a bit dizzying, but I couldn't really complain—it was the nature of this job.

Lucian started the engine, and the three of us drove away from the mansion once more.

Sue connected her phone to the car, then threw it back at me. "Choose some music," she said.

I browsed through her playlists, holding back a snicker at some of the names—*Workout*, *Hype*, *Songs Lucian Hates*, *Songs Dario Hates*, *Chill Vibes*. Feeling like I needed something to give me more energy, I ended up choosing the *Hype* playlist.

"I would have chosen *Songs Lucian Hates*, but this is fine too," Sue said.

Lucian didn't say anything, but his lips pulled up slightly. Curious, I opened that playlist to see what type of music Lucian disliked.

"Not a fan of heavy metal?" I asked.

"That's not music," Lucian said.

"Ouch," Sue said.

I handed the phone back to her, and Sue started looking through pictures of the murder scenes. I glanced away from the photos of blood-splattered floors. The afternoon sun had managed to break through the mist and bathed the highway with bright rays.

My phone buzzed. I fished it out of my pocket.

Is your boss still holding you hostage or are you free to see a movie tonight? Liz had texted in our group chat.

We promise we won't talk about book spoilers, Aura added.

A cold dread seeped into my heart, turning it into ice. I burned with the need to tell them about the killer and that they were in danger. But even if we caught the killer, I would never be able to tell them the full truth. For the rest of our lives, we would be the prey of ancient beings that hid among us—and my friends would never know that.

Still busy, I texted back.

I didn't wait to see their reply as I put the phone away.

"Your mom?" Lucian asked.

"No, my friends," I said.

"They must hate me," Lucian said. He turned to Sue. "Isa's friends think I'm the worst boss in the world for keeping her so busy."

"Sounds about right," Sue muttered.

I laughed, and Lucian smiled. But the dread continued to spread from my heart to the rest of my chest.

The rest of our short ride was in silence. We arrived at the scene fifteen minutes later, stopping at an abandoned warehouse with rusted metal walls.

"They should be here already," Lucian said as he slowly drove up to the entrance.

"They're behind the building," Sue said. "They probably don't want anyone to see the police cars."

We found the police cars parked between the warehouse and a slim one-story building. The three of us exited the car and made our way to the three officers huddled together next to one of the cars. The female officer I had talked to earlier raised a brow when she saw me but said nothing.

"Thanks for getting here so quickly," she said to Lucian. She motioned to the building, and we followed her inside while the other two officers stayed behind.

"Victim went out with her friends last night but never came back," the officer started as she pushed open a creaking metal door. "Her friends have a phone-tracking app, and when they tracked hers here, they called us."

I didn't miss the sidelong glance Lucian cast at me. The officer continued talking, but her voice faded into the background. I pulled out my phone and opened the tracker app. Liz was in her apartment, probably working since she had a remote job. Aura was at her company's offices. I didn't have Mya's location, which sent a ripple of fear through me.

Tell me more about your trip. I texted her just so I would know she was fine.

The warehouse's oily odor pulled me out of my thoughts, because the scent choked the air out of my lungs. The large room was completely empty. I didn't spot any blood or inscriptions, or a body. The officer opened another door—which revealed a large room with some boilers at each side—and pointed at the floor. A circular grate had been pulled to the side to reveal a dark hole.

Sue sighed next to me. "Please tell me that doesn't lead to the—"

"Sewers," the officer finished. She pulled out a flashlight, placed it in her mouth to hold it with her teeth, and began climbing down the ladder.

Muttering a curse, Sue went after her. A powerful stench washed over me as I stepped closer. I breathed through my mouth as I descended the ladder. My hands trembled slightly as I gripped the cold, rusted metal. I was careful as I stepped on the wet ground and walked toward Sue, whom I barely saw in the dark as my eyes adjusted.

The water sloshed against the narrow ledge where we stood. The dark, murky liquid reflected the dim light from the officer's flashlight. It felt like standing on an underground sidewalk next to a flooded street that smelled of rot and decay. Shadows danced on the damp, mold-encrusted walls, and the occasional drip of water from the ceiling echoed like a sinister countdown. A few squeaks echoed in the distance, making me startle so that my heart pounded in the oppressive silence.

Sue cursed again when the beam of light landed on a body a few yards away. The pale skin was carved with tiny inscriptions, many more than the ones on the other victims. Her entire body was like a piece of paper ripped from a book. One arm lay submerged, and the rest of her limbs were twisted in unnatural positions. The bloated face was so disfigured I couldn't make out the facial features. I glanced away as bile rose up my throat, but taking deep breaths wouldn't help because of the horrible smell.

Lucian stepped away from the ladder and came closer to me. He hesitantly laid a hand on my shoulder, his eyes tracing me. His attention snapped back to the officer when she began speaking.

"We found her in the water less than an hour ago," she said. "But with the bloating, it's hard to pinpoint exactly when the murder happened." She slid the beam of light away from the body. "Then we found this."

Lucian's grip on my shoulder tightened, and I pushed away my nausea to follow the police officer's flashlight. I hadn't looked too closely at the wall behind us, but with the flashlight illuminating it, the words seemed to glow. Lucian finally broke his grip on me as I walked closer to the wall.

"The killer must not be very tall," Lucian observed.

The words came up to the top of my head, but at that height, the handwriting was already messy. The officer moved her flashlight to the side and revealed hundreds, possibly thousands, of words scratched crudely on the wall.

"Why would the killer write them here?" Sue asked.

No one had a response.

Greek, Latin, and Egyptian words were jumbled together in incoherent sentences that weren't even written in straight lines. Forcing my legs to remain steady, I walked down the length of the sewer. I kept my eyes on the wall, not daring to glance at the body behind me. With every step, the carvings became messier and more like doodles until they ended with a sentence written in English.

Long live the lost god.

Ice seemed to flow through my bloodstream. Who was the lost god? And why had this sentence been written in English? The officer's flashlight settled on something under that sentence—eleven tally marks etched deeply into the wall like stab wounds.

"Do you think these are—"

"They're counting the victims," Lucian whispered.

"That's more than we've found," Sue said.

"Have you searched through the rest of the sewers?" Lucian asked.

"Not yet," the officer said.

Lucian stalked away.

"Wait," the officer said. "I don't think we should—"

Electricity crackled in Lucian's hand, bright enough to illuminate our surroundings in twisting white light. Lucian's eyes shone white as he glanced back, reminding me, and everyone else, that he wasn't just a vampire.

He was a demigod.

"I'll be back," he said before rounding the corner at the end.

"Hold up," Sue said as she raced after him.

After a second of hesitation, I followed them too. The ground was slick with slime, and one misstep would send me tumbling into the foul waters. The female officer cursed, then ran to catch up to me. We three women rounded the corner but didn't find any bodies or words scratched on the walls. Our footsteps echoed down the length of the sewer, occasionally interrupted by the scurrying and squeaking of rats. I hoped someone was keeping track of where we were going because I quickly lost any sense of direction. The tunnel seemed to close in around us, the ceiling lowering and the walls narrowing, as if the sewers were alive and intent on swallowing us whole.

"What's that?" Sue asked as she pointed at something on the ground.

I stopped, and the officer's flashlight settled on what Sue had seen. I crouched down next to soggy sheets of paper that had been left bunched up against the wall. After a second, I noted what had caught Sue's attention—a large Egyptian symbol on one of the pages.

Lucian's flickering light faded as he rounded another corner, leaving us in a little island of light from the flashlight. Sue grabbed the dripping papers and tried to separate them. Half of the bunch ripped off and splatted onto the damp ground, but I was able to make out some details.

"Looks like pictures of Egyptian parchments," I said. "Wait."

Sue stopped trying to pry the pages apart.

"I can't be absolutely sure," I said, "but I think these might be from the Fine Arts Museum in San Francisco."

"How do you know?" the officer asked.

"I recognize the top part of the plaque under the parchment. I helped set those up during an internship when they expanded the Egyptian exhibit," I said.

The officer took a few pictures with her phone.

Sue turned to her. "Would be good to get camera footage from the museum and try to find the woman who matches the description the last victim gave you."

The officer nodded. "It might take awhile to get through all the footage from the past days, or even weeks, but we'll have a team assigned to this."

The air vibrated as Lucian rounded the corner. I stood up slowly as he advanced toward us, electricity skittering off his skin like thrashing white snakes.

"Lucian," Sue said carefully. "Calm down."

The officer eyed him, but she didn't back down.

"I didn't find anything," Lucian said, his voice raw. "But the other victims could be here. We have to find them."

Sue's hair began to drift upward, and a second later my hair did, too, as if gravity had become lighter in the room. Lucian's eyes began to shine brighter.

"We'll find them," Sue said. "Now calm down before you hurt someone."

Hesitantly, I stepped forward.

The officer glared at me as if to warn me.

"Lucian," I said.

His eyes met my own. The pit of my stomach dropped at the searing power in his gaze. But his light dimmed, gravity seemed to return to normal, and the electricity in his hands shrunk until it was only a few wisps of light circling around his hands.

He closed his eyes, breathed deeply, then opened them again. "Let's get back," he said.

Sue grabbed the dripping papers, and the four of us quietly made our way back to the carvings on the wall. Two more officers were already there bagging the body.

My phone buzzed, the sound too loud in the sewers.

`Oh my god, I have so much to tell you. You remember Ray from the marketing team . . .`

I exhaled with relief, then put the phone away without bothering to read the rest. Sue began climbing the stairs while Lucian's gaze stayed fixed on the tally marks, his eyes drilling into them as if he could shoot lasers that would burn them off the wall. But my own attention strayed back to the English sentence. It had to mean something important. The killer may not have made sense—and they were clearly insane—but there was a certain intention to the words on the wall, the tally marks, and the English sentence that begged me to find how they were all connected.

I didn't have an answer as I climbed up the ladder and left the warehouse, but I wouldn't stop until I found one.

12

I SAT cross-legged on the floor inside the basement office, my computer on my lap and a ridiculous number of loose pages and sticky notes scattered around me, when Lucian returned from the police station. The lights flickered slightly as he walked into the room.

"Anything new?" he asked.

"No," I said.

Lucian leaned against the wall opposite Dario and me. Even though vampires didn't need sleep, Lucian seemed tired. His raven hair was disheveled in a tangle of dark strands. The light in his eyes had dimmed as if obscured by heavy clouds, and a wild sort of haze seemed to sparkle off him.

After the warehouse, I had returned to finish translating the inscriptions from the latest victim and the ones we had found on the wall. But the newer inscriptions were nonsense. Random words had been mashed together without a clear pattern. Dario had helped me transcribe the text from the pictures, but it had still taken several hours to get through everything. I had also reread the Book of the Dead but hadn't found any mention of a lost god, making me wonder if the killer had made that up.

"What I don't understand," I said while setting my computer next to me, "is why the killer is doing all this." I motioned at the sticky notes and pictures. "If the killer is a vampire, and all you need to do to turn a human immortal is bite them, drain their blood, and feed them yours, then why do this ritual?"

Lucian folded his arms across his chest. "If the killer were human, I would have said that they were trying to find a way to achieve immortality without having to be bitten by gods or half-bloods. But I've been wondering about that, too, and trying to think of a motive for a half-blood killer. I still think it's tied to death and immortality, but I don't know what they're trying to do specifically."

"I suppose," Dario said, his eyes darting across the sticky notes and pictures, "that there could be someone out there who wishes they could make their favorite humans immortal without having them inherit their power. It would make those humans less dangerous to them and easier to control."

"So just creating a lower-born vampire?" Lucian asked.

Dario shrugged. "Maybe."

I wondered if that was motive enough for all these murders. But what other motive could the killer have? I glanced at Lucian but couldn't read anything from his expression.

"Did you discover anything new?" Dario asked.

"The killer is being quite evasive," Lucian said. "Camera footage is unreliable everywhere we go, and we haven't picked up any distinctive scents at the scenes."

"Do the bite marks match?" Dario asked.

"No," Lucian said. "The new ones were too ragged and wide, which indicates the victim was bitten while she was still alive and struggling." He walked closer to the pictures, eyeing them closely as if they would reveal a hidden clue. "No saliva samples from the bites either, so the killer must have washed the wound."

"Anything from the museum footage?" I asked.

"Not yet," Lucian said. "That might take awhile, but we were able to confirm that the pictures you found are from the Egyptian exhibit in the Fine Arts Museum here, so at least we have that lead."

Sue walked into the room and stood next to the door, looking at the wild mess of notes around me.

"So what's the plan now?" Dario asked. "Do we wait to see if the museum cameras caught something?"

Lucian blinked slowly, his gaze trained on the floor as he breathed deeply. The lights flickered again. Dario glanced at him as if afraid Lucian might do something worse than mess with the electricity.

"We should be doing more," Sue said. "Maybe we need to try something more drastic."

"Maybe," Lucian said, his gaze still distant.

"Like what?" I asked.

Sue didn't respond.

"Any suspicious activity from the strays?" Dario asked.

Lucian shook his head. "We're starting to track some of the smaller covens in the area. It would be good to get your perspective on them since you've met a few."

"I wouldn't say I know them well, but I've crossed paths with some of them," Dario said.

"Any of them have a blond female vampire with a scar on her chin?" Sue asked.

"Not that I know of," Dario said. "But it's been awhile since I've seen them so they might have new members. I can help you build profiles for these covens if that's helpful."

Sue nodded. "Yeah, let's get that started."

The two of them walked out of the room.

Lucian took a deep breath while straightening his back, and his gaze slid to me. "How are you holding up?"

"I'm good," I said.

Lucian didn't seem convinced.

I sighed, then stood up, leaving my computer on the floor. "It's a lot to take in, but I'm getting through it."

"Have you eaten dinner yet?"

I looked at my phone. It was already night again. How were the hours slipping by so fast? I had discovered Lucian was a vampire this morning, but it felt like days ago.

"Dinner would be good," I said.

"I'll go with you," he said. "I need a break."

We headed to the kitchen together. I was in no mood to cook, so I grabbed some chicken parmigiana leftovers that someone, presumably Dario, had left in the fridge and heated them in the microwave. I considered asking Dario to teach me to cook as we walked back to the dining room, where I sank down on a chair and started eating.

"I'm sorry," Lucian said.

"For what?" I asked.

"For forgetting you're human," he said. "It's been so long since—I don't remember what it feels like."

"You don't need to apologize. I should be taking better care of myself." I paused. "How old are you? If you don't mind me asking."

Lucian gave me half a smile. "Trust me, you don't want to know."

"Young enough never to have learned Latin, Greek, or ancient Egyptian because they weren't relevant anymore?" I asked.

I knew I was tiptoeing on ice, but the curiosity to discover how old Lucian was and where he came from was overwhelming.

"In my culture, writing and reading were considered inferior to the spoken word, so even though those languages were around, I didn't learn them," Lucian said. "And later on, I never got into Latin mostly because I hated the Romans."

I nearly choked on the chicken. That meant he must have been over a thousand years old, which my mind had trouble processing. I continued eating, and Lucian watched me as if it was the most important thing he had to do. My cheeks grew warm, and he glanced away.

"Sorry," he said again. "I didn't mean to make you uncomfortable. It's just that . . ."

"What?" I prompted.

"I like watching you," he said. "And before you think that's creepy, let me explain." He leaned back in the chair. "An important part about being a detective is understanding the behavior of both the killer and the victim. I have no problem understanding the behavior of killers. I've hunted down enough of them that I know how and why they behave and act in certain ways. And whenever it's a vampire killer, it's even easier for me to understand them." His eyes settled back on me. "But I've lost my connection to the victims. It becomes harder for me to understand them. I don't need to eat or sleep. I don't need to shower, although I still do it sometimes." I chuckled, and Lucian smiled, then kept going. "I would like to believe that I still understand humans. But the truth is that I don't. Understanding behavior is not about being observant. It's about being empathetic, and I've lost that empathy, as I'm sure you've experienced." He crossed his arms over his chest. "I don't think I understand people anymore when they're not trying to kill each other. That's quite sad."

He glanced at my empty plate.

"I'll leave this in the kitchen," I said as I stood up, then cursed myself for having interrupted a deep conversation with Lucian. He felt comfortable opening up to me, and I didn't want him to feel like I was shutting him out. I quickly washed the plate and left it in the rack, then walked back to the dining room where Lucian was standing.

"Would you like to go for a walk?" Lucian asked.

My instinct was to not go outside when it was dark, but with a demigod it seemed silly to worry that anything would happen. And I didn't expect Lucian to have any ill intentions.

"Sure," I said.

I picked up my jacket from the coat hanger next to the entrance and zipped it tight. The air outside was bitingly cold. It didn't seem to bother Lucian, who only wore a dark, buttoned shirt. We walked toward the line of trees.

"You mentioned that you felt like time was slipping from your fingers like water," Lucian said. "That's exactly how I feel.

I've been alive for such a long time, and will likely live longer, yet I still feel the pressure of time weighing on me as if I'll run out of it, and that once I do, I'll wonder if my life was worth living."

"You've helped a lot of people and saved many lives," I reminded him.

"But time killed them anyways," Lucian said. "Killers will never disappear, and death won't either. Sometimes I wonder what the point of all of this is." He turned around to face me. "Sorry, you probably don't want to hear me feeling sorry for myself."

"It's okay to feel vulnerable," I said. "And you sometimes need to let that out. It's not fair that you should carry that on your own."

"I'm not sure if vulnerable is the right word," he said. "I'm just . . . lost. Still trying to figure out who I want to be."

If Lucian had been alive for over a thousand years and still hadn't figured out his life, then what was my hope?

Under the canopy of entangled branches blocking the moonlight, the trees appeared like skeletal shadows. We walked in companionable silence for a while until Lucian found an over-turned trunk and then we sat down. Some stars were still visible above us like glitter scattered on a fabric of twisted knots. I felt so small in that moment knowing that I was but a speck of dust in the universe and that my life was nothing but the blink of an eye to Lucian.

He breathed in deeply, and I looked at his chest. "Is your heart still beating?" I asked.

A dark curl fell on Lucian's forehead as he smiled. "Yes."

"Hmm."

"Don't believe me?" Lucian asked as he raised a brow. "Feel it."

"I . . ."

He raised an eyebrow as if issuing a challenge to prove him right. Slowly, I raised my hand toward his chest. Lucian didn't move as I placed my hand directly over his heart. His heartbeat pulsed powerfully against my palm. Warmth spread through my skin with every beat. I pulled my hand away, my own heartbeat racing furiously inside my chest. I looked back into his eyes, which glowed like two silver rings. If I could have stared at them all night, I would have.

What was I thinking? I ripped my gaze from him. Lucian was a god and technically my boss, I reminded myself, which made me feel slightly guilty. And what was he thinking? He should have been looking for the killer, not sitting with me in the forest. Yet there was something special about our interactions, a certain authenticity to our conversations that I really enjoyed as if we had known each other for much longer, even if I had only met him a couple of days ago.

"What's your favorite season of the year?" Lucian asked.

"Fall," I said. "It's not too hot nor too cold, and I love watching the trees change color."

"I also enjoy the fall," Lucian said. "I hate summer though."

"Is it true that the sun and heat bother vampires?" I asked. "I've seen you out in the sunlight, so I guess that's probably not true, but where does that myth come from?"

Lucian shrugged. "It's easier to get away with murder at night when people are sleeping, which is what most vampires did. I guess people observed that and started making assumptions and theories. But I don't hate the sun. I only dislike the heat. It's uncomfortable."

"Agreed," I said. "What do you do in your free time when you're not hunting killers?"

"I'm always hunting someone," Lucian said. "Like I said, killers never disappear."

"But what would you do if you weren't?" I asked.

"I don't know," Lucian said. I felt his gaze on me, and against every instinct that told me not to, I looked up to meet his eyes.

Heat spread inside of my chest as if one of Dario's solar spheres had lit up inside of me.

Lucian looked up at the sky. "Have you ever seen the stars?" he asked. "I mean, truly seen them?"

"No."

He smiled. "Walk with me."

Lucian led me back to the mansion even though I had expected us to stop at the clearing. We ascended the stairs to the top of the house, came out on the roof, then stood on a flat ledge next to one of the gables.

"It does look beautiful," I said as mist curled out of my mouth while I admired the dark dome of stars uninterrupted by clouds.

Lucian extended his hands above his head. The sky seemed to shift as if he had removed a dark lens that had been hovering over us. The light from the stars intensified at once as if the atmosphere didn't exist and I was standing directly below them. I gasped as they twinkled like jewels glinting in the sun. The effect disappeared after a few seconds, and Lucian let out a long breath.

"That was beautiful," I said, unsure of how he had done that. "Thank you."

Lucian smiled again, dimples digging into his cheeks. "I miss seeing the stars," he said. "They used to be bright like that before, and I watched them every night."

"It's tragic that we have lost that," I said. I sat down, still looking up.

Lucian sat down next to me, our legs brushing.

"What else do you miss?" I asked. "Food?"

Lucian huffed. "No. I never have. The amount of time it takes to think about food, get food, prepare food, and then eat food multiple times a day is ridiculous."

I chuckled. "That's true."

"I used to drink a lot of tea though," he said. "My mom used to make it with her herbs. Now tea doesn't taste like anything."

"I've never been much of a tea person," I admitted. "I like coffee better."

"I never tasted coffee as a human," Lucian said, "so I can't relate to all the wonderful things people attribute to it."

"You already seem to have all the benefits of caffeine without having to drink it, so you're not missing out on much."

Lucian laughed, looking up again. "I miss . . ." In that moment, with his back hunched slightly and his eyes opened wide as he stared at the night sky, Lucian didn't seem immortal. He looked much younger, like a young boy staring at the stars in wonder. "I miss the moments that I took for granted—having a conversation over a meal, going shopping at the market, sleeping in on a rainy day. When your only necessity becomes drinking blood, life becomes duller."

"It must be hard," I said.

I thought about the people I loved dying while I remained alive and about not being able to at least pretend to have a normal life because, at some point, people would notice something strange.

"It's not all bad," Lucian said, "but sometimes I do wish I would've had a human life."

"What would you have done as a human?" I asked.

Lucian shrugged. "I ask myself that question every decade and my answers are always different. Back when I was born, I would have likely become a warrior, then married and had a family. Now there are so many things you can do, but I'm not sure what I would have done in this era." He exhaled and mist curled out of his mouth. "It doesn't matter, I guess. No point in wishing for a life that wasn't meant to be mine." After another long pause, he turned back to me. "What do people our age do for fun nowadays besides read romance books?" he said with a smile.

"Ah, well, we play beer pong and rage cage to get drunk, go dance at parties and clubs, or hang out at cheap restaurants," I said jokingly.

"Beer pong?" Lucian asked.

"You've never played?" I asked.

"No," he said.

"We have to someday," I said. "All we need is beer, a Ping-Pong ball, and a table."

"That should be easy to find," Lucian said as he stood up.

"Oh, you mean we're playing now?" I asked.

Lucian shrugged. "Why not? Might as well enjoy our youth while we have it."

He offered a hand and pulled me up. Our hands held for a second longer before he let go.

"Well, your youth isn't going anywhere," I said.

We walked back into the house, and I followed Lucian around as he grabbed a stack of some expensive-looking glasses and took us to a large storage room next to the kitchen.

"Dario is a bit of an impulsive buyer," Lucian said as we walked past some Halloween costumes, a mini football table, a drum set, and a stack of comic books.

Covered in a thick layer of dust, the Ping-Pong table lay on the opposite side of the room. Lucian placed the glasses on the surface, then flipped his hand. A gust of wind blew the dust off.

"We don't have beer, but we do have a lot of wine," Lucian said.

"That works."

Lucian left the room while I arranged the glasses on both sides of the table. Once he returned, I poured the wine in the glasses as Lucian watched.

"Okay, we each stand at opposite sides of the table. We have to throw the ball at the glasses, and if it falls into one of them, the other person has to drink from that glass."

Lucian eyed the glasses. He grabbed the Ping-Pong ball that had fallen off the side of the table, wiped it clean with his shirt, and bounced it a couple of times. He threw it toward my side, and it plopped into one of the glasses.

"You have good aim," I said as I fished the ball out and drank the wine.

I threw the ball to the other side but missed his glasses. Lucian threw again, and the ball fell into another glass.

"That's not fair," I said as I drank more.

Lucian laughed as we continued playing a few more rounds. His aim never missed, but I only got him to drink twice.

"So this is what people do for fun?" Lucian asked.

"Yep," I said. "I swear it's more fun when there's music, and colorful lights, and more people to cheer you on."

He chuckled, bouncing the ball on his side of the table in a rhythmic beat. "I think I liked what we did for fun in my times more."

"What did you do?" I asked, my head feeling lighter as the alcohol started kicking in.

Lucian held the ball. "Songs and stories were the main form of entertainment. Usually songs told a story. Wandering entertainers would come into our town and play at the local tavern. People listened to their songs, and we danced to them." He set the ball down. "We had real dancing, not whatever it is people do now that looks like they're convulsing."

I burst out laughing.

"What kind of songs did you like?" I asked as I pushed the glasses back and sat on the edge of the table.

Lucian walked away from the table and rummaged through the room until he found a guitar-looking instrument.

"It's a lute," Lucian said as he looked at my confused expression. He dragged a stool closer to me, then sat as he tried out the strings. "Not a good one but it should do the trick."

He started playing. The strings thrummed out of tune, making Lucian wince, but after a few more moments the strings seemed to behave under his fingers, and a song began to flow from them. The lively tune filled the air like fiery sparks. Lucian began singing in the same language he had sung last time. His rich voice never fell out of tune as the song's pace quickened, and I could almost imagine people laughing as they tried to keep up with the rhythm. Lucian's gaze became distant as if lost in his own song. It ended after a minute, and Lucian clutched the lute. "I'm a bit out of practice with this one."

"That was beautiful," I said.

"Hmm," he said. "Maybe I need to play that when you're sober and ask again."

I laughed. "I'm serious. You sing and play very well. Did you ever perform live?"

Lucian nodded. "Like I said, the spoken word was considered more powerful than the written one, so singing was important. It was how we shared our history with the newer generations. That was how my mom taught me about our ancestors."

"That's pretty cool. And you said people danced too," I said as I stood up.

"We did." Lucian stood and placed the instrument on the stool.

"How?" I asked.

Lucian went still, eyeing me for a second. Then he stepped closer. "Put your arms on my shoulders," he instructed. I did as he said, feeling the warmth of his body. His hands rested on the small of my back, making my breath hitch slightly. "We used to dance around in a wide circle, which we can't do here."

Between the Ping-Pong table, the drum set, and the mini football table, there was only a few feet of space for us to move in. Lucian stepped to the left, then back, and to the right, then forward. I followed him as best as I could, trying to not trip over myself. Lucian grabbed one of my hands and twirled me around slowly. My head spun for a moment before his hands settled on my back again.

"I swear it was more fun with the live music, the dresses, and the candles and torches lighting up the room," he said.

"That must have been nice," I said without breaking my gaze away from him.

We continued to dance, falling into a slow rhythm. It was easy to forget everything else but him. In that moment, we weren't working on a murder case. He wasn't a detective, and I wasn't a translator. We were something else together—something that felt more real.

"What else do people our age do nowadays?" Lucian asked after a few moments of silence.

I smiled. Lucian's grip tightened on me as he tipped his head closer to mine. Our lips met. The soft kiss made my stomach flip over. I didn't know how I had expected Lucian to taste but was surprised at the sweetness in his mouth. I let my hand travel to his jawline, then threaded my fingers through his hair. Lucian inhaled sharply, his lips pressing harder against mine. I placed my hand on his chest again. His heart beat against his rib cage like a drum. I hesitantly slipped my tongue into his mouth, but he didn't pull away. I slid it against his teeth but didn't feel the fangs and figured that they probably only came out when he fed. Lucian pulled away from my mouth and planted a soft kiss on my neck, gently cradling the back of my head.

"Lucian?" Sue said from somewhere in the house. "McGowan is calling. They found another victim."

Lucian sighed. "I have to go," he whispered, but he didn't pull away from me. He seemed to hesitate before he pressed another kiss onto my lips, then finally stepped away.

I let go of him.

Lucian walked toward the door as disappointment spiked through me. I shouldn't have felt that—we were supposed to be solving a murder, and there was another dead girl we hadn't been able to save. Our eyes met again.

"Good luck," I said.

"Thanks," he said. Lucian gave me one last smile before he stepped through the door.

13

"HAVE YOU SEEN LUCIAN?" I asked Dario the next morning as I walked into the basement office.

I stopped at the threshold to take in the mess around Dario. Sticky notes were spread out all over the boards, and a few of them had fallen to the floor. Dario's hair was disheveled as he furiously scribbled on a new note. He raised his head to meet my gaze and blinked.

"Is it morning already?" he asked.

"It is," I said.

"Oh," he said weakly. "I didn't notice." A wild glimmer shone in his eyes.

"Are you okay?" I asked.

"Why would you ask?" Dario said in a clipped tone. He seemed to catch himself, then lowered his head with a sigh. Dario turned back to the chaotic mess of sticky notes. "I don't know."

I stepped closer to Dario. "Do you want to talk about it?" I asked.

He ripped his gaze from the board and his eyes slid to me. "Talk about what?"

I didn't respond but simply looked at Dario expectantly. If he wanted to share something, he would.

"It's just . . ." He exhaled, his chest deflating like a balloon. "I've seen gruesome murders but nothing like this." He shook his head. "A maniac trying to force immortality on others by carving symbols into their skins is just . . . I can't find a word to describe how horrible I find this. It angers me so much. These girls had families, friends, partners. They had their entire lives ahead of them. And now they're just"—he motioned to the boards—"and immortality shouldn't be forced upon anyone. But they didn't even get immortal lives, and now, they're just dead."

"It is horrible," I said.

Dario let his arms dangle at his sides. "We'll find whoever did this."

"We will," I said. "I'll go upstairs to find Lucian and see if he discovered anything new last night."

Dario nodded, then began reorganizing some of his sticky notes as I walked out of the room. I wandered through the house, visiting the library and Lucian's study, but he wasn't around. I wondered if he could he be in his room, but I didn't even know where that was.

As I made my way through the first floor again, I found Sue inside a small living room.

"Have you seen Lucian?" I asked her.

"He's at a crime scene," Sue said without looking up from her phone as her feet dangled from a reading chair. "Why?"

"Just wondering," I said.

Sue glanced up. "Is there something you need to tell him? You can tell me, and I'll let him know."

"It's not anything specific," I said. "I was just wondering if you discovered anything last night or if you have the new inscriptions ready for me."

Sue eyed me for a few seconds. Something in her gaze shifted.

"We're waiting on the police to send pictures of the inscriptions," Sue said as she stood up. "But Lucian wanted you to look at the new crime scene too."

"Yeah, sure," I said.

"Good," Sue said with a smile. "Grab your jacket."

I followed Sue out of the house and into the car. We drove in silence as I rested my head on the seat and looked out the window.

Sue didn't have the GPS on—maybe she was old-fashioned like Lucian—and she seemed to know exactly where we were going.

After about forty minutes, Sue began to slow down as we approached a run-down neighborhood. Graffiti and large cracks marred building walls, and trash littered the sides of the narrow street. Neon lights flickered against dark bricks, marking a bar that seemed to be open. Outside, a group of people stood smoking, their faces illuminated by the sign's pulsing glow.

Sue continued onward, entering what seemed like a residential neighborhood. The houses hadn't fared any better with boarded-up windows and walls with flaked-off paint. I would have assumed they were abandoned if not for lights shining through windows or clothing hanging to dry from shutters. Sue's gaze set on a house on the far right. Its once-white paint was now peeling and chipped, revealing grimy, weathered wood underneath. Weeds and vines crawled up the walls, their tendrils snaking around broken shutters. The roof sagged in the middle, and shingles lay scattered on the overgrown grass.

Sue stopped in front of the house. I assumed this was the new murder scene and hoped it wasn't the victim's residence. It was more likely that she had been brought here. Sue unbuckled her seat belt and exited the car. I did the same, walking carefully through tall grass.

Sue motioned to the open front door. "You can check inside while I inspect the shed behind the house."

"What am I supposed to do?" I asked.

Sue shrugged. "Try to find some clues."

"Is Lucian inside?" I asked.

"He should be," Sue said before she began walking around the house toward the shed.

I was careful to not step on any broken glass on my way to the front door. Inside, the musty smell of neglect hung heavy in the air, and dust covered most of the wooden floorboards. The floor had been disturbed in some sections as if someone had recently walked on it.

I patted my side where I had placed the Taser pen Lucian had given me. I had the knife in my other pocket. I didn't expect the killer to come back to their last murder scene but still felt anxious.

After taking one hesitant step forward, the floor creaked underneath me, but I forced myself to follow the trail of footprints despite my battering heart. Upon closer examination, I realized the footprints seemed too small to belong to Lucian. Maybe they belonged to the victim or even the killer. I shook off a chill.

I walked into a hallway with several open doors on both sides and peeked into the first room. Spiderwebs draped every corner, and clumps of dust dotted the floor like acne bumps, but there were no traces of blood nor any strange inscriptions on the walls.

Staring down the length of the hallway, I wondered where Lucian was. I considered shouting his name but hesitated. Nervous in the eerie silence of the abandoned house, I walked into the next room. Adrenaline spiked into my veins as my eyes locked on the words scratched on the walls. A stool had been placed against the wall where the words reached up higher. Compared to the sewers, these inscriptions were cleaner, more elegant. I didn't spot any tally marks or the strange English sentence we had seen last time. I pulled out my phone with trembling hands and took pictures of all the inscriptions, then walked out of that room.

I explored the next room. Scratch marks covered the floor as if heavy furniture had been dragged across it. A glimmer caught my eye and drew my attention to a piece of black paper on the floor. Its lack of dust suggested it had been left there recently. I picked it up, noting the intricate vines and grapes in gold foil that framed the small paper. At the center was the number 5,480.

From my jacket, I pulled out the torn piece of paper that I had forgotten to put away after Lucian gave it to me. The black piece's gold frame was of the same design. It couldn't be a coincidence that we had found the paper at two crime scenes. I wondered what that number meant.

I pocketed both pieces. Making my way back to the main room, I noticed a closed door right next to the front entrance that I had missed before. Maybe Lucian, and the murder scene, were behind it. The handle was painfully cold when I touched it, and the door creaked when I swung it open. I entered another empty room with a staircase at the back leading to the second floor. Just as I was about to climb the stairs, footsteps echoed behind me.

"Lucian?" I asked.

I turned around. My heart dropped to my stomach when I realized it wasn't Lucian who was standing by the door. The woman seemed to be around thirty with silky blond hair, hazel eyes, and a ragged scar cutting through her chin.

"Hello," the woman said with a sweet voice that didn't match the vicious gleam in her eyes. She smiled, showing off a pair of fangs.

14

PANICKED, I FROZE. The vampire in front of me matched the description Ana had given us. Why had she come back to the murder scene?

"What's your name?" the woman asked.

She took one step forward as I took one back, and I nearly stumbled on the stairway. The woman's gaze seemed to eat me up hungrily as she said, "Well, I don't know which god I have to thank for bringing you here."

My heart beat in a panicked frenzy, and even though my instincts screamed at me to run or to pull the silver knife from my pocket, my mind became foggy.

"You might want to beg them for help before thanking them." Lucian's voice was dangerously calm.

I hadn't heard him come into the room, and from the way the woman startled, it was clear she hadn't either. Lucian stood at the doorway, his eyes two rings of lightning. The woman bared her fangs and hissed at him. A growl cut through the room, silencing her. Lucian's fangs shot out of his mouth. They were considerably longer than hers—like two spears jutting out from his lips.

The ground began to tremble. Dust from the ceiling rained down as the wooden house groaned. Blinding white light curled around Lucian's hands. My eyes stung from the brightness, so I squeezed them shut. A thunderous boom blasted through the room, making my ears ring painfully. The light was gone after a moment, but my ears continued to throb. For a few seconds, the ringing enveloped me like hail pounding on my head.

Two strong hands gripped my arms and pulled me up. I hadn't realized I had fallen to my knees. Lucian's eyes traced over me. His mouth was moving, the fangs gone, but I couldn't hear his words. He shook me gently, and the ringing stabbed my head. Lucian pulled me into his arms and carried me out of the room. The last thing I saw before leaving was a body that had been charred.

"Drink," Dario said as he handed me a cup of tea while I sat in the mansion's kitchen. He had been buzzing around me to make sure I was alright after retrieving a first aid kit complete with bandages, aspirin, and wound closures and even using a heart rate monitor, pulse oximeter, and blood pressure machine on me. My heart rate had been alarmingly high, and my oxygen concentration had been lower than average due to a low blood pressure. Dario assured me that those readings were normal during shock and that we could check them again in a few hours. He had also thrown a cozy blanket around me.

After Lucian had driven me back to the house and left me in Dario's care, he had asked Sue if they could talk in private. I hadn't seen them in the thirty minutes since. Part of me was disappointed that Lucian hadn't come to check on me, but maybe he had other important things to do now that we had caught the killer.

The police had arrived at the scene right as Lucian carried me out of the house. Even though we had left right after, they had called to say they found a few bodies with carvings on them in the basement. While it was impossible to confirm fingerprints from a charred body, everyone was positive that the woman had been the killer since she had matched Ana's description.

"Thanks," I said to Dario as I took a sip from the tea. It burned its way down my throat and warmed up my chest.

"Are you sure you weren't hurt?" Dario asked as his eyes swept over me once again.

I shook my head, which made it pound. I winced. "The blast just hurt my ears and gave me a headache."

Dario clenched his jaw, staring at the door where Lucian had disappeared. "He shouldn't have taken you there."

"He didn't," I said. "Sue did."

Dario opened his mouth to say something, then closed it as his eyes flashed. He pressed his lips together, and I didn't know why he was mad. Sue couldn't have known the killer would return to the scene. I took another sip from the mug, placed it on the table next to me, then wrapped the blanket tighter around me to try and stop myself from shivering.

Dario extended his hand to me. I stared dumbly at it for a second, then realized he wanted me to hold it. I grabbed his hand, and he gently closed his fingers around mine. Warmth immediately enveloped me like a soft embrace.

We didn't speak as his warmth wrapped tighter around me. The headache subsided, and my heart finally stopped echoing inside of my ears. We remained holding hands in silence for a long while until I began nodding off. Then Dario escorted me back to my room.

Even though I was exhausted, I took a long shower—as if that could erase the memories from the last few hours of the electricity sizzling across the room and the burnt body lying on the ground. I shut those images away, pulled on my pajamas, and finally collapsed onto the bed.

My head hit sand instead of a soft pillow, and I began sinking into the desert. I tried to move, to pull myself away, but couldn't. The sand burned against my skin as if trying to pierce every pore in my body. I continued descending, deeper and deeper, until full darkness swallowed me whole. Something lay at the bottom of that darkness. Something I had lost. The sand continued to pull me downward, the temperature dropping. Then one of my hands touched something cold yet soft—skin.

Someone else was buried in the sand with me. I had to get him back to the surface, but I couldn't move. I tried to grab him, to take hold of anything, but my hand remained motionless, lying limply on his bare skin. Something shifted underneath me as if the sand was liquifying and flowing turbulently around me. I opened my mouth to scream but the metallic taste of blood swept over my tongue and rushed down my throat, drowning me and pulling me away from him. No, I thought, I couldn't lose him again.

He's dead, a voice said. *You can't bring him back.*

The sand bit into my skin, consuming me slowly. He couldn't have gone far. The earth couldn't have swallowed him that fast.

Let the dead stay dead, the voice said.

I couldn't. I wouldn't.

His hand gripped mine back.

I bolted upright, my sweaty pajamas sticking to my body. My lungs puffed out hoarse breaths, and my entire body trembled. Fog drifted outside the window, slightly dimming the morning light. My head was heavy with exhaustion even though I had slept through the entire evening and night. I took a deep breath through my clogged nose and lay back on the bed, pulling the blankets up to my chin as I nestled in their warmth. I didn't have enough energy to drag myself to the bathroom for a tissue to blow my nose. I closed my eyes and just lay on my side but couldn't fall back asleep. My mind spun with thoughts.

The last few days had been too much, and I hadn't fully processed it all. But now the killer was dead, and my job was done. In the end, my translations hadn't helped to find the killer or to learn what her intentions had been. That made me feel slightly useless.

My thoughts went back to two nights ago. Would Lucian still want to see me now that the case was over? Would he leave the city as he hunted down new killers?

To avoid thinking of those questions, I got up from the bed, took a quick shower, and changed into my clothes. I roamed the house but couldn't find the others and decided to go down into the basement. They would probably be dismantling the boards and throwing out or archiving all the notes. Voices began drifting toward me as soon as I started walking down the steps. Finally catching their conversation, I stopped before I came into view.

"I don't understand why you're so mad," Sue said in a flat tone. "We hadn't made any progress. It only took a few minutes for the killer to come out when Isa walked into the house. You should have used her as bait sooner. Wasn't that part of the plan when we hired her?"

The words hit me like a stone in the face. I stood completely still for a second before anger rolled through me. I stomped back up the stairs.

"Isa?" Lucian called out. "You knew she was listening," he hissed.

I didn't wait to hear what else he had to say as I hurried back to the bedroom and shut the door behind me.

"Isa," Lucian said as he knocked on the door.

"Is it true that you were planning to use me as bait?" I asked.

Two nights ago, Sue had suggested we try something more drastic, and Lucian had been desperate to find the killer.

"I didn't agree with Sue's idea," he said.

"But you still let her do it," I said.

"I didn't realize what she was doing until you were already in the killer's lair," Lucian said.

So Sue hadn't even taken me to a normal crime scene. She had known, or had at least suspected, that we were in the killer's lair, and she had let me walk inside alone. I wondered how they had tracked the killer there. Had Lucian already been inside the house when I entered? Or had he only arrived after the killer came out? If he had gotten there even a minute later, I might not have survived.

I quickly packed my belongings, angrily shoving them into my duffel bag.

"Isa, please," Lucian said. "I wouldn't have put you in danger to lure the killer."

I swung the bag over my shoulder and walked out of the room. Lucian stood in the middle of the hallway, his eyes wide and pleading. I glared at him. Even after everything I had learned about him and the murder case, I had trusted him. I should have listened to the police officer's advice.

Brushing past him, I headed down the stairs. Had he even cared about the translations? Or was using me as bait the only reason he had hired me? Had he cared about me? He had promised to protect me, but now I understood that my safety had never been his priority. My heart squeezed painfully, and my eyes stung with tears, but I refused to cry in front of Lucian and swallowed the lump in my throat.

Lucian grabbed my arm, his grip solid as a metal clamp. I whirled to face him.

"Let go," I said.

Lucian opened his mouth to say something.

"Let. Go."

And he did while saying, "I would have never put you in danger."

"Well, you did."

"Can we talk about it?" Lucian said as he stepped in front of me.

"No."

I walked out the front door and hurried to my car, afraid he would chase after me. I climbed into the driver's seat and threw the duffel bag behind me, then turned on the engine and backed away from the mansion.

Lucian stood at the entrance, watching me leave. Our eyes met through the rearview mirror for a second before the trees blocked him from my view. I didn't look back again as I drove away.

15

I HAD FOUND HIM too late. His body lay on a stone table, and grief shattered me like a sledgehammer pounding me to pieces with each rhythmic beat. His tanned brown skin had turned pale as parchment as if death had bleached him.

The silver knife trembled in my grip. I had failed to save him, but maybe I could bring him back to me. I held his arm, his skin cold and clammy, and wrote the first inscription on his shoulder. His skin was smoother than any parchment I had worked with, and the words flowed easily from me onto his skin. A few drops of blood dribbled from the cuts, but most of his blood had already been drained. Someone knocked on the door, but I ignored them. I couldn't get distracted now. The knock came again but more forcefully.

I awoke with a start and then lay still on my own bed. The knock came again. I glanced at the clock on the nightstand. It was already evening, but I could have slept for another full day.

"Isa?" The voice was muffled by the door, but I recognized her immediately.

I pushed back the sheets and rushed to the door. The light from the hallway outside made my eyes sting with pain, but I couldn't help the smile that extended my lips.

"You look like shit," Mya said. Her red-brown hair was tied back into a braid. The freckles splashed on her pale face seemed a shade darker than I remembered.

"I feel like shit," I responded, moving to the side to let her in.

Mya managed to keep the smile on her lips as she surveyed the stack of dirty dishes in the sink and the empty pizza box that still lay atop the dining table. We had been roommates our first two years of college, and she had always been very particular about cleanliness.

Mya crinkled her nose. "I've been worried about you spending the last few days holed up in here." She turned back to me. "Do you still feel sick?"

Mya wasn't close friends with Liz or Aura, and I hadn't told her about the new job, but I didn't want to explain any of that.

"I'm not sick anymore, just tired," I said.

I pushed away the image of Lucian standing in the doorway, his gray eyes digging straight through me. Had I overreacted by just leaving like that? Maybe, but I had every right to feel angry for having been used as bait. Either Sue had really acted without Lucian's knowledge or they had planned it together. And I had to admit that Lucian had seemed genuinely apologetic.

Maybe I would go back to the house at some point, assuming they were still there. I had forgotten my backpack, notebook, laptop, and dictionaries in the library. That would give me a good excuse to return. Or maybe Lucian would come over to drop them off.

I rubbed my face. Thinking about him was already giving me another headache.

And as if money would prompt me to forgive him, he had paid me double what we had agreed to. I couldn't complain about that and had transferred some of it to my parents. They had protested, but I made it clear that I didn't want or need the money back. Of course, I had lied, saying that I had been offered a full-time position as a private translator and would receive a consistent income and that I could spare sending some money to them. I didn't even know if private translators existed, but my parents had believed me. And at least the extra money would give me more time to find another job.

"Isa," Mya said.

"Huh?" I pulled out of my thoughts.

"We're going to a bar tonight," Mya said.

"What? No," I said.

Mya crossed her arms. "You promised we would go out again when I came back from the trip."

"I don't feel like going out right now."

"You'll feel like it when you take a shower, get dressed, and walk out that door." Mya pointed at the front door for emphasis.

I simply stared back at her.

"Come on, Isa," Mya pleaded.

I shifted from one foot to the other. The last few days had been a fever dream, and I was exhausted. But I had rested so much already that I knew more sleep wouldn't help. Maybe going out was what I needed to get some space from what had happened and to decide what to do about Lucian.

"I'll clean all the dishes and sweep the floor while you get ready," Mya said.

"Fine," I said.

Mya smiled.

An hour later, the two of us exited my apartment, and Mya drove us to the Mission District.

"Where exactly are we going?" I asked.

"To a restaurant and then barhopping," Mya said.

"But where?" I asked.

"They've opened some cool places we haven't been to before. I met some guys at one of the new bars last week, and I invited them both tonight."

"What?" I said. "You didn't tell me more people were coming."

"They're nice"—Mya took a left turn—"single, and hot."

I clenched my teeth.

"Come on. Going on a date won't kill you."

"It might," I muttered. How would I know they weren't bloodthirsty vampires? Instinctively, I buried my hand in my pocket and brushed my fingers against a cold silver handle. I couldn't stop the anxious writhing in my stomach. After everything that had happened in the last few days, I couldn't blame myself for being worried. And Mya didn't understand the danger that would surround us for the rest of our lives.

"We'll be fine," Mya said. "You'll stop feeling paranoid when we get there and meet them."

As we drove further into the city, Mya told me about her trip. She had a job at a tech startup that was rapidly expanding. They created or managed some kind of software—I didn't fully understand what they were doing, but Mya was happy and had been traveling a lot to make sales pitches or something. But there was always some drama with her team.

Once at our destination, Mya parked in a garage, and we walked down the ramp together. The streets were buzzing with activity even though the sky had already turned fully dark. Mya pointed down the street, and I spotted a wooden terrace edged with plants. Spheres of light hung above the terrace and illuminated it in a dim light.

Two men stood outside of the restaurant. One of them waved to Mya. The other man turned around, and both of them smiled at us. I forced myself to smile back. One of them had close-cropped hair and small eyes under thick eyebrows. The other man was half a head taller with dark hair and eyes. His nose was slightly crooked with a faint scar running down its side.

"This is my friend Isa," Mya said, then she pointed at the two men. "These are Sam and Liam."

Mya leaned closer to Sam, the man with small eyes, and I wondered how soon they would start dating.

"We should grab a table," Liam said.

The four of us walked up the steps onto the terrace, and a young lady led us to a table. The other three ordered some drinks, but I asked for water.

"Come on, Isa," Mya said. "Don't you want a mango margarita?"

"I don't feel like it tonight," I said.

"We don't need to be drunk to have a fun time," Liam said. He turned to face me. "So, Isa, where are you currently working?"

Mya tensed slightly and took a long sip from her drink. "I'm still looking for a job," I said.

"What are you interested in working in?" he asked.

I shrugged. "I want to be a translator. I like translating ancient languages."

"Cool," Liam said.

The conversation shifted toward Sam and Mya, who talked about how they had met after they bumped into each other on their way to the bathroom. I kept my gaze focused on them, trying to ignore Liam as he kept staring at me. I didn't want to stare back even though I wished I could have analyzed him properly, but I knew the two men were just human. Liam had that scar on his nose, and his cheeks had a few spots with acne. Sam's back was a bit hunched over, and his skin was flushed red.

I hadn't realized how perfect Lucian, Dario, and Sue's skin had been. There had also been something in their eyes that made them shine a bit as if their irises were a window to their powers. Lucian's eyes had been especially bright, sometimes shifting like thunderclouds.

My phone buzzed. It was Aura, again, asking how I was doing.

I'm free later tonight. I texted back because I could tell Mya that I was feeling sick again and then bail out after we ate dinner. I would feel slightly guilty for leaving her, but if she already knew Sam, then she would be fine. Do you and Liz want to come over for a movie? I can also go to your place.

The reply came less than a minute later. We'll be at your place in 2 hours. We expect a full debrief on what's been happening with your new job.

My stomach clenched. I would have to make up something to say. I put my phone away while apologizing and mumbling about my mom. We ordered some food, and the conversation continued to drag on with mundane topics. While in the middle of discussing a new TV show, police sirens interrupted us. I startled, my heart racing furiously, as the images of the bloated body in the sewers and Ana's blood pooling around her body flashed through my mind.

"You okay, Isa?" Mya asked.

"Yeah," I said, almost shouting as the police cars drove past us. "It's loud." I expected the sirens to fade in the distance, but they stopped abruptly. Blue and red light reflected on the lamps above us. I turned around. The police cars had parked next to the restaurant. People around us began murmuring, but after a few seconds, the restaurant turned up the music and people went back to their conversations. Liam, Sam, and Mya began to speak louder over the noise.

"Isa," Mya said, making me turn around again. "Remember that time when Arnav was drunk and fell into the fountain after celebrating finishing one of our finals?"

"Yeah, I remember," I said. "You almost fell in after him."

Sam laughed. "I'll be sure to keep you away from fountains when you're drinking."

Mya laughed.

I turned around again, but the police cars were still there. The officers hadn't entered the restaurant, so whatever the problem was, it wasn't here.

"Are you feeling okay?" Liam asked.

It took me a moment to realize he had spoken to me. I forced a smile on my lips. "Yeah," I said. "Just wondering what all that is about."

Liam shrugged. "Maybe just a drunken brawl. There's a lot of bars on this street."

I took another sip of water. Even though I had already finished the sandwich I had ordered and some of the fries, I still felt hungry. But I didn't want to order more if the others weren't going to.

The blue and red lights sparkled off my glass when I set it down. "I'm going to the bathroom." I didn't wait for anyone to respond as I got up from the table. I approached a waiter, who pointed me to the side of the restaurant. I took a little detour to pass by the front entrance and glanced toward the police cars.

I stopped, my heart racing wildly. The female police officer I had met before was standing next to one of the cars with a phone pressed to her ear. Her eyes carefully analyzed the building next to us.

I should have just kept walking because whatever was happening wasn't my problem anymore. But I couldn't. Something inside me pushed me to exit the restaurant, walk down the steps, and make my way to the officer.

Her eyes immediately widened when she saw me, and she waved at me to come closer. Not a good sign, I thought.

She ended her call and said, "Can't say I'm glad to see you because I would rather you be doing something else with your life than helping Holt. But maybe you can get in touch with him because he isn't answering my calls."

I refrained from saying that Lucian had never given me his phone number and that I was probably not the right person to contact him.

"What happened?" I asked as I followed her gaze to the glass building that towered above us. Colorful lights spilled from the topmost floor, making me think there was a rooftop bar or club.

"There's been another murder. Same MO," she said, then pulled me toward the building. "Come on."

PART IV

THE
COMPETITION

16

WOLF STEPPED ON dried blood as he made his way to the other side of the bare room, where faded wallpaper peeled in long, curling strips from the wall. The scent of blood drove him mad as the *Aether* demanded he drink. It had been a couple days since he had drunk that man's blood at the alley, and he still felt the craving for more.

"Sorry for the mess," Jan said as he walked ahead of Wolf. He had the appearance of a twenty-year-old man with copper-brown skin and small dark eyes. Barely sparing a glance at the blood, Jan walked with long, determined strides.

Wolf stepped through a door at the end of the room and carefully surveyed the people before him. It was clear from the way the other two straightened when Jan came in that he was their leader. A girl who looked around twenty-three stood against the wall on the far right. She had fair skin and long auburn hair braided to the side. Her feline eyes traced over Wolf. A man of around the same age sat on a worn leather couch and flicked a small knife between his fingers. A baseball cap hid his hair and shaded his eyes, but Wolf knew he was staring at him. Dust swirled in the air and slightly masked the scent of blood, making the *Aether* calm into a steady flow. The midday sun shone through windows that revealed a run-down garden with crumbling vines and flowers.

"I found a stray roaming the streets," Jan said with a smile as if he had rescued a puppy from a dark alley.

"He's old," the boy with the baseball cap said. "I mean, we're all old. But he looks physically old, like in his thirties. Y'all know what I mean."

They seemed to be American, and Wolf wondered why they had moved to Europe.

"We don't judge people based on their physical age," Jan said like an older brother scolding a younger sibling.

Wolf analyzed them in silence. He suspected everyone in the group had been recently turned. They were children but children with fangs, a lust for blood, and enough strength and speed to make them a menace to humans.

"What's your name?" the girl asked.

"I'm Rick," Wolf said.

"That's an old man name," Baseball-Cap guy said. "If you want to join us, you need to choose a cooler name."

Wolf chuckled. "Who said I wanted to join you?"

Jan's smile dropped, and silence filled the room for a couple of seconds. "You would be lucky if you did," Jan said, the smile creeping back.

"Would I?" Wolf asked. "Or would you be the lucky ones?"

Baseball-Cap guy laughed. "Why would we be lucky to have an old señor with us?"

"He's fourth-generation," Jan said.

The girl leaned closer to Wolf.

Baseball-Cap guy straightened his back and finally removed his cap, revealing close-cropped hair and wide dark eyes. "How do we know that's true?"

"I saw him turn a brick into gold," Jan said, his eyes sparkling.

"What coven do you come from?" the girl asked.

"The Helios Coven," Wolf said, which should have been obvious since that was the only coven with such a power, but this group didn't seem to be familiar with Athatos history. And as he had expected, they also didn't know that only second- and third-generations from that coven could turn objects to gold or that Helios would have never let anyone with that power leave him.

"The Helios Coven," Baseball-Cap guy repeated as he flicked out his little knife again. "Those are the superrich Italians, right? One of the twelve ruling covens?"

Wolf nodded. He also physically looked like someone from Helios's family, which was why he had chosen that coven as a cover. Whenever someone got bit by an Athatos, or by other immortals, their physical appearance usually changed to assimilate to the immortal whose blood they had drunk. Wolf realized this group probably didn't even know that either.

"Why aren't you with your coven?" the girl asked, stepping closer to him.

"Anyone fourth-generation or below is not allowed to live with their covens anymore. That's the law of the twelve rulers," Wolf said.

He assumed the others were at least seventh- or eighth-generation. Power and strength were inherited in an exponentially negative curve, so he didn't expect this bunch could do more than lift a motorcycle with their bare hands. They could obviously never join one of the Athatos covens.

"We could use someone like you," Jan said. "And I think you could use a group like us."

Wolf crossed his arms over his chest. "Why?" He motioned to the room and to the outside. "You don't even know how to clean up after yourselves." He chuckled. "I'm not interested in living in a frat house."

"We're not a frat house," the girl said.

"A sorority then," Wolf said. "I expected some phi gamma alpha whatever to be etched on the door."

A tense silence blanketed the room.

"You know what I have," Wolf said. To prove his point, he touched the wall behind him. Instantly, the wooden boards turned to gold, gleaming with the sun. Wolf pressed his hand harder, and the gold spread like a wildfire to consume the wood and burn it into a shiny, smooth surface. He didn't take his hand off the wall until it had all turned golden. Wolf's breath caught. He flexed his hand and faked a pained expression.

"What can you offer me?" Wolf asked.

He could sense their desperation. They were young, insecure, and scared. Behind the bravado Jan put on, they still didn't know how they fit into the world. Part of Wolf pitied them.

The three youngsters looked at each other.

"That's what I thought," Wolf said. "Thanks for the invite, Jan, but I think I'll just let myself out."

"Wait," the girl said.

Jan glared at her, but the girl seemed to communicate something to him through her eyes that made Jan's shoulders square up.

"We might have something that could interest you," Jan said. He turned to the Baseball-Cap guy, who nodded in return. "The opportunity of a lifetime."

"This sounds like a terrible job recruitment ad," Wolf muttered.

"Have you heard about the competition?" Jan asked.

"What competition?" Wolf asked.

The three friends exchanged another glance, then nodded to each other.

"You can't tell anyone about this," the girl whispered as if the vines outside had ears.

"I don't have any friends to talk to anyways," Wolf said dryly.

"A competition started a few days ago," Jan said.

"What type of competition?" Wolf asked.

"A competition to kill the gods," Jan said with a smile.

Wolf blinked, then laughed to conceal his shock. The window vibrated slightly, but the others didn't notice. Wolf pressed down on the *Aether*.

"The gods can't be killed," he said. "And if someone has found a way, one of the gods would have killed them by now."

"Oh, but there is," Jan said. "There's an ancient manuscript that details how to take immortality away from the gods."

"Which manuscript?" Wolf asked.

"The Book of the Dead," the girl said.

Wolf's heart smashed against his chest, and his muscles strained as he tried to reel in his power and avoid destroying the house and everyone in it. Thankfully, nothing broke.

"The what?" Wolf asked.

"The Egyptian Book of the Dead," Jan said as if it were obvious. "It holds the key to kill the gods."

"The coven that decodes it first and figures out which parts of it kill the gods wins," Baseball-Cap guy said.

"And how are you planning on decoding it?" Wolf asked.

"We've been observing a couple of other covens," Jan said. "They've been carving out inscriptions on humans to try and get the right combination of passages from the Book of the Dead. If it works, then the human will combust into ashes. As far as we know, no one has decoded it, but we think we're close."

"They've also been using Latin and Greek translations since some Egyptian translations became lost and only survived in those two languages," the girl added. "So the truth might be hidden there."

Wolf struggled to not let the horror of the situation show on his features.

"If the competition is real, then why haven't I heard of it?" Wolf asked.

"He's being very careful about who he tells," Jan said.

"He who?" Wolf asked.

Jan shrugged. "I've never seen his face and don't know his name. We just know he started the competition to finally get rid of the gods. It's time those old bastards stopped bullying us."

"If he's being careful about the competition, then why did he tell you?" Wolf said. "No offense."

"He's only told those he knows who are fourth-generation or lower and who hate the gods," the girl said. "So we don't expect news of this to be circulating widely. Not yet at least."

Wolf rubbed his chin, the stubble rough against his palm. "How many covens are part of this?"

Jan shrugged. "Could be dozens, maybe more."

The air grew thick with another uneasy silence.

"But what's the point?" Wolf said. "You kill the gods and then what?"

"Then we can build a new world with our own rules," Jan said.

"And," the girl added, "there might be a way to steal the gods' powers and take it for ourselves."

Those were the most delusional statements Wolf had ever heard, and he tried to look pensive instead of frustrated.

"How long has this contest been going on for?" Wolf asked.

"It officially started five days ago," Jan said.

Gabriel had been killed the same day the competition had begun. A cloud passed over the sun and darkened the room, making it as somber as Wolf's emotions. When he had seen the picture in the newspaper of a dead body with inscriptions carved in Egyptian, he had known it was related to Gabriel's death somehow. But he hadn't expected all this.

Wolf met each of their gazes. "And you want me to help you win this competition?" he asked. Wolf knew that someone with powers like the ones he had shown could give this small group an advantage over larger and more powerful covens—even if it was a rather useless power, in his opinion. But anyone fifth-generation and below had always hyper-fixated on having some sort of power beyond the strength, speed, and long life that they had already been given.

"We can split the power from the gods," Jan said.

Wolf refrained from saying that he didn't believe power could be split up like a piece of cake. "And why wouldn't it be a better idea to win the competition on my own?" Wolf asked.

The girl tensed.

Jan smiled. "Because we've stolen from the Louvre Museum some segments of the Book that we think hold the right passages."

Baseball-Cap guy nodded. "Those are some of the most ancient segments, which are more likely to have the right inscriptions."

Wolf didn't even want to ask how they had managed to do that and thought it might be a bluff.

"You see," Jan explained, "the Book of the Dead is a collection of many texts that have been reproduced over time, but they all stem from the same source. And that original text holds the power. It's basically a spell that was written by one of the gods in ancient times. If we can find out which passages are the original ones, and in which order they should be written, then we'll be able to win the competition."

"You won't get very far on your own, Rick," the girl said. "We have an advantage over other covens and feel confident we can win."

"So?" Jan asked. "Will you join us?"

Wolf cocked his head to one side, pretending to consider Jan's proposition. Jan couldn't see the rage that boiled Wolf's blood and made the *Aether* storm inside of him. The wall behind Jan and his friends began to shift, but no one except Wolf noticed. Rafe seemed to step out of the wall, although Wolf knew he had only made himself invisible. Rafe's eyes turned into two emerald rings burning with enough force to make the sun explode.

Like a liquid being sucked out of the room, the gold coating the walls receded into the corners and revealed the wooden panels once again. Jan startled, Baseball-Cap guy's jaw slackened, and the girl immediately tensed. It took Jan another full second to turn around. He stumbled backward, away from Rafe's unnaturally wide smile.

"You—" Jan turned toward Wolf, then back to Rafe. His face drained of color at the same time his friends' faces did.

"Who the hell are you?" Baseball-Cap guy asked Rafe as he stepped away from him.

Green tendrils of power twirled around Rafe. Jan's eyes widened as the truth struck him.

Rafe's smile extended a bit more, like a crocodile attempting to grin. "The Norse used to call me Loki." Rafe turned to Wolf. "They're all yours."

"Wait, wait, wait." The words stumbled out of Jan's mouth. "We can take you to the man organizing this. We can help you." His dark eyes frantically looked around the room as if trying to spot a hidden exit route. "Please, uh, Rick. Or whatever your real name is."

Wolf's power raced through his veins like a stampede waiting to trample out of his body. But Wolf held it back. It had been so long since he had used his power to kill someone. Would he be able to contain it if he let it loose? Or would it take a life of its own and continue destroying like it had last time?

"Oh come on," Rafe said.

Jan tried to bolt for the door next to Wolf, but Rafe reacted first. His body exploded into the form of a giant black wolf. He cut off Jan's head with a single bite. The girl screamed but was silenced when Rafe bit her neck and smashed her limp body against the floor. Baseball-Cap guy stood stunned as Rafe turned back to him. Rafe growled, then tore him to pieces. It was all over in less than a minute.

With his sinister green eyes and his muzzle dripping with blood, Rafe eyed Wolf. "Why do you insist on making yourself weak?" Rafe asked.

Before Wolf could respond, Rafe pounced, pushing Wolf so hard that he smashed through the wall and crashed on his back. Wolf coughed as Rafe circled him. The smell of dry blood wafted into his nostrils, and the pull in his chest grew stronger, making him dizzy. His fangs shot out, and Wolf suppressed a growl of frustration.

The *Aether* stirred within him, demanding fresh blood. He tried to smother it, but some dripped out. The house began to shake, the wooden boards groaning.

"I remember more than most of the others, I think," Rafe said. "You used to destroy cities and demolish armies with little more than a thought. What changed?"

I lost control and nearly destroyed the world, Wolf thought.

But of course, everyone had forgotten that. Only myths and legends of that day remained, and in everyone's memories, it had been some external threat that had caused all that destruction, not Wolf.

"I don't understand you," Rafe said.

Wolf got to his feet. Rafe lunged forward again, pushing Wolf through another wall and sending him rolling on the muddy ground outside.

"You want to find Gabriel's killer, put an end to this rebellion, and protect the Athatos, but you can't even defend yourself," Rafe snarled. "You'll have to fight eventually."

"I know," Wolf said.

Rafe bared his deadly, sharp teeth. "I hope you do, or you'll end up like Gabriel."

Fear shot through Wolf. The wooden house burst, sending splinters flying everywhere. He breathed deeply and tried to calm down.

Wolf wouldn't let Death claim him. He had fought so hard to keep their immortality safe—he would do anything to keep it that way. Even if that meant destroying more than he could save.

A swirling green cloud enveloped Rafe, and a few seconds later, he was a man again. He offered a hand to Wolf.

Wolf took it and let Rafe pull him back to his feet.

"This isn't good," Rafe said. He used his sleeves to wipe the blood off his face. "The rebellion has already started and has spread further than we thought. And there is someone manipulating these half-bloods from behind the curtains. We need to find out who started the competition."

Wolf nodded.

"And what does the Book of the Dead have to do with anything?" Rafe asked as he tucked in his shirt. "I didn't even remember it existed."

"I don't know," Wolf said.

But Wolf knew exactly how the Book of the Dead was related to Gabriel's murder. Jan and his buddies had been dangerously close to finding the truth that Wolf had spent the last few millennia hiding. The original copy of the Book of the Dead didn't exist anymore—Wolf had burned it to ashes ages ago and had thought he was the only one who remembered the true importance of it. But the Book of the Dead was only half of the ritual. Jan and his friends had been completely oblivious to the other half—one that Gabriel's killer must have known to be able to destroy him. But why tell these half-bloods only half of the truth when they could have all the information needed to kill an Athatos? Wolf let his confusion filter through his emotions.

"The competition and the human murders are a smoke screen," Wolf said. "These half-bloods have no idea how to actually kill us." Wolf paused as he followed that line of thought. "The killer knows Gabriel's murder can't stay a secret forever, and they want the Athatos to turn their attention to the rebelling half-bloods so they can stay hidden longer."

Rafe considered this. "Maybe," he said. "I'm surprised none of the Athatos know about this yet." He paused. "Or I guess they could be pretending not to know, if they're behind this."

"Do you think the half-bloods, or the real killer, are planning something for Dionysus's party?" Wolf asked as the thought came to him. "It doesn't seem like a coincidence that it's happening tomorrow."

Rafe didn't immediately respond. "It's likely," he said. "It is the biggest party of the year."

Wolf refrained from saying that he suspected Dionysus might be the next target. He knew Rafe must be thinking the same thing. A public display like that would openly start this war even if the half-bloods didn't kill Dionysus. The true killers were getting ready to sow chaos and brew a conflict that would leave thousands dead.

"If we're fast, we could be in and out of the Underworld in a couple of hours or less," Wolf said. Days in the Underworld were hours in the Upperworld. "We would have enough time to come back to the party and deal with the half-bloods there once we know who's behind this."

"We better arrive early then," Rafe said.

The killers could let the rebelling half-bloods cause as much chaos as possible before stepping into the spotlight. Or they might strike first before the Athatos even realized that they could be killed and could begin taking precautions against an attack. Either way, Wolf knew that Dionysus's party would brew something big. They had to be ready for anything—and they needed to know how Gabriel had been killed so they could prevent the same from happening to the rest of them.

Rafe walked back to the car. Wolf followed him.

"I'm just going to say this now," Rafe said as he placed his palms on the hood. "I'm holding back from going on a killing spree because I understand it's to our advantage that whoever is behind this doesn't know we're onto them. But"—Rafe paused—"once we know who killed Gabriel, and how, I'll destroy any half-blood who's involved in this competition." Rafe's gaze darkened. "I'm not holding back."

Because Rafe had finally found a good reason to kill the half-bloods without suffering repercussions from all the other Athatos,

Wolf knew the party would turn into a bloodbath. "I wasn't expecting you to," he said.

"I'm hoping you won't hold back either," Rafe said with a smile.

"I might not have a choice," Wolf muttered.

"Then let's go hunting," Rafe said. "We'll need more blood."

The *Aether* thrummed inside Wolf's veins in response. That old fear still clung to him, but he wouldn't risk getting killed like Gabriel had. It was time for the *Aether* to be free again.

17

"BUT THE KILLER is dead," I said as the police officer opened the door to the Mission District high-rise.

"I think we're dealing with multiple killers, Isa," she said as we made our way through the lobby. "We've received three calls tonight for three different murder scenes. The only thing that has changed is that a couple of the victims are men." She pressed the elevator button. "We have a whole family dead too."

The doors slid open, and we got in. The officer pulled out her phone and swiped through dozens of pictures. My head began to spin.

"New York, Las Vegas, Austin, Chicago," she said. The pictures showed different victims with inscriptions carved into their bodies. "These last three are from here, and there might be more we haven't discovered."

I took deep breaths to force my stomach to settle. It was a terribly unlucky coincidence that I had found my way right back into the middle of this murder case.

"I think this started in San Francisco," she continued, "but it's expanded to other cities. We didn't even realize it until a couple of hours ago when I got a call from a friend at the Las Vegas Police Department after a macabre scene in one of the casinos," she said.

"Do you think the killers are all—"

"Vampires?" she said. "Yes, which is why we've been trying to get in touch with Holt. He usually doesn't take long to respond so he'll probably be here soon."

The elevator dinged, and the doors opened. We had arrived at a hallway with a couple of police officers already there. They moved to the side to let us walk through a door. When we entered a lounge, colorful lights flashed around the empty room, making me slightly dizzy. Drinks and plates still lay on the tables. Dark velvet couches lined one side. Spilled drinks and food littered a marble dance floor at the center of the room. The bar on the left displayed a wide array of bottles, all of them lit up with pink light that shone through the panel behind them.

We continued through the lounge until we arrived at the men's restroom, where two other police officers seemed to be keeping guard. The body was next to the row of sinks. A wave of nausea slapped me, and I bit my tongue as I breathed deeply. The man lay face down in a pool of blood, his torso uncovered. Crude Egyptian hieroglyphs had been carved onto his pale skin. The man's mouth was still open in a scream, his blank eyes gazing toward the wall.

The female officer opened her mouth to say something. Just as she did, the radio blared something. I couldn't make out what the person on the other side said, but it sounded urgent.

"The killer is trying to escape," she said. "Stay here."

"Wait. I don't—"

She ran from the bathroom, leaving me alone with the dead man. My heart drummed against my chest, and blood rushed inside my ears. I should have run after the police officers, but I would probably be in more danger wherever they were going. I stood awkwardly in the oppressive silence, but then leaned closer to the body and analyzed the inscriptions while trying to forget they were etched on a dead man's back. Compared to some of the pictures Lucian had showed me, these inscriptions were messier. I could make out some of the hieroglyphs, but others were completely incomprehensible. Still, I figured they were from the Book of the Dead like the other murders.

One killer engraving inscriptions from the Egyptian Book of the Dead on their victims was bad enough, but multiple killers around the country made this truly baffling. We had never really discovered why the Book of the Dead had been important to the killer and whether they were trying to find another way to achieve immortality.

"You seem too young to be a police officer," someone said behind me.

I whirled around, my heart lurching into my throat.

A young man stood leaning against the doorframe. He wore a dark navy suit and white shirt. Blood stained his cuffs. His dark eyes glinted.

Fear threatened to paralyze me again, but I didn't let it take hold. Sue and Lucian weren't here to help me this time.

The man walked closer to me, his steps dangerously slow and calm. He didn't take his eyes off me as he stopped a couple of feet away to lean against the sink. There was something terrifying in the way he looked at me—I wasn't a person to him, merely a meal or a toy.

He opened his mouth to say something.

I pulled the silver knife from its sheath, lunged toward the man, and slashed at him. He nimbly moved to the side, and I only managed to cut his upper arm. He screamed while I bolted out of the bathroom. My legs burned as I raced forward, and my surroundings blurred past me.

I found the elevators again and rammed the button multiple times. We were on the fourteenth floor. One of the elevators was still in the lobby, and the other was on the fifth floor. The lifts weren't going to make it in time. I raced to the end of the hallway and pushed a door open, then rushed down the stairs. I had made it two floors down when a door above me burst open. I didn't dare glance up.

My feet had just stepped on the landing of the eleventh floor when two strong arms wrapped around my torso. I tried to slash the knife again, but he pulled it out of my hand with another scream and tossed it to the side. The man hissed as his other arm pinned me against his chest. I let out a choked scream. He clamped a hand on my mouth, his palm blistering and bleeding from the silver.

"Bold," he whispered. "I like that."

He pulled me backward as I struggled in his grip. He used his back to push open a door, and we entered a new room. My phone buzzed, but I couldn't pull it out of my back pocket. I tried to scream, but his hand was clasped so tightly around my mouth that I worried he might break my jaw. The lights were all out, and glass doors at my sides were closed. The man let go of me by throwing me to the side. I landed roughly on a carpet, then pushed myself to my feet as the ground swayed beneath me.

Looking around, I noticed that couches flanked me on either side in the small lounge. Lining the right side, glass walls and doors led to conference rooms, while a large TV hung on the left wall. Behind me, a floor-to-ceiling window revealed the glittering cityscape outside. The man stood blocking my only exit.

"I wasn't planning on killing you until you attacked me. Now I'm going to enjoy it."

"He'll kill you if you hurt me," I said.

The man cocked his head to one side, the gesture more animal than human. "He who?"

"Lucian Holt."

He dropped his smug grin.

"He's here to investigate the crime scene," I said.

A smile cut through his face. "If Holt wants me, he can come get me."

He slowly walked around the couches. I stepped away, but my back hit the window. I stepped to the left but stumbled. The man lunged forward, grabbed me by the neck, and pushed me against a wall. My throat closed up as my head burst with pain.

"You can't fight me," he said. "Humans were made to fight other humans, but you weren't built to fight something like me."

Fangs shot out of his mouth as he opened it wide. A bolt of fear slammed through me, roaring like a beast. Lightning thundered through the room. Everything shattered—the windows and the glass walls—it all broke to pieces. His grip loosened from my neck as he was thrown backward. The ground cracked beneath him as he hit the floor. Gravity shifted around us, throwing the furniture around in random directions.

I fell to my knees, breathing hard. The man pushed himself back to his feet. Tiny shards of glass glinted off his skin and blood slid from his face. I pulled the Taser pen from my pocket, clicked on the switch, and lunged at him, aiming for his upper hip. He screamed as the pen connected with him, and he stumbled backward. Then he stepped outside the window and fell to the street below.

I sank back to my knees, breathing raggedly as if the shards of glass had found their way down my throat and into my lungs. Time passed. Hours. Minutes. Seconds.

"Isa," Lucian shouted. I turned to face him as his hands wrapped around my shoulders.

"I'm okay," I managed.

Lucian pulled me to my feet, then glanced around the room as if stunned. It seemed as if a tornado had swept through.

"Come on," he said.

But my body felt so heavy, and my head was spinning. Lucian wrapped one arm around my waist and lifted me into his arms. He stepped over the broken glass as if he were walking through sand. His heart thumped wildly. Somehow, it still surprised me that he really had a heartbeat. He set me down when we got in the elevator.

"Can you walk?" he asked. He pulled off his shoes and unceremoniously dumped them on the floor. The soles were encrusted with shards of glass.

I nodded. Still, Lucian held my shoulders to keep me steady as we rode to the lobby.

"Thank you," I said, "for saving me again."

Lucian's face was unreadable. "No need to thank me," he said. "I didn't do much this time."

Except just shattering the room to pieces, I thought.

His expression became strained. "I'm sorry," he whispered. "I promised I would keep you safe, and I failed you—twice."

"You didn't," I said. "I would have been dead today without you."

"I know you don't believe me anymore," Lucian said. "But I won't break that promise again."

I risked a glance to meet his gaze.

"I promise you," he said. "I will keep you safe."

I nodded, unsure of what to do with his promise.

18

"WAIT, WAIT, ISA," the female police officer—I now knew she was named Esther—said to me in the police station. "You did what?"

"I slashed him with a silver knife," I said, "then shocked him with a Taser pen, and he fell out the window."

"Wow," another police officer, Andrew, said. "A natural born vampire hunter."

"Are vampire hunters real?" I asked.

"No," Esther responded. "Vampires are too powerful for that."

The murmurs and voices inside the police station died down as Lucian walked inside. He had stepped out briefly to call Sue.

Esther, six police officers, and I had gathered in a tight circle around a large screen at the back of the room. Esther had told me that only this group knew the truth, and I had seen these officers at the previous crime scenes.

"Alright, let's get started," Esther said after Lucian joined our group. She used a remote to turn on the TV, which showed a map of the United States with red dots marking the locations where victims had been found. I swallowed the lump in my throat as I counted the dots. There were over two dozen.

"I think we all now know that this is not an isolated murder case," Esther said. "The initial killer had been targeting women aged fifteen to twenty-five, but other killers don't seem to have that preference. The MO, however, is the same. They carve Greek, Latin, or Egyptian inscriptions on the victims. Sometimes the victims are still alive while this happens, and other times they're already dead. Since the last killer we caught was a vampire, we believe the other killers are as well, but only some of the victims have bite marks."

"What do the inscriptions say?" a young male officer asked as he scribbled on a notepad.

"We're still working on it," Lucian said before I could respond.

I didn't know why he didn't share our discoveries but trusted that he had his reasons. He looked at the map, his eyes darting from one red dot to the other.

"So what's the plan for finding the killers, Holt?" Esther asked.

"We need to know exactly where the murders started," Lucian said. "They could have begun somewhere else without us being aware of it. Talk with other police stations, government agencies, or whatever other contacts you have. I need to know exactly where this is happening and if it has spread to other countries."

"You think this might be international?" Esther asked.

Lucian was silent for a couple of seconds. "I've never seen anything like this before," he said. "Strays and groups of vampires don't coordinate to kill humans the same way, especially not like this. Most of the victims' blood wasn't drained, either, so we're not dealing with a physical craving, a need to feed, or even a tendency toward violence. Something is affecting their behavior, and behaviors tend to be contagious. If it's happening here, I have no doubt it might be happening in other places. This is a wildfire, and it's spreading fast. We need to pinpoint where the fire started."

The officers nodded, some of them taking notes and starting to talk to each other.

"I don't know if we can keep the press out of this for much longer," an officer said from the back. "The murder at the nightclub caused a big stir, and multiple people saw the body. Someone will connect the dots soon and realize it's happening nationally."

Lucian exhaled. "If the press asks you anything, try to be as vague as possible while mentioning you're actively working to find the killer."

Esther nodded. "I'll keep an eye out for any news."

"We'll continue deciphering the inscriptions to understand the killers' motives while you track down the origin of the murders," Lucian said.

"Keep me in the loop," Esther said.

"You too," he responded.

Lucian turned in my direction and motioned toward the door with his head. I waved goodbye at Esther, who waved back, and I walked out of the station with Lucian toward his car parked out front. I climbed into the passenger seat, and we rode in silence for a few moments.

"Are you still willing to help? I think your translations will be key to cracking this case," Lucian said. Then he added, "I can pay you."

It wasn't about the money anymore. This was bigger than us, and I couldn't go back to my normal life knowing I could help find these mad killers.

"I'll help," I said. "Can I pick up some stuff from my apartment before we go back to the mansion?"

"Sure," Lucian said.

Just as we were driving off, my phone rang.

"Where are you?" Mya asked. I realized I had several missed calls from her.

"Sorry, I started feeling sick and left," I said.

"You could have just said so. You didn't have to bail on us." Her tone was angry, but I didn't have the emotional energy to deal with it.

"I'll make it up," I said.

"Feel better," she said in a clipped tone before hanging up.

Lucian said nothing as I put my phone away. I could deal with Mya once this case was over. I clasped my hands together to stop them from shaking.

"Why didn't you tell the police about the Book of the Dead?" I asked.

"Part of being a detective is knowing what to share and what not to," Lucian said. "Knowing about the book won't help their search, but it will help ours." Lucian gripped the wheel tightly as we switched lanes. "I'm sorry, Isa, for using you as bait. I would not have put you in that situation unless you had consented to it and we had a solid plan. Trust me, I'm furious at Sue for what she did, and she regrets it."

"But you considered it," I said.

Lucian's jaw clenched. "We did, at the very beginning, but I didn't think we would need to do that. But again, I wouldn't have done it if you hadn't agreed to it, and I knew I could protect you." He glanced at me. "I'm sorry," he repeated.

I didn't respond. A simple *it's fine* didn't seem appropriate. We arrived at my apartment a few minutes later. Lucian parked in the garage and came with me this time. He walked a few steps behind me, giving me some space. We climbed the stairs to the third floor, then walked down the hallway.

I was turning the corner when a voice shouted, "There you are!" Liz nearly tackled me to the floor with a hug.

"Look who's back," Aura said as she flung her arms around me.

I had completely forgotten I had invited them over. They pulled away from me a second later. Aura seemed about to say something, but immediately shut her mouth. By her expression, I knew Lucian had just walked around the corner to stand behind me.

The two girls glanced at me, and my face grew warm. I had never felt so embarrassed in my life.

"Uh," I said to Lucian, "these are my friends, Liz and Aura." Then I motioned to him. "And this is . . ." I didn't know what to say.

"Her boss," Lucian said.

Well, that was definitely *not* the right thing to say.

Lucian must have realized that, too, since his face flushed slightly. Aura and Liz's eyes drilled into me. I glanced up at Lucian, silently asking for his permission. He seemed to understand what I meant, and he nodded. I looked back at my friends.

"Can you keep a secret?" I asked.

"Sure," Aura said.

I walked closer to the door and fumbled with my keys. I turned back to Lucian. "I'll be back in a few minutes."

He nodded again.

Aura and Liz didn't take their eyes off him until we got into the apartment and I closed the door.

"You're sleeping with your boss?" Liz exclaimed.

"No," I hissed, my face becoming even hotter. There was no way Lucian hadn't heard her.

"Then why is he here?" Liz pointed at the door.

"I would sleep with him if he were my boss," Aura said.

They both snickered.

"Is that why you were staying at his place overnight?" Aura asked.

I rubbed my face. "No."

A knock on the door made us all startle.

"Isa?" Mya's voice sounded through the door. "Just wanted to check in on you."

I exhaled, opening the door. Mya's eyes were wide with concern as she looked at me. Lucian still stood in the hallway a few feet away from the door, and Mya glanced at him before I moved to the side to let her in.

"When did you two get here?" Mya asked Liz and Aura.

Lucian's eyes softened with a pitying look as I closed the door again.

"Who's that?" Mya asked.

"Isa's boss," Liz said.

At the same time Aura said, "Isa's new boyfriend."

They both laughed again. Mya's eyes opened even wider, then she glared at me.

"Don't worry, Isa," Liz said through tears as laughter shook through her. "We'll keep your secret."

"That's not the secret I wanted you to keep," I said.

"Is he actually your boss?" Mya asked.

"Yes," I said. Before Liz or Aura could add another inappropriate comment, I continued. "He's a private detective, and I'm helping him solve a murder case."

That finally got everyone's attention.

"What?" Liz asked.

Keeping out anything related to gods and vampires, I told them what had happened these last few days.

"Oh shit." Aura clamped a hand over her mouth.

Liz's dark skin had paled, and Mya was hugging herself tightly. A few seconds of tense silence gripped the room.

Aura turned back to me. "How are you holding up?"

"I'm alright," I said. "I'll be better when this case is over. But in the meantime, please take more precautions to stay safe until we catch the killers."

The three of them nodded. I exhaled, my heart feeling a bit lighter knowing that my close friends were aware of the danger. I walked to the side of my bed and picked up the duffel bag I hadn't even unpacked.

"I need to go," I said.

Liz stared at the bag. "So then, you're not sleeping with him?"

Mya glared at her, but Aura chuckled.

"Oh, look. She's blushing," Liz said.

"Stop that," Mya said. "This is serious."

"I know," Liz said. "But he's hot."

"He's only a few years older than us, so I don't think it matters that much," Aura added.

I ignored them. "Please just stay safe."

They sobered up again. The four of us walked back to the door and stepped outside. Lucian hadn't moved. He glanced up as we walked out, giving no indication that he had heard our conversation.

"Alright," Mya said. "I'll see you all later."

"I just made a new group chat," Aura said. "Everyone text when you're back home safe and text in the morning and at night for the next few days, just in case. And we also have each other's locations if something happens."

I nodded, and the others did too. I gave the three girls a hug, and they all walked down the hall together, disappearing as they turned a corner in the hallway.

"You have very caring friends," Lucian said.

"I know," I said with a smile.

Hopefully, this nightmare would be over soon, and I wouldn't have to worry about them. Lucian took the duffel bag from me, and neither of us spoke a word as we followed the same path back to the car. We drove in silence for a while, the streetlights making shadows dance on Lucian's face.

"I don't understand why multiple groups of vampires would be so obsessed about giving humans immortality," I finally said. "What do they gain for themselves?"

"I've thought about that too," Lucian said. "Something isn't adding up."

"And what would happen to the killers if news of the murders starts to spread?" I asked. "I assume that because most humans don't know vampires exist, you want to stay hidden from the public. Do vampires have rules that make killings like these illegal?"

"Something like that," Lucian said. "Several ruling covens created a set of laws."

"Dario mentioned he used to belong to one of those covens," I said. "But he didn't explain much more."

"There are twelve ruling covens in total," Lucian said. "Hera, Morrigan, Anubis, Helios, Aphrodite, Prithvi, Quetzalcoatl, Dionysus, Sin, Ame-No-Uzume, and Njord."

"Aren't you missing one?" I asked.

"I am," Lucian said. "I'm not sure who the twelfth ruler is. I don't think a lot of people do."

"Why?" I asked.

"Legend says that they purposefully hid themselves from the world to avoid confrontations and power struggles, but that they're still out there ruling from the shadows." Lucian glanced at the rearview mirror. "These twelve covens each have different responsibilities in the world, but they govern over it together, and they created a set of laws for all gods and half-bloods to follow. Like you said, we want to stay hidden from the public. If humans knew we existed, then they would take better care to hide or fight us, which would make feeding harder. So making sure no one exposes our secret is one of our most important laws." He turned around to look at the cars behind him before switching lanes and driving onto the highway. "When someone breaks that law, there are consequences. Punishments tend to vary depending on the ruling god of that area, but the gods keep each other accountable for the most part, which makes them always enforce that law. I'm guessing one of the gods and their covens will take notice of this, if they haven't already."

"Why don't you just tell them and let them deal with this if it's that big of a problem."

"Because they're all part of my suspect list," Lucian said. "Someone influential is behind the murders, and I don't trust any of them."

He exited the highway, then parked on the side of a deserted street.

"You once asked me why I had become a private detective," Lucian said, leaning back on the seat. "I wasn't completely honest before."

"Okay," I said.

"I just—" His voice caught. "I want you to know the truth, if we're going to keep working together. You deserve that much."

I nodded.

"My blood was powerful," Lucian said. "My human blood," he added after a second. "Some humans are just born with blood that attracts vampires like mosquitoes are drawn to light. It's rare, but it happens." He turned his gaze toward me. Even in the dark, his eyes gleamed silver. "I know what it's like to be hunted. I know what it's like to be afraid of monsters that others think are just a myth." His gaze became distant. "One of the gods found me when I entered their temple pleading for help after running away from a vampire who had wounded me." Something in his eyes lit up like lightning forking through dark clouds. "I don't remember who it was. I keep trying to, but it's as if that memory has been broken. I only remember this god said they would grant me one wish." He exhaled, throwing his head back until it rested against the seat. "I wanted to be safe from the monsters who hunted me. I wanted to be free to roam the world without the fear of them killing me." Lucian closed his eyes. "So that's what I asked for. I said, I wish to be safe and free from the monsters who are hunting me." He opened his eyes again, but they had lost their spark. "So the god bit me," he whispered. "They sucked the blood out of my body until I was dead. Then they made a cut on their wrist and fed me their blood."

Silence settled between us for a long while. I didn't know what to say to him. I didn't think there was anything I could say.

"They fulfilled my wish, but it turned me into the same monster that I had feared and loathed for so long," Lucian said. "I wish I could have had someone protect me during my human life." He met my eyes then. "That's why I do what I do. I can't save everyone, but I can save as many as I can from the same fate I had—or an even worse one." A charged silence sizzled through the car for a long moment. "I became a monster, so I figured I might as well be the monster of monsters."

"I don't think you're a monster," I said.

A slight smile spread on Lucian's lips. "I am, Isa," he said softly. "Don't convince yourself I'm not. I just hide that monster better than most."

"I mean it," I said. "The way those two vampires looked at me—they only saw me as a meal and nothing more. You said that you had lost your empathy toward humans, but you haven't. You still see us as people, as individuals whose lives are worth something. That makes you more human than you realize."

Breaking his gaze away from me, Lucian was quiet for a second. "Thank you," he finally whispered. He took a deep breath, then started the car again.

Dario had told me Lucian had never revealed how he had been turned, but now, he had confided that information to me. I locked it away in my chest like a treasure. I knew this was his way of apologizing, and it was worth more than saying sorry a hundred times. He cared about keeping the promise he had made to me, because he wished someone would have made that promise to him. I trusted he would keep it, even if that meant bringing out the monster within him.

19

"GLAD TO HAVE you back," Dario said as he rolled some dough.

It was eleven at night by the time Lucian and I arrived at the mansion. I had been hungry, and thankfully Dario had already made some creamy pasta that I heated in the microwave and devoured. We were now waiting on his famous focaccia bread.

Sue walked into the kitchen and sat at Lucian's side.

"I detected some weird activity from the three covens you mentioned, Dario," Sue said.

"What did you discover?" Lucian asked.

"They were all packing up, ready to leave," Sue said.

"Where to?" Dario asked.

"The first coven was going to Paris," Sue said. "Those in the second coven were discussing how many vampires they each knew around the Paris area, and the third coven was talking specifically about attending a party there."

"Really?" Lucian asked. "They were all talking about Paris when you spied on them?" His brows drew together. "That seems strangely coincidental."

"Is there something important happening in Paris?" I asked.

"Not that I know of," Lucian said.

"Maybe we should go there to investigate," Sue said.

Lucian shook his head. "Not yet. I still want to figure out why—"

"The party," Dario exclaimed. He gripped the wooden rolling pin so tightly it burst in half and released a small cloud of flour.

I turned to Lucian and Sue, but they seemed equally as confused as me.

"What party?" Lucian asked.

"Every year, Dionysus holds a huge party in his castle outside of Paris to celebrate his birthday," Dario said. He looked at his digital watch. "It should be happening tomorrow night. If I remember correctly, this year he turns 5,480 years old."

"Wait a second," I said. I unzipped my jacket, dug into my pocket, and pulled out the dark paper decorated with gold foil. The number 5,480 glinted in the light.

"Where did you find that?" Dario asked.

"In that house, the killer's lair." I turned to Lucian. "I forgot to show you this afterward." I pulled out the other ripped paper and laid it down. "And we found this piece at the first murder scene I visited."

"Is that an invitation?" Sue asked.

Dario nodded.

"I've never seen one," Sue said.

"I don't think you're the type of attendees Dionysus would invite," Dario said as he looked at Sue and Lucian. "No offense."

"Who usually goes to the party?" Lucian asked, his gaze intense enough to burn through wood.

"The twelve ruling covens are always invited," Dario said. "And it's usually an honor for minor covens to attend since very few of them ever get the chance to go. I've never seen any strays at the party though, so I'm not sure why the killer would have had this." He brushed the broken pieces of the rolling pin to the side. "But the three covens in this area have never been invited, as far as I know."

Lucian's eyes whirled like a storm. "What if the killers were all invited this year?"

A tense silence sliced through the room.

Dario opened his mouth, closed it, then opened it again to say, "That's a big accusation, Lucian."

"Our suspect is someone who could have started a behavioral shift so big it spread out like wildfire," Lucian said. "Who's the only god who can make people go mad with lust or go on a killing frenzy?"

"But they've never done anything like this," Dario said.

"That doesn't mean anything," Lucian said. "They have the power to do it, and the evidence is pointing at them right now."

Dario turned to Sue.

"I have to admit this doesn't look good for Dionysus's coven," Sue said. "A killing frenzy starts a week before his big party, the stray killer is invited, and so are minor covens who are usually not."

"It could be a coincidence," Dario said. "And if it weren't, Hera and her coven would have seen something. She would never let this slide by. They would have put a stop to the murders already."

"Why hasn't she though?" Sue asked.

"I . . . don't have a good answer to that," Dario said. "I'm only saying that it would be strange if one of the twelve was involved in this killing frenzy. They have no reason to be a part of this."

"Do you really think that's true?" Lucian asked. His eyes darkened like black clouds bursting with lightning. "You're telling me none of the twelve, or any of their half-bloods, would want to find another way to give humans immortality?"

Dario's eyes glinted with a golden blaze. The lights above our heads flickered, and the room began to warm up. I glanced at Sue, but she seemed equally as confused at the dark tension traveling between the two men.

Dario broke his gaze away from Lucian. "We need to get into that party," Dario said.

"Agreed," Lucian said.

Dario huffed. "You're not the kind of invitee that would be expected to attend."

"Neither are you," Lucian said.

The lights flickered again. Sue was deathly silent, her eyes narrowed in concentration as if she could expand her power to hear their thoughts.

"And it seems like a lot of unusual invitees will be showing up this year," Lucian said. The intensity in his eyes faded. "Are you willing to go back in there, Dario? You don't have to. I can take this."

Dario stared at the deformed piece of dough. "If the twelve are really trying to find another way to give humans immortality, then you know my answer."

Sue narrowed her eyes further.

"Still," Lucian said, "this is not your responsibility."

"It's not yours either, Lucian," Dario said.

One of the bulbs sputtered out, casting a corner into a shadowy darkness.

Lucian exhaled. "Then I guess we're both going."

Dario raised a brow. "You're not the type of date I would bring to the party."

That earned a laugh from Lucian. "Sue and I can go together, and you can go with Isa."

Sue seemed to like that idea, because a faint smile edged up her lips.

I blinked. "I'm going too?" I asked. "Isn't the party just for vampires?"

"Human guests can go if they're accompanying an influential half-blood," Dario said, then shook his head. "This isn't going to work though. We only have one invitation, and each invitation is only valid for one couple."

"Sue and I keep this invitation," Lucian said as he snatched it from the table. "You can ask someone from the Coven of the Sun to give you one."

The table cracked under the weight of Dario's palms.

"You're going to see them there anyway," Lucian said. "Might deflect some of the tension before the party."

"Yeah," Dario said, casting his head down. "I think you're right."

"The Helios Coven can give you access to the party, but if you play them right, we might be able to get some information from them too," Lucian said. He turned to me. "And we need you there because you're the only one who can understand the ancient translations and help us figure out how the Book of the Dead fits into all of this."

I nodded.

Dario exhaled, then raised his head again to look at Lucian. "It might be better if only Isa and I go to the party," he said. "They all hate you, Lucian." His words were gentle but cut the air like a blade. "With you there, it might make the situation worse if anyone guesses you're after them—if they don't already know you're involved in this."

"I know exactly what I'm doing if I go to that party," Lucian said, his eyes sparkling. "I'll make everyone nervous. People make mistakes when they're nervous, and when they make mistakes, they show their hand."

Dario and Lucian held each other's gazes in what felt like an intense blinking contest. A brittle silence enveloped us, crackling with unspoken tension. Dario closed his eyes, took a deep breath, then opened them again to look at me.

"You're walking into a den full of lions," Dario said. "Is that something you're willing to do?"

"My promise still stands," Lucian said before I could speak. "I will protect you from any harm."

"We're not supposed to show we know each other," Sue said. "No one knows Dario joined us."

"I don't care," Lucian said as he kept his gaze fixed on me. "If any of us are threatened, then I will strike, and to hell with everything else. I want to stop the killers, but I won't do it at the cost of any of your lives."

Dario raised a brow, but then nodded slowly.

"I'll go," I said as my stomach tightened. I had already committed to this.

"If you go with Dario, everyone will think the two of you are together," Sue said.

"Are you alright with that, Isa?" Dario asked. "I mean with pretending the two of us are together."

I glanced at Lucian, and he nodded.

"Sure," I said.

"I suppose that settles it then," Lucian said. He turned to the wall clock. "We have less than twenty-four hours before the party. We should leave soon."

My stomach clenched again.

Dario looked down at his dough and sighed. "The focaccia will have to wait for another time."

I stood on the terrace, the stars obscured by a heavy mass of clouds. The private plane would pick us up soon, and there was nothing to do now but wait.

"Don't go out alone at night," my mother had said. I had texted her saying that I would be going to Paris for work, and she had immediately called back despite the late hour.

"I won't," I said.

"I just checked the weather, and it will be colder than in San Francisco, so pack your winter clothes. Wear several layers."

"Yeah, Mom."

"You let me know when you land and get to the hotel, okay?"

"Okay," I said.

"You have fun. Love you."

"Love you too, bye."

I had hung up and looked at my friends' group chat again. Everyone had made it back home alright. I had texted them I was going to Europe to follow some leads, just in case they saw my location there. No one had responded, and I assumed they were already asleep.

"Are you alright?" Lucian said.

I turned just as he closed the door behind him and walked over to me.

"Yeah," I said.

"I know this is a lot," he said.

"It is," I admitted. "But I can't walk away from this."

"I understand," he said. Lucian leaned against the railing and looked out at the dark sky. "I need to ask you something, Isa, because this might be the last time we talk in a while."

I turned to face him, but his eyes were set ahead.

"Like I told you," he said, "I didn't have a choice when I lay dying, and I swear I will do everything I can to prevent you from getting hurt. But if something does happen, I want to know what your choice is."

My heart lurched in a thunderous race. Lucian finally met my gaze, his own alight with its unnatural brightness.

"I . . ." I didn't know. Lucian Holt had just offered me immortality if my only other option was death.

"I made you a promise," Lucian said. "I'll protect you, however I can, but I would never do anything against your will."

Blood rushed inside of my ears so loud that I could barely hear my own thoughts. If death came for me, would I choose to cheat it?

"I don't know," I admitted. "I'm sorry. I just—"

"It's okay," he said. "I knew you probably wouldn't have an answer."

"Then why ask?"

"Because no one ever asked me," he said. "Just think about it. But hopefully, it won't come to that."

"Hopefully," I said.

A breeze swept past us, making me shiver. Lucian, as always, seemed unbothered by the weather.

"How long has it been since you went to a party?" I asked.

Lucian huffed. "Too long. If we don't count our little wine pong party downstairs."

I laughed, and he did too.

Our eyes met for one second. Two. Three.

There was something familiar about those eyes as if I had been staring at them for centuries. A small smile spread across my lips, which made Lucian smile too.

I leaned closer. Lucian tipped his head down. Our lips met and heat ignited inside my chest. I didn't care that we were working together. We had already crossed that line. And even though I didn't know whether I wanted immortality or not, at least for tonight I knew I wanted him. I threaded my fingers through his hair, and his arms wrapped around me, pulling me closer. His lips parted and I pushed my tongue into his mouth. He moaned, his grip tightening on my waist. His tongue brushed against my teeth, then the top of my mouth, making me inhale sharply. He pulled his head back slightly.

"I really, really like you," Lucian whispered into my ear.

"Why?" I asked.

Lucian's hot breath slid against my neck. His grip didn't slacken as his gaze captured mine.

"Because you're the first person who has truly seen me in a long, long time," Lucian said. "Maybe it's because you didn't know what I was in the beginning. But even after you discovered the truth, you never saw me as a monster. You"—he leaned closer until our lips were inches apart—"for the first time in a really long time, you made me feel human." His hands tightened around my waist.

"I think others assume that because I'm ancient and powerful I don't feel anything anymore. And maybe for a time, I didn't want to feel the pain of loss or even feel lost. But you made me realize that it's alright to feel and that feeling doesn't make me any less strong."

He brushed a strand of hair from my face and pulled it behind my ear. "I once heard someone say that life passes by faster the older you get, and it's true. Centuries start to feel like years, then months." His palm cupped my cheek, making the heat in my chest burn even hotter. "But this last week has felt longer than the last decade." He kissed me softly. "And it's those little moments like talking while you eat, sitting outside on the terrace, playing that stupid wine game, singing, or just talking about random things that made me feel like I was alive and not an immortal monster built to kill other monsters." He kissed me again. "I still don't know who I want to be, but I like who I am around you, and I want to be more of that."

He brushed his thumb over my lips, sending spikes of desire through me. I pulled his head down until our lips met again. He dragged his tongue over mine as his fingers dug into my skin. Lucian grabbed the back of my thighs and pulled me up. I wrapped my legs around him as he started walking back into the house. Even with his eyes closed and his lips locked on mine he seemed to know where to go. We walked down several hallways until we arrived in what I assumed was his bedroom. Lucian closed the door and pushed me against the wall.

I gripped Lucian's shirt and started unbuttoning it slowly. As soon as I finished the last button, Lucian pulled the shirt off and cast it to the side. I pressed my palm against his bare chest, feeling his heart again and the heat of his body. The hard muscles in his chest flexed under my touch.

Lucian gripped my jacket and swiftly peeled it off, then grabbed the edge of my sweater, pulled it over my body, and let it fall. I pulled my hands back and undid my bra. It hadn't even hit the floor before Lucian placed his mouth over my breast and licked it softly. I gasped as his tongue rolled over my nipple in gentle strokes. My fingers buried in his hair as desire began burning hotter at my core.

He pulled back slightly and kissed my chest, then my collarbone. His lips left a trail of kisses up my neck. Lucian abruptly pulled back, nearly making me fall and sending a shot of adrenaline through me as I found my footing again.

"What's wrong?" I asked.

Lucian breathed deeply, his head turned away from me. I stepped closer to him and spotted the fangs protruding from his mouth.

"Sorry. Instincts." Lucian stumbled over the words. "But I wasn't going to bite you. I just . . . can't always control when they come out."

I placed my hand on his cheek and forced him to face me. He cast his gaze down. "I understand if you feel uncomfortable and want to stop," he said

I kissed him.

He pulled back slightly. "Are you sure?"

"I trust you."

He pulled me closer until our chests pressed together, and the strong beat of his heart throbbed against me. When he kissed me again, I dragged my tongue over his fangs. The tips weren't as pointy as I had thought and didn't hurt my tongue. In that second, I realized that it was the force of the bite that could tear through flesh. But that thought disappeared as Lucian brushed my hair back and kissed my jaw, then my neck as he held the back of my head with his palm. My heartbeat pulsed where he pressed soft kisses, his fangs softly brushing against my skin.

Lucian pulled me up, carried me toward the bed, and laid me down gently. He sat at my side and closed his eyes, breathing deeply until the fangs retracted a few moments later. When he opened his eyes again, his irises were sizzling. He pushed himself onto his knees and unbuttoned my jeans, then slowly pulled them down, his gaze never breaking away from mine. After he gently tugged at my underwear, he cocked his head to one side. I nodded, and he pulled them down too.

Lucian held on to my thighs with his hands, gently nudging my legs apart. My fingers threaded into his hair as his head settled in between my legs, which rested on his shoulders. His tongue slid slowly through my entrance, then found my clit and moved over it in circles. I moaned, feeling a tight pressure building up inside of me as he continued with slow licks. Lucian slid one finger into me, and I dug my fingers into his scalp. He slid in another finger and started pumping slowly, then fast as his tongue continued to move in slow circles.

Release shattered through me, and I screamed his name. My ragged breaths filled the room as I lay limply on the bed. Lucian let my legs drop slowly, then he crawled over me. His eyes were burning with light when he smiled, then he pressed his lips over mine to make me taste myself. I pulled him closer, dragging my tongue over his teeth again.

Lucian pulled back. He kneeled next to me and unbuckled his belt, then pulled down his pants and boxers. He was already hard as he leaned over me again. He slid his tongue over the edge of my lips as he nudged my legs apart with his knee.

I traced my hands over his back, his muscles flexing under my fingers. Lucian looked into my eyes. I nodded. Our lips met again. Then he pushed into me slowly. I gasped into his mouth as he sheathed himself completely inside of me. He pulled back a little, then pushed in again with a moan, pulled back a little more and pushed in. We fell into a slow rhythm, which became faster as Lucian pumped more vigorously.

He leaned back, kneeling on the bed, and pulled my legs over his shoulders. While he gripped my thighs as he thrust into me, one of his fingers pressed down on my clit and rubbed it gently with my own wetness. Pressure built inside of me once more. Lucian hissed, his fangs shooting out again as his eyes glowed brighter. His grip tightened, and Lucian roared my name as he came inside of me, setting off my second orgasm. Waves of pleasure washed over me.

Lucian closed his eyes as he exhaled slowly, his hair curling over his forehead as he continued to hold me tight. My heartbeat echoed inside of my ears as I tried to make my breaths even out. Lucian opened his eyes, his irises glowing in a silver blaze. He loosened his grip on me as he pulled back, then leaned forward and wrapped me in an embrace. He kissed me softly on the forehead and on the lips. We lay entangled for some time hearing each other's breaths. After a few minutes, his fangs retracted again. I kissed him, and he pulled me closer to him.

"I don't want to lose you," Lucian whispered. "I need to know what your choice is, Isa."

I didn't respond.

"If something happens to you, I need to know I have your permission to save your life."

I thought about that, really thought about it for a moment. What would I do if I became immortal? I would still be around to see my parents for some years, and I felt sure I could come up with something to explain why I didn't age. And I would have something I had felt for a while was in short supply—time. Time to figure out who I wanted to be and what I wanted to do. Time to explore the world if I wanted to. Time to learn anything new that piqued my curiosity.

But I was getting way ahead of myself. Maybe nothing would happen tomorrow and I would continue being human. But if something did happen, was I willing to lose my life for this case?

"Bite me," I said. I raised my head to meet Lucian's gaze. "But only if something bad happens to me and the only other choice is death."

Lucian nodded. "I promise."

His arms tightened around me. "And if it doesn't," Lucian said, "if everything at the party goes alright and you continue being human, then I still want to be with you."

"I don't really know where I'll be after this," I said. I thought I would probably be back in my apartment looking for another job.

"It doesn't matter," Lucian said. "I'll be wherever you are. I can help you apply to more jobs until you find something that you really like, wherever that is, and we'll be together."

"What about your job?" I asked.

"I could take a break," Lucian said.

"Are you sure?" I asked.

"Yes," he said. "I've already had a shot at building my life, and now I want to help you build yours so you can become the person you want to be."

Tears welled in my eyes as my throat tightened. "I would like that."

Lucian kissed me on the forehead. He stroked my hair, softly rubbing my scalp. I closed my eyes and felt the rise and fall of his chest until it was time to go.

20

DARIO FIDGETED WITH his tie as we drove through the streets of Paris. A black van had picked us up from a private hangar, and the driver had informed Dario we would be meeting with Ernesto for dinner. Now Dario shifted his weight on the backseat and rubbed his palms together while his gaze flicked to the driver again. We both sat in nervous silence for about half an hour before we arrived at a hotel.

I wasn't sure if we were staying there but didn't have time to ask as a valet quickly ushered us into a restaurant at the side of the lobby. The tables were spaced out generously, giving diners a sense of privacy. Tables dressed in crisp white linen stood out sharply from the black walls. Gliding silently between the tables, the waitstaff matched those colors with white shirts and black pants.

Dario visibly stiffened when his gaze landed on a man a few tables away, a man whom I assumed was Ernesto. I stepped closer to Dario as we walked toward him. Ernesto rose, towering at least two heads above the waiters around him. My heart ran into a sprint. He was over six feet tall, and his muscles strained against the tight button-down shirt. His arms were as thick as both of mine combined. Ernesto's hair was close-cropped, but even in the dim light of the room, it still shone golden just like his beard. He was built like a hero born to slay a dragon, and I wondered how people could mistake him as human. His sparkling blue eyes settled on me, and a smile cut across his face, making the skin around his eyes wrinkle.

Ernesto stepped forward and gave Dario a hug. "It's been a long time, brother," he said in a deep voice that rumbled around him.

Dario hugged him back. "I know."

Ernesto's eyes settled on me again. "And who is this young lady?"

"This is Isa," Dario said, stepping closer to me.

Ernesto extended a hand to me. "It's very nice to meet you, Isa."

I took his hand, and he gently shook it. "It's a pleasure to meet you too."

The three of us sat down at the table, and the waiters immediately brought us menus. Dario busied himself reading, so I did the same. A minute later, a waiter was back with a small notepad.

"Could I get the salmon carpaccio and the artichoke dip please?" Dario asked.

The waiter nodded as he jotted that down.

Dario turned to me.

"Could I get the tomato bisque please?" I asked.

The waiter nodded again, then walked away.

Ernesto chuckled. "You still have your appetite."

Dario shrugged. "A little."

There was an awkward second of silence.

"So," Ernesto said. "How have you been? What have you been doing these past years? And how did you meet this lovely lady?"

I simply smiled.

"Well," Dario said. "I moved to California."

"I heard California is a good place to be right now. There's a lot of . . . fresh opportunities," Ernesto said.

Dario stiffened slightly but nodded. "It is. There are a lot of interesting things to do—a lot of outdoor activities, and the weather is also pretty good."

Ernesto nodded, his gaze subtly shifting to me for a second.

"You definitely look better than you did before," Ernesto said. "And I'm glad to see you've finally moved on."

I didn't miss Ernesto's eyes pausing on Dario's empty ring finger, then moving back to me. My stomach clenched, but I managed to maintain my expression neutral. Dario couldn't hide the flash that simmered in his eyes for a split second before he smiled.

"You still haven't told me how you met," Ernesto said.

"I went to college in California," I said. "We met while I was out hiking. I'm not a very outdoorsy person and got lost on a trail. Dario found me, and we began to see each other afterward."

Ernesto laughed, flashing his white teeth. "That's sweet." He didn't comment on the fact that Dario was a bit too old for a college student, but I supposed that because he was a vampire, age wasn't really the main concern. "What did you study?" he asked.

"Classics, Egyptology, and art history," I said.

Dario's smile widened. "She's an expert at reading ancient Greek, Latin, and Egyptian."

"A very educated young lady," Ernesto said.

I wasn't the best at reading people and knew Dario would probably be better at detecting Ernesto's shifts to see if this info had caused some interest.

"What do you do?" I asked Ernesto even as my heart sped up.

"Our family owns banks," Ernesto responded.

"Which ones?" I asked.

"Most of them," Ernesto said. "Our family invented the first bank, way back when, and ever since, we've kept control of most banks around the world."

"Oh," I said. "That's cool."

"Dario here was a really good banker. Everything he touched turned to gold," Ernesto said with a wink.

"A lot of us have that golden touch," Dario replied, his voice tight.

"Not as good as you," Ernesto said.

A short silence extended between them like a taut wire.

"So how is everyone?" Dario asked. "I hope the family has been doing well."

A waiter poured water in our empty glasses, then walked away.

"Not much has changed," Ernesto said. "There are no new members, and we've managed to maintain things civilly with Morrigan's children."

"That's good," Dario said.

The waiter brought our entrées, and Dario and I ate while he and Ernesto discussed more about their coven. I didn't think any of it was relevant to our search but still listened, just in case.

"Are you planning on coming back?" Ernesto asked.

The question held enough weight that it fully pulled me back into the conversation. Dario tensed next to me. He glanced at me once, then quickly looked away. Ernesto must have noticed the look, because he leaned closer to us.

"We would be happy to have her join us if she's important to you, Dario," Ernesto said. "We just want you to come home."

My blood turned to ice under Ernesto's stare, and I couldn't hide the surprise in my face.

"She's still young"—Dario shot another quick glance at me— "and should live a bit more before committing."

Hiding my trembling hands under the table, I forced myself to smile and nod.

Ernesto eyed me as if fully assessing me for the first time. "If you choose to come back, I'll turn her myself."

Dario's eyes widened. "We'll consider that too."

My heart echoed inside of my ears, and I was too stunned to say anything.

Ernesto leaned back in the chair. He pulled out a black piece of paper from his pocket and handed it to Dario. "The others will be happy to see you at the party tonight. I hope we can reconnect."

Dario nodded as he took the invitation.

Ernesto stood up from the table. "I need to head out now," he said with a glance at his watch. "Tell the waiters to charge your meal to my card."

"Thank you," Dario said.

"Of course," Ernesto responded. "I'll see you in a few hours."

Dario nodded, and Ernesto walked away from us. Neither Dario nor I dared to say a word as we finished our meal and then left the restaurant.

Dario exhaled loudly as he sat on a bench. After dinner, we had walked to a nearby park to talk.

"I'm sorry," Dario said. "I'm so sorry you're part of all this mess."

"I chose to be a part of it," I said.

Dario shook his head slowly but didn't say anything.

"At least we got the invitation," I said.

"At the very least," Dario muttered.

I glanced at his clenched fists, eyeing his empty ring finger as I remembered Ernesto's words. Dario noticed me staring.

"They let my wife die," Dario said, his voice hollow. "One of Helios's daughters took a liking to me, so she kidnapped me and turned me immortal to be her partner. But I didn't want that. I had a wife, a family, and a life I enjoyed." The pain in his eyes made my heart ache. "So she kept me locked away and didn't let me out until my wife had died of cancer. It took her away quickly, and I wasn't there for her." Dario ran his fingers through his hair. "I hate them. They didn't stop her when she locked me away and kept me as a pet. They claimed they didn't know, but I know they did and just decided to look the other way. After she let me out, I only stayed with their coven because I had no idea where to go or what else to do. But I found the courage to leave one day. Lucian found me, and"—he choked on his words—"I have no intention of going back."

A breeze swept past us, filling the silence with rustling branches.

"I'm so sorry, Dario," I whispered.

He looked at me. "I'm only doing this to find the killers and figure out if they're actually trying to find another way to give humans immortality." He pushed himself off the bench. "We'll figure out how to get us both off the hook later, but I just wanted you to know what type of people you're dealing with. Don't let their smiles fool you."

I nodded. Dario began walking, and I followed close by his side. "She's dead now, by the way," he said after a minute. "The woman who turned me, she was second-generation, a demigod technically. She was killed in a fight against Morrigan's coven, so you don't have to worry about her." Dario looked up at the sun. "Ernesto is also second-generation. He was the first one who Helios turned millennia ago. That's why he offered to be the one to bite you, so you could become third-generation and be part of the Coven of the Sun."

Ernesto had made the offer so freely, even though I knew they didn't give that away to anyone. They must have really wanted Dario back if they were considering taking me in too.

Lucian's promise found its way back to my mind like a caress, and I made a dedicated effort to not let my thoughts of him distract me.

"So tonight, who can we expect to see at the party?" I asked.

We had talked about it briefly back at the mansion, but I wanted to go over that information with Dario.

"Dionysus and all his coven will obviously be there," Dario said. "We're close to them. They're like our cousins, so we should be able to get some information from them. The other main covens will also be present. Stay away from Morrigan's though. We still have bad blood with them. We should also not hang around any lower-generations, or else we might attract unwanted attention." A cloud passed over the sinking sun, making the temperature drop a few degrees. "You'll be able to tell the covens apart by the rings they have on their left pinky finger. Each of the ruling covens has a different color and crest. The lower-generations won't have rings."

"Does a god rule over all the covens, even the lower-generation ones?" I asked.

"The politics of our world are complicated," Dario said. "Generally, only second- and third-generations are allowed to remain in covens ruled by a god or goddess. If a fourth-generation is turned, they are usually shunned from the coven since their powers are weak."

"That seems—"

"Brutal, harsh, unethical? Yes, yes, and yes," Dario said. "Some covens accept anyone from their descendance, but the most powerful covens don't—especially the twelve rulers."

That made me feel uncomfortable. I assumed some people were turned against their wills, so it seemed unfair that they were excluded from the family that was responsible for giving them immortality.

"Beyond the twelve, there are still hundreds of covens ruled by other gods," Dario said. "But it's become more popular to make independent covens, small families who band together but aren't under the rule of a god or goddess, like Lucian, Sue, and me. And then there are strays, individuals who live on their own."

That certainly seemed like some convoluted politics.

"This system has created a lot of resentment from those who get turned against their will and are forced to join a coven and from those who are turned and then cast away." He exhaled slowly. "Second- and third-generations usually don't interact with lower-generations, which is why we'll try finding information from the twelve covens while Lucian and Sue spy on the rest."

I nodded. Now I understood their plan better. Dario and I walked in silence, the crunch of the gravel the only sound. He paused to look at some wildflowers growing over the grass, then glanced at his watch.

"Let's go pick up your dress and my suit," Dario said. "Then we'll get ready for the party."

"It shouldn't be too bad," I said.

"Yeah," Dario replied.

We both knew it was a lie.

PART V

THE
PARTY

21

WOLF HAD BOUGHT new clothes in Paris for the party—a marine blue, three-piece suit with a white shirt. He had opted to not wear a tie, but to leave the top of his shirt unbuttoned. As he and Rafe drove down a long driveway, Wolf's memories of the last time he had worn a suit tugged at him. The wooden gazebo materialized inside his mind. The fairy lights had given her skin a golden glow in the night, making her look like a star as they danced together. It had been days before he had left. A sharp pain twisted inside his heart. The car windows rattled slightly. He breathed deeply. Soon, he told himself. Once he found answers and knew how to protect her, he would find her again.

The car slowed to a stop as they arrived at the entrance. A valet opened the door. Wolf suppressed a growl as Rafe, in the form of a scarab beetle, trampled across his chest. Rafe had started out hidden in his pocket but had migrated into his shirt while Wolf was lost in his thoughts, and there was nothing he could do to take Rafe out of there without drawing attention to himself.

Even if all the Athatos attended the party, they wouldn't look twice at Wolf. He had kept a low profile for centuries by taking advantage of their fragmented minds to convince them he wasn't a threat.

Rafe was another story. All the half-bloods knew who he was. Even though Rafe could have shape-shifted to look like another person, arriving with someone else would make people ask more questions. It was easier if it seemed Wolf was on his own.

Wolf buttoned up his suit as he exited the car and handed the keys to the valet. At Rafe's insistence, he had drunk more blood the night before. The *Aether* pulsed powerfully through his veins, nearly drowning out the beat of his heart. He would have to be very careful to not let it out before it was time.

Dionysus's home was smaller than he remembered, or maybe his imagination had rendered it bigger since he had last visited. The castle stood at the top of a hill that commanded a view of the countryside. A field of yellowed, withering grape-vines stretched out around the hill, struggling against the cold weather. The castle walls rose into sharp towers against the night. Light flooded out of every window and encased the castle in a dim halo against the night. Wolf remembered that inside were twenty bedrooms, each with their own closets and bathrooms. The castle also had a library, drawing room, sitting room, and of course, a large ballroom. It was an impressive home but nothing compared to the temples Dionysus had lived in a couple thousand years ago.

Wolf ascended the steps to the main entrance, eyeing the people around him. He didn't recognize a single face. Most clothing items were little more than scraps to cover certain body parts. Wolf pulled out his invitation before arriving at the front door. A man wearing a bright red mask looked at it for a couple of seconds, then waved Wolf inside. Wolf pocketed the invitation and walked into the party. Two grand staircases flanked the main room, one on each side, curving upward to meet at a shared landing on the second floor, opposite the entry. Three massive chandeliers hung from the ceiling and dispelled any shadow that may have lingered. Wolf noted the chandeliers had candles instead of electric lights.

Some people stood or sat on the staircases, but there was no one on the second floor. Wolf wondered if the other floors were off-limits. He also noted that very few people had rings on their pinky fingers. Wolf found it strange that Dionysus had invited so many lower-generation half-bloods, unless his coven had something to do with the murders and the half-bloods here were participating in the competition.

The *Aether* pulsed strongly in Wolf's chest, drowning out the chatter. With one blink, he could have destroyed the room and everyone in it.

After taking a deep breath, he walked to the other end of the foyer and entered a wide hallway painted in red and gold. People milled about in the corridor, talking and laughing in pairs or small groups. They stared at Wolf as he passed, then murmured behind his back. He ignored them. Even though Wolf had contained his power, he knew the others could still sense part of it—it was impossible to hide that he was an Athatos after having drunk so much blood.

The hallway opened into a massive ballroom. Wolf paused for a second. The ballroom was nearly the size of a soccer field, and half-bloods from most of the ruling twelve covens were present. Wolf counted at least twenty-five from Dionysus's coven, many more than he had seen before. There were four members of the Helios Coven, seven from Anubis's, and six from Morrigan's. The Twelfth Coven was missing, which wasn't strange given that they had distanced themselves from everyone else. He counted a handful from the remaining covens, but Hera's coven was also missing. A swirl of anxiety clutched his stomach. The lights flickered for a second. Hera must have known something was going to happen during the party and hadn't wanted her coven to be a part of it. Even though he tried to not worry about her, he couldn't bring himself to fully ignore that she was already involved in this rebellion somehow.

After sweeping his gaze through the room, his eyes settled on Dionysus at the very back of the room. He sat on a throne at the center of a raised stage. Dionysus had made himself look young, no older than a twelve-year-old boy. His tawny brown skin gleamed golden, and his eyes glowed red and purple. A woman wearing a revealing red dress sat on his lap, but Wolf didn't recognize her.

Rafe scuttled to his abdomen, poking at Wolf's skin with his little legs. Wolf understood the message—he had to focus on their mission. But first, he wanted to have a little chat with Dionysus. Wolf walked to the other end of the room, edging around people and being careful not to touch them. Some of them glanced at him, but no one approached him. Wolf climbed the steps that led to the throne, and a couple from Anubis's coven gawked at him as if he had just violated a sacred law. Dionysus's eyes immediately trained on Wolf, but his gaze softened a second later.

"Hey," Dionysus said. "It's been a long time."

"It has," Wolf said as he walked closer.

Dionysus smiled, dimples forming in his chubby cheeks. While it seemed that he fed diligently, his childish appearance told Wolf that Dionysus's mind was quite fragmented.

Dionysus turned to his children around him. "Everyone, this is . . ." His eyes glazed, turning foggy.

"Wolf."

"I like the name," Dionysus said. "I decided to change mine to Max. It's more modern."

"Wolf," the woman on Max's lap drawled. "Which one of the old gods are you?"

Max narrowed his eyes. "I don't even remember." He laughed. "It's been so long. I remember you used to own sheep."

"Yes," Wolf said. "I watched over shepherds."

Rafe scratched Wolf's chest, and Wolf could sense his amusement.

"Right, right," Max said.

Wolf wondered whether Max's children truly understood how broken their minds had become.

"Are you going to be sitting here all night?" Wolf asked.

He was aware that Max was in danger but could only do so much to help him before he spoke to Gabriel.

"Maybe," Max said with a shrug.

"I hope you don't mind me wandering off."

Max waved his hand dismissively. "Treat this as your own home."

Wolf bowed his head in acknowledgement, then stepped down from the stage and walked toward the exit, feeling the weight of everyone's stares on him. He was fully in the incognito mode he and Rafe had planned for. As soon as people began referring to him as the old god of shepherds, they lost interest. He heard a few mocking laughs and chuckles. His power stirred within him at the insults, and the lights flickered again, but he pushed the *Aether* back down.

Not yet, Wolf thought. Let them believe he ruled over sheep.

Rafe began scratching his stomach, but Wolf wasn't sure what that meant, so he continued making his way around the first floor to find the kitchen. Then Rafe scrawled something on Wolf's chest using his tiny insect legs.

Wolf was barely able to discern what Rafe spelled out, but he thought Rafe had spelled *talk* on his skin.

But Wolf figured they could talk once they found the secret entrance to the Underworld. He tried to find waiters or waitresses carrying food trays but spotted none. Was it too early for dinner? Or maybe it was too late, and he had missed it.

Rafe bit Wolf's nipple. A light above him burst. Wolf clenched his teeth as he contained the urge to squash the bug. Rafe spelled *talk* out again. Wolf quickly went back into the main foyer and walked up the stairs to the second floor. He roamed dimly lit corridors until he was sure they were alone. Rafe crawled out of his shirt, up his face, and into the crevices of his ear.

"People are nervous, some are afraid," Rafe whispered.

"They are buzzing with anticipation, waiting for something big to happen."

Wolf's gut clenched. "How many of them?"

"Most of the lower-generations," Rafe whispered. "A few from Max's coven too."

"What about the other main covens?" Wolf asked. "The second- and third-generations?"

"A few from Anubis's coven are also very nervous," Rafe said. "But most others from the ruling covens are bored. It's as if they had been forced to come here."

"And Max?" Wolf asked.

"His emotions were difficult to read," Rafe said. "I can't tell if he's involved or not."

Before Wolf could ask why Max's emotions had been hard to read, Rafe scuttled back into his shirt. Wolf heard the footsteps a second later as a beautiful woman rounded the corner. She wore a long sparkling silver dress that hugged her body tightly. It glinted brightly as she walked toward Wolf. She cocked her head to one side.

"I didn't expect to see one of the gods here," she said. She had light purple eyes and tanned brown skin. Wolf made an effort to not glance at the plunging neckline of her dress.

"I thought I would come by for some fun," Wolf said.

The woman reached out and straightened Wolf's shirt, which had rumpled a bit when Rafe had crawled out. Her pinky finger had a ring that marked her as one of Max's children. "What kind of fun are you looking for?"

Rafe was smart enough to remain completely immobile on Wolf's back, but Wolf couldn't stop his heart from racing forward. The woman must have heard it because she smiled. As long as she didn't hear, see, or sense the beetle, Wolf considered it a win.

"Have we met before?" Wolf asked.

"I'm sure you would remember if we had," the woman answered. "I'm Ariadne."

"Wolf." He extended his hand, and she shook it, her grip firmer than he expected. Then he remembered she was Max's wife. Wolf hadn't attended the wedding, so he didn't expect Ariadne to know who he was.

"Where were you heading?" Ariadne asked.

"I was just exploring," Wolf said.

"I could give you a tour, if you would like," Ariadne said.

Wolf was about to say that he was fine, but Rafe tapped on his back before scrawling *follow her.*

"So?" Ariadne asked.

Wolf realized he had taken too long to respond while he waited for Rafe to finish the message. "Sure," Wolf said. He didn't know what Rafe had detected in Ariadne's emotions but decided to trust him. Ariadne turned her back to him, and he followed her down the hallway.

"Which one of the old gods are you?" she asked without turning to look at him.

"One of the forgotten ones," Wolf said with a sigh. "I used to watch over shepherds and teach humans how to take care of their cattle." It wasn't fully a lie—he had done that once.

Ariadne didn't respond. She led him down a series of corridors until they arrived at a set of large double doors. She pushed them open. Their footsteps echoed inside the room as Wolf admired the floor-to-ceiling bookshelves at his sides. The door closed behind his back.

Rafe seemed to have turned to stone, and Wolf's instincts told him he was in danger. He understood why Rafe had asked him to follow Ariadne. She thought he was the weakest of the gods—an easy target. The power inside of him began to curl out of his chest, but he pressed down on it. Not yet, he thought.

"Do you come in here often?" Wolf asked without looking at Ariadne.

"Sometimes," she responded. "We have over a million books, all manuscripts that Dionysus has collected since his childhood."

Wolf knew it was a lie. Dionysus had never collected any books. One of his children must have done it, because Dionysus had never been fond of reading. Ariadne must have expected Wolf's memories to be as foggy as her husband's.

"I remember that," Wolf said. He finally turned to face Ariadne, who hadn't dropped her smile. Wolf slowly walked toward her. "Is that all?" he asked in a low, taunting voice.

"Is there anything else you would like me to show you?" Ariadne asked.

Wolf finally dared to let his eyes travel below her neckline. "Maybe just one thing."

Ariadne stepped closer to him, nearly closing the distance between them. "Are you sure?" she asked, her breath brushing against his neck.

Wolf smiled. "You tell me."

Wolf saw the flash of the knife before his brain fully processed what it was. The *Aether* shot out of him like a lance, piercing Ariadne through the chest. Her hand froze, the knife inches away from Wolf's chest. The knife clattered onto the floor.

Wolf struggled to keep his power from exploding out of him and ripping the entire room to pieces. He channeled the *Aether* into Ariadne's body, which instantly began to crack with lines of fire as if lava were bursting out of her. She opened her mouth to scream, but no sound came out as her body disintegrated into flaming ashes. The molecules around him vibrated, and heat spread through the room. Wolf sank to his knees, clenching his jaw as he tried to contain his power. It was like trying to use his hands to push back against a breaking dam.

"What the hell is this?" Rafe asked, his body human again. He picked up the knife from the scattered pile of ashes and held it away from him as if it were poisoned. "It's engraved with ancient Egyptian."

Wolf had feared as much.

He extended his hand, and Rafe handed him the knife. Wolf examined the long blade—made of pure silver—and flipped it to the other side. The metal had tiny Egyptian words carved into it that spelled out a very specific section of the Book of the Dead.

"Shit," Wolf said.

The knife gleamed red with sudden heat. Wolf crushed the knife inside of his palm, the metal dripping from his hand and onto the floor like silver water.

The *Aether* sprang out of Wolf's body before he could even attempt to contain his fury. Wolf screamed as it burned through his veins. The particles around Wolf began to stir, their energy increasing. The room heated up. One by one, the books disintegrated into ashes, releasing a burst of energy from them that further intensified the heat in the room.

It felt so good to destroy those books, like Wolf could finally scratch an itch that had been bothering him for days.

When Wolf took a deep breath, his nostrils burned with the tang of ash. Rafe had crouched down where he had previously stood, and still covered his face with his hands. When Rafe finally raised his head, fear slithered in his green eyes. The bookshelves were all empty now, spilling black ashes like dripping blood. But something had been left behind on one of the bookshelves.

Wolf rushed to it, Rafe close at his heels. The two men stopped before one of the bookshelves, their eyes glued to the object lying there—the thing Wolf had tried, and failed, to destroy many times.

Shit, thought Wolf.

"Disgusting," Rafe said. "Whose hand is that? And why is it in the library?"

Osiris's rotten hand lay before them. The skin had turned into a watercolor gradation of yellow, black, and purple. White bones peeked out from some sections where the skin had become so thin it had cracked.

Stray half-blood Jan and his buddies hadn't known about Osiris, but Dionysus's coven did—they knew what they needed to kill an Athatos. Wolf had been in real danger, and that realization sent a cold shiver rippling down his spine.

How had Dionysus's coven found the hand? Had they also stolen the head and the leg that Gabriel had been guarding? Could more body parts be hidden somewhere in the castle?

Wolf's mind whirled, trying to tie together all the loose threads. Had Dionysus's coven killed Gabriel? They could have since they knew what they needed. But were they powerful enough to have killed Gabriel? He was too strong, and they had never been able to influence the minds of the Athatos. They couldn't have made him go into a mad frenzy that could have weakened him enough for them to kill him. Wolf was still missing something.

Wolf picked up the hand, then shoved it into a pocket.

Rafe cocked his head to the side. "That looks awkward," he said. "You might want to put your own hand in your pocket too. The worst people will think is that you have a massive hand in there."

"You knew she was planning to kill me," Wolf snarled.

The bookshelves rattled, spilling more ashes like a spewing volcano.

Rafe threw up his hands. "I knew she wouldn't," he said. "I didn't sense anyone else on the second floor, and Ariadne is no match for you. She thought you were weak, and I was curious to see what she would do to try to kill you." He spread his arms wide. "Isn't that why we're here—to figure out how they killed Gabriel? Now we know they used a silver knife with inscriptions, which I'm assuming are from the Book of the Dead and which means that the Book of the Dead is truly connected to all of this somehow." His eyes settled on Wolf's pocket. "Any ideas on how that's related to this?"

"Let's go," Wolf said in between gritted teeth while trying to force his power to settle down. "We need to find that entrance."

He placed his hand inside his pocket. Making direct contact with the rotten hand was disgusting, but he had no other choice. It looked like he had a phone, or maybe a thick wallet in his pocket, but Wolf didn't think anyone would guess he had another hand.

"Alrighty," Rafe said with a smile.

Wolf blinked, and Rafe disappeared. He spotted the scarab beetle on the floor, picked him up, and placed Rafe on his shoulder. Rafe made his way into Wolf's shirt again as he walked to the door. After opening the door slowly, Wolf didn't see anyone outside. He quickly stepped out, closed the door behind him, and hoped that no one would go into the library during the party. Just to be sure, he pressed his palm on the door. A small trickle of the *Aether* snaked out of him. The wood expanded, growing out of the frame and stretching further inside of the library. Wolf couldn't see it, but he could feel the wood curling into the walls and the floor to brace the doors in place.

With the library taken care of, Wolf made his way down the hallway. He brushed some ash off his hair, but at least his suit hadn't stained. He tried to appear calm. He knew rushing around would likely heighten suspicions. Now he just had to find the kitchen, and Rafe would create an illusion to clear out everyone for a few minutes while they found the entrance to the Underworld.

Wolf arrived at the large staircase again but took a second to assess the crowd below. The attendees drank and laughed, and live music blared somewhere off in the distance. As Wolf descended the stairs, a waiter approached him and offered him a glass of wine. Wolf took it, then quietly followed the waiter as he made his way through the foyer. Since there had been only one glass left on the waiter's tray, Wolf assumed the waiter would go to the kitchen to get a full tray. As he shadowed the waiter, Wolf pretended to look around the house and admired statues and paintings around him that he hadn't noticed when he first walked in.

When he made it to the other side of the room, he saw the waiter walking toward a corridor that extended to the left and below the stairs. Before leaving the foyer, Wolf glanced toward the entrance to eye the newcomers. He nearly choked on his wine.

Walking through the main door was the one person Wolf hadn't expected to see at the party.

22

WEARING MY NEW purple dress, I held Dario's arm tightly as we entered Dionysus's party.

The bodice of the dress hugged me tightly before expanding into luxurious layers of amethyst silk. A flower lace pattern on the back and long sleeves gave it an elegant touch. Dario wore a matching purple tie with his black suit. I had opted to wear comfortable shoes, which were not the most aesthetically pleasing, but in case of an emergency, I would be able to run. And since the shoes were hidden under the long dress, I figured not many people would notice.

On his left pinky finger, Dario wore Helios's golden ring. It had a crest that depicted a sun with twelve bright rays undulating out of it. He had been reluctant to put it back on but knew that he needed to play his part.

Three large chandeliers hung above our heads. Gold leaf and paintings decorated the ornate walls. Statues stood at the edges of the room, silently admiring the throng of people gathered inside. Even though Dario insisted we had arrived early, the large foyer was already heavily crowded. My eyes darted around as I tried to spot the rings from the twelve ruling covens, but I didn't see a single one. Everyone was clad in elegant suits and lavish gowns and adorned with glittering jewelry that flaunted an ostentatious display of wealth.

Half-bloods turned to look at us as we passed them by. Some of them stared, probably noting I was human. But they gave us a wide berth when they noted Dario's golden ring. I tightened my grip on his arm, feeling their burning glares at my back.

"Dario," a female voice said.

We stopped as a tall woman in a peach dress placed her hand on Dario's arm. I noted the rose gold ring on her pinky. Chatter cut off abruptly. The music ceased. Everyone froze where they had been as if the woman had stopped time.

"Hello, Jia," Dario said curtly.

Her skin shone with a dim radiance as she smiled at Dario and glanced at his ring. "I thought you had left the Sun Coven."

"I did for a while," Dario said.

"What made you come back?" Her eyes slid to me, then back to Dario.

"I have my own reasons," Dario said.

She squeezed his arm. "Well, do let me know if you need anything. It's nice to see you again."

She took her hand off his arm, and time resumed its course. Jia walked away, throwing one last glance at Dario before disappearing into the crowd. Dario released a long breath before we continued.

We walked through a large hallway and arrived at the ballroom. I gawked at the vast space, big enough to nearly fit a soccer field, with hundreds assembled inside. Small clusters had formed and all conversations seemed to mingle together as they echoed off the walls. At the very end stood a throne raised on a stage. A youth lounged on it talking to a woman who sat on his lap. I didn't need Dario to tell me that was Dionysus himself. I had never met a god before but immediately knew what he was. He shone with a strange radiance. It was almost like a vibration that made my skin tremble just by being in his presence.

Dario gently nudged me forward, and I spotted a small group of people wearing golden rings on the left. I didn't see Ernesto but assumed he was somewhere. A woman in the group looked in our direction and waved at Dario. Two men turned around to face us, their expressions hard as stone.

"Dario," the woman said before giving him a gentle hug.

"Hello, Estelle," Dario said with a smile. He looked at the other two. "Rufus, Bruno."

The two of them dipped their heads in acknowledgement.

All four members of the Helios Coven, Dario included, had golden blond hair. I wondered if Helios had preferred to turn people who physically looked alike or if the transformation had changed them.

Rufus looked around twenty and had perfectly combed straight hair. His dark eyes were like two chips of obsidian. A small scar ran from his upper lip to his cheek, which seemed to widen when he smiled at us.

"Ernesto told us you had found someone," Rufus said with a slight Italian accent. "I didn't realize she was so young." He inhaled sharply. "Her blood is good, it should—"

"Not here," Estelle interrupted, gently laying a hand on his chest. Her blue eyes sparkled like the ocean under the midday sun, and her cheeks dimpled slightly with her smile.

Bruno nodded in agreement. His hazel eyes had only landed on us briefly before turning to the rest of the room as if searching for any threats that might step close to us. He gave me the impression of being the group's guard dog.

"There are more lower-generations here than in previous years," Dario commented.

Rufus huffed. "I just said the same thing. This year, Ariadne took care of the invitations."

"But why would she invite more of them?" I had never heard Dario speak in such a tone that suggested the lower-generations were no more than filthy rats.

"Something about all of us being one people, and blah, blah," Rufus replied.

Recalling that Ariadne was Dionysus's wife in mythology, I assumed it was the same person he spoke of. I also wondered why she had chosen to invite the stray killers. Such an action reinforced Lucian's theory that their coven was involved in the murders.

"Ariadne is trying to be more inclusive," Estelle said.

"You think it's a good idea?" Rufus asked.

"I think the segregation between the top generations of half-bloods and everyone else should be addressed, but I don't think this party is the right way to do it," Estelle said, keeping her voice low.

Dario seemed to consider this.

"I still don't see anyone from Hera's coven," Bruno mentioned, his tone raspy like grinding stones.

"Maybe she had a vision that this would be the most boring party ever and warned her children not to come," Rufus said.

"Or maybe she knew there would be a lot of lower-generations milling about and purposefully decided to make a statement by not showing," Dario said.

"Hmm," Bruno said as he pondered that.

"She wouldn't do that," Estelle said.

Rufus shrugged. "She doesn't even let third-generations remain in her coven, only seconds, so it wouldn't surprise me," he said. "By not showing up, she's making a statement to remind Dionysus that only those of purer blood should be around the Athatos."

I remained silent as I heard them talk. It was slightly terrifying to see how much their society hinged on the generation they belonged to.

"I didn't expect to see you here," someone said behind us.

Rufus's eyes flashed golden and so did Bruno's, as if the sun had ignited inside of them. Estelle became rigid. Dario slowly turned around. I released my hold on his arm to face the woman who had spoken. Her skin was pale as the moon, and her hair curled around her head like threads of midnight. She had a long face with curved eyebrows and full lips. Her black eyes drilled into Dario.

"I heard you went on a little vacation." She pronounced the last word sharp enough to draw blood. "But no one expected you to come back." Her eyes traveled past him toward the three others standing behind him.

Rufus stepped to Dario's other side, his golden eyes scathing hot. "Leave," he said.

The woman raised a brow. "I just came by to say hello, Rufus, no need to get defensive about it." She raised a glass to her lips to take a sip, displaying her black ring with a Celtic knot as a crest—Morrigan's coven. She turned back to Dario. "You look good, Dario. I think this is the first time I've seen you without dark stains under your eyes."

Rufus growled, a deep rumble that made the air tremble. A few lower-generations who had been standing close by moved away. Others began looking in our direction or murmuring as they glanced at us over their shoulders. Rufus's eyes burned an even deeper shade of gold, and the air around us warmed as if I had stepped onto a hot beach. The woman smiled back, flashing her pearly white teeth. Her black eyes glinted gray, but it wasn't like the lightning that swam in Lucian's eyes. It was the gray of skeletons trying to claw their way out of a black ocean. Death itself lay on the other side of her gaze.

"You heard Rufus. Leave." Ernesto's voice was calm, but threatening.

Fear flashed in the woman's eyes as her smile faded. After a second, her smile reappeared. "Ernesto," she said. "You grew back the beard."

I risked a glance behind me and nearly flinched as Ernesto stepped around me. His eyes shone so brightly my own stung just glancing at them. Heat rippled out of him in sharp waves. It wasn't the warmth Dario had shared with me but a painful, searing hotness.

"Hold up, hold up," another voice rang out nearby. A young

man broke through the crowd and stepped toward us. His skin was tawny brown, and his eyes shone with a red-purple gleam. The young man had the appearance of an eighteen-year-old with a blob of curls around his head. "No fights are allowed. You all know that."

Rufus and Ernesto glared at the woman, who only raised her hands in a shrug.

"I only came to say hello to Dario," the woman said.

The young man's eyes widened at the sight of Dario and gleamed a brighter shade of purple. "Dario," he said, "it's been a long time. We should catch up. How about we get a drink together?"

"Another time," Ernesto cut in, glaring daggers at the young man.

"Another time then," the young man repeated in a sarcastic tone.

He walked away from us, and I realized that the woman had left too. Ernesto looked at the rest of the people assembled in the room as if daring anyone else to come closer to us.

"They're like vultures," Estelle said.

"Yeah," Dario said in a tight voice.

Ernesto looked around us. "Why are there so many lower-borns here? Let's go somewhere else. The second floor is off-limits, so we can't go there."

"Why?" Rufus asked. "It's never been closed off before."

Ernesto shrugged. We followed him out of the ballroom and through a series of hallways, and I couldn't stop myself from glancing into the rooms we passed by. In one, a woman danced with remarkable grace, her movements fluid and captivating as she twirled and spun in a colorful dress with intricate patterns and bright hues. Thick smoke permeated another room where half-bloods lounged on plush chairs as they smoked from a shisha and chatted in lively tones. A set of open double doors revealed a large indoor pool surrounded by intricately carved marble columns. I quickly averted my gaze when I realized most people there were fully naked.

After a few minutes, we arrived at a small living room with an ivy-covered wall. Opposite to that was a large window that framed a statue garden outside.

"Finally," Rufus said. "Some peace."

I sat next to Dario on one of the couches. Estelle exhaled as she plopped down on a couch, and Rufus let out a sigh when he sat next to her and placed a hand over hers.

"This year's party is a mess," Bruno said. "It seems that everyone got an invitation. I spotted some eighth-generations in that pool."

"Ugh," Ernesto said. "I remember when it was only the twelve covens." He turned to look at me. "This party used to be exclusive. Dionysus started it to celebrate his birthday and only invited close family members, which mostly consisted of the other gods and the twelve ruling covens." He looked out the window, carefully eyeing the statues. "But over time, the gods stopped coming, and Dionysus began inviting lower-borns. It became a social competition to gain entrance to the party. But this year, he's gone overboard. He might as well have ditched the invitations altogether and just opened the doors to everyone."

"Ariadne was the one who decided," Estelle said.

"That makes it even worse," Ernesto said. "Dionysus is becoming more and more like a child instead of taking control of his family."

"We shouldn't talk about him while we're in his house," Estelle said. "Remember the walls have ears here."

A second of silence passed.

"But this is the first time in four years that an Athatos shows up. Now that was a surprise," Rufus said.

"Another god is here?" Dario asked, leaning forward.

"He goes by the name Wolf," Estelle said. "The old god of shepherds or something."

Rufus huffed. "He looked weak."

"He looked handsome," Estelle said, which earned a glare from Rufus, and in turn, made her smile.

"Never heard of him," Dario said with a frown.

Rubbing his face with his palm, Ernesto didn't seem to find the appearance of the old god interesting. "What do you think about all of these lower-borns, Dario?" he asked.

The question seemed to weigh heavily in the air.

"I think it's strange so many of them were invited," Dario said. "I'm not buying the whole argument that we are all one people."

"That's what I said," Rufus said. "It's as if Dionysus and his coven have a secret political agenda going on."

"I don't like this either," Bruno muttered.

Ernesto remained silent, watching the conversation unfold. His body was stiff like a lion about to spring forward to strike, but I wasn't yet sure who the prey was.

"Would it look bad if we leave early?" Rufus asked. He turned to me. "We can say she's feeling sick or something. Humans get sick constantly, don't they? Hera's coven didn't even show up so we wouldn't be the only coven missing."

"Trust me, I would rather be anywhere but here." Ernesto rubbed his beard. "But I would rather not anger Dionysus's coven, especially not while our relationship with the War Coven is so tense."

"We can wait until the midnight reveal, then leave," Estelle said.

"The midnight reveal?" Dario asked.

"Something about a big surprise," Rufus said as he waved his hand dismissively. "Don't know what it is, but Dionysus's coven seems excited about it."

I had the feeling the big surprise might not be a pleasant one.

The door burst open. Ernesto was immediately on his feet, his palms balled into fists. He uncurled them when a young woman entered the room. Her eyes were the same red-purple color as the young man who had talked to us previously. She appeared to be about my age and wore a short red dress that hugged her figure tightly. Her auburn hair fell below her shoulders in rippling cascades. A variety of golden bracelets encircled her wrists.

"The party is out there you know," she said as she pointed at the open door.

"We know," Rufus said. "We came here to take a break from all the noise."

"You didn't complain about the noise last year, Rufus," the girl said.

"Last year there weren't so many loud lower-generations," Rufus replied.

The girl laughed. "I didn't realize their presence irked you so much." She glanced at me. "If you're hanging out with a human, I don't see why you couldn't tolerate their presence."

"Don't compare her to them," Rufus said.

The girl turned to me. "I'm Irene, by the way. Nice to meet you."

"I'm Isa," I said after clearing my throat.

Irene didn't close the door behind her as she stepped closer to us. Bruno and Rufus eyed her, but Estelle was smiling.

"Is that a new necklace?" Irene asked as she looked in Estelle's direction.

"A gift for our two-hundredth anniversary," Estelle said as she glanced at Rufus, who didn't break his gaze away from Irene.

I had forgotten for a second how old these people were and couldn't imagine being married to someone for that long. Irene laughed as she looked in my direction as if reading the thought off my expression. "Time passes by faster than you think," she said. Her eyes flitted to Dario. "Maybe one day you'll celebrate that many years of marriage."

Dario didn't respond.

"But seriously," Irene said as she swept her gaze through us, "what are you doing hiding in here? You should be drinking and enjoying the night."

Ernesto exchanged a glance with Rufus. "Yeah," Ernesto said. "We should all get some drinks."

"Actually," Dario said, "I told Isa you had a grand library, and she's excited to see it."

Irene's gaze slid to me.

"I studied classics and Egyptology in college and love translating ancient texts, so it would be fun if I got to see some original manuscripts," I said.

I could feel the burning glares from everyone else in the room, but my eyes were only on Irene.

"What kinds of texts do you like?" she asked.

"Ancient Greek and Latin, but I'm also pretty good at translating Egyptian," I said.

Irene smiled. Something hungry and dangerous glinted in her eyes. "Looks like you found yourself an interesting match, Dario," she said with a wink at Dario, who gave her a smile.

"What kinds of texts do you have, if you don't mind me asking," I said.

"We have a few originals," Irene said. "Homer, Plato, Aristotle, Virgil, Ovid, and many others."

"What about Egyptian manuscripts?" I asked.

"Are you looking for one in particular?" Irene asked.

"Not really," I said.

Irene was thoughtful for a second. "Well, we did recently acquire a small fragment of the Book of the Dead, if you're interested in reading that."

I managed to keep my heart rate from spiking into a furious roar. "That's cool," I said. "I would love to see it."

She clasped her hands together, making her bracelets clang. "I could make an exception for you."

"Sure," Dario said. "We would love that." He turned to the

others. "We can meet you back in the ballroom once we're done looking at the ancient books."

Ernesto seemed highly annoyed, and so did the others. "Fine," he said in a clipped tone. "We'll see you later."

The Helios Coven members seemed clueless about the murders, but Lucian had been right—Dionysus's coven was involved somehow.

"Follow me," Irene said as she led us out of the room.

I held Dario's hand tightly as we walked out of the room together. My heartbeat echoed furiously inside of my ears while we followed Irene through dimly lit stone corridors.

"I'm so glad you made it to the party, Dario," Irene said. "We sent you an invitation but weren't sure if you had received it since you move around a lot."

Dario's grip tightened on my hand. Irene finally stopped at a wooden door with vines carved at the edges. She opened it and motioned us inside as she switched on the light. I was not surprised to find it was not the library. My ears pulsed with the pounding beat of my heart at the sight of the black stone table in the middle of the room. Dried splotches of blood formed a macabre pattern on its surface.

"There's so much we need to discuss," Irene said, then closed the door.

23

WHEN THE DOOR clicked shut, Dario inhaled sharply. I thought he probably smelled the blood when he gripped my hand tighter.

"This is where we take the bodies for experimentation," Irene said. She stepped around us, scanning our faces. "You don't need to pretend like you don't know what I'm talking about."

"Of course," Dario said, his tone much calmer than I felt.

"How convenient that you found someone who can translate Greek, Latin, and Egyptian." Her smile widened. "That's an unfair advantage over everyone else. You would be surprised how few half-bloods know those languages. With our extended lifespans, you would assume that they would learn something new, but most of them don't even know basic Latin." Irene glanced back at the bloodied table. "Have you come close to figuring out the right inscriptions?"

"We're not sure," Dario said.

I shook my head as fear began to take hold of me. The images of the victims flashed through my mind—Ana dead on the cement floor, the unnamed body rotting in the sewers. How many victims had been killed here?

Irene sat on the edge of the table, bracing her hands against it. "I really shouldn't be doing this, but there's no one else from the Helios Coven involved in the competition, so I'll make an exception. I don't think the others will mind."

Dario's grip on my hand tightened again at the word *competition*. So that was why multiple covens were involved in the murders and why they had become more reckless. But what were they competing for?

Irene pushed herself off the table and walked to one side of the room.

She retrieved a blank piece of parchment from one of the drawers, then placed it on the table. "How about you write the inscriptions that you think are the correct ones?"

"I . . ." Blood rushed inside my ears. "I don't have them all memorized."

"Give it a try," Irene said with a sly smile. "Then we can talk more."

I knew we wouldn't be getting any more information unless I managed to write something. Dario let go of my hand. I looked into his hazel eyes, and he gave me an encouraging nod. I turned to the blank parchment, and my mind became just as empty. Irene handed me a pen, and my hand shook slightly as I held it.

"Just give it a try," Irene said. "This isn't meant to be a test or anything."

But we all knew that it was. I took a deep breath and closed my eyes.

A competition. That was why the victims had been killed. But why use the Book of the Dead to find a new way to make humans immortal?

That's why I had come to the party—everyone else had their part to play, and answering that question was mine.

I opened my eyes again, and my heartbeat steadied. The rest of the room seemed to fade into the background. The tip of the pen touched the parchment, and words began flowing out of my mind as if they had become muscle memory. I defaulted to Egyptian. Other covens might have believed that Latin and Greek translations could work, but I knew they wouldn't. Those symbols didn't hold as much power as the Egyptian hieroglyphs with which the Book of the Dead had been written.

Even though my mind was blank, my hands knew what to do. Something inside of me squirmed in discomfort, and a sense of wrongness settled within my stomach. I became aware of how closely Irene was watching me, her gaze never leaving the parchment.

I stopped writing abruptly, and my breath hitched, making me cough. Dario gently placed a hand on my shoulder. I glanced down at what I had written, at the beautiful hieroglyphs on the page. A shiver trembled through me. The passage was incomplete. It was missing a couple of key sentences, but I didn't want Irene to see them. I wasn't sure how I knew the right sentences, but for the first time since I had started helping Lucian, my mind seemed to instinctively understand it.

"Sorry, that's all I know," I said.

For a few seconds, Irene didn't answer. Dario stepped closer to me and protectively pulled me to his side.

"It's backward," Irene commented.

"Sorry?" I asked.

"You have most of the passages, but it's all written backward," Irene said. "Which would have the opposite effect."

I looked down at the parchment again, but whatever moment of inspiration I'd had was gone. The characters seemed incomprehensible to me now.

The opposite effect, I thought.

Then the truth crystallized in my mind. Despite the warmth emanating from Dario, a wave of cold slammed into me.

"Of course," I said. "I got used to seeing them in that order from the Book of the Dead. This is the order needed to give someone immortality."

"Yes," Irene said.

"But we need the reverse order to take away immortality." My tongue felt numb as those words floated out of my lips. Dario stiffened next to me. That idea hadn't even settled in my head before I asked the next question. "How will we know if we have the right words?"

"The correct reversed spell rips a soul out of the body, making it disintegrate into ashes, and the spell works in humans as well as gods," Irene said. She glanced back at Dario. "It was a brilliant idea for you to make the others believe you were considering rejoining their coven. They want you back so badly they can't see how much you hate them. I can't blame you, Dario. They destroyed your life."

She walked over to one of the cabinets and crouched down as my mind finally caught up with her revelation. The inscriptions in the bodies had also been reversed. Words had power, and the order of those words had power too. The competition, and this entire murder case, wasn't to give immortality but to destroy it. Maybe there was more than human blood keeping the ancient gods alive. What had they actually discovered five thousand years ago?

Irene stood up again, holding a small, tattered parchment in her hand. She gave it to me, and I skimmed through the hieroglyphs.

"Don't worry," Irene said. "Once Helios is dead, you can come back to us and we'll protect you. You're not alone. Not anymore." She stared directly into Dario's eyes, her own gleaming with purple light. "Are you ready, Dario?"

The room was gripped by an unsettling silence, which tightened around us like a noose.

"Of course I'm ready," Dario finally said. He smiled, flashing his fangs. I almost startled away from him and the deadly, uncharacteristic gleam in his eyes.

Irene smiled. "Good. Let's go to the library now so we don't make the others suspicious. I'll gift you a book if you want one, Isa."

"Thank you," I managed.

I handed the parchment to Dario, who carefully placed it inside his suit pocket.

My heartbeat echoed inside of my ears like a pounding war drum as we walked out of the room and through the hallways. We made our way back into the main room, which was just as crowded as it had been when we had arrived. Dario and I followed Irene toward the stairs and slowly began climbing them.

"Feel free to stay in the library a bit longer if you want," Irene said when we were halfway up the staircase. "Just make sure you're back in the ballroom before midnight. You won't want to miss what will happen then." The smile she flashed made my blood chill.

What if they were planning to kill one of the gods at midnight? Was that why so many lower-generations had been invited? If they killed Dionysus in front of the ruling covens, it would incite a war. But that would expose the half-bloods in other covens who were planning to kill their gods, so they would lose the element of surprise. And what about the competition? Had someone already won? Dionysus's coven seemed to have figured out the right verses.

I glanced back at Dario, at that terrifying coldness in his normally warm gaze. Was he actually considering killing Helios? I didn't know if he hated his old coven enough to end their lives. And what would Lucian do once he realized the truth behind the murders? Would he protect the gods and fight on their side, or would he be the one who helped bring their downfall?

What would I do? This wasn't just a murder case anymore. I wasn't just protecting the lives of humans who had been brutally murdered. This was a war between creatures powerful enough to destroy the world.

Before my mind could continue spinning with questions, a ripple of silence slashed through the main room. We stopped at the top of the staircase and turned just as Lucian and Sue walked hand in hand into the party.

Sue wore a marine-blue velvet dress that held her waist tightly before falling loosely below her knees. It curled like ocean waves as she walked with her chin raised high. Lucian looked dashing in an impeccably tailored suit. It was a few shades darker than Sue's dress, the color of the sky right before it turns black with night. His dark hair was combed back, and his gray eyes seemed to sparkle like two diamonds. Sue held on tightly to Lucian's hand as they slowly cut through the room with the crowd parting to let them pass.

My chest burned at the sight of him and in a wave of clashing emotions. I wanted to be in his arms again, away from the castle and safe. But the idea that we could just come into the party to gather information and then leave seemed like a fading dream now. One way or another, midnight would turn into a bloodbath.

I mentally willed Lucian to turn to look at me and Dario and notice my panic so he could realize that there was something wrong, but he didn't even spare us a glance. Expressions of fear, surprise, anger, and curiosity mingled among the other invitees as Lucian passed by them.

"You invited Holt?" Dario asked in a surprised tone.

"Yes," Irene said with a smile. "He's one of our special guests tonight. I was wondering when he would show up."

24

MY HEART SANK into my chest, and I exchanged a quick glance with Dario.

"Well, come on," Irene said as she turned back. "Let me show you the library."

Dario and I had no choice but to follow her up the stairs. I really hoped Sue had been listening to what Irene had said. How had Irene known Lucian would come? Had someone left the invitations at the murder scenes to lead him here? But why would they invite Lucian if he could expose the murders and put a stop to them?

The voices died down as we wove through the hallways until we arrived at a grand set of double doors.

"Here we are," Irene said. She pushed on the door, but it didn't budge. "Hmm," she said and tried again. The door squeaked, but it didn't give way. "The library isn't usually closed. Maybe one of my siblings locked it to avoid any guests wandering into it to look for the Book of the Dead." She turned back to us. "I apologize for that. But feel free to come back any time to visit."

"Sure," I said.

We walked back to the staircase, but Irene's expression seemed troubled—her brows knitted tightly together and her lips pressed into a thin line. She didn't talk to us again as she quickly descended the staircase and became lost in the crowd.

Dario led me back to the ballroom and cut through the crowd to get to the Helios Coven. They were staring at Lucian as if he were a wild tiger on the loose. Up on the stage, Dionysus didn't seem to have noticed the shift in everyone's mood, and he laughed with a young girl who stood leaning against his throne. The rest of his coven had gathered around him, and they were eyeing Lucian with open curiosity. Ernesto's eyes snapped to Dario as we walked closer to them.

"We're leaving right after midnight," Ernesto whispered in a hushed tone.

Dario glanced at his watch. Midnight was less than fifteen minutes away.

"You should come with us," Ernesto said.

Dario's gaze bounced around the room, and he pressed his lips into a thin line. I glanced back at Lucian and Sue. They were talking to a lower-generation couple.

"Dario," Estelle said, pulling his attention back to her. "Are you coming with us after the party?"

"It's fine if you're not ready to come back to Italy," Ernesto said, "but we want you to stay a bit longer so we can talk. We can send Isa back to California."

Dario tightened his grip on my hand. I could see the debate within his eyes—a war was brewing, and he was trying to decide which side he was on. Lucian and Sue weren't here so he could make a plan with them. Dario had to make a choice for himself.

"I'm not joining the Coven of the Sun again," Dario said. "Ever."

Rufus glared at Dario, Estelle's shoulders slumped, and Bruno tensed. But Ernesto didn't seem surprised because his expression remained calm.

"You let my wife die without me," Dario said. "And you let Beatrice abuse me for decades." He seemed taller now, his eyes burning like the sun. "I can't forgive you for that."

"This is not the time and place to discuss this," Rufus hissed.

"This is the perfect time, actually," Dario said in an angry whisper. "I won't rejoin your coven." He took a deep breath. "But I also don't think you all deserve to die."

"What are you talking about?" Ernesto's brows furrowed together.

Bruno balled his palms into fists.

Dario leaned closer. "We're all in danger, and unless we act right now, Helios's coven will fall."

So Dario was going to help his old coven. Despite everything they had done to him and all the suffering they had put him through, he wasn't going to make them pay for it. I gave his hand a gentle squeeze, hoping he would feel my support, small though it was. Dario was not a man consumed by revenge, which was something that couldn't be said for most people on the planet—vampires and humans alike. I admired him for that.

"What kind of danger are we talking about?" Ernesto asked.

Before Dario could say anything else, the ballroom door closed with a bang. It seemed like everyone at the party had gathered inside, and the ballroom was much fuller than it had been moments ago. Lower-generations kept their distance from us and from the other ruling covens, but they were pressed together in the remaining available space.

A voice boomed through the crowd: "Good evening, everyone. I hope you're enjoying the party." I didn't recognize the man who walked onto the stage. He had dark skin and curly black hair. Like the rest of his coven, his eyes shone red and purple. Behind him, Dionysus seemed surprised, and I assumed he had no idea what his coven had been up to. "Ariadne was supposed to give this speech, but it seems we have lost her somewhere. So my apologies for my terrible public speaking skills." A few chuckles echoed in the room. The man cleared his throat. "As promised, we have a very special announcement and surprise prepared for tonight." He paused, surveying the people in the room. "As you may have noticed, there are many more attendees this year. That was done for a purpose. Because every single half-blood here tonight shares something special."

249

Dario pushed me behind him as if he expected the room to blow up at any moment. The Sun Coven noticed, and all four of them took up defensive positions. Ernesto and Rufus stood next to Dario, and Estelle and Bruno stepped closer to me, blocking my sides protectively. Their eyes began to glow golden, and heat wrapped around me. I felt so utterly defenseless and powerless as I braced myself for what would come next.

"Tonight marks the beginning of—"

The ballroom door burst open. Ernesto's breath hitched when he turned toward the man standing at the entrance.

I immediately knew the man was a god.

He towered one head above everyone else. The white shirt under his black suit was unbuttoned at the top, revealing a muscular chest underneath. His midnight black hair seemed to glow as it reflected the golden light from the room. Shining like two emeralds, his eyes had a sharp edge to them that could draw blood with one stare.

"Happy birthday!" the god shouted to Dionysus as he spread his arms wide.

Someone near us said, *Loki*.

"Rafe!" Dionysus's voice rang through the silent room. "I haven't seen you in years."

Rafe smiled. Anyone would have noticed his smile wasn't human. It was too big, too wide, and with too many teeth, like the jaws of a crocodile about to snap someone in half. The god walked toward Dionysus's throne slowly, glancing left and right. It was like seeing a jaguar walk into a pen of sheep. At the other side of the room, Lucian and Sue had gone still, their eyes wide. Rafe ascended the stage, and the two gods embraced each other, completely ignoring the man who had been giving the speech.

Rafe pulled away from Dionysus.

"I'm so happy you came," Dionysus said. "The party is just getting started."

Rafe's smile widened even more, slashing across his face. "Actually . . ." He turned toward the crowd, and absolute silence filled the room as if the air itself were holding its breath. "I'm sorry to announce that this party is over."

A second of confusion rippled through the crowd. Then the room exploded with green light.

Screams drowned out the silence.

PART VI

THE
UNDERWORLD

25

WOLF'S HEART THUMPED in irregular beats, betraying his terror. He had been to the Underworld only once before, and the memories of that journey threatened to overwhelm him.

A body broken in pieces—Wolf inhaled.

A mouth torn open in a scream—he exhaled slowly.

Eyes devoid of life yet burning with revenge—Wolf continued to breathe deeply and vanquished the memories, locking them deep in his mind where he had kept them for the last few millennia.

Osiris's hand inside his pocket felt heavier, and Wolf could have sworn it was twitching. Even the *Aether* had quieted down inside of him as if it, too, had been paralyzed with fear. Death seemed to be hovering, waiting over them like a cloud. This was why he had brought Rafe, Wolf reminded himself. Rafe would take them through the Underworld and out of it.

The tunnels they walked through looked like the ragged intestines of a dark beast. Wolf could walk ten steps and move one yard or one mile because time thinned and stretched as if it were made of rubber, and space was no better. Gravity shifted around him, sometimes pulling him down and sometimes up or to the sides. Light came from the ground as the molten heat inside the center of the planet escaped through the cracks.

But Wolf barely paid any attention to their surroundings as his thoughts drifted back to the person he had seen at the party— the one person who shouldn't have been there. Wolf would have to make a new plan once they left the Underworld and be careful about it so no one could realize what he was up to.

Wolf tripped on something and nearly stumbled to his knees. Rafe spun around and caught his arm before he could fall. The cracks beneath their feet that bled with red light bathed Rafe's face in a sinister glow.

"You alright?" Rafe asked.

Wolf nodded but knew Rafe could sense his tumultuous emotions—the fear, rage, and sorrow that clashed with each beat of his heart and shredded his chest into ribbons. Wolf took a deep breath and tried to clear his mind. One thing at a time, he reminded himself. He needed to focus on finding Gabriel, then he could worry about the rest.

Wolf exhaled again, then nodded once more to Rafe, who let go of his arm. The two of them continued their journey in silence. After what felt like an interminable amount of time, they came upon a heavy metal door. Wolf glanced at Rafe, who slowly approached the door. It had no handle or knob—only pure iron blocked their way to what lay on the other side. Feeling the intense gaze of something watching him, Wolf nervously glanced over his shoulder. He couldn't spot anyone.

Rafe pressed his palm on the metal door. It shifted as if it had turned liquid. Figures began emerging from the surface, then dipped back into the depths of the door. One face remained above the surface at the same eye level as Wolf and Rafe. The figure watched them silently. Its eyes swirled like two silver whirlpools.

Then the figure spoke. The hairs on Wolf's neck prickled at the sound of ten people whispering at the same time. It wasn't a language that Wolf understood, which was rare since he had been around long enough to learn most of them. It must have been one of the death languages and beyond Wolf's power. Rafe responded, his voice a rough whisper compared to the silky-smooth voices of the figure. The two of them exchanged a few sentences, then the face disappeared below the surface. After a couple of seconds, the door swung inward.

Rafe pressed a finger to his lips, indicating to Wolf to be silent. The two men walked through the threshold. They moved through a black hallway lit by dark red torches. The stone walls had no windows, and Wolf didn't spot another door as Rafe led them deeper into Alec's house. He really hoped they wouldn't run into anyone.

The old death god had become very fragmented, making him a threat to any living creature, which was why he remained exiled in his underground castle and forbidden to return to the Upperworld. Gabriel had been the one to enforce the exile. Maybe Alec had murdered him and started the competition. He had forced all his immortal children to remain with him, so it wouldn't have surprised Wolf if they had joined his plan. They definitely had the power to weaken and kill Gabriel.

His wife Persephone was still allowed in the Upperworld though, and she constantly traveled between the two worlds with her own coven. In Wolf's opinion, she was far more dangerous than Alec. The dead liked her better, which meant she was the one who truly held their power. He hoped that she wasn't involved in Gabriel's murder.

After awhile, Rafe stopped and motioned at Wolf to do the same. Wolf's heart thundered in his ears. Rafe pressed his palm on the wall at their side and closed his eyes. The wall began to shift. Rafe's eyes moved under his eyelids while he made a silent incantation. The black wall vanished as if it had never been there. Rafe opened his eyes, and the two of them walked briskly down the new hallway until they reached a spiral staircase at the end. Rafe began stepping down, and Wolf followed him but eventually lost sight of Rafe.

Down and down they went. Even though Wolf was used to seeing clearly at night, they were surrounded by a blackness that threatened to bring out more of Wolf's buried memories. The *Aether* stirred, responding to his anxiety, but he suppressed it. His mind became muddled as they continued downward, the darkness pressing on him like a giant hand squeezing his body.

After what seemed like several eternities, they finally reached the bottom of the staircase. Wolf nearly stumbled onto his knees when he didn't find the next step, but Rafe held his arm to prevent him from falling to the ground. He wasn't sure if they were allowed to speak now, but just to be sure, he didn't thank Rafe out loud. The other man remained immobile, his hand still gripping Wolf's arm. It took Wolf a few seconds to notice the pale blue glow at the other end of the room. It was a halo of light surrounding a rectangle—a door, Wolf realized, with light spilling from its edges.

Wolf didn't need Rafe to tell him this was the Gate. The last time Wolf had been to the Underworld, he hadn't used this entrance, which was much less terrifying than the other one. Rafe pulled Wolf forward, and the two of them made their way to the Gate. It had seemed close, but after walking for over a minute, Wolf realized that wasn't the case. The glow had intensified to a blue-gray hue, and he could finally see Rafe again. His dark hair looked gray in the light. As they continued walking to the Gate, Wolf had to crane his neck to see the very top of it. The Gate wasn't solid, or at least it didn't seem solid. The blue-gray light shifted like mercury, making little swirls and ripples.

Even if Wolf had found a way to make it to the Gate on his own, he wouldn't have been able to cross through it. Only the dead and death gods were allowed on the other side. And Rafe. Even though he was not naturally a death god, Rafe's shape-shifting powers allowed him to be able to handle death magic, which was essentially a transformation from one life to the next.

Rafe took ahold of Wolf's hand, and Wolf felt Rafe's power flowing into him. It was like poison burning through his veins. Wolf bit back a grunt. His body tingled while going numb. He began to feel lightheaded as if his soul had detached slightly from his body. Rafe pulled Wolf through the Gate. One moment Wolf had been facing the light, then the next second, his feet were submerged in ice-cold water. Wolf hissed as the water bit into his ankles. They had arrived at one of the death rivers, but Wolf wasn't sure which one. Fear pounded through his body like a second heartbeat, and Wolf instinctively gripped Rafe's hand harder.

"It's alright," Rafe said in a playful tone as he squeezed back. "I won't let go."

Rafe's face had turned ashen gray, and when Wolf looked at his own hands, he realized his skin was the same color. Rafe pulled him forward as they waded through the water. Fog hovered right above the river, but never touched it, and surrounded them. The scene was just as Wolf remembered it—cold, barren, and depressing.

Wolf shivered.

A dark figure wearing a dark hood came into view. He stood on a little wooden barge.

"Charon," Rafe said. "How are you doing, old friend?"

They were at the River Styx, Wolf concluded.

Charon did not respond, his face hidden deep inside the hood so Wolf couldn't read his expression. Rafe jumped onto the little boat and pulled Wolf aboard. The raft wobbled underneath them. Charon stared silently at the men from the other end of the barge.

"Hey, look, we need a favor," Rafe said. "A good friend died and we need to visit him." Charon remained silent. "I brought a gift for you to take us there." Rafe dug into his pocket and pulled out a golden coin and a little jar filled with blood. Charon greedily snapped the jar from Rafe's hand and gulped down the blood. He threw the jar overboard, and it splashed into the river. He then plucked the coin from Rafe's fingers. Charon pulled an oar from the water and began paddling.

Wolf and Rafe sat down. The water sloshed at their sides as the little boat cut through the river. Wolf had never met Charon and had only heard about him from others. He knew Alec brought him fresh blood every now and then for Charon to retain his power.

Rafe began humming, but Wolf didn't recognize the tune. And although Rafe's grip never slackened, Wolf hated that the other man had so much power over him in the Underworld. If Rafe wanted to get rid of Wolf, all he had to do was let go of his hand. Doing so wouldn't kill Wolf, but it would make it a challenge to escape, and he didn't have the time to fight his way out. But even though Rafe liked to challenge him, Wolf didn't think he wanted to get rid of him—not yet at least.

The fog didn't reveal anything, and he wondered how wide the river was. The oar dove deeply into the water as Charon rowed.

After another immeasurable amount of time, Wolf spotted land in the distance—a little island with nothing but black sand. Rafe had closed his eyes but opened them when the fog cleared from the island as if he had sensed it. The little barge seemed to move faster as they neared the shore. Rafe stood, then jumped off the boat and onto the little island. Wolf did the same.

"Could you come back for us in a bit?" Rafe asked Charon.

Charon nodded, or at least Wolf thought he had nodded when he saw the hood bob slightly. Charon paddled away, the fog slowly consuming him.

"Did you bring the artifact?" Rafe asked.

Wolf nodded. He used his free hand to dig into his suit pocket and pulled out a golden ring. It was a plain golden band, the same one Gabriel had worn since marrying Hera thousands of years ago. He had never stopped wearing it, not even after Hera had left him to start her own coven. It was the only item that had been left behind after Gabriel's body had disintegrated into ashes.

At the very center of the tiny island, Wolf placed the ring on the ground. For a long moment, nothing changed. The air hung still around them, the fog immobile. Even the water remained unperturbed, reflecting the fog like a smoky mirror.

"It can take awhile," Rafe said after a couple of minutes had passed.

Wolf's heartbeat painfully throbbed against his chest. He knew he was still in time to see Gabriel's soul before it fully departed, but his anxiety still crawled through his gut.

Rafe squeezed his hand reassuringly. "Patience," he said.

More minutes ticked by, minutes that seemed to stretch even longer as Wolf's body continued to tingle with Rafe's power.

The golden ring began to tremble. It seemed as if a ghost was attempting to lift the ring but wasn't quite strong enough. Wolf tightened his grip on Rafe. One moment, the ring was quivering in the air, and the next second Gabriel was kneeling on the ground as he attempted to pick up the ring.

"Gabriel," Wolf said as he exhaled the breath he had been holding.

Gabriel looked up, then stood at his full height with the ring on his palm. He looked exactly as he had before his death. Gabriel's white hair was like silken strands of lightning, the same color as his neatly trimmed beard. His eyes were two silver orbs of thunderclouds. He had a big, long nose in his rectangular face that was edged with a sharp jawline. Gabriel stood half a head taller than Wolf and Rafe, but his back was hunched and made him look smaller.

"Wolf," Gabriel said. Even his voice had lost the rumbling power it had once held. "I don't know how I got here and haven't been able to leave this island. Every time I try, I end up right back here."

Wolf's breath hitched painfully, and he couldn't come up with a reply. Gabriel's eyes finally landed on Rafe.

"Why is he here?" Gabriel asked.

"I'm here to deliver some good and bad news to you," Rafe said. "The good news is that I'm here to help. And the bad news is that there's not much I can do to help because you're dead."

Gabriel blinked. "What?" He turned to Wolf as if he had misunderstood.

"You're dead, Gabriel." Wolf forced the words out of his lips, his throat tight. "Someone killed you."

"That's impossible," Gabriel said, shaking his head.

"Do you remember anything before you got here?" Wolf asked. "Do you remember what you were going to tell me when you called?" Wolf's heart pounded against his chest as if trying to break his rib cage into pieces.

Gabriel frowned, his bushy eyebrows drawing together. "I remember you came to see me a couple of weeks ago. You were looking for Osiris's leg, which I was assigned to guard, and you said someone had stolen his head."

Wolf tensed, all too aware that Rafe was listening carefully. Gabriel didn't continue, his frown burrowing into his skin like widening cracks.

"Who were you with before coming here?" Rafe asked.

Gabriel's gaze became distant, then he startled as if he had been electrocuted. "He said he was from the Twelfth Coven," Gabriel said.

"The Twelfth Coven?" Wolf asked.

"Do you remember who the god of that coven is?" Gabriel said.

Wolf opened his mouth to respond, then realized he didn't know the answer. Who was the ruling Athatos of the Twelfth Coven? He knew they existed, but they had kept to themselves for the last couple centuries or so. Still, he should have known who they were. It seemed strange that he couldn't recall that information and that it had seemed perfectly normal that he didn't remember. Wolf had perfect memory unless—

Horror tore through Wolf.

"I always did wonder why our memories became so foggy," Gabriel said. "It wasn't time that wore us down. It was the Twelfth

Coven. They were the ones who fragmented our minds so they could hide from us."

"That's impossible," Wolf whispered.

"How?" Rafe asked at the same time in a louder tone.

"Not sure," Gabriel said. "He acknowledged they used that power a century ago to erase themselves from our memories so they could hide while they discovered how to destroy our immortality. He also only referred to the ruler of the Twelfth Coven as the lost god." Gabriel shook his head slowly. "I don't know why he even revealed that much though."

Because he knew you wouldn't walk out of that conversation alive, Wolf thought.

"They must have been the ones to start the competition then," Rafe said.

"What competition?" Gabriel asked.

Rafe explained what he and Wolf had discovered in the last few days, while in stunned silence, Wolf tried to piece together what Gabriel had just told him. Something was wrong. Very wrong. Wolf knew with absolute certainty that it hadn't been the Twelfth Coven who had fragmented the minds of the Athatos. But then, how could he explain that he remembered nothing about them and that it had seemed perfectly normal until now?

"Do you remember if he attacked you?" Rafe asked.

Wolf pulled out of his thoughts, and noted Rafe hadn't said the word kill.

"Yes he . . ." Gabriel trailed off again, lost in his memories. Rafe's grip on Wolf's hand tightened. Gabriel cocked his head to one side.

"Do you remember?" Wolf said.

"I do, it's just . . ." Gabriel scratched his beard. "It doesn't make sense."

"It doesn't have to make sense," Rafe said.

"He . . . just . . . seemed to absorb my power," Gabriel said.

Wolf looked at Rafe who looked back at him as if he was just as confused as Wolf was.

"I threw a thunderbolt at him," Gabriel continued, "but he seemed to suck it into himself and then threw the bolt back at me. That had never happened before. Not even my own children can absorb my power."

Those words pierced Wolf's mind like a lance, and everything fell into place.

"The Twelfth Coven can mirror our powers," Wolf said.

"It seemed like that, yes," Gabriel said. "He never used any of his power, but instead reflected mine whenever I attacked."

So that's how they had overpowered and killed Gabriel, Wolf thought. They had used his own power against him.

Wolf's muscles cramped with terror.

"It's brilliant," Rafe muttered. "If they can absorb and deflect our powers, then they can infiltrate anyone's coven and have as much power as any Athatos." He turned to Wolf. "The Twelfth Coven must have infiltrated Dionysus's coven."

Wolf nodded. He wondered if all of Dionysus's coven was in on this or just certain people who were from the Twelfth Coven. But who could be the ruler of the Twelfth Coven with the power to do this?

Rafe scratched his cheek with his free hand. "If they can only absorb and deflect our powers, then how did they fragment our minds?" he asked. "Whose power did they mirror for that?"

"I . . . I don't know," Gabriel said. He released a long breath. "We need to get out of here so we can stop them."

Wolf exchanged a look with Rafe.

"You can't," Wolf said.

"Why not?" Gabriel asked.

"You're dead," Wolf said. "They killed you."

"No. They couldn't have. I . . ." Gabriel trailed off. "Can't you get me out of here? I can't—this can't be my end. There must be something we can do to take me back."

"I'm afraid there's nothing we can do, brother," a dark voice said. Wolf whipped around to find Alec standing right behind them. Alec wore black pants but didn't have a shirt. His muscled chest was like a sculpted piece of marble. A black veil covered Alec's face completely. After one of his fragmentations, Alec's powers had also cracked, so anyone who stared directly into his eyes would instantly drop dead. He couldn't harm any of the other Athatos, or his own children, but Wolf knew he preferred to cover his eyes just in case. It wasn't like the death stare of Morrigan's children, who were only capable of killing someone who had killed another person. And their power only worked during a battle. But Alec could kill anyone, anytime—all he had to do was look into their eyes.

"Alec," Rafe squeaked. "I hope you don't mind we let ourselves in."

"You could have knocked," Alec said.

"We didn't know if we could trust you," Wolf said.

"Fair," Alec responded.

"Did you know about this?" Rafe said, motioning to Gabriel.

"No," Alec said. "I didn't see him here until I followed you two fools." He turned to Gabriel. "If what you say is true and it's the Twelfth Coven who fragmented our minds, who can absorb any of our powers when we use them, and who have now found a way to destroy our immortality, then we must kill all of them."

"There has to be a way to bring me back so I can help," Gabriel said. "I can't stay here forever." His eyes rippled, and Wolf felt profound horror, which made his gut squirm.

"There is no way that I know of," Alec said.

Gabriel's eyes pulsated as if pleading with them. "Where will my soul go? Will I remain here?" he asked, his voice cracking like glass. "Where did Osiris go when he died before we discovered how to attain full immortality?"

"I . . . do not know," Alec admitted.

But Wolf knew.

Death was different for the Athatos than for all other mortal creatures and half-bloods. The Athatos had cheated Death for millennia, and Death wasn't happy about it—Death had created a special place in the Underworld for them, one not even Alec knew of. Wolf became dizzy and had the sudden urge to throw up as memories of that place threatened to surface from his mind. He pushed them away. He wasn't dead. He would do everything in his power to avoid ever going there.

"There has to be something you can do to help me," Gabriel pleaded with Alec. "You rule this place."

"Death is beyond my rule," Alec said. "I'm merely the one who keeps order here."

Wolf had never seen Gabriel so defeated. Wrinkles spread through his face, and his hair thinned. He didn't have much time left.

"If I don't find a way out of here, could you do me a favor?" Gabriel asked, turning to Wolf.

Wolf nodded. Gabriel handed him the golden ring.

"Tell her I always loved her," Gabriel said, "and that I wish we'd had more time together because no amount of time would have ever been enough." Gabriel exhaled, his chest deflating. His cheeks began to hollow as if an invisible vacuum were sucking him out of this world slowly. "Also tell her that I hope she's happy, and that I'm proud of how she has led her coven and ruled over others."

"I'll tell her," Wolf said, his throat so tight he barely managed to get the words out.

"Do you think she knew I would die?" Gabriel asked.

"No," Wolf said. "The Twelfth Coven probably mirrored her power to hide the future from her so she couldn't intervene."

But Hera must have known something bad was happening, Wolf thought. She hadn't sent her coven to the party, and he wondered if she knew about the Twelfth Coven.

"Will I ever see any of you again?" Gabriel asked.

"I do not know," Alec said.

Grief pounced on Wolf's heart. He had never been close to Gabriel, but seeing his dying soul made Wolf's eyes sting with tears. Gabriel had been their king and one of the most powerful Athatos. This is what Death had done to him—reduced him to nothing more than a frail spirit.

"Maybe it isn't all that bad," Alec said. "Maybe you'll like the next world."

Wolf knew that he wouldn't. Only suffering awaited the Athatos on the other side.

Gabriel nodded with that hope to cling to. "I suppose this is goodbye then."

"Not yet," Rafe said. "You still haven't told us who killed you. There's nothing we can do to bring you back to life, but trust me when I say that I'll make hell look tame when I find whoever did this to you."

"I would enjoy bringing hell to the Upperworld," Alec said. He turned to Gabriel. "I would like my exile to be terminated, and I know my children would also enjoy seeing the sun again."

"Can you trust them?" Wolf asked Alec. "How do you know they won't turn on you?"

"Don't they resent you for forbidding them from leaving the Underworld?" Rafe said.

"I never did such a thing," Alec said. "They all chose to stay with me. If they wanted to leave, or to kill me, they could have done so."

"I officially terminate your exile," Gabriel said.

The air shifted slightly around them. So Gabriel hadn't lost all of his power, Wolf thought.

"Fantastic." Rafe smiled.

Wolf, Rafe, and Alec turned back to Gabriel.

"Give us a name," Wolf said. "Who was the last person you saw before you died?"

They waited in silence. Gabriel jolted again and bared his fangs, his eyes roiling. Wolf's grip tightened on Rafe's hand, and Rafe almost crushed his fingers.

"Lucian Holt," Gabriel said like a clap of thunder.

26

"ISA!" DARIO'S VOICE rose above the screams of all the others in Dionysus's ballroom as blinding green light enveloped the room. Dario pressed against me, and my back hit the wall. The light dimmed after a moment. I peeked behind Dario's shoulders. Terror flowed through me like a tidal wave.

Rafe's body twisted at unnatural angles and expanded like a butterfly breaking out of a cocoon. Tendrils of green lightning twisted around him. Rafe's head reached the ceiling, his body ten times the size it had been before. Black scales grew on his skin, gleaming green as they reflected the light. His fingers elongated into deadly sharp claws, and wings sprouted from his back, blocking Dionysus's throne from view. Horns grew from his head like an obsidian crown. Rafe opened his eyes, revealing emerald storms within them. The dragon's roar shook the room like an earthquake.

Vines curled toward the dragon and around his legs. Ribbons of red-purple light glimmered around the children of Dionysus as they extended their hands toward the vines. They had gathered at the center of the room and formed a tight cluster.

The dragon laughed as the vines tightened on him. "You truly forgot why people once used to call us gods, didn't you?" He inhaled sharply, then exhaled a large column of green fire that devoured Dionysus's children.

"No!" Dionysus cried from somewhere behind the dragon.

A scream burst out from the right. I turned just as someone slashed a woman's throat with a knife. My mind processed everything slowly as if I were watching the scene in slow motion. The woman's rich brown skin and yellow dress stained with red blood surging from her neck.

A blinding lance of lightning struck the man with the knife, sending him off his feet and flying into the air. He crashed through the wall on the opposite side of the room above the main entrance. Coils of lightning twisted around Lucian's hands as he bared his fangs and stood in front of Sue.

Three others gathered around the fallen woman, their faces slack as they tried to stop the bleeding. One of the men roared. The ground trembled. Chandeliers swayed above us. The floor cleaved in half, creating a deep gash in the middle of the room that fell into darkness. People scurried away from the edge as chunks started falling into the void. Others had begun rushing out of the room while screaming. The dragon looked at the widening crack and cocked his head to one side.

"Loki!" Dionysus yelled.

The dragon picked up the little god and held him tightly. Green fire shot from Loki's mouth as he burned the ceiling. He launched himself from the ground and broke through the roof with a crash that sent charred pieces of the ceiling raining down on the ballroom. The dragon's roar filled the air once more.

Dario pushed me through a hole that had been burnt through the wall. I forced my feet to move as we ran down a hallway with the Helios coven. The screams faded in the distance.

"What the hell is happening?" Rufus asked.

"Let's just get out of here," Ernesto said.

Three of Dionysus's remaining children rounded the corner and blocked our path. A tall man stood in the middle, his eyes swirling in a red-violet storm. He menacingly bared his fangs.

"Otto," Ernesto said. "What are you doing?"

Otto smiled.

Ernesto inhaled sharply. His eyes were tinged purple at the edges. He bared his fangs and growled, but the purple kept drowning out the gold in his irises.

"Let go of his mind, Otto," Rufus growled.

Ernesto turned to Rufus and Bruno, a deadly glint in his now fully red-purple eyes.

"Otto?" Estelle gasped as her eyes widened.

Ernesto growled at Rufus, his eyes swirling with a violet haze.

"Stop this right now, Otto, or I'll rip you apart," Bruno hissed.

Dario stood frozen in front of me, watching Ernesto advance toward the rest of his family.

The temperature abruptly dropped ten degrees. My breath caught in my throat as the cold slapped me like an iron hand. A man over seven feet tall appeared at the end of the hallway behind Dionysus's children. His skin stretched too tightly over his bones like a rubber mask about to rip. The man only wore dark pants and held a black veil in his hand. Where his eyes should have been were two black voids that seemed ready to suck me inside of them. He met my stare, and something inside of my chest burned.

"Close your eyes," Bruno shouted.

The god ripped his gaze from me just as the children of Dionysus turned toward him. They barely managed to open their mouths before they dropped to the floor like stalks of wheat cut by a scythe. Ernesto stumbled forward, and I turned my attention back to him as he fell on his knees.

"What?" he mumbled as the red-purple haze vanished from his irises.

"Close your eyes!" Bruno repeated.

I closed my eyes so tightly that my eyelids began to tremble.

"Children of Helios," the god said. His voice seemed to come from the depths of the earth, rumbling like an earthquake attempting to form words. "Are you with or against the gods?"

"What?" Ernesto said again.

"What are you talking about, Hades?" Rufus said.

"Hmm," Hades said. My bones vibrated with the strength of his voice. Even though I wasn't looking, I could tell he had moved to stand in front of me. His presence was overwhelming, a rippling vibration radiating out of his body in waves.

I whimpered as one of his cold fingers slid down my cheek. He held my chin, his nails digging painfully into my flesh. Then he let go, and his presence diminished.

"You can open your eyes now," Dario said.

I opened them, my body shaking. Even though the temperature in the room had returned to normal, my chest felt encased in ice.

"You didn't look into his eyes, did you?" Dario asked me.

"If she had, she would be dead," Bruno said.

"What's Hades doing here?" Estelle asked as she clung to Rufus. "Wasn't he exiled?"

No one responded.

We turned back to the children of Dionysus, who now lay immobile on the floor. Their eyes had become milky white as if bleached. Otto had fallen at a twisted angle, one of his arms folded underneath him.

"Why would they turn on us?" Bruno asked.

"Because you're loyal to Helios," someone said behind us.

It was the woman from Morrigan's coven we had met earlier. She held a large sword in her hand—it dripped blood.

Ernesto growled, his eyes blazing.

"What does that have to do with anything?" Rufus asked.

"The lower-generations have started a rebellion to overthrow the gods and the twelve ruling covens," she said. "We found traitors in our coven who tried to kill the rest of us. All of Dionysus's children betrayed him except for two of them, and about half of the Anubis Coven has turned on the others." Drops of blood had splattered onto the floor into a small puddle. "The rebels claim they have found a way to kill the Athatos."

"That's impossible, Maeve," Ernesto said. "The gods can't be killed."

"Impossible or not, they've started a war," Maeve said.

"Shit," Rufus said.

I wondered how she had discovered all that information so quickly. Or had she known about this before?

"Helios might be the only coven that's still intact," Maeve said. She glanced at Dario, and the others did too. A rumble escaped from Bruno's lips.

Dario paled. "I never planned on killing Helios."

"The timing of your return indicates otherwise," Rufus said with a growl.

Ernesto's eyes burned. The ground shook slightly under our feet. And somewhere in the distance, the dragon roared.

"Why did you come to the party tonight?" Ernesto asked, his tone brutally calm.

"I'm helping Lucian Holt solve a murder case," Dario said.

Rufus and Estelle exchanged a glance. Ernesto narrowed his eyes.

"I've been living with Lucian Holt and Sue Lee since I left you," Dario continued. "Recently, there were a series of murders in San Francisco and then all over the United States. The killers were half-bloods who were carving ancient Greek, Latin, and Egyptian texts into the victim's skins. Lucian was investigating the murders. We found Dionysus's invitation at a couple of the crime scenes, so we knew the killers would be gathering here for something. We came to investigate. Irene told Isa and me that they were killing humans to practice how to kill the gods by using spells from the Book of the Dead. I was trying to warn you when it all went down."

A second of silence burned through the room.

Ernesto slowly turned to me. "Is what Dario said true, Isa?"

"Yes," I said. "Lucian hired me a few days ago to help him solve the murders because I'm a translator."

"So you and Dario aren't dating?" Rufus asked.

"No," I said.

Ernesto glanced at Dario, who shrugged.

"Lucian Holt is insane," Bruno muttered.

"He's saner than any of you," Dario said.

Rufus snorted.

"So Holt is not fighting for the rebels?" Maeve asked.

"No," Dario said. "He wouldn't join anyone who murders innocent humans."

Bruno growled at Dario and bared his fangs.

"I'm not one of the rebels," Dario insisted. "Why do you think I warned you we were in danger?"

"I believe you, Dario." Ernesto said.

"I don't," Bruno said.

"I do," Rufus said. "This Lucian Holt story is so crazy he couldn't have made it up."

"What if he and Holt are both rebels trying to infiltrate our coven?" Bruno said.

The castle shook again. The lights flickered.

"I believe you, too, Dario," Maeve said. "But don't make me regret that. One move against us, and I'll cut you in half."

Dario nodded.

"We need to fight together," Maeve said, her gaze sliding to Ernesto. "Even if we're more powerful than the lower-generations, they outnumber us, and some of our own have betrayed us. We're at a disadvantage."

Ernesto nodded. "I agree. They've taken us by surprise, but we need to fight back in a united front."

Maeve smiled. "Alright. Let's move."

If I had felt useless before, then I felt even more useless now. There was absolutely nothing I could do to help. I was just a bystander watching the chaos unfold around me. It had been a mistake for me to come. I had thought that I could handle it— that I could walk into a world of beings a hundred times more powerful than I and outsmart them to help Lucian. But there was nothing I could do to help win this war.

"Isa." Ernesto's voice pulled me out of my thoughts. "You'll be alright. We'll get you out of here."

I nodded numbly. Dario took my hand, and his warmth spread through me. He nodded, and I nodded back. His eyes turned golden, and so did the eyes of the others in the Helios Coven. Ernesto was the most terrifying—a glare from him could have seared someone to ashes. Maeve's eyes swirled gray like liquid iron.

Ernesto led the way down the hallway past the three corpses Hades had left in his wake. We had just rounded the corner when a roar split through the air. A dark shape lunged from the shadows at Ernesto, knocking him flat on the floor. The being had the head of a black jackal and the body of a man, and it fell on top of Ernesto. Dark tendrils curled out of the beast's sides like extra limbs. Ernesto pushed the creature away with tremendous force. A stone wall cracked as the jackal's back smashed against it, and the tendrils vanished in a blink. The beast fell to its knees but was quickly on its feet again.

As Ernesto struggled into a sitting position, a thick ray of golden fire burst from his palm. The jackal roared as the fire hit its face and seared its skin into a bloody, charred mass. It tumbled backward. The jackal's howls were cut short when golden light burst from Rufus's hand and pierced the creature's chest. It crumpled to the floor with a smoking hole in its torso.

Bruno held out a hand to Ernesto and pulled him back to his feet.

"Behind you," Dario shouted at Maeve.

She swung her sword just as a woman stepped out of the shadows in the corridor. Maeve's sword slashed through her chest a second before Bruno's fire singed the left side of her body and consumed it in angry flames. She dropped with a loud thud, her body unmoving and burning brightly.

Dario pulled me forward and we started running through the hallways. Screams, roars, and howls occasionally echoed back to us. After a minute, a string of voices grew louder ahead of us. Maeve and Ernesto took up defensive positions at the front as we rounded the hallway.

"Oh gods," Maeve said as she kneeled.

A young girl sat against the wall, holding a bloodied hand over her abdomen. A man with silver-white hair kneeled next to her.

"Move your hand," he said.

The girl let her hand drop limply to her side. The man placed his palm over the gaping wound. I noted the white ring on his left pinky finger. The man's eyes rolled back into his head, and they began to shine with blue-white light. Ernesto and Rufus guarded our sides as the rest of us stood watching. Bright silver light poured out of the man's hand. The girl whimpered, but the blood that had stained her dress disappeared as if it had been reabsorbed by her skin. The man pulled his hand away and blinked a few times until his eyes returned to normal again.

"Who hurt you?" Maeve asked. She gently placed a hand on the girl's shoulder.

"Someone from my coven," the man answered bitterly as he stood again.

"Who?" Maeve asked again.

"Eli," the man responded.

"We really can't trust anyone, can we?" Estelle asked.

"Let's keep moving," Ernesto said. "We need to get out of this castle."

"I don't think it's much better out there," the man said as he stood up, then helped the girl stand too.

The two of them joined us as Ernesto and Maeve led us through more hallways. The castle felt interminable. Whenever I thought an exit would be around the corner, we simply found another dark corridor. The cracked stone floor, washed-out walls, and splintered wooden doors seemed to belong to a different castle than the one I had seen during the party.

We had been walking for about five minutes when the castle shook, sending us all tumbling down. Dario helped me to my feet. He pulled me to the right before the floor fell into a dark pit. A large gash cut through the ground, separating me and Dario from everyone else. It began widening, consuming bits and pieces of the floor and swallowing them.

"Run," Ernesto shouted from the other side.

I didn't get to see what the others did as Dario and I sprinted away. I stumbled as the ground shook with a roaring rumble, but Dario held my arm and pulled me forward. Walls cracked and small pieces of stone drizzled from the ceiling. I hissed as one piece fell sharply on my head. I glanced back and my heart nearly lurched out of my chest. The ground continued to fall into the darkness, the gash racing toward us. At the end of the hallway, we had to turn left. The nearby wall crumbled, gobbled up by the gaping void. Dario pushed open a door on the right and pulled me into a room. We rushed to the far end.

The shaking stopped. Abrupt silence settled around us, interrupted only by my ragged breaths. A flickering lamp on the ceiling pulsed as erratically as my own heartbeat. Dario slowly stepped toward the door, and I did too. A few inches past the threshold, the floor dropped steeply into darkness. The dust was so heavy in the air it obscured our surroundings like gray fog. But I was still able to make out the doors and sections of walls that clung precariously to the ceiling and hovered over the void.

A dim gray light glimmered ahead of us. Dario pushed me behind him. I peeked around his shoulder as the long light floated toward us. Only when it was ten yards away was I able to discern a translucent face.

"A ghost," Dario whispered.

The ghost's neck was broken, its head bent to the left. Its mouth was open in a terrible, silent scream as its hollow white eyes stared at us. The rest of the ghost's body swirled like glowing gray mist. It stared at us for a few moments, then turned to the side and began drifting away until it vanished in the dust.

"Hades must have summoned it," Dario said as we stepped away from the void and back into the room.

"Can it hurt us?" I asked.

"Maybe," Dario said. "Let's not find out though."

A closed door on the opposite side seemed like our only way out. We began walking toward it, but the light above us extinguished. Something shifted at the edge of my vision. An orb of golden light burst from Dario's palm and cast the shadows away, but it was too late. A man with flowing dark hair had already used the shadows to step into the room. I hid behind Dario, feeling useless again.

"I'm disappointed in you, Dario," the man said. "Why are you fighting for the gods when they were the ones who took everything from you?"

The light hovering on Dario's palm intensified, heating up the room.

"Their time is over," the man said. "Now it's our turn to rule."

Dario roared. Shadows curled out of the man, then shot toward Dario and wrapped around him like ribbons of fog. The room went pitch-black, then light glowed inside the darkness like golden lightning forking through black clouds. It burned through the shadows, making them evaporate. The man screamed as Dario extended his hand in front of him, and a ray of light shot from his palm and into the man. His suit on fire, the man bellowed. Dario stepped forward and pushed the man with such force that he was thrown beyond the door and disappeared into the void.

Dario breathed raggedly as I tentatively stepped toward him. He whipped around, his eyes burning. The golden glare disappeared, replaced by a familiar amber as his gaze met my own. A small orb floated above his palm to light the room again.

"Are you alright?" he asked.

I nodded.

"Good," he said. "Let's keep moving."

He opened the door on the far side of the room. Our footsteps echoed off the smooth walls that rose into a curved ceiling. We stopped briefly to glance at the bare room when someone else stepped inside. Dario's light intensified, revealing a woman who had come from a side corridor. Her hands and mouth dripped with blood.

"Hello, Dario." She smiled, her teeth red. "We really hoped you would join us. It's a terrible waste that you haven't, considering how powerful you are."

Dario tensed as the woman took a step closer.

"We know you have a secret, Dario," she continued. "Helios would have never let you walk away unless he was afraid of you." She cocked her head to the side. "What makes a god afraid?"

Dario held the orb of light with both hands. The orb expanded, and loose filaments of light churned between his palms. Dario screamed and spread his arms. Golden fire burst from the orb and raged forward like an avalanche of flames. I expected the woman to burn instantly. Instead, the fire flowed into her as if she had absorbed it like a black hole. The room plunged into darkness. It lit up again when two orbs of light hovered on the woman's palms. She smiled as her eyes shone gold.

27

"WHAT THE HELL?" Dario whispered as he looked at the woman who had just absorbed his fiery attack.

The woman smiled devilishly, but she wasn't looking at Dario—she was glaring at me.

"No!" Dario shouted.

The woman threw a roiling wave of flames toward us. Dario extended his hands to try to stop it. I turned away, shielding my face. My heartbeat roared inside of my ears, thumping furiously as if I could survive by sheer force of will. I expected the heat to envelop me at any moment.

It never did.

I turned back. Dario stood in front of me, his hands still outstretched. The woman's smile had disappeared and was replaced by a frown. She glared in our direction, her eyes a normal shade of brown again.

"How did you do it?" she demanded.

A golden orb of light flared over Dario's hand again, but he hesitated.

"Come on," the woman said as a smile danced back into her lips. She lunged forward, and Dario threw the fire like a cannonball. The woman caught it with her hand. Threads of fire twisted around her arm like squirming worms of light. Dario and I backed away.

"What is she doing?" I asked.

"I don't know," Dario said.

Something crashed close by, but the woman's gaze never broke away from us. Her eyes began to glow a dark shade of gold once more. The air crackled around us, and wind swept at my hair.

The wall behind the woman crumbled down with a burst. Lucian walked out of the hole, his eyes shining as electricity twisted around his hands.

"Wait, no!" Dario shouted, but Lucian had already shot a bolt of electricity toward the woman with a deafening blast. The electricity sizzled toward her, and the woman caught it with her free hand.

She smiled, then shot the golden fire toward Lucian and the bolt of electricity toward Dario.

"No!" he shouted.

Everything moved slowly as if time had slowed into a crawl. Lucian lurched to the side to avoid the lance of fire, and Dario shielded us both with his body as lightning shot toward us like a ragged arrow.

Before the bolt could hit Dario, it turned back sharply as if it had bounced off a mirror. The same happened with the ray of fire that soared toward Lucian, and the flames leaped back toward the woman. She didn't even manage a scream before thunder and fire charred her into ashes.

Lucian stood immobile watching the woman's remains with a cold expression as Dario and I breathed heavily.

"Where's Sue?" Dario asked.

"Outside," Lucian said. He walked toward us and placed a hand on my cheek. The heat of his touch traveled through my body. "Are you alright?" he asked, his long fangs protruding dangerously from his mouth. His eyes searched into my own as his other palm enveloped my hand.

I threaded my fingers through his. "I'm alright," I said.

Lucian searched my face again, but finally nodded. He turned to Dario, who looked intently at our locked hands. Dario quickly glanced away.

"This isn't just a murder case," Dario said.

"I figured," Lucian said.

"They're planning to take away the immortality of the gods and kill them. They were practicing with the human victims," Dario continued. "Did they tell you about that? Did they try to recruit you for the rebellion? Irene said she was expecting you here."

Lucian frowned. "Some of the half-bloods we spoke to seemed to be expecting me here, too, which I found strange. But no one mentioned anything about killing the gods. Did they try to recruit you?"

Dario nodded. "And I chose to not help them."

The ground trembled slightly beneath us. Lucian's grip on my hand tightened. "Good," he said. "Now let's get out of here."

"What about the killers?" Dario asked.

"I'll make them pay for what they've done," Lucian said. "But now is not the time."

"And what about this rebellion?" Dario said. "Half-bloods are picking sides."

Lucian didn't respond right away. He looked at the woman's charred body. "I suppose I've already chosen my side."

Following Lucian's gaze, Dario nodded slowly. "Have you ever seen that type of power before?" Dario asked as we began to walk toward the hole on the wall.

"No," Lucian said. "But whatever she had intended clearly backfired."

"I worry about the next time when it doesn't," Dario said.

"You think there's more like her?" I asked.

"Maybe," Dario said.

Lucian didn't respond, his eyes set ahead. The next few hallways were marred with cracks on the walls and ceilings, and the floors were littered with broken objects. We finally arrived at a large door. Lucian raised his free hand and extended it toward the door. It exploded outward from a bolt of lightning. Lucian let go of my hand as we stepped outside. Screams echoed through the night. My heart galloped wildly as I took in the scene before us, the battle bathed in an eerie glow from the castle's remaining lights and the bright glow of the moon.

Twisted shadows swirled around a vampire. He flicked his hand, and a long, sharp shadow pierced another half-blood through the chest like a sword thrust. With a sweeping motion, he directed another shadow to cleave a woman in half. She quickly sidestepped, narrowly avoiding the lethal strike. The earth beneath him shifted and began to swallow him as if quicksand had appeared below his feet. The shadow that had impaled the other half-blood vanished, and the dead man fell limply on the ground. The shadowy half-blood shouted, trying to claw his way out of the ground, but the earth consumed him whole. The woman kneeled at the dead man's side and cried.

Maeve fought before us, moving with frightening speed. The sword seemed weightless in her hand and cut through bodies as if they were made of gelatin. Her eyes swirled gray, releasing a dim flash of light every time enemies came too close. That light seemed to kill them immediately as if she could deliver death with one stare.

The children of Prithvi were scattered throughout the battlefield, their eyes glowing a deep brown. No one ever managed to get close to them. Roots sprung up from the earth and tore vampires to pieces. The ground cracked open and devoured bodies before closing again like a gaping wound stitched together.

Further away, a man and a woman stood back-to-back, their palms spread before them as their eyes glowed blue-green. They had rings, but I didn't know what coven they belonged to. Three vampires holding knives converged on the couple. The woman squeezed her fist, and a vampire fell to his knees gasping for air before Maeve rushed over and cut off his head with her sword. The man flipped his wrist, and a powerful wind sent the two other vampires flying off their feet and crashing into the castle walls.

Lucian watched the battle but made no move to join in.

Then the sun appeared above us as if we had stepped into a summer day. I shielded my eyes from the brightness. Screams erupted around me, and only when the heat lessened and light dimmed did I dare to open my eyes.

Ernesto floated ten feet above us, hovering inside an orb of red and golden light. Bodies had been charred and burned beyond recognition, and grapevines had crumbled into piles of ash. But the vampires fighting on our side, or at least the ones I assumed were on our side, were all unharmed.

Ernesto's burning glare settled behind me, and I turned to see a group of at least a dozen vampires running away from the battle. Ernesto flew to them, passing right above my head with a wave of heat. When he got to them, he stopped, extended his arms in front of him, and screamed. As if bursting from a dam, a stream of golden fire erupted from his hands and blazed like a hungry beast eager to devour. The flames quickly drowned the group in flames. Ernesto let his arms drop at his sides, and the fire died down.

A roar tore through the night. From out of the ground, a wave of darkness surged and crashed into Ernesto, making him fall from the sky. The darkness re-formed into a fifteen-foot-tall figure with the head of a jackal and the body of a man.

My ears rang as two swords clanged against each other. Close to where Ernesto had fallen, Maeve fought someone from her own coven, a tall man with long, fiery red hair. Someone growled to our left, and I turned just as a woman lunged toward us. Dario extended his hand and shot out a ray of fire that set her entire body in flames before she could reach us. Shouts, screams, and growls erupted around us once more as the fight continued. The hulking black jackal stepped closer to Ernesto, who struggled onto his knees with a cough.

Lucian roared, drowning out every other sound.

The air quivered.

Lucian extended his hand and a thick bolt of electricity shot out, striking the black figure squarely. The darkness dispersed, revealing a man lying face up on the ground with a gaping hole burnt through his chest.

I expected Lucian's pupils to glow silver, as they had done before, but they didn't—his eyes shone pure white. He levitated into the air as if gravity held no power against him. Rising high, he became a tiny figure in the sky. Lucian raised his arms, and the sky responded to him. Dark, thundering clouds materialized above him and spread out like a formless figure with twisting white veins. The wind picked up, making me shiver. Dario stepped closer to me, his warmth hugging me in a tight embrace. The lightning intensified, casting our surroundings in ghastly white light.

The man who had been fighting Maeve was pulled into the air screaming. As he rose toward the clouds, multiple bolts of lightning struck him at once. His dead body dropped to the ground a second later.

My hair floated up around me. I began feeling much lighter as if I were being pulled up. But the force wasn't strong enough to lift me from the ground. The earth rose around us, tearing free in large chunks and rising into the sky like drifting balloons. Lightning struck down like twisted swords. Some chunks of earth remained suspended in the air, while other pieces smashed back onto the ground and crushed people beneath them. I held on to Dario's arm as the ground shook violently.

Lucian still hovered in the air as a halo of white light extended around him. Chunks of earth continued to rip themselves from the ground. I covered my ears as lightning crackled furiously around us for what seemed like minutes.

The lightning and wind stopped, thrusting us into silence and darkness. Gravity returned to normal, and my knees buckled. Dario caught my arm before I fell. Large craters surrounded the castle, and several bodies lay strewn about.

Lucian slowly descended back to us. His power wasn't just lightning, or even storms, but nature itself responded to him and bent to his will. The vampires who were still alive eyed Lucian.

I realized this was the reason why no one dared step in his way when he hunted down half-bloods. No one was powerful enough to stop him—maybe not even the gods themselves.

Lucian quickly scanned the crowd until he saw me. He sighed. I wanted to pull him into an embrace, get away, and forget this night had happened. But Lucian walked over to Ernesto, who was still on his knees, and offered him a hand. Ernesto hesitated for a second, then took it and let Lucian pull him back to his feet.

The two of them made their way back to us.

"Where are the others?" Dario asked.

"They're helping the wounded on the other side of the castle," Ernesto said. "Sue was there too."

Lucian walked closer to me and seemed about to say something when a shadow blotted out the light from the moon. A second later the black dragon landed on the ground. His green eyes settled on a woman a few yards behind us who wore a torn pink dress.

Loki bared his teeth. "Traitor," he hissed at her.

Lucian squared his shoulders at the accusation, eyeing the woman. A man stepped between her and the dragon. White light formed in his palm, and the air around him seemed to warp strangely as if he were pulling space into a vortex.

"Don't you dare touch her," the man said.

"She's a traitor," Loki said with a growl. "She doesn't belong to your coven."

The dragon lunged forward. Loki's jaws opened with exaggerated slowness, his giant teeth dripping with blood and saliva. Before Loki could swallow them both, the woman pulled the man to the side. Time resumed its course, and Loki's jaws closed around empty air.

Loki hissed as his head snapped back to the man and woman. The dragon inhaled, then exhaled a wave of green fire. The woman stretched her arms in front of her. She absorbed the flames, sucking them in through her palms. Her eyes glowed green. The dragon stopped, then stepped back as a dense orb of green light floated between the woman's hands. I could have sworn the dragon smiled when the woman screamed. She spread her arms, and the green fire raced toward us like a rampaging tsunami.

"No!" Ernesto screamed, but even with his arms outstretched before him he couldn't stop the green flames.

Loki roared so loudly the clouds seemed to tremble, but that sound was drowned out by the crackling fire closing around us in a wave of poisonous heat. I closed my eyes and felt something twist inside of my chest. The heat vanished, and when I opened my eyes again, the fire was already moving away from us as if time had turned backward. The woman opened her eyes wide, the green light inside of them extinguishing. The flames enveloped her and the man. They screamed, but no one attempted to douse the green fire as it killed them.

Silence hung densely in the air for a couple of seconds.

Then a thunderous roar boomed out of the castle. The earth shook so violently that it sent me sprawling to the ground. Loki shrieked, and out of the corner of my eye, I spotted him taking off into the night sky.

The castle began glowing with a strange red hue.

"What the . . ." Dario said.

The mighty towers and walls exploded and crumbled down like sand. Lucian pulled me to my feet and away from the castle as it continued to shatter into heaps of dust. The structure disintegrated entirely in only a few seconds.

"What the hell was that?" Ernesto asked.

No one responded.

Something felt wrong as ashes drifted down from the sky.

Lucian pulled me closer to him, holding my waist tight as his eyes began to shine with dim white light.

Black-red tendrils burst from the smoldering castle ruins, making us startle and move back. As soon as the tendrils touched the vineyard on the other side of the castle that had been left untouched by Ernesto's fire, they turned into a fiery blaze. But the black-red fire seemed unnatural and more like a special effect trying too hard to appear real. The flames spread like a dark curse as they ate through the grapevines without even leaving ashes in their wake.

It all stopped abruptly, the flames vanishing and leaving the earth barren. Lucian turned to Dario, who glanced at Ernesto, but they seemed equally confused about what that might have been.

I breathed hard, my heart beating fast against my chest.

"Are you alright?" Lucian asked me.

Trembling, I turned to face him and nodded.

His eyes traced me carefully, then he nodded back and let go of me. Turning toward the other vampires who had begun to gather around us, Lucian seemed about to say something.

I didn't see the dragon until it became visible just as it snatched Lucian from the ground with its clawed hand. It launched back into the sky with a powerful flap of its wings, gone so fast that no one had time to react.

"Lucian," Sue yelled as she raced toward us.

Lucian and the dragon disappeared inside of the clouds, which crackled with thunder. After a few seconds, the sky went quiet again.

"Lucian!" I screamed.

Only silence responded.

PART VII

THE
NAME

28

WOLF FOLLOWED THE HALF-BLOOD out of the ball-room door. The man had been the first to run when Rafe turned into a dragon. Wolf almost lost the half-blood through the maze-like corridors, but Wolf's sharp nose followed his scent with ease. Wolf burst through another door and found himself outside the castle, the cold night air howling around him.

The half-blood glanced behind him, noted Wolf was still after him, and muttered something under his breath. Even though they were separated by about fifty yards, Wolf was rapidly shortening the distance between them. The man veered to the left toward a large greenhouse, and Wolf followed.

Rafe roared. Even though the sound was muffled through the many castle walls, the sound still made Wolf's bones vibrate.

The half-blood ripped open the greenhouse door and dashed inside. Wolf arrived there seconds later but stopped at the thresh-old when he beheld him sitting on an upturned pot a few feet away. The man breathed heavily, but he didn't move when his gaze landed on Wolf.

Moonlight filtered through the clear panes, casting a ghostly silver sheen over the rows of plants and the man's dark skin. The air was thick with the scent of wet soil and the sweet aroma of nocturnal blooms.

The man didn't stand up as Wolf stepped closer to him.

"Hello, Wolf," he said. "I'll admit we weren't expecting you at the party. But now that you're here, we might have some fun."

Smiling, the man stood up. Wolf realized too late that the man had probably lured him here. An explosion shook the ground. A roar echoed through the night. The man looked up, but Wolf didn't dare break his gaze away from him. A dragon-shaped shadow slid through the greenhouse, and Wolf knew Rafe had flown away according to their plan.

"You shouldn't have come," the man said, turning his attention back to him. "We both know you're not strong enough to fight me." Wolf didn't answer, and the man continued. "Erasing memories is a useful power, Wolf, but it won't help you win this war."

Wolf couldn't contain his surprise.

The man flashed another smile. "Oh yes, we know what you're capable of."

Wolf cocked his head to one side.

"You break people's minds and erase their thoughts," the man continued. He seemed eager to show off how much he knew, like insecure people always did. "You can make people turn dumb and stupid. Look at Dionysus. He's nothing more than a blood-thirsty child now."

After what Gabriel had said, Wolf had assumed the Twelfth Coven knew all about his power. But he had been wrong. They only knew about part of his power—the part they had used but not the full extent of what he was capable of.

"Where is the leg?" Wolf asked.

The man raised an eyebrow. "Ah," he said, "you're the one Zeus was working with. I would have assumed he had partnered with a more . . . powerful god. Or maybe it was his plan to use you to erase everyone's minds to forget about Osiris completely. I suppose that was smart. Or it would have been smart, if he hadn't fallen into our trap."

The *Aether* began to thump in Wolf's veins like a second heartbeat. He was quick to push it away, but he couldn't contain the deep growl that rumbled through his throat. That only seemed to excite the man more, because his eyes twinkled.

"You should leave," the man said. "You're no match for us, Wolf, and it would be unfortunate to have to kill you after everything you've done to help us. Zeus couldn't fight us. What makes you think that you can?"

Wolf couldn't help but savor the moment. It felt good to be underestimated—it would make everything easier. Wolf lunged forward and crashed into the man. They both fell as pure rage darkened Wolf's vision. A pot crunched underneath the man, and earth splattered on the floor. Wolf roared, and his fangs shot out of his mouth. He didn't need his power to kill someone—even without it, he had always been one of the strongest Athatos. He sank his fangs into the man's neck and ripped away a chunk of flesh. The man screamed and struggled underneath Wolf as blood gurgled out of his mouth. The *Aether* stirred within Wolf, bursting to get out, but he reined it in.

Warm blood dripped from his mouth. The blood tasted bitter, unlike the sweetness of human blood, so he spat it out. The man had gone pale, his lips tainted with his own blood.

"The leg," Wolf snarled as he pinned the man's hands at his sides. "And the head." Wolf crushed his wrists, and the man howled in pain. Wolf leaned down, bit the man's ear off, then spat it out. The man screamed and continued to wriggle, but Wolf didn't budge. Wolf hissed at him, and the man whimpered.

Not so powerful now, are you? Wolf thought.

The ground shook violently underneath them, the earth groaning. Wolf didn't move, even as plants began falling off the tables. The trembling stopped after a few moments. Glass shattered behind Wolf. Without breaking his hold on the man, he swiveled his head around.

Rafe calmly walked toward him, a smile on his face. "There's the Wolf I remember. I knew you still had it in you." He looked at the man. "Hello there."

Wolf turned back toward the man. "Where are they?"

"I don't know," the man said. "I wasn't involved in the theft. I swear." Bursts of blood had sputtered out of his lips while he spoke.

Wolf turned to Rafe.

Rafe nodded.

"Please," the man begged. "I can give you other information. I can help you."

Rafe shook his head.

Wolf opened his jaws wide and clamped his teeth around the man's neck, slashing through flesh and bone. The head rolled to the other side of the greenhouse, leaving a trail of wet blood over the spilled earth. Wolf pulled himself to his feet, bitter blood dripping from his mouth in rivers. Rafe simply stared at him with an amused expression.

"Where's Dionysus?" Wolf asked.

"Away from here and safe," Rafe said.

"Good." Wolf trotted back toward the castle.

"Alec already killed a half-blood from the Twelfth Coven, and I ate another one a few minutes ago," Rafe said casually. "We're missing four more."

Wolf and Alec had been careful to note anyone who had absorbed Rafe's power inside the ballroom when he had shifted into a dragon. The signals had only been little twirls of green around their bodies, but it had been enough to confirm the truth about Gabriel's story. Wolf pushed away the image of Gabriel's last terrified expression before he had faded within the thick mists of the Underworld.

"Where are we going?" Rafe asked as they arrived at the castle again. "The battle is moving outside."

"Make us invisible," Wolf ordered since it wasn't a power he was particularly worried someone would mirror.

Wolf expected a retort or question from Rafe, but the other man said nothing as he air-warped and shielded them both from the sight of others yet kept them visible to each other.

Wolf broke through a door, and they went inside the castle. Cracks cut through the walls. Broken objects and furniture littered the floor. Wolf spotted a faint gray light at the end of the hallway. He and Rafe approached the ghost carefully. Its neck was bent in half, its mouth open in a scream. While the ghost's blank eyes revealed no emotion, Wolf felt that it wanted them to follow it.

The ghost turned around, and they trailed it through several hallways until they arrived at the hole that had cleaved through the castle. He guessed that the rift happened when someone from the Twelfth Coven absorbed power from Prithvi's coven. Some walls and the ceiling still clung stubbornly to each other, seemingly hovering above the void. The ghost floated over the hole and vanished inside a room on the other side.

"No!" a man shouted.

Wolf recognized the son of Helios's voice.

His heartbeat roared inside his ears, and the *Aether* swirled madly inside of him. Wolf scanned his surroundings to try to find a way to the other side. He could try to jump over the rift, but it was a very large distance. Rafe exhaled loudly next to him. Wolf felt Rafe's strong arms wrap around him, and before he could ask what he was doing, Rafe pushed them both into the void. Wolf screamed as they fell. Then he heard the powerful flap of wings as Rafe carried them back up to the other side. Rafe crashed through a wall, and they landed roughly on the floor. Wolf coughed as dust sprang up around them. Rafe's black wings pulled back into his body. Wolf noted his suit wasn't torn, and wondered if that was an illusion.

Wolf walked toward the open door at the other end of the room and stopped at the threshold. Rafe joined him a second later. A young woman, the son of Helios, and a woman Wolf recognized as part of the Twelfth Coven stood in the middle of the room. The traitorous woman held an orb of flaming light on her palm, her eyes shining a dark shade of gold. Threads of fire entwined her arm. The child of Helios stood before the young woman protectively. Before Wolf could even think about intervening, the air crackled with electricity. The wall behind the traitor crumbled down, and Lucian Holt walked out of the hole.

"Wait, no!" the child of Helios shouted.

It was too late. Holt had already shot a bolt of electricity toward the Twelfth Coven woman. She caught it with her free hand and flashed her teeth with a hiss. Then she threw the golden fire toward Holt and the bolt of electricity at the young woman and the child of Helios.

"No!" Wolf roared.

Wolf didn't realize he had surged forward to intervene until Rafe's arms wrapped around him and pulled him backward. The *Aether* smashed against his chest, and he used every bit of strength he had to contain it. A surge of helplessness choked the air out of his lungs.

Helios's son turned his back to the woman and shielded the girl with his body. Holt launched himself to the side to try to avoid the fire. Then something strange happened. Wolf felt the shift in the air. The bolt and the fire bounced back toward the woman as if they had hit a mirror. The Twelfth Coven woman widened her eyes as fire and electricity surged back to her. She didn't even manage to scream before her body blasted into ashes.

Wolf stood still for a second, the truth stunning him. Holt and the child of Helios looked at each other. They began talking, and Wolf found it hard to follow their conversation as he became lost in his own thoughts. A minute later, the three of them walked out of the room.

"What the hell was that?" Rafe asked. "It mirrored back." He raked a hand through his hair.

But Wolf knew exactly what had happened. He exhaled, and adrenaline pumped in his veins as a new plan formed in his head. His eyes lingered on the hole where Holt had disappeared, and he became furious.

"Don't touch Holt," Rafe said.

"He killed Gabriel," Wolf said. "We must destroy him."

Rafe's eyes glowed green. "Let me play with him for a bit. After I'm done, he's all yours." Rafe glanced at the scattered pile of ashes. "I wonder what Holt's connection to the human girl is. They seemed . . . familiar with each other. Maybe we can use that to our advantage."

Wolf analyzed Rafe's expression carefully. "What are you planning?"

"You tell me your secrets, and I'll tell you mine," Rafe said.

Wolf exhaled. Fine, he could fight that battle after they were done with this one. He would worry about Holt later, who seemed happy to pretend he was fighting against the rebels.

"We need to kill the remaining members of the Twelfth Coven," Wolf said.

"What's your plan?" Rafe asked.

Wolf quickly explained what he was thinking, veiling the truth he had just discovered with careful lies.

"Shouldn't be too hard," Rafe said. "I wonder how the child of Helios is doing that."

"Just make sure he's close to the human girl," Wolf said. "If she's threatened, he'll use that power to save her like he did here."

Rafe nodded. "Will do." He took a deep breath. "Well then, I'll see you in a bit."

Rafe dropped their invisibility, and they left the room in opposite directions, Rafe going back to the void and Wolf heading to the hole on the wall. Wolf helped wounded people escape from the castle and carried them outside. He dropped them off in the garden where the Coven of the Moon had gathered to heal others. Some of Morrigan's children were also at the garden guarding the healers and the wounded. Fire shone in the sky like a sun, the earth shook, and the clouds rumbled with thunder as the fight outside raged on.

Wolf went back inside even though he knew there were no more wounded in the castle. He stepped inside a large atrium. The glass ceiling had shattered, and the broken shards crunched under Wolf's shoes as he walked toward the center. The castle shook. Claws of lightning tore at the sky as the battle continued outside. But Wolf paid little heed to that. He had his own battle to fight.

The rebels stepped out of the shadows—he knew they had been waiting for him. Wolf counted them quickly—a son of Anubis, a daughter of Prithvi, a daughter of Aphrodite, five from minor covens, and three lower-borns. The lower-generations carried themselves differently as if they had something to prove to the rest of the world. Their eyes shone with what he deemed as defiance because they were the underdogs who now led a revolution.

"Well look who we have here," the son of Anubis said. He stood on the upper floor of the atrium with two others while the rest encircled Wolf on the bottom floor. "The god of shepherds."

Snickers echoed around him.

Lightning crackled above. A loud boom followed, and the earth shook violently. The son of Anubis jumped over the railing and landed in front of Wolf. Glass crunched under his feet. The man's dark hair flowed to his shoulders in glossy waves. Shadows expanded around him, then shot toward Wolf, sending him tumbling to the floor over shards of glass that tore through his suit. The *Aether* responded instinctively, but he pulled it back toward him.

Not yet, Wolf thought.

He coughed, then pushed himself to his feet again.

"Do the other Athatos remember that it was the god of shepherds who erased their memories?" the son of Anubis asked.

"Tell us," the daughter of Aphrodite said from the upper floor.

But she couldn't compel Wolf to do anything. He had been one of the few who was immune to Aphrodite's charms, although the rebels didn't need to know that.

"No, they don't," Wolf responded in a strained voice.

"Wolf," a woman said behind him.

He turned around and faced a tall woman with bright red hair and skin light as porcelain. The red and purple in her eyes had faded, revealing pale blue eyes underneath. On her left hand she wore a red ring from Dionysus's coven.

"We've heard so much about you," she said.

"Good things I hope," Wolf said.

The woman smiled. Wolf was still missing one of the members from the Twelfth Coven, and he hoped they showed up soon or else it would ruin his plan. The other two half-bloods on the upper floor of the atrium jumped down. They seemed hungry, lusting for murder. Wolf assumed one of them had a silver knife and knew the right words to carve into his body to kill him. Death seemed to be waiting in the shadows and eager to claim him.

"Aren't you going to fight back?" the red-haired woman asked. "You could erase our minds and escape."

Another wave of shadows crashed against Wolf. Black surrounded him before his back collided against one of the pillars on the side of the atrium. The stone pillar cracked with the impact, and Wolf dropped to the floor. More chuckles spread through the room. Wolf groaned, then pushed himself back up on unsteady legs. Someone pushed him from behind. He stumbled to the center of the atrium and fell to his knees.

The woman's eyes sparkled as she smiled. "What's your real name?" she asked.

Wolf didn't respond. He was so old that his true name had long ago been forgotten. The few myths that spoke of him never quite got the details about him right either. Even his power had never been properly explained by the ancient humans who had once worshipped him, but modern humans had come closer to describing Wolf's power.

They called it *entropy*.

Ancient humans had only known it as *chaos*, but most of them had misunderstood what chaos meant. Even now, chaos had a bad reputation, but entropy was closer to Wolf's nature.

Humans had recently discovered that the universe was moving toward disorder, and that any physical, chemical, and biological reactions that occurred had to create disorder in some way. So ancient humans had been half right. Chaos did increase disorder, and therefore, followed the principle of entropy. But then why did creation happen? If everything moved toward chaos, then why did atoms, molecules, and cells form ordered structures? It was, in theory, a violation of the natural laws, except that those creations, in turn, created more disorder around them. Chemical reactions involved the movement of molecules and the breaking and forming of chemical bonds, which contributed to the overall increase in entropy. In biological systems, the process of metabolism and energy transfer also involved the breaking down and building up of different molecules, which resulted in a net increase of disorder in the environment around them.

Energy always dispersed in the universe to increase randomness.

That's exactly what the *Aether* was—a force that drove the universe into disorder. Wolf had leveled buildings, towns, and empires, creating chaos around him. He had also used his power to create things, but as time passed by, it had become harder to create than to destroy. That's why he had decided to stop drinking blood and starve his power—because entropy radiated out of him in waves, and one way or another, his surroundings always moved toward disorder. Sometimes it made plants grow or increased the temperature in a room, but more often than not, things blew up around him and accidents tended to occur. Other times, more dramatic things happened.

Like the near end of the world.

A roar boomed through the air. For a second, he thought that it was Rafe's signal, but the sound seemed different somehow, almost as if—

A dragon landed on the corner of the atrium, its wings spread wide. The dragon's gray scales reflected the moonlight.

"Hello, Wolf," the dragon said.

The others around him backed away but still surrounded Wolf in a loose circle.

Come on Rafe, Wolf thought.

Time was running out for him. The dragon leaned closer while keeping a grip on the roof with its claws. It was big, but not nearly as large as Rafe. The dragon bared its teeth, and hot mist drifted out of its nostrils. The other half-bloods waited—they assumed Wolf wouldn't leave this castle alive. The dragon opened its jaws. Fire glowed at the back of its throat.

A roar sliced through the night, powerful and deep.

Wolf felt the subtle shift as a wave of power passed through him. The *Aether* stormed within him, rushing through his veins.

Wolf was the god of creation.

He was the god of destruction.

It was time to set Chaos free.

Wolf roared as the *Aether* blasted out of him. At the same time, fire shot from the dragon's mouth toward Wolf, but it never reached him. The fire exploded back in a wave that made his eyes sting. It slammed against the castle walls, setting the dragon afire in a red blaze. Engulfed in flames, the dragon lost its grip on the roof and tumbled into the atrium.

The red-haired woman came from behind Wolf and extended her arms, trying to absorb his power. Her irises darkened into a color that had previously only existed within Wolf's eyes—black shinning with a red glow. The tendrils of the *Aether* that shot out of Wolf and twisted around her were like a black liquid reflecting a bright red light from a different source. She spread her palms toward him. A dark wave surged in his direction. For a split second, he worried his plan hadn't worked, but only for a split second. Wolf's power bounced off him again, then crashed against the woman. She let out a guttural scream before her body disintegrated to ashes.

The dragon shrieked, the fire still consuming its skin. Wolf didn't know how much time he had left before the other power stopped working, but he didn't lose a single second. The *Aether* happily danced inside the fire, and the flames turned dark red. They became hotter and brighter, eating through the dragon as if greedily devouring its flesh. The monster let out one last roar before it went still.

Everyone else had frozen.

Wolf smiled as he turned his head to face each of them in turn. His gaze eventually landed on the child of Anubis. Shadows expanded around him like a blooming black flower. Wolf's fangs shot out. He roared, and the sound echoed off the walls.

The *Aether* responded and lurched toward the son of Anubis. The half-blood's shadows tried to block the *Aether* but failed. The *Aether* cut through the darkness like scissors slicing a velvet fabric, and it pierced the man through the chest. He convulsed, his skin cracking as red light burst from his body. He disintegrated into a burst of ashes a moment later.

The others tried to run, but Wolf didn't give them a chance. He screamed again, and the *Aether* burst from him in rivers of black and red. It surged toward the rebels, making their bodies twitch and twist before they started to dissolve. They screamed, but not for long before they drowned within his power.

It felt so good, like exhaling after having held his breath for years. His heart pulsed in tune with the *Aether*, and for the first time in centuries, Wolf felt truly alive as an exhilarating thrill burned through his veins. The ground cracked underneath him. Walls began to crumble like sand. Objects shattered into particles. The entire castle came crashing down around him until there was nothing left but smoldering ruins. The *Aether* continued to propagate like a hungry beast demanding to be satiated. It ate through the vineyards, disintegrating them. Wolf began to feel the pull from the stars above him and from the heated core at the center of the planet.

Stop, Wolf told himself.

The *Aether* kept going. The ground beneath him continued to tremble. Wolf could bring the sky crashing over the earth and burn the ocean in a blaze. He could make the sun burst and eat this world or make planets change their orbit and send the universe spinning into chaos.

Stop! he commanded.

The *Aether* pulled back into his body like a rubber band snapping into its original shape. Wolf coughed, feeling his body again. He was on his knees, fire burned around him, and ashes dripped from the sky.

Hera's words echoed inside his mind—*you will be the one who destroys this world.*

Not this time, he thought to himself.

It could start with just a castle, then expand to a small village or town, then to a city, a country, and the world. It was so easy to climb that ladder.

So frighteningly simple.

And Wolf had discovered long ago that physical objects were not the only things that could cause entropy to increase. Disordered minds also created a more disordered environment—that's how he had fragmented the minds of others. The first time he had done so hadn't been on purpose, and he had broken the Athatos' minds more violently than he had intended. Afterward, it had been hard to repair the damage, and the Athatos had blamed their immortality for the state of their minds. They had said that was what old life did. It broke their minds under the weight of time.

Wolf had felt guilty about what he had done, but there were some dangerous secrets that he couldn't let them keep. As Wolf glanced up at the ashes falling from the sky like snowflakes, he wondered once again how that secret had slipped into the hands of the Twelfth Coven. He supposed it didn't matter much at this point, even though it made his stomach sink with dread. All that mattered now was that he stopped the Twelfth Coven before they caused more damage. And tonight, Wolf had discovered the key to destroy them. His little experiment here had proved how it could be done. Now he needed to make sure everything moved into the right place.

The most critical part of his new plan had just begun.

As hot ash prickled his skin, he stood. Wolf brushed the ash from his hair and walked out of the castle. There was much work to be done.

29

THE CUP OF TEA trembled in my shaky hand. A couple of hours had passed since the end of the battle at the castle, and we had left with the remaining survivors. I took another flavorless sip, then held on to the cup tightly because of the warmth seeping through the porcelain. I had changed out of my dress and into the winter clothes Estelle had given me, but I still felt the chill of the night clinging to me. Dario sat at one of my sides, and Sue sat at the other with her arms crossed tightly across her chest.

Ernesto, Rufus, Estelle, and Bruno sat on the couch in front of us. Bruno stared at Dario as if he wanted to beat him to a pulp. Rufus's fangs still hadn't retracted. Estelle's only reaction had been to open her eyes wide as Dario told them all the truth. Ernesto had maintained a neutral expression while he listened to Dario.

Even though Dario had already told his old coven about Lucian and the mysterious murders that had led us here, he had filled them in with the details. Once spoken out loud, everything seemed to weigh more heavily on me. What the hell had I gotten myself into?

One of Quetzalcoatl's children entered the room.

"Any news, Ixchel?" Sue asked.

The woman shook her head. "We flew for a while but didn't find any trace of Lucian or Loki. Sorry."

The light in Sue's eyes dulled, and my own heart squeezed painfully. Ixchel left the room, most likely heading downstairs to where the surviving half-bloods had gathered.

Ernesto exhaled. He undid his tie, letting it hang limply around his neck. "We need a plan," he said. "I'm damn sure this isn't the end of it. There must be more lower-generations who are in on this, and I'll bet they're rallying to strike again." He lowered his voice. "And I think the ruling covens might still have traitors among them that plan to kill the gods whenever they get the chance." He looked at Dario. "I need to know if we can count on you."

Dario exhaled. "I'll fight on your side. But like I said, I won't rejoin the Coven of the Sun. I hope you can respect that."

"If we hadn't respected your choice, we wouldn't have let you leave," Ernesto said. He looked at the others, and they nodded in agreement.

"Good to know where you stand," Bruno said bitterly.

"So what now?" Rufus asked. "We need to warn Helios, obviously, but what happens after?"

"We get ready to fight," Ernesto said. "We figure out which other covens are still standing, and we form alliances."

"I need to find Lucian," Sue said.

"He might already be dead," Rufus said. "Loki is not the merciful type."

I gripped the teacup so tightly that my hands throbbed in pain.

Estelle glared at Rufus. "Lucian Holt is a powerful ally," she said.

"Yes," Ernesto said. "But I'm not risking our lives for his."

"You don't have to." Sue stood up. "I'll get him back"—she glanced in my direction—"and take Isa far away from here."

"Far away where?" Estelle asked. "She'll be much safer with us."

Sue's eyes narrowed.

"I think Isa should go," Dario said. "I don't want her caught in the crossfire."

Ernesto glanced at me, one of his brows shooting up in question.

"I'll go with Sue," I said.

"Suit yourself," Ernesto said before he stood too. "We leave for Italy in thirty minutes. We'll meet you downstairs, Dario."

Dario nodded. We waited for the others to walk out of the room. The air began to vibrate. I was about to ask what was happening, then realized Sue must be using her power to shield our conversation.

"Where will you be going?" Dario asked as he stood.

"I think it's best if we don't tell you," Sue said. "I wouldn't want anyone reading your mind or your heart to discover the truth."

Dario clenched his fists. "I guess that makes sense." He glanced at me. "I'm so sorry you got involved in this, and I hope to see you again once this is over."

"I hope so too," I said.

I placed the cup on the table beside the couch and stood. Dario hesitantly stepped closer to me, and I gave him a hug. His arms wrapped around me, flooding me with warmth.

"Please stay safe, Isa," he said.

"You too," I said before I pulled away.

Dario smiled at Sue, who also gave him a tight hug.

"I'll bring him back. I promise," she said.

"I know you will," Dario said. "When this is over, I'll cook us all a fancy dinner."

"I'll make an exception to eat," Sue said.

The air stopped thrumming, and Sue motioned at the door with her head. "Let's go, Isa."

Dario smiled. "Go."

Sue and I exited the room, but not before one last wave at Dario. The half-bloods downstairs didn't spare me and Sue more than a glance. Ernesto gave us a car, and Sue drove us away from the large house. I didn't even know who the property belonged to, but it was too late to ask.

There was little traffic as the city still slept.

"So where are we going?" I asked.

The simple thought of hiding and waiting until Sue came back with Lucian made me anxious.

Sue smiled. "Even though everyone else, including Lucian, seems to think you're too young and weak to be part of our world, I think you're strong enough to handle it." We stopped at a red light, which bathed Sue's face in an angry glow.

"So we're not going to a safe place?" I asked.

"The safest place to be is with me and Lucian. I don't trust the Helios Coven to not bite you, and there's no one else I would trust to take care of you while this all plays out." Sue finally turned to face me, and the stoplight turned green. "So we're going to save Lucian together."

I exhaled the breath I had been holding.

"Good," I said. "Let's go then."

Sue stepped on the gas and the car surged forward into the dawn.

30

AS I WOLFED DOWN scrambled eggs while Sue stirred her coffee, I wondered if she would eventually drink it. The low murmurs from a couple sitting next to us were the only other noises in the small café. The window on the left revealed a run-down garden on the opposite side of the sidewalk, its plants and shrubs squeezing through rusted metal bars like prisoners trying to escape.

Sue checked her phone again, tapping her foot on the floor. The cook standing behind a counter began humming a song while the waiter wiped down a glass case containing several pastries.

The clear door near us opened. Sue's foot stopped moving as she gazed at the man who had just walked in. His dark eyes swept through the café before settling on Sue. A brilliant smile broke through his face, contrasting starkly against his rich brown skin. He walked over to us and took the seat between Sue and me.

He analyzed me. "Who's your new friend?" he asked.

"This is Isa," Sue said. "Isa, meet Jean."

"Nice to meet you," I said.

He turned back to Sue, his friendly smile expanding. But something felt off about that smile—its edges were too sharp—as if he were about to slice someone with a bite.

"I need your help with something," Sue said.

"I've been doing well, thanks for asking," Jean said. "I finally bought a house in the countryside. You're welcome to come whenever you please. I've quite missed your—"

"Does Loki have any properties around the area?" Sue asked.

Jean's smile disappeared, his lips crushing into a thin line. Sue held Jean's gaze steadily, her face expressionless.

"Should I ask why you and Holt got tangled up with that psychopath?" Jean asked.

"No."

"Hmm." Jean tapped his fingers lightly on the table.

I silently finished eating my eggs.

Jean sat back, crossing his arms. "There's a tiny island close to the coast of Le Havre. Loki uses illusions to keep it hidden from humans so that boats crash into it and he can prey on sailors." Uncrossing his arms, he grabbed Sue's coffee and took a sip. He immediately spat it out, then glanced behind his shoulder to make sure the waiter and cook hadn't seen him. "Gods this is awful." He coughed. "Anyway, I don't know much more about the island, but I'm sure you can use your power to know where it is."

Sue nodded. "That's helpful. Thanks." Her expression softened. "You should lay low for a while."

Jean's gaze sharpened. "Why?"

"Just stay away from the Athatos and their covens," Sue said.

Jean stared at her for a long moment, then finally nodded.

"I'll see you around," Sue said in a clear dismissal.

Jean stared at her for another moment before standing. "See you around. Be careful out there."

"Always."

Jean exited the café. We left a few minutes later.

Sue drove northwest, toward the coast of the English Channel. The dense city buildings eventually disappeared as the countryside dominated the landscape. Patches of green and yellow grass mixed like a watercolor painting. Skeletal trees and bushes with dangling green leaves intermingled with each other as the fall season lost its battle against winter.

We only stopped once so I could use the restroom and buy some snacks, but most of our drive was in silence. I should have been exhausted but had never felt more awake. The image of Lucian being snatched from the ground like a toy kept replaying in my mind. Lucian was powerful enough to fight the gods, but I still worried about him and hoped Loki hadn't hurt him.

Eventually, we pulled into a parking lot next to a deserted beach. We stepped out of the car, and I zipped my jacket tight. Fog as dense as cotton had settled over the ocean, preventing me from seeing into the distance.

"What if Loki is still a dragon and tries to kill us?" I asked.

"I can use my power to hide us," Sue said. "We'll be silent."

I wished I could feel as confident as Sue sounded.

"Come on," she said.

We walked out of the parking lot and made our way to some docks. Sue studied the boats, then stopped before a little motorboat. She jumped into it.

"What if the owner comes looking for it?" I asked.

Sue shrugged.

I stepped onto the boat, which wobbled beneath my feet. Sue untied it from the dock and looked around for the keys. She found them hidden under the seat.

"Do you know how to drive this thing?" I asked.

Sue only smiled in response.

We rode in silence as we set out into the Channel. The air around us began vibrating as Sue used her power to mask us. I nervously sat on the back bench, my mind creating various twisted shapes from the fog—a hollow face, a hand, the tail of a snake.

"I can hear the waves washing onto the shore," Sue said after awhile. I couldn't see anything and narrowed my eyes in the direction we were heading. After another minute, the island appeared before me as if it had surged up from the waves. A crumbling castle stood shrouded in fog like a large bug caught in a thick spiderweb.

Sue closed her eyes, then snapped them open. "I only hear one heartbeat inside the castle. I think it's Lucian."

"What if it's not?" I asked.

"We run," Sue said.

The boat hit the sand. Sue turned off the engine and jumped out. I hesitantly stepped onto the sand, then hurried to catch up to Sue. A large hole, like the gaping mouth of a dead monster, greeted us as the entrance to the castle. Sue stopped at the threshold, closing her eyes.

"Follow me," she whispered.

We stepped into the castle, the air still vibrating. The moist dark walls dripped with water like the skin of a slimy beast. Pale light that filtered through cracks and ragged holes that could have once been windows cast uneven patterns on the floors and walls where patches of moss clung. The fog outside seemed to seep through the very stones of the castle to blur our surroundings.

My chest tightened as we lost ourselves in the hallways. What if the heartbeat Sue had heard was Loki and not Lucian? What would the god do if he caught us? I suppressed the chill that snaked down my spine. What if we didn't find Lucian here? Where else would we look for him? What if Loki had hurt him, or worse, killed him? My hands began to shake. I buried them inside my coat pockets.

We wandered through vast, empty halls where the ocean had begun to reclaim its territory. In some rooms, seawater pooled on the floor. The water lapped gently against the stone, filling the castle with a quiet, persistent tide. Seaweed had begun to form a slimy carpet in other rooms, and I was careful to not slip. The remnants of a grand staircase, now crumbled, hinted at the once-majestic scale of the structure.

I couldn't tell how old the castle was. It could have been here for centuries. I didn't spot any words or text carved on the walls or a single statue or any other sort of decoration that could have given me a clue about who had built the castle.

After awhile, Sue stopped in front of a staircase leading down into a gloomy darkness.

"He's down there," Sue whispered.

"Are you sure it's Lucian?" I asked.

Sue didn't respond. She began to descend the stairs. I took a deep breath before following her. The smell of rot and decay burned through my nose. I pressed my sleeve over my face as my heartbeat pulsed in the tips of my fingers. The room at the bottom was pitch-black. Sue pulled out her phone and turned on her flashlight.

I startled, my pulse racing uncontrollably. Human skeletons lay piled against the walls. They gleamed in the light as if Loki had eaten every bit of flesh and licked the bones clean. Sue pointed to the other side of the room. Lucian was locked in a cell at the far end. Relief swept through me.

Sue and I hurried to him. Lucian sat with his back to the wall. A pair of silver shackles bound his wrists.

"Lucian," Sue said, but he didn't move.

Terrified, I gripped the bars tightly and looked at him. He was still breathing, but he didn't open his eyes. His suit wasn't torn, either, and I didn't spot any blood or wounds.

"The silver is weakening him," Sue said. "And Loki may have done something else to him." She stood a foot away from the cell, and I assumed she didn't dare to come any closer to the silver bars.

A large lock kept the door shut. I shook it. A clang resonated across the room, but the lock didn't budge. "I don't suppose the key is just lying around here somewhere," I said.

"It wouldn't hurt to look," Sue said. "Let's hurry before Loki decides to come back. Search the rooms on the third floor while I look around the first and second floor."

"Okay."

I hurried back up the stairs, feeling acutely exposed without Sue's anti-noise bubble. Every breath I took seemed amplified like gusts of wind echoing through the stone corridors. My footsteps reverberated ominously, each one a thunderous clap that seemed to shake the very walls. My heartbeat pounded like a giant drum, and with each beat a booming beacon, I feared I would summon Loki back to the castle.

I reached the second floor using the crumbling grand staircase. But the stairs to the third floor had been reduced to a broken mass of stones, and I climbed them carefully, taking support from the mossy wall. I stood at the landing for a couple of seconds, catching my breath. The wall opposite me was missing. Apart from the waves washing onto the shore, no other sound penetrated the dense fog.

I began walking through the hallway on the right, which had two wooden doors. They seemed new, were polished smoothly, and had gleaming silver doorknobs. The first room had a small chair and desk—the only pieces of furniture I had seen so far. I walked across the hallway into the other room, then halted.

A tall man stood with his back against the wall, his eyes locked on me. His smooth skin glowed dimly, and so did his golden hair and dark eyes. He was handsome in the same way Loki had been—dangerous and deadly like a lion. Power emanated from him in sharp waves. I took a step back. How hadn't Sue heard him?

"Hello," he said. His powerful voice made my bones tremble.

Surely Sue would hear him and come help me, I thought.

"Are you looking for this?" He held a key in his hand.

I stepped back closer to the door, but he was quicker and blocked the exit.

"Not so fast," he said. If eyes could eat, his would have gobbled me up. They were black like a universe without stars. But something shimmered under the surface. Tendrils of red light glowed in his eyes like a twisting snake encircling his pupils. "I was hoping you would come," he said.

31

"WHO ARE YOU?" I asked him, then regretted saying anything.

He smiled. But it wasn't a predatory smile like Loki's. His smile seemed genuinely friendly, which made my stomach twist and fear coil tightly around my spine in warning.

"My name is Wolf," he said.

Helios's children had mentioned his name. Wolf had been at the party last night, and now he was here. I took a step back, but unless I jumped out the window, there were no other exits. Where was Sue?

"I was expecting the child of Helios to come with you," Wolf said. His tone was casual, but his eyes lit up.

I wondered why everyone was so interested in Dario. I thought back to how the rebel woman had taunted him. What kind of secret could Dario be hiding?

"He's around," I said.

Wolf smiled again as if he could smell the lie. He extended his hand. A key lay on his palm. "Take it."

"Why?" I asked.

"You need it to free Holt."

"Why are you helping me?" My heart pounded heavily.

I glanced out the window, but if I fell out, the jagged rocks would crush me to pieces. Wolf moved, pulling my attention back to him. He had stepped away from the door and was eyeing me.

"Take the key and get Holt out of here," Wolf said more urgently now.

It felt like a trap—it was a trap. But what else could I do? I wasn't leaving without Lucian. Hesitantly, I stepped toward Wolf. He stood still, his eyes never leaving my own. Very slowly, I took the key from his palm. Wolf withdrew his hand as if I had electrocuted him, making me startle.

"Sorry," he hissed in between his teeth.

"Why are you helping me?" I asked again.

Wolf smiled once more, but this smile was different—it seemed like the smile of a predator who had just captured its prey. My heart shot backward with fear.

"It's all part of the plan," Wolf whispered.

His eyes flashed red.

My vision blurred as if the lens I was looking through had cracked into thousands of pieces. The ground opened up beneath my feet, and I fell. Then kept falling. And falling. Deeper and deeper I went into a vast ocean of darkness. Then I spotted something below, a tiny fragment of light that awaited at the bottom of the infinite blackness. The light widened, like a broken window leading back into the world. I smashed through it, and my vision came into focus, the broken pieces mending together.

A gust of wind howled in the castle hallway as I stepped away from the room. I hurried down the stairs to find Sue. I couldn't believe my luck. The key had just been lying on a table. Sue wasn't on the second floor, but I found her on the first, wading through water in a room with a missing wall where the waves washed onto the submerged floor.

"I found it," I said excitedly.

Sue jumped out of the water, her shoes squeaking as they dripped. "This seems a bit too easy," she said. "Like we're being set up."

"You were the one who expected the key to be around here somewhere," I said.

"I know," she said as we walked out of the room and back to the staircase. "Still, it's weird that Loki would leave him here like that. But Loki is a strange god so he could have just dumped Lucian here for no reason."

"I guess," I said.

We lit our phone flashlights before we descended the stairs, and I pointedly avoided looking at the skeletons. I walked to the cell, my hands shaking, but I managed to insert the key in the lock and turn it. My heart made a little jump when the lock fell to the floor with a clank. I swung the door open and hurried inside.

"Lucian," I said, kneeling at his side.

I placed my palm on his cold cheek. His eyes moved below his eyelids, but he didn't wake. My gut twisted. I glanced down at the shackles, and his skin was red as the silver burned his skin. The restraints didn't seem to have a keyhole.

"We'll worry about that later," Sue said as she glanced at the shackles. "Let's just get out of here. We'll have to carry him. You grab him under the arms, and I'll take his legs. I don't want to touch the silver by mistake."

I hoisted Lucian up, my arms straining, then walked backward out of the cell. My back began to ache when we reached the stairs, but I pushed away the pain as we pulled him up the steps and through the castle. My heart battered against my chest as if some unseen timer was counting down the seconds until our luck ran out and Loki returned. The sand crunched under my shoes as we walked away from the castle, its cracked openings gazing at us like empty eye sockets in a giant spider's skull.

Heaving, we carried Lucian all the way to the little boat, then set him down in it. I sat next to him to catch my breath and glanced back at the lonely castle. The fog covered most of my view, so the castle appeared to be floating within the clouds. I wondered how long it would take Loki to realize Lucian was gone. Would he come after us once he figured it out?

Sue started the engine, and we quickly rode away. I propped Lucian into a sitting position and rested my head on his chest. He was alive and seemed mostly unhurt. I pressed myself closer to him, letting Lucian's heartbeat throb against my cheek. I wasn't sure what I had expected from our rescue mission, but I certainly hadn't expected it to be this easy. Sue was right. Something felt wrong—but this entire situation was strange. Why had Loki taken Lucian in the first place? Why lock him in a dungeon and leave?

We rode in silence back to the mainland. After leaving the boat where we had found it, we carried Lucian to the car and drove away. I kept glancing back at the coast, but nothing came chasing after us. I finally let myself exhale with relief.

"What should we do now?" I asked.

"We should wait for Lucian to wake up, then decide what to do," Sue said.

I glanced back. Lucian's head lolled back, his expression soft with sleep. I took another deep breath to make my anxiety ebb. Lucian was safe now. Whatever happened now we would face it together.

"Where will we go in the meantime?" I asked.

"We own a house a couple of hours away," Sue said. "We can rest there for a bit."

"Rest sounds good," I said.

Now that my body didn't feel in imminent danger, exhaustion began to overtake me, but I forced myself to stay awake. I could sleep once we got to their house.

My parents called me halfway through our drive. They asked for pictures, but I told them I had been too busy to take any. Then they shared some stories from their dinner with our neighbors. It was a mundane conversation, which felt strange after everything that had happened. After the call, we stopped at another gas station so I could use the restroom and buy more food. Then we continued onward. Lucian didn't wake up or give any indication that he would anytime soon. Sue glanced at him through the rear-view mirror every few minutes as if that would somehow pull him back into consciousness.

The place Sue mentioned turned out to be another grand mansion nestled in the countryside. A tall stone wall encircled the property, and Sue pressed a code to open the ornate wrought iron gate. At the entrance stood a rectangular fountain, its surface reflecting the gray sky like liquid iron while water gently rippled from a central statue. Large, meticulously trimmed hedges bordered the house, though some leaves had shriveled, turned brown, and scattered across the ground. The mansion itself loomed majestically with tall windows and ivy climbing its stone facade. A gravel path led to the grand entrance flanked by neatly arranged flower beds that added a touch of color to the otherwise muted landscape.

After parking, Sue and I exited the car. We dragged Lucian to the entrance and had to lay him on the marble steps while Sue opened the front door. My arms trembled with Lucian's weight as Sue directed me through the mansion. Our shoes squeaked on the elegant marble floors that were polished so smoothly that our reflections rippled as we passed by. We walked through opulent hallways, past rooms adorned with plush velvet furniture in rich hues of emerald. A dining room was dominated by a sparkling crystal chandelier that cast dazzling patterns of light across the room.

I felt like my arms were about to rip out of their sockets by the time we finally dragged Lucian into a small bedroom and laid him on the bed. I panted, my arms burning and my lower back pulsing with pain.

"You should sleep, Isa," Sue said. "You can take the room next to this one."

"I'll stay here with Lucian," I said.

"Okay," Sue said, sounding a bit hesitant.

"What about the shackles?" I asked.

"I'll look around to see if there's anything we can use to take them off."

"Okay."

I took a quick shower, then changed back into my clothes because the closet was empty. When I returned to the room, a steaming cup of tea waited for me on the nightstand. I drank some of it, and the tea burned down my throat and heated up my chest. Then I climbed into bed next to Lucian. I lay next to him, brushing his hair off of his face. He would be alright, I assured myself. We just had to remove the shackles. I placed one hand on his chest, feeling his heart.

His heartbeat seemed to travel through my own veins and link us together. That rhythmic pounce followed me to the desert as I buried my hands inside the sand, digging slowly. He was still trapped under the dunes. My cheeks were wet with tears that evaporated with the scorching heat of the sun.

Stop. A hand settled on my shoulder, and his shadow blocked my view. I looked up. His golden-blond hair had grown longer and was in a small bun at the base of his skull. He kneeled next to me, his dark eyes boring into mine.

He's gone.

"No," I replied. "He's still here. I can bring him back again."

You can't. He whispered softly.

He pulled me into an embrace, and I melted into his arms, my head resting against his chest. He held me close and pulled me away from the dunes. The dry sand turned to ocean waves licking at my feet. The void in my chest was still there, an ever-present wound that would never heal, but he was with me now holding my hand.

Still, the desert beckoned me. He was waiting for me, his heartbeat summoning me. I dug for him again, but it was nighttime now. The heat had gone, replaced by a cool breeze that swept at my hair.

Stop. He placed his hand on my shoulder. This time his grip was stronger, almost painful. *He's gone.* His tone was angry, but I couldn't help myself.

"I can bring him back," I said.

If he comes back, then the rest of us will die.

I shook my head. He was wrong, and even if he had been right, I didn't care. He hauled me to my feet.

You need to stop. You're putting all of us at risk.

But he wasn't strong enough to stop me. I blinked, and he was gone. I was on my knees again, digging and digging and digging. I dug until the gaping hole I had created began swallowing me.

"Where are you?" I called out. He didn't respond. I kept falling deeper into the depths of the sand, its grains hot against my skin. Then my foot touched something soft. It moved underneath me, and the beat of his heart was weak but present.

Then I stood next to a stone table looking down at him. My heart tore itself apart at the sight of him. I had stitched him back together, but his soul was gone. No. I could bring his soul back into his body and keep it there forever. His heartbeat echoed through the room, reverberating in my bones.

"Isa," someone shouted, but their voice was so far away. "Wake up."

I ignored them. I couldn't get distracted now.

My knuckles turned white as I gripped the knife harder. I had already written the inscriptions on its blade. I leaned closer to him as the torches on the walls brightened, their flames surging to life. The inscriptions were still on his body. All I had to do was retrace them.

"Please," the distant voice said.

I took a deep breath, then lowered the knife. The metal tip

touched the center of his chest. A burst of energy tore out of me, traveled through the knife, and sank into his flesh.

"Wake up," the voice insisted.

His heart stopped beating.

32

"ISA, WAKE UP."

A cough shook my body so strongly I almost retched. Air rushed into my lungs that felt bruised and torn. My vision blurred as bright light seared into my eyes, making them sting. I coughed again.

I lay on my side on a cold, hard floor. Hadn't I fallen asleep on a bed?

I startled into a sitting position, my heartbeat pulsing in my throat.

"Isa," Lucian said.

He kneeled on the other side of metal bars. His eyes wide, he looked down at me.

"Lucian," I croaked, then coughed again.

My head snapped side to side as I took in my new surroundings. I was locked inside a cell, with Lucian in the one adjacent to me. The entire room was coated in silver, each surface reflecting the bright white lights in the ceiling and casting harsh glares that created an almost blinding brightness. Three empty cells were across a narrow corridor.

"What?" I managed to say. "No, we . . . how did we get here?"

"I was about to ask you the same," Lucian said.

Where was Sue? Had we been ambushed in the new mansion? I crawled toward Lucian. The bars were wide enough for me to slide my hand in between them. With his silver shackles clanging softly, he folded his fingers around my palm. Red blisters dotted his hands.

"What's the last thing you remember?" Lucian asked.

With my throat still aching, I told Lucian how Sue and I had rescued him, how we had brought him to their countryside mansion, and how Sue had left some tea for me after I had showered.

"What did the tea taste like?" Lucian asked.

"I don't remember," I said. "Do you think—"

"It was probably drugged."

"By whom?" I asked.

"I don't know," Lucian said, his hand tightening around mine. "We're still in the mansion. I built this room a few years ago, but I have no idea who dragged us here or what they could have done with Sue."

"Maybe she escaped," I said.

"Maybe," Lucian said.

I crushed Lucian's hand as panic began to overtake me. Had someone attacked Sue while I was showering and then left the tea on the nightstand? But why not just attack me too? I wouldn't have been able to do much against a vampire anyway. And who would have done this? The rebels behind the murders? Loki?

"Can you break us out of here?" I asked.

Lucian shook his head. "Not with the silver shackles. They've weakened me considerably, and they prevent me from using my power."

My heart seemed to beat out of rhythm like in a spasm.

"I'll get you out of here," Lucian said, pulling my attention back to him. Dark stains had set below his eyes, and his face looked gaunt as if the silver had sucked out chunks of his flesh. Yet his irises still shone brightly. Lucian opened his mouth to say something else but was interrupted when the door at the end of the corridor swung open.

Lucian let go of my hand to stand. A growl rumbled out of him, his fangs bared. A man slowly walked toward us. He had the appearance of a twenty-five-year-old, but his white hair made him look older. His eyes shone like moonlight. A small boy walked in behind him, eyeing Lucian with open interest. Both completely ignored me as if I was nothing more than a potted plant left to wilt and die.

"Hello, Holt," the man said.

"What do you want from me?" Lucian asked.

The little boy smiled. It was such a feral expression that it made me pull further back into the cell.

"Did you wonder why Loki took you?" the man said.

Lucian balled his fists. "He accused me of murdering Zeus. But I think I would have remembered doing that."

My mind foggily processed the fact that a god had been murdered.

"I'm sure you would have," the boy said.

The boy's body began to transform. It elongated like rubber to match Lucian's height. His hair color, eyes, and facial features shifted as if they were made of dough. A couple of seconds later, Lucian's clone stood right in front of us.

Lucian chuckled. "I'm your scapegoat then."

"You always were," the other Lucian said, except his voice didn't match Lucian's. It was missing the thunderous intensity Lucian spoke with, but I doubted anyone who hadn't met him would notice. "You hate the gods. You always have. You hate Zeus, specifically, because he's the one who bit you, abandoned you, and refused to accept you into his coven because he was scared of you."

Lucian said nothing.

"And now you've escaped the castle where Loki kept you prisoner, and you will continue leading the rebellion against the gods," Other Lucian said.

Lucian's face reddened. "I don't understand how blaming me for murdering the gods will help you."

Other Lucian smiled. "You don't have to understand."

"Why not just kill me if you plan on stealing my identity anyway?"

Other Lucian grinned. "You'll see soon enough." His eyes finally landed on me. "And we'll keep her, too, to make sure you behave. We've heard you've become . . . close."

"Touch her and there will be nothing left of you but ashes," Lucian hissed.

The white-haired man smiled. "You just have to do exactly what we say, and she'll be fine. But if you dare disobey us, then . . . we'll take a bite."

The room seemed to tilt on its axis, the world warping at each terrified heartbeat that slammed against my chest. For a moment, everything faded into the background except the roaring of my heart.

A few hours ago, we had been free of Loki and had escaped all the horrors of the night before. My mind couldn't process that we were now trapped and with little hope of escape.

The white-haired man turned to the open door they had come through. He glanced back at Lucian, and a smile cut through his face like a curved gash.

"We'll give you some privacy," he said.

The two walked away.

I angled my head toward the door but couldn't see who or what was on the other side. Lucian stepped closer to the bars. I heard the slow footsteps before Sue came into view. I glanced over her body for any signs of injury, but she seemed unharmed with not a hair out of place. Her dark eyes were set on Lucian, and my heart sank at the expression of hatred that twisted her face.

Lucian stiffened. "Sue, what did you do?"

She simply stared at him for a few seconds, and then she said, "You never really saw me, Lucian. I spent all of those years at your side, and you never saw me."

"What are you talking about?" Lucian asked.

Then it hit me. Sue was in love with Lucian. I felt stupid for not noticing that before. Lucian also loved her, I had no doubt of that, but he just didn't love her how she wanted to be loved.

Lucian must have realized this at the same time I did. "Sue," he said as he shook his head. "I didn't . . ." He hung his head low for a moment, then raised it again to meet Sue's glare. "I gave you everything I could," he said. "I'm sorry that wasn't enough for you."

Sue's eyes turned glassy. She slid her gaze away from Lucian, and the full brunt of her hatred fell on me.

"This is between you and me, Sue." Lucian's tone darkened. "Let her go."

A single tear fell from her eye and slid down her cheek. She walked away. Every step seemed to push into my chest, pressing in until I felt I couldn't breathe. The door banged closed.

Silence settled inside the room so densely that I would have been able to slice it with a knife.

"Isa," Lucian said.

I turned to him and saw his eyes sizzling, expressing what I could only assume was terror. He kneeled, and I dragged myself closer to him, sliding my arm between the bars again to hold his hand.

"Let me bite you," he said.

33

MY BREATH CAUGHT in my throat as I held Lucian's hand.

"It's the only power I have left to keep you safe," Lucian said.

"I . . ." My heart rate spiked into a race. The odds of getting out of this situation alive were low.

"Let me bite you now while I still have the chance."

I imagined Lucian's fangs sinking into my flesh and sucking out my blood before feeding me his own.

He would do it. Lucian would turn me immortal.

But even though I had agreed to let him turn me if something happened, the reality of it made my heart race from horror. I wasn't just choosing immortality. I was choosing to become a being who needed to kill humans to survive. Was that something I was willing to live with? Was I willing to take countless lives to sustain my own?

Hot tears streamed from my eyes and slid down my cheeks.

"I can't," I said, trying to pull my hand away.

Lucian held tight for a moment before letting go.

"I'm sorry," I said as a sob shook through me. "I can't."

"I understand," Lucian said. "But I still wanted to offer that option."

Our eyes met again. There was no reproach in his gaze, and for the first time, I was able to read something from Lucian's expression that I hadn't been able to understand before.

Hate.

Lucian hated himself. That's why he had felt lost for so long. He hated what he had become and had to live with that hate every day of his immortal life. Even if it meant losing me, he wouldn't force that same fate on me.

"I'm so sorry," I said.

Lucian slid his hand through the bars, careful not to touch the silver. With the shackles, only part of his palm peeked into my side of the cell. I held his hand again, our fingers interlacing.

"There's nothing for you to be sorry about," Lucian said. "I should have never taken you to the party."

"I chose to go," I said.

"I'll find a way, Isa," Lucian said. "I'll find a way to keep my promise."

"I know," I whispered back.

The door swung open again. The white-haired man walked in accompanied by a dark-haired girl who seemed to have been created from shadows. They both wore thick leather gloves. The man opened my cell door. I let go of Lucian and pressed myself against the far wall, but the man grabbed my arms and pulled me to my feet. His fingers dug painfully into my flesh.

"You know you can't escape so don't even try," he said.

He pushed my back against his chest. The air sang as the girl unsheathed a silver blade and handed it to him. My heart dropped to the floor. Lucian roared.

"Calm down," the man said. "We won't hurt her—yet."

He held the silver blade lightly, but I knew it would take less than a second for him to slice my throat open.

"One move against us and she dies," the girl said.

Lucian said nothing.

The girl opened Lucian's cell door and motioned for him to come out. He slowly stepped toward her, but his eyes never left me. The man made sure to keep some distance between me and Lucian as they led us down several hallways until we arrived at a large circular room with a domed glass ceiling that revealed the cloudy night sky above us.

Five other vampires were already there. They cheered when we walked in. I didn't spot Sue among the small crowd and wondered if she had left.

"About time," a red-haired girl said.

With one arm around my waist to keep me pinned against him, the white-haired man pulled me to the side. Lucian was led to the center of the room where another pair of shackles lay chained to the floor.

Lucian paused before reaching them. The man raised the knife, letting it hover inches away from me. Lucian bared his fangs but took the last few steps toward the shackles. Other Lucian chained his ankles, a mocking smile twisting his face.

"Who wants to go first?" the red-haired girl asked.

A tall woman standing next to her bared her fangs with a wild smile, but it was the shadow girl who stepped forward and sized up Lucian with a glare. She balled her fists and delivered a blow to his face. A crack echoed through the room. Lucian staggered back.

"No," I shouted.

The white-haired man tightened his grip on me, and the cold kiss of a blade pressed against my cheek. Lucian's eyes snapped back to us, blood squirting from his obviously broken nose, but he did nothing to defend himself as the girl's boot connected with his leg and sent him tumbling down. Lucian's blood splattered on the white marble floor. The girl smiled, then stepped back.

A white-haired girl walked toward Lucian. She pressed a hand to his cheek. He flinched. Silver light flowed out of her palm and sank into his skin. The blood immediately disappeared from his face as if it had been reabsorbed by his flesh. The light faded from her hand as she stepped away.

"Who's next?" the red-haired girl asked.

A bald man with bulging muscles stepped forward. Lucian eyed him warily but didn't even make the effort to stand again.

"You probably don't remember me, Holt." The man's voice sounded like stones grinding against each other. "But I remember the day you killed my brother."

"I remember him," Lucian said. "I never forget a face. He was an ugly bastard just like you."

The bald man stepped forward and kicked Lucian in the face, then continued kicking him even as bones crunched.

"Please, stop!" But my voice was drowned out by the cheers that had erupted in the room. The bald man continued to kick Lucian like a soccer ball for a solid minute. When he walked away, he left bloody footprints behind.

"Lucian!" I shouted.

"Go check on your boyfriend," said the white-haired man as he let go.

I rushed to Lucian's side. He had curled himself into a ball but turned to me when I laid my hands on his arm. His face was swollen, flushed a deep red and covered with streaks of blood. One eye was nearly shut, a dark purple bruise blossoming around it. A gash on his cheek oozed. His nose looked painfully crooked and dripped blood into his mouth. Lucian's suit had torn, and the white shirt was splattered with dark red stains.

"Lucian." My voice caught painfully in my throat.

Jeers and laughs erupted around me.

"I promised you," he whispered. "You will get out of here alive, with or without me."

Tears slid down my cheeks. I knew he would keep that promise even if it ended up killing him. Rough hands pulled me backward.

"No," I shouted. "Don't hurt him anymore!"

My hands were wet with Lucian's blood, and the smell of it was so strong that a wave of dizziness washed over me. It was an overwhelming sensation, like gravity pulling me out of my body. Every sound faded away, and my heartbeat slowed. The scent of

Lucian's blood traveled deep into me as if it belonged inside my heart.

I promise I will keep you safe from the monsters that hunt you.

Lucian had promised me that.

No.

Wait.

I was the one who had promised him safety.

My hands had been wet with his blood, as they were now. He had been hurt, and terrified, and dying. Lucian now lay on the floor, but he was immobile, his last words echoing inside of my ears. His blood was everywhere, the scent so strong that it pulled me like the sun pulled the earth around its orbit.

His broken body lay inside a torchlit temple. The flickering light illuminated his bloody white shirt. His dying human heartbeat filled my ears. The frantic immortal heartbeat vibrated inside my bones.

Those monsters will never hurt you again.

I licked Lucian's blood from my hands. It was a familiar taste—it tasted like my own blood.

Something deep within me cracked, shattering into a million fragments and releasing something that had been buried inside my mind. At first, I didn't know what it was—it was just an echo, a small, faint beat calling me from the depths of oblivion. Then the echo materialized into something solid.

Tell me my name.

Names had power, not only over others, but over yourself too. That's what I had lost inside of myself—me. A hundred names rushed through me like a violent river.

I was none of them.

I was all of them.

They were the little pieces that made the whole, each

reflecting a different part of me like shards of a mirror. But I was broken into so many bits that they made no sense to me now, like watching a hundred movies at once trying to figure out how they were all connected.

Tell me my name.

"Isa," I whispered. But it felt wrong. That name held no power. It was a mortal's name.

Tell me my name.

I was the one who had written those words in the Book of the Dead to remind myself to remember.

Tell me my name.

"Isis," I said.
I screamed as pain shattered through my head.
And the world around me shattered too.

34

MY PARENTS WAVED at me from the car as I entered my new college dorm.

I sat in the front row of the lecture hall for my first class, trying to keep my hands steady as I took notes.

The night soon turned into day, and I still hadn't finished all my homework.

Mya and I sang karaoke, barely able to say the words over our laughs.

Aura, Liz, and I giggled as we hid between the library stacks reading a silly book we had found.

The memories of the last five years flashed through my eyes as if I had been an observer letting someone else take the wheel while I just rode along. The couple that I had made into my parents had been so heartbroken when their daughter had died that their minds had been easy to influence with memories of me. For the first time in a long while I had felt loved. Truly loved. I had been happy to forget the rest of my life and wrap myself around that love.

My father, who was not my father, had asked me what I was passionate about.

I hadn't known.

Maybe that was why I had chosen to start a new life as a college student. That was the age when humans discovered what they wanted to do with their lives. But four years later the question had still haunted me. What was I passionate about? Ancient civilizations and languages weren't a passion but a nostalgia of better times when we had ruled the world—before we were forgotten. Before we grew old and hungry. Before we became addicted to the taste of human blood to keep us young and powerful.

For the longest time I'd had no purpose, ever since I had realized that I couldn't bring Osiris back to life and that we couldn't be together forever as we had promised each other we would be.

Lucian had asked me who I wanted to be.

I had been attracted to him from the moment I set eyes on him. I wasn't sure how destiny had driven us together after so long. I hadn't seen him in centuries, but the love I had felt for him before was still warm inside of me. I had loved Lucian ever since he stepped into that temple begging for help. The light inside of him was so bright and had so much promise that he deserved another chance to achieve his full potential. That's what I had given him when I fed him my blood.

But now I knew he wasn't happy with the new life I had gifted him. He hated the monster I had turned him into. I hated the monster I had become, too, hating it so much I had shattered into a million pieces to become hundreds of different personas to forget about it.

Who do you want to be? Lucian's question echoed inside of my head, demanding an answer. I could still choose to become something I didn't hate.

"I'm a translator," I whispered.

That's what Isa had discovered. And that's who I really was at my core.

The laws of the universe were a language, one I had learned to understand and manipulate. Life, death, nature—they were commands woven into the fabric of reality.

Lucian had said it was time to give a voice to those who can't speak anymore. But it was more than that. Being a translator was about being a vessel of the words of the universe and helping those words materialize into reality.

I opened my eyes again.

Time froze.

Lucian lay curled into a ball as the red-haired girl bared her fangs at him, her hands already bloodied. The rest of the group formed a tight circle around them, their eyes shining, their expressions enraged.

I looked away from the scene to the empty air above us—except it wasn't empty. The *Aether* filled the space around us. We were all fish living inside its waters. The *Aether* permeated the entire universe. We were one big, expanding tank.

Wolf was the only Athatos who could directly control that power, but he had never truly understood it—had never seen it as more than the force that drove creation and destruction. But the *Aether* was also the language that tied reality together. It was an electric energy that bound the laws of science into the physical plane and connected them to the spiritual realm.

Hesitantly, I reached out to that power. It was already moving through and around me. But being aware of it for the first time in a while—giving it a name and a voice—made it react to me. It coursed through my veins like a second circulatory system because the *Aether* was the universe's blood. Yet I couldn't make it directly influence the world around me, not without something to hold its power in place and to make its energy manifest into this physical reality. Using my hand, I drew a symbol in the air, one I had written many times. Symbols were the vehicles through which the *Aether* could be manipulated by someone to fulfill their desires. To a certain extent, anyone could manipulate the *Aether* with words, but not everyone had the power to make it alter the laws of reality.

I was the only one who could—I was the universe's translator, and I could use that power to save lives as much as I could to take them.

The symbol shone brightly in the air, casting all the shadows away. Blinding white light exploded from the symbol, making the half-bloods around me fly backward until they hit the walls. Lucian still lay in the center of the room, his body broken and bloodied. I hurried to him, kneeled by his side, and placed my hands on his chest. Using my nails, I carved a crude symbol on Lucian's skin. Soft light escaped from the symbol, then wrapped around him in a gentle embrace. His body immediately responded by pulling blood back into his body and closing his wounds. The symbol healed itself and its light vanished. Lucian moaned, but he didn't open his eyes.

Something moved at my periphery. I pushed back to my feet, standing protectively over Lucian. The eight vampires around me formed a loose circle.

"What the hell?" Other Lucian asked.

Anger rolled through me like a spiked wheel. He didn't deserve to have Lucian's face. The *Aether* rushed around me like a violent river. I drew another symbol in the air to pull the *Aether* into its shape. I flicked my hand, and the symbol flew toward Other Lucian. As soon as it came in touch with him, he burned to cinders.

The other vampires stood frozen, staring at the spot where Other Lucian had vanished in a blaze. Then their gazes slowly traveled back to me, and their eyes opened wide.

I had been hiding under a human's skin for too long, and it had become too easy to pretend I was one.

But not anymore.

Tonight, I would step into the skin of the monster I hated to save Lucian.

The red-haired girl attacked first by sending a wave of fire toward me. I recognized the power she bore from Agni. The fire was different from the sun-energy of Helios. This was more destructive, raging with life. I drew another symbol, pulling a current of the *Aether* into it and changing the fire's course to the white-haired man. The fire burned his skin like old parchment, and he crumpled to the ground. The white-haired girl screamed. The bald man stepped forward with his fangs bared.

I quickly traced more symbols in the air, each of them shinning with blazing white power, then I unleashed them. The bald man flew backward, tearing through the wall until he crashed onto the ground somewhere outside. White moonlight came out of a girl's hands. Instead of striking me, it curved back to pierce through her own body like a blade. There was no blood, no visible wound, but she dropped down as if her heart had been torn out.

Shadows twisted around me, but the darkness evaporated as soon as it touched my skin. A young girl hissed as more shadows bloomed around her. The tall woman and the red-haired girl stood at her sides. I drew one more symbol. The red-haired woman lunged forward, but she remained hovering in the air. Gravity inverted, and all three of them floated up from the floor as they screamed. The symbol exploded with a burst of power, and they were all thrown through the walls.

I glanced down at Lucian, who lay sleeping on the floor. His face looked so peaceful, almost childlike. I kneeled at his side and scratched a symbol on each of the manacles. The chains vibrated, then shattered into pieces and scattered over the floor. I leaned over him, resting my head on his chest, and listened to his beating heart. I hugged him closely.

Electricity crackled in the air as one of the symbols still burned brightly. Strength zapped out of me as my mind began to crack again. I tried to deactivate the symbol, but it felt like trying to control a limb that wasn't attached to my body anymore. The house creaked and groaned. The ground trembled violently. I hugged Lucian tighter. I wouldn't lose him like I had lost Osiris. I wouldn't leave him again. But why had I left Lucian last time? Had he left me? That memory was wrapped in fog.

A boom shook through the house. Glass shattered. Stone crumbled. The world around me broke into as many pieces as my own mind. The air trembled. The sky roared with thunderous fury. The earth shook until everything on it collapsed into a heap of stones. But nothing touched us. Lucian and I remained lying at the center of the destruction.

Why couldn't I remember why Lucian and I had separated?

As soon as that question flowed through my mind, my thoughts became muddy as if they were encased in amber. A pair of glowing red eyes flashed through my mind.

Wolf.

But as soon as his face materialized, it left me like a nightmare after awakening. I was falling asleep again. The pain in my chest eased. I hadn't even noticed it was there until it left me.

I'm a monster, Lucian had said. I had said.

But I wanted to become something better with him. Together, we could give a voice to the voiceless and save more lives than the ones we had to take. Even if we never met that one person we did save, I could endure that—with Lucian, I could live that life.

As those thoughts drifted through my head, I was pulled deeper into my human slumber again with the *Aether* slipping away. I tried to stay awake. Lucian needed me. The Athatos needed me. Yet the pull was so strong, and my mind so weak, that I couldn't stop myself from breaking again.

Lucian's heart thumped against my cheek, lulling me with its rhythmic beat as oblivion swallowed me once more.

35

A SLIGHT VIBRATION made my skin tremble. My eyes fluttered open, and I groaned as I sat upright. My head pounded, and I wondered if I had a concussion. The world around me came into focus, but it still took a few seconds for my eyes to adjust to the darkness.

Sue stood at the opposite end of the small space. Lucian was on the left, his wrists and ankles bound with silver chains. We bounced up sharply, then dropped back down. The roar of the engine drowned out my frantic heartbeat. I realized we were in a truck. When I turned back to Sue, her stare burned into me.

I couldn't remember how we had gotten here. Sue had betrayed us, and the other vampires had been hurting Lucian while I was being held back, completely powerless and unable to help him. That's where my memories stopped. Maybe I had been knocked out.

I wasn't bound by chains or tied up, but I knew Sue would kill me if I tried to free Lucian or escape. I met her gaze, which hadn't broken away from me, and I tried to find the Sue I had met back at the mansion. Yet that person seemed to have been corroded by anger and jealousy into someone different.

Lucian groaned. The chains clanked at his sides as he moved slightly. His eyes slowly opened. He exhaled when his gaze settled on me, then his irises twisted with lightning as he glared at Sue.

"How did you do it?" Sue asked him.

Lucian didn't respond.

"You blew up the house and killed everyone in it," Sue said. "I knew you were powerful but didn't think you would be capable of that while chained and weakened."

Lucian's face remained neutral, but his eyes flared. I couldn't remember when he had blown up the house but didn't doubt that he had done it. The chains bounding him rattled, but they didn't break.

"I would advise you to not use your power from this moment onward," Sue said.

"Why?" Lucian asked.

"Because they'll absorb it and use it against you," Sue said. "They'll use your power to kill her."

Terror twisted in my chest.

Lucian growled, making the air crackle. "Don't you dare touch her," he hissed.

"We won't hurt her as long as you behave," Sue said. "And he may find Isa useful enough to keep her alive."

"He who?" Lucian asked.

I wondered what they could possibly want from me. If the killers had already decoded the Book of the Dead and killed one of the gods, then they didn't need me. I was just leverage against Lucian.

"Starting to get soft with her?" Sue asked mockingly.

Lucian clenched his jaw. He stared down at the chains again as if his gaze could cut through them. Then he turned back to Sue. "Which coven are you really from?" he asked.

The truck came to a stop, and someone banged on the back door. I wasn't sure I wanted to know what was on the other side.

"Welcome to the Twelfth Coven," Sue said.

She opened the door.

PART VIII

THE
WAR

36

FIVE YEARS AGO

WOLF AND ISIS lay in bed together. They had woken up awhile ago, and after making love, had remained in each other's arms as the morning sun found its way around the shutters. Isis's head rested on Wolf's chest, and he absently wove his fingers through her hair. She pulled her head back to meet his eyes. Her gaze seemed troubled.

"What's wrong?" Wolf asked.

She didn't answer.

"Did you have another dream?" Wolf asked hesitantly.

She nodded slowly.

Wolf didn't need to ask what the dream had been about—it was always the same one. A pang of jealousy cut through him, but he quickly suppressed it, afraid she would be able to read his emotions. The room began to warm up as the sun rose higher above the horizon.

"What if there's a way to bring him back?" Isis whispered.

"There isn't," Wolf said, trying to make his tone sound gentle yet forceful. "You tried, and it didn't work."

"But," Isis said as she pushed herself into a sitting position, the blankets falling around her and exposing the rest of Wolf's torso, "he came back once before, even if it was temporary. I don't remember why the magic failed, but I could try again."

Wolf's heart began to thump harder against his chest as he sat up too.

"Isis," he said, "it's been five thousand years. You need to move on."

How many times had he told her that? How many times had she gone down this lane of thought? How many times had he been forced to fragment her thoughts? Wolf was getting tired of it.

Isis shook her head. "I try," she said, pulling her legs up to her chest, "but he keeps appearing in my dreams and calling me to him. He's still there. It's not too late."

"It won't work," Wolf said.

Isis's eyes flashed. "I'm powerful enough to bring him back."

He knew she was.

Before he could say anything else, Isis swung her legs around and stood up from the bed. She began to get dressed. Wolf exhaled. He pushed the blankets away and put on his clothes. Isis walked to the door, but Wolf held her arm, forcing her to face him.

"Let go," Isis said.

"I can't let you do that," he said.

"Why?" Isis asked, her eyes swirling. "Are you jealous?"

Wolf was jealous. He had given her everything, but he had never been enough for her. He never would be. The mortal man she had fallen in love with and turned immortal hadn't been enough either. But this went beyond his jealousy. There were much more powerful forces at play.

"No," Wolf said. Maybe this time he should try a different approach. "I'm opposed to the idea because if you bring him back, then the rest of us will die."

Isis blinked. "What?" she asked. "Why would the rest of us die?"

But even as she said it, understanding dawned on her face, and Wolf knew she was remembering the secret he had made her, and every other Athatos, forget millennia ago.

Osiris's death had been a sacrifice to give the rest of them a new, immortal life. But Isis's unwavering love for him, and her desire to bring him back to life, would be their ruin.

Wolf couldn't let that happen.

"I still love him," she whispered.

Those four words shot out of her mouth like bullets to his heart. A tear slid down her cheek, and Wolf used his thumb to wipe it away before cupping her cheek with his palm.

"I know," Wolf said. "But you can't have it all. Either he lives or the rest of us do."

More tears streamed from her eyes. "Maybe we don't deserve to live."

"You don't mean that," Wolf said. His gut twisted.

"It's been too long, Wolf," she said. "I don't—we've lived far more than was ever intended for us. I'm tired. I don't know what to do with my life anymore. The world has moved on without us," she said as her voice cracked. "But time hasn't erased the pain of his absence. I just want this to be over."

Wolf shook his head. His heartbeat echoed in his ears. How could she not be terrified of Death? Humans died and were reborn, but it was inconsequential to them because they had no power to lose. But Wolf knew that the Athatos weren't reborn. There was a special place in the Underworld for them, one not even Hades knew of. But of course, she had forgotten that place existed. Wolf had made sure of it or else she would have already tried to rescue Osiris.

"Aren't you tired too?" she asked. "We've spent the last few years doing nothing. We're just sticking around because there's nothing else we can do. We don't belong here anymore."

Her words cut his heart like blades, but Wolf told himself it wasn't true.

"Just because you feel that way doesn't mean the rest of us do," Wolf said.

"Oh really?" she said. "Tell me one thing that's worth living for."

You, Wolf thought.

He couldn't bring himself to say that aloud. He knew she loved him, but not as much as he loved her. And there were others she loved more.

Wolf took a deep breath. He had thought that if he explained the truth, then she would see the logic in it and abandon her obsession with Osiris. Now he understood that she never would. Isis was a threat to their existence. She would destroy their immortality to bring Osiris back. He couldn't let that happen. Death was peeking at him from around the corner, but he wouldn't let it come any closer.

Isis pulled her arm from his grip and began to walk away from him.

"Wait," Wolf said. "I'm sorry."

Isis turned around.

Wolf stepped closer to her. "I'm sorry," he repeated. Wolf cupped her cheek again, wiping her tears away. He leaned down to kiss her and taste her soft lips one last time.

Wolf pushed into her mind, the *Aether* coursing through her body like blood. It was like an invisible hammer crushing her mind and memories. She whimpered, feebly trying to push away. Wolf held the back of her head with one hand and her waist with the other, kissing her deeper. Wolf didn't hold back as he destroyed her mind. He couldn't let her remember anything this time—not even him.

It was over in a few seconds. Wolf finally pushed away from her. Isis stared blankly at him, like a child who had just awoken from sleep. Wolf's eyes burned with tears, making his vision blur.

He loved her. He had always loved her. But that love would doom them all. He had to leave her for some time to let her pretend to be human and build a life for herself—and let her find her own name this time. Once she was deep inside that life, Wolf would come back for her, making it seem like a chance encounter and letting her fall in love with him again. Hopefully this time, her mind would be broken for longer, and he could enjoy his time with her without Osiris's memory looming over them like a shadow.

He left the beach house and didn't stop when the dying sun came down over the horizon. He continued onward even when the golden rays of dawn came back.

Isis would be alright. Like the other fragmented gods, she would find her way among the humans. Maybe they could give her the life purpose that she so dearly wanted. In the meantime, there was much more of the world for Wolf to explore.

PRESENT DAY

Feeling exhausted from the events of the last twenty-four hours, Wolf climbed into the car with a sigh.

After destroying Dionysus's castle, he had flown with Rafe to an island where they had interrogated Lucian Holt. It quickly became clear that Holt had been framed for Gabriel's murder. Someone from the Twelfth Coven must have shifted to look like him and then mirrored Gabriel's power. Holt was the perfect scapegoat since he publicly hated the gods and had never joined any of their covens. Wolf theorized that Dionysus's coven had lured Holt to the party to drive him mad so he would unwittingly kill Max. That would have officially unleashed the war, and the attention of the Athatos would have been on Holt and the lower-generation half-bloods instead of on the infiltrators of their own covens. And if Hera had seen Gabriel's murder in a vision, she would have seen Holt, too, so no one would have known he had been manipulated into this mess.

It was a brilliant plan.

Too bad he and Rafe had turned it upside down.

Wolf knew the Twelfth Coven would want to capture Holt to continue using him as a scapegoat, and Wolf had used that to his advantage for his new plan. He still felt the nervous shock at having seen Isis again—the one person he hadn't expected at the party. But he had known she would come to the castle to save Holt.

Yet her presence and having to tiptoe around her to not reveal he knew her had left him drained. The mere sight of her after several years had made him burn with desire. He had wanted nothing more than to pull her into his arms, take her away from this war, and show her how much he loved her.

But he couldn't risk revealing her identity. She had become much younger during this fragmentation, and her features had changed somewhat, but he had loved her too much and for too long to not recognize her. He had made a tremendous effort to not show he knew her during the battle at the party, and he was glad no one had realized she was the one who had instinctively counteracted the Twelfth Coven's mirroring powers and not the child of Helios. That would be good—they would direct their attention to him instead of her.

That was perfect for the next part of Wolf's plan when the Twelfth Coven took her captive with Holt—she would be able to destroy them from the inside. Everyone would think she was just a human girl thrown into the middle of their chaos, when in fact, she was one of the most powerful Athatos to ever be born.

Isis would be his Trojan horse, his bomb slowly ticking as she remembered herself. He knew it wouldn't be long.

Letting her get captured was a risky gamble, and his heart ached at the thought of her being in danger. But this was the best plan he had to destroy the Twelfth Coven without them suspecting anything.

Once this was all over, Wolf would find Isis again and live by her side once more. And he would make sure Holt didn't intervene.

Wolf didn't even know how they had found each other again. It had been another considerable effort to not strangle Holt on the spot when he took Isis's hand. The *Aether* had burned angrily in his veins, but Wolf had suppressed it.

He turned the car's key, and the engine roared to life. The passenger door opened, and Rafe climbed in.

"What are you doing here?" Wolf asked. "I thought you were busy hunting down lower-generations and ripping out their throats."

"Where's Holt?" Rafe asked.

Wolf shrugged, but the *Aether* sensed danger and prickled his skin.

Rafe sighed, rubbing his eyes. "She wants to talk to you," he said. "She's already waiting for us at the ruins."

"You contacted her?" Wolf asked, trying to decide if he was angry or not.

Rafe didn't respond.

Wolf considered this for a moment, then stepped on the pedal. They drove in silence, but Wolf's power was ready to strike if Rafe decided to do anything. After a couple of hours, they finally arrived at the ruins. Wolf stepped out of the car and banged the door shut.

There were no tourists in sight. This place was too ancient for them to even consider it a sign of an intelligent civilization. It had once been a grand palace, the home of all the Athatos, but it had long ago crumbled, and was now no more than rocks and boulders strewn around.

She stood in the middle of the ruins wearing a thick black jacket. Wolf and Rafe approached her slowly.

"Hello, Hera," Wolf said.

She had never changed her name.

"Wolf," Hera said. She turned to Rafe. A smile edged her lips.

"Hello, love," Rafe said as he walked toward her. He planted a kiss on her lips.

Shock rolled through Wolf's body as they pulled away from each other. Rafe smiled at Wolf. The *Aether* swirled in Wolf's veins as he balled his fists.

Rafe pulled out a ring from his pocket—Gabriel's ring—and handed it to Hera while whispering something into her ear. She eyed the ring for a few long moments, but her face didn't betray any emotions. Her power did though. The sky began to darken, and thunder rumbled inside of it, mighty and powerful.

"You lied to me," Wolf snarled at Rafe.

"I did," Rafe said. "I'm not single."

"Why didn't you tell me about this?" Wolf asked.

"We didn't trust you," Hera said.

"Why?" Wolf asked.

"Are you seriously asking that?" Hera said. "You're the one who originally fragmented us, making us all forget how we became immortal. And whenever one of us didn't do as you liked, you broke our minds again. We became weak because of you. The Twelfth Coven was able to kill Gabriel because they used your power of making us forget to hide from us."

Wolf tensed at the accusations. He wondered how Hera had recovered her broken memories. He suspected that her visions helped her remember things her mind had forgotten. "Everything I've done has been to keep us alive."

"I know," Hera said. "But the end doesn't justify the means, Wolf. And your actions may end up killing us all in the end. I once told you that you would be the one to destroy this world. I still have that vision."

Wolf didn't know what to say.

"I trust him," Rafe said, placing a hand on Hera's shoulder. "We need him."

"Need me for what?" Wolf asked.

"Where's Isis?" Hera asked.

Now Wolf understood why Rafe had been following him around for so long and why he might have wanted to keep Holt close after interrogating him and finding him innocent.

"She's not with me," Wolf said.

"I can see that," Hera snapped. "But you're the one who last saw her, and Isis is the only one powerful enough to defeat the Twelfth Coven. That is, of course, assuming we can help her remember who she is."

Hera could have used her power, but the future had never been clear around Wolf and Isis since they could both change the future faster than she could keep track.

"Wolf, where is she?" Rafe asked.

Wolf hesitated for a second. "I let her go with Lucian Holt and Sue Lee, so I assume the Twelfth Coven has taken her and Holt captive."

"What?" Rafe exclaimed. "How would she"—his eyes widened in shock—"she's the one who counteracted the Twelfth Coven's power, not the son of Helios. That was her."

A hiss escaped from between Hera's teeth. "Do you have any idea the danger you've put her in?"

"She'll be fine," Wolf said, although anxiety tied itself into a knot in his stomach and made the *Aether* stir again. "She's the only one whose power they can't absorb and who can counteract their mirroring. I let her infiltrate the Twelfth Coven so she can destroy them from the inside."

"And you think she's strong enough to do that?" Rafe asked as his eyes glowed green. "She looked human. Smelled human. She's in deep—too broken to be able to defend herself."

"She has Holt with her," Wolf said. "He'll protect her." Those words tasted bitter on his tongue. He could protect her better than Holt, but he wouldn't be able to infiltrate the Twelfth Coven.

"He didn't recognize her as Isis," Rafe said.

"He didn't?" Hera asked, then gave a bitter laugh. "Oh, you jealous bastard."

Wolf only exhaled in response.

Hera composed herself, her jaw ticking as she clenched her teeth hard. "We need a new plan to stop him."

"Who?" Wolf asked.

Hera raised a brow. "You still haven't guessed who the god of the Twelfth Coven is?"

Rafe smiled.

"I assumed you would have known," Hera said. "Don't you remember what happened a hundred years ago?"

"No," Wolf said. Now he knew how frustratingly awful it must have felt to have his memories fragmented.

"Isis is the Athatos of the Twelfth Coven," Hera said.

Wolf blinked in surprise. Isis?

Hera chuckled. "Confused?" she asked. "I'll clear up some things. Isis is the Athatos of the Twelfth Coven, but she's not the one who started this war."

"Then who did?" Wolf asked.

"When he found us, he tried to kill you first, Wolf, but Isis used her power to protect you," Hera continued. "So he murdered all of her coven right in front of her—except Holt because he was too powerful. You tried to fight back, but he absorbed your power, amplified it, and fragmented everyone's minds."

Wolf didn't remember any of that.

"He's highly unstable and volatile, and we believe he doesn't fully remember us," Rafe said. "Isis must have known that, too, when she fought him. But he remembers enough to hate us, and his sole purpose has become to destroy our immortality."

"Why? Who is he?" Wolf asked.

Hera continued. "Some lower-generation half-bloods found him and realized that his bite could turn humans immortal and give them the ability to absorb any other power. They fed him lies, telling him that he was the lost god of the Twelfth Coven. They knew that was a mysterious story that would propagate and lure more people to them, since by then, everyone had forgotten Isis was the goddess of the twelfth throne." Hera's eyes glowed. "This moment is the time they've been waiting for. And they've been patient, slowly infiltrating other covens over the last century and building their army while the rest of us continued with our normal lives."

"Who?" Wolf asked, desperation edging his voice.

Hera eyed him carefully. "Do you know what awaits us when we die?"

Memories began filtering through Wolf's mind—screams, pain, and darkness.

"I know it's different for us than it is for humans," Wolf said, trying to keep his voice steady and the *Aether* from bursting out.

"It is," Hera said. "Humans forget everything and are reborn again. We're not."

Wolf's heart began thundering like the lightning above his head.

"Death changes us, transforms us through pain. Imagine living in a torment for millennia, and all you have are your last memories." Hera stepped closer to him. "Have you guessed who's behind this now?"

Wolf nodded, trying to swallow the lump in his throat. The earth shook as lightning struck the ground.

"He found another way to cheat Death, and he's come back for revenge." Hera's eyes flashed with silver light. "Osiris has returned."

ACKNOWLEDGMENTS

THIS BOOK STARTED as an idea that one day just popped into my mind. I found the concept of vampire gods intriguing, so I started writing it. And though it took me awhile to find the story I wanted to tell, eventually everything fell into place, and I found the perfect characters and a plot that transformed that idea into a new world I felt very excited to share with others. Throughout this journey there have been so many people who have supported me, and I am very grateful for each of them.

The first person I want to thank is Rain. You believed in this story before anyone else did (even before I fully believed in it), and have continued supporting me for nearly two years as I took this from an idea to a whole book. I won't ever be able to thank you enough for that.

Bry, you were also there from the very first post and have continued to follow along since then—thank you.

Jennifer, you've liked every single one of my videos for over a year (and have amassed an ungodly amount of power). Thank you for your support and all your fun messages.

Timmy, happy late birthday, and thank you for being so supportive of this series, for your messages, and for your interactions with my content.

Kat, thank you for being Kickstarter backer #2, and for all your kind messages and continued support.

Kiana, thank you for following me along in this journey and for interacting with the content I have posted (you have also collected a dangerous amount of power).

To Maria for being Kickstarter backer #1.

I also want to thank every single one of the seventy Kickstarter backers for supporting this story and for all the excitement you have shown for it. Being a writer can be a bit lonely in the sense that all this remains a daydream in my mind and a document with words until someone else reads it and experiences this world through their own imagination—so thank you for being here for this journey and making the time to meet my characters and immerse yourselves in this story.

Daniel, you've always been a great advisor and friend. Thank you for always supporting my writing (and everything else I do). And for being Kickstarter backer #3.

Gargi, you have no idea how much I appreciate the friendship we have built over the years, and that no matter what crazy story I come up with, you're always there to support it.

Rodri, my fellow writer friend, thank you for your continued support. It's been very exciting to see you grow as a writer as well.

Klaus, thank you for ordering this book from the other side of the world, and for all our conversations as we grow into this entrepreneurial world.

Sophie and Patrick, you were the ones who got the Kickstarter one hundred percent funded, and receiving that notification was such a thrill. Sophie, thank you for being such an awesome mentor, friend, and book buddy. Patrick, thank you for being an awesome co-worker and for all your support throughout these last few years as a Lilie mentor.

Yessenia and Josselyn, we will argue about dirty dishes, cleaning, and quiet hours but we're always there to support each other and I love being silly señoras together.

Pam, thank you for this awesome friendship and for always supporting my writing since the first book I published.

Denise, it's officially been twenty years of friendship. Thank you for supporting this book and for all the great times we've had together.

Jonathan, you're the best mentor I could have asked for. I can't thank you enough for all your support these last few years and for helping me get where I am today.

Mel, for being one of the sweetest people I know and always being there to support me. Thank you for this wonderful friendship.

Alejo, for understanding me in a way that few people can, and for always being there for me.

Sof, I love listening to your podcast voice notes and that even while living in different countries we can still be a part of each other's lives.

Val D, for always supporting my crazy ideas no matter where you are.

To the Hilatino group: Rosa, Eric, and Mario. Thank you for being such amazing, fun friends and being there to support me. And to Daniel for being a great lab mentor and friend.

Even though my books are self-published, I still have a wonderful team helping me each step of the way to bring these stories to life.

Ally Machate, thank you for all the support you have provided these last ten years.

Harrison Demchick, I continue to learn something new and improve with every book I write thanks to you, and I will always be grateful for your support and your dedication as an editor to help me grow as an author. It's nearly been ten years working with you and I'm really grateful you've been there throughout this journey.

Julie Haase, for always keeping everything running on track and for all your support with my books.

Karen Stoff, for catching all the little (and some bigger) mistakes I made throughout the manuscript and helping refine the writing.

Emily Hitchcock and Clair Fink, thank you for being so responsive to my many questions and emails, and for guiding me through the publishing process and helping me bring these books to the world.

Augusto Aguilera and the D'signLab team, for designing another stunning cover, and also for providing so much support throughout this entire process. I will never stop being amazed at all your creativity.

I also have such an amazing family that has supported my writing for the last ten years.

Mom, for helping me discover my voice as a writer and for supporting me since the very first book I ever wrote.

Dad, for being my #1 fan, and for your support not only with my stories but in my life and career too.

Abu, for being the kindest person I know and always being there to support us through everything.

Caro, for reading the shitty first drafts I wrote and saying they were good. And for reading all the final drafts too. You're my best friend and I'm so grateful to be sisters. Thank you to Gerard too, for all your support.

And thank you, dear reader, for being part of the world of The Fragmented. *An Echo of Oblivion* is only the beginning of this story.

So choose your coven wisely.

Don't miss out on Sofi Aguilera's
STAR BLOOD series

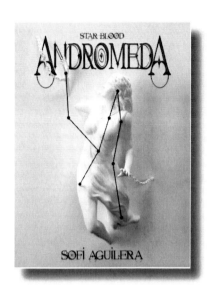

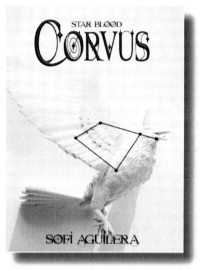

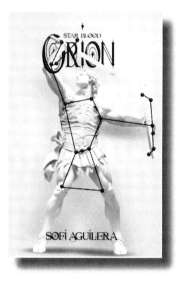

ABOUT THE AUTHOR

AT SEVENTEEN, SOFI BECAME Mexico's youngest published author. She is the author of *The Lost Origin*, *Star Blood*, and *The Fragmented* series. She won the award *Writers of Tomorrow* and was named one of the most influential women in Mexico by *Quién* magazine at nineteen. Sofi wants to keep one foot in the future and get involved with technologies that are making fiction turn into reality through science. She holds a BS in Bioengineering from Rice University and has worked at Hilton Lab doing research in epigenetic engineering and synthetic biology. Sofi currently works in venture capital, looking for startups transforming the world.

Made in United States
North Haven, CT
20 December 2024

63295558R00224